Pride Comes Before a Fall

Also by Virginia Heath

MISS PRENTICE'S PROTÉGÉES

All's Fair in Love and War

Look Before You Leap

THE MERRIWELL SISTERS

Never Fall for Your Fiancée

Never Rescue a Rogue

Never Wager with a Wallflower

The Discerning Gentleman's Guide

Redeeming the Reclusive Earl

Miss Bradshaw's Bought Betrothal

The Scoundrel's Bartered Bride

Her Enemy at the Altar

His Mistletoe Wager

That Despicable Rogue

THE WILD WARRINERS SERIES

A Warriner to Protect Her

A Warriner to Rescue Her

A Warriner to Tempt Her

A Warriner to Seduce Her

THE KING'S ELITE SERIES

The Mysterious Lord Millcroft

The Uncompromising Lord Flint

The Disgraceful Lord Gray

The Determined Lord Hadleigh

THE TALK OF THE BEAU MONDE

The Viscount's Unconventional Lady

The Marquess Next Door

How Not to Chaperone a Lady

A VERY VILLAGE SCANDAL

The Earl's Inconvenient Houseguest

His Maddening Matchmaker

A Wedding to Stop a Scandal

Pride Comes Before a Fall

A Novel

VIRGINIA HEATH

ST. MARTIN'S GRIFFIN
NEW YORK

This is a work of fiction. All of the names, characters, organizations, places, and events portrayed in this work are either products of the author's imagination or used fictitiously.

First published in the United States by St. Martin's Griffin, an imprint of St. Martin's Publishing Group

EU Representative: Macmillan Publishers Ireland Ltd, 1st Floor, The Liffey Trust Centre, 117–126 Sheriff Street Upper, Dublin 1, D01 YC43

www.stmartins.com

Designed by Gabriel Guma

The Library of Congress Cataloging-in-Publication Data is available upon request.

ISBN 978-1-250-89611-7 (trade paperback)
ISBN 978-1-250-89612-4 (ebook)

First Edition: 2026

10 9 8 7 6 5 4 3 2 1

For Jean Fullerton

A great friend and fellow writer of HEAs, who is unwaveringly there to commiserate with when this writing lark gets hard

Pride Comes Before a Fall

Chapter ONE

WHERE IT ALL BEGAN, EIGHT YEARS BEFORE . . .

Portia Kendall hadn't just so much had an epiphany as an earth-shattering, mind-blowing, seismic, life-changing revelation.

The sort that, as she stared sightlessly at her still unfamiliar bedchamber ceiling, upended her life and everything that she had been brought up to believe. The sort that left her uncharacteristically speechless and floundering. And angry. So justifiably furious that she could barely hold it all in.

"Are you all right, Portia?" From the bed squeezed beside hers at Miss Prentice's School for Young Ladies, her new friend Kitty rubbed her sleepy eyes. She took in the flickering stub that remained of what had once been their bedtime candle, and then the waning moonlight bleeding through the window as dawn beckoned, and frowned.

"No," Portia whispered, still dumbstruck but mindful that their two other friends, Georgie and Lottie, were fast asleep in the same dormitory. "I'm . . . I've . . ."

How exactly did one calmly articulate the sheer magnitude of the despicable injustices that she had recently been enlightened to within the yellowed pages of the battered pamphlet she had brought up to bed? A nondescript and dull-looking missive that had been gathering dust on the shelves in the small library here at this well-respected school in Mayfair—her new home for the last week. A pamphlet that she'd hoped would bore her to sleep in this strange bed.

Except it had done the opposite and kept her awake all night instead.

Because it explained so much.

"I've been reading this." Portia lifted the booklet so that Kitty could see it. "And I think it has just changed my life."

"*A Vindication of the Rights of Men.*" Her friend screwed up her face with distaste as she whispered the title aloud. "By Mary Wollstonecraft—whoever she may be." *A genius!* That's what Mrs. Wollstonecraft was! "Sounds as dull as dishwater."

"That's precisely what I had hoped it would be." Needing to vocalize, albeit in hushed tones, some of her outrage at all the new and troubling knowledge she now possessed, Portia rolled on her side to face her friend. "But instead, the scales have fallen from my eyes." An understatement. "They have been wrenched from them actually, and I am incensed as a result. Seething, in fact." That dusty little pamphlet had lit a fire in her belly. "At society, the rotten aristocracy, the shameful way they treat the rest of the population, and my blithe and naïve acceptance of the constructs that they have collectively used to control me—to control *all* of us—for time immemorial."

In truth, Portia already had a chip on her shoulder about the fickle nature of those she was supposed to curtsy in subservience to without the help of Mrs. Wollstonecraft. It was difficult not to when Portia and her mother had been evicted from their gamekeeper's cottage on the Earl of Corston's substantial estate within weeks of the untimely demise of her father—the gamekeeper. That was his reward for fifteen loyal years of service. The skinflint Corston had even halved Papa's promised pension, and then only paid it for two years, so his widow had been instantly plunged into poverty. But promises were only binding while people lived, the earl had explained dispassionately, mere days after their world had fallen apart. They had to understand that the pension was supposed to be for her father and the new gamekeeper would need their cottage. A grand estate could hardly function properly without a gamekeeper, after all.

And of course, she and her mother had accepted that as the way of things, because it *was* the way of things. People like them were disposable. Interchangeable. Replaceable. That was the lot of those born to serve and always had been.

They had scrimped and saved to rent a cramped and leaky cottage where poor Mama had struggled to make ends meet ever since. And they had accepted their situation gratefully. So pathetically gratefully that Portia now tasted acid at the very thought of it. Because that's what lowly people did when they had no other choice.

Or believed that they had no other choice.

Because they were just the pawns in the chess game, and always sacrificed first by the more important pieces who used and abused them without a single care or any moral consideration.

The scoundrels!

"Isn't it a bit late—or far too early—to be seething?" Kitty yawned again. "Especially when you've struggled all week to sleep in a strange bed." Her friend reached out to stroke Portia's shoulder. "Only I don't think seething is conducive to sleep."

While Kitty made a valid point—because Portia had barely managed a couple of hours a night since leaving her home in Somerset—she was suddenly wider awake than she had been in years. Her pulse was racing and her blood was pumping. Like a racehorse champing at the bit, she knew that she had been profoundly altered and galvanized by the shocking words printed on those old pages.

Who knew that a few simple words could be so powerful? Clearly the pen was mightier than the sword just as the old adage claimed!

"How on earth can I sleep now that I know how corruption and manipulation have robbed me of all my freedoms!" She was more hissing than whispering now, knowing she was one of the few enlightened. Although how it was possible that total societal reform hadn't happened already, when Mary Wollstonecraft had penned her excellent essay seven years before Portia had even been born, beggared belief. "We are being used, Kitty! Used and abused and lied to. Subjugated by the wrongly privileged, simply to maintain the status quo which they've managed to unjustly keep for millennia!"

A travesty that could not be allowed to continue when people were suffering all around them!

"Portia." Her friend released a heavy sigh. "I think all your insomnia has finally caught up with you and you are delirious. You need to go to sleep. *We* need to go to sleep. So, hand me that pamphlet which has incensed you so, and we'll discuss whatever it is that has enraged you tomorrow when we are both more refreshed and rational." Kitty tried to grab it, but Portia snatched it from her grasp.

"Mrs. Wollstonecraft states that people should be judged on their merits, Kitty, and not on their birthrights. Birthrights, I might add, that all those pompous dukes and pious earls and hedonistic kings probably stole from someone else at some point in history anyway. Yet because of them—because they have stolen *all* our power and control our government—we have to survive by living off their meager scraps. Bowing to our supposed betters lest they take their frugal largesse away and leave us to die in the gutters!"

"Look around you, Portia." Kitty huffed her impatience as she swept her arm to encompass their shadowy Mayfair bedchamber. "We are hardly living on frugal scraps or in the gutter, so please shut up so that I can go back to sleep. We've got a deportment class at eight, and I promised Miss P faithfully that I would actually arrive to my first lesson on time today."

"But don't you see that is part of the problem? The entire premise of this school feeds into the corrupted facade we are all forced to exist behind. We aren't just being taught duty, decorum, diligence, and discretion at all times." Otherwise known as the Four *D*'s, the cornerstones of Miss Prentice's teachings and the mantra she had repeated almost hourly since the afternoon post had dropped Portia outside this school on Half Moon Street seven days ago. The school where, for reasons known only to Miss P, Portia had been handpicked, out of the blue, to train to be a governess. "We are being taught our place, Kitty. And worse, we are being indoctrinated into not only accepting it—but being grateful for the opportunity to serve our oppressors rather than question their authority or push for reform."

"If this is a dreadful facade"—Kitty gestured around the pretty, cozy room again—"I am utterly at peace with it. Just as I am utterly at peace with learning the Four *D*'s so that I can become one of Miss P's coveted protégées. Because everyone knows that a protégée can command twice the normal salary from one of our *oppressors* than any run-of-the-mill governess could. In fact, I actually consider myself quite fortunate at this very moment and so should you. Most girls of our station would give their right arms to become a protégée."

"Doesn't the injustice of *our station* bother you?"

"Not as much as it currently bothers you." Her friend rolled over so that her back faced Portia. "Read your silly pamphlet till your eyes bleed if you have to, but in the name of all that is holy, kindly shut up so that I can head back to dreamland." Kitty's head burrowed beneath her pillow in an attempt to do just that and groaned when Portia yanked it away.

"We need to change the world, Kitty, just like Mary Wollstonecraft says. We need to end the aristocracy's prolonged tenure of tyranny that is held together with nothing but pomp, tradition, and our oppressors' lies." She raised a righteous finger and jabbed the air. "We need to shout the truth from the rafters and stand up for the rights that those with ill-gotten hereditary power work so hard to deny us. It is our civic responsibility, as the next generation, to save all future generations from their suffocating and soul-destroying influence. Surely you can see that?"

"Right at this precise moment, all I want to see is the back of my eyelids, but if you want a revolution, by all means go ahead and start one." Kitty yanked her pillow back and flopped back down on it. "But don't blame me if you end up guillotined for it!"

And there was the rub!

Dare question the oppressors and you'd probably end up punished for it. It was a vicious cycle that would not stop until a few brave souls stuck their heads above the parapet and enlightened the rest of the oppressed to both the truth and the alternatives.

"Perhaps I will start the revolution." Because they had never guillotined people here in England. They didn't even chop people's heads off nowadays either, so she wouldn't allow fear to put her off doing what was right. Reforming the entire system from the top all the way down to the bottom was a daunting prospect for a sixteen-year-old girl with no actual prospects—but Portia had never shied away from a challenge. Especially when it suddenly felt like her overwhelming destiny to rise to the occasion. "And perhaps, when I've freed you and the rest of the working masses from the shackles of servitude, you'll thank me for it."

When Kitty failed to reply, Portia poked her in the ribs. "I shall not rest until I do it, Kitty Blackstone, and I will. You mark my words."

Although quite how a down-at-heel gamekeeper's daughter from Somerset was going to do all that when she grew up was anyone's guess.

Then it came to her—her second epiphany of the night—she would use her words just like Mary Wollstonecraft! And those words, those irrefutable, truthful arguments, would be relentless until the world listened and agreed to change things.

The days of entitled earls and detestable dukes controlling everything were numbered.

She was so inspired, she got up and went in search of a pen and some paper and, to mark her epiphany, set about writing her first-ever essay. Putting all her tangled thoughts on paper, organizing her arguments and backing them with evidence.

Blithely unaware of how just the significance of writing it all down was going to end up changing her life in ways that she couldn't yet imagine.

Chapter
TWO

THE CITY OF BATH, LATE MAY 1821 . . .

Portia's tummy was doing somersaults as she walked across Pulteney Bridge toward the less-populated outskirts of Bath. The bulk of her nerves were due to excitement at the new challenge ahead, but there was enough self-doubt and fear to make her question the unpopular and very hasty choice she had just made. Because while her three best friends, Kitty, Lottie, and Georgie, had all wished her well on her adventure, they had also made no secret of the fact that they agreed wholeheartedly with Miss Prentice. That it was rash to potentially throw away everything for an impassioned whim.

Aside from the fact that she didn't have any clear idea what she was letting herself in for, giving up a well-paid position as a governess in Mayfair to become the temporary assistant editor of *Equitas*, the reforming periodical that Portia had written periodically for these past five years, was a huge and reckless gamble. One that Miss P had urged her repeatedly to reconsider. "Principles are all well and good, dearest," she had said with a shake of her head, "but they do not pay the bills. And who is going to employ you here again in Mayfair when those principles are exposed?"

Miss P was right, of course.

Always a committed overachiever, Portia had worked hard since she had graduated Miss Prentice's School for Young Ladies to excel as much as a governess as she had a political writer. Furthermore, unlike Kitty and Lottie, who had frequently managed to get themselves dismissed, she had a largely unblemished record as a governess. But that wouldn't mean a thing if word of her involvement with this newspaper ever leaked out—which it doubtless would with her name printed in it weekly.

Thanks to a tumultuous few years, the government and the majority of the ton saw *Equitas* as the enemy. An instrument of sedition and the mouthpiece of radical revolutionaries who wanted to crush the aristocracy and destroy the very fabric of British society. At best, she would be branded a troublemaker of the highest order if her words and deeds caused the authorities consternation. At worst, she would be tried as a criminal! In the last five years alone, two of the newspaper's former editors had been imprisoned. One on trumped-up charges of treason, which had been quickly dropped, and the other for incitement to riot. That the latest one of those, whom she was so hastily replacing, looked to be imminently sent to a penal colony in the New World was a cause of grave concern that she couldn't ignore. Nobody would employ a governess with a criminal record, and she sincerely doubted anyone would need one if she ended up transported to Botany Bay.

And if all that wasn't gamble enough to make her question her snap decision to come here, as much as it galled her to admit it—even to herself—she also had to factor the problem of her sex into the equation. Reformers liked to think of themselves as an egalitarian bunch; however, it was no coincidence that all the leaders of the movement were men, and men, as a general rule, tended to think of women as the weaker sex.

Portia had constantly been pushed to the rear as a result. Relegated to creating pamphlets or writing other people's speeches, rather than taking on the more important and influential role at the forefront of the movement that she craved. It did not matter that she had a unique and convincing way with words, or that she was twice as clever and had worked twice as hard as any of the men she tirelessly campaigned beside at the United League for Reform's headquarters—this was ultimately still a man's world. That she had been given the position at *Equitas* simply because her predecessor had just been arrested and was currently awaiting trial in a Bristol prison did not help her plight either. Portia was the last-minute, make-do replacement while the men in charge waited either for the original candidate to be released or, if he was sent down, for a more suitable male replacement to be found. Hence, they had been at great pains to caveat her position here at the newspaper as only "temporary."

Yet despite those many obstacles, here she still was.

Because she felt in her gut that this was her chance to shine.

To make a real difference in the war for reform.

Because principles mattered.

The truth mattered.

The rights of men—and women—mattered.

Because she believed too passionately in the cause to not take this risk and because, even after she had debated all the pros and cons in a soul-searching essay to herself that had extended to ten whole pages, she had come to the irrefutable conclusion that this was the right thing to do.

She walked down to the quay and scanned the row of ramshackle buildings, comparing them to her instructions. The office of *Equitas* wasn't easy to spot, but then she discovered it was the shabbiest warehouse of the lot. She wasn't surprised by that. The United League for Reform ran on a shoestring and the newspaper had to move thrice since it had been forced out of London three years ago. There weren't many respectable landlords who would rent space to "trouble," especially trouble that infuriated the government.

She wasn't surprised to find the well-hidden door locked either, to keep trouble out, so she knocked and waited as excitement fizzed.

"Who is it?" The voice inside sounded wary.

She took a second to straighten her shoulders, pull herself to her full height, and enjoy the significance of this moment because it had been a long time coming. "Miss Portia Kendall. Your new assistant editor." An achievement she was beyond proud of, because now her words would travel the length and breadth of the country every single week—the assistant editor of *Equitas* always, always, always wrote the opinion piece that sat at the very top of the newspaper.

What sounded like twenty bolts shifted before the door was flung open to reveal a smiling man with thick spectacles and a mane of curling gray hair. "You drew the short straw, did you? My condolences." He beckoned her across the threshold. "But you are very welcome nonetheless. For my sins, I am William Stowe." He held out his hand and she smiled, a little in awe, as she shook it. "Editor in chief of this scandalous and seditious rag."

"I know who you are, Sir William. I've been reading your articles and essays for years." Sir William Stowe was up there with Mary Wollstonecraft, as far as Portia was concerned, and one of the main reasons she had done everything in her power, including some unbecoming begging, to be here so fast.

Academic.

Lawyer.

Orator and writer extraordinaire. This eccentric-looking old man was an unwavering, unapologetic legend of the reform movement. "And I didn't draw the short straw, sir—I volunteered." The chance to work alongside one of her idols and soak up some of his genius, albeit temporarily, was too good an opportunity to miss.

"Ah . . . the folly of youth." He chuckled as he bolted the door behind her. "Did nobody ever tell you to never volunteer for anything as it is invariably a mistake that you will live to regret? I take it you are full of vim and vigor and principles and as keen to get cracking as I have been assured that you are?"

"Of course."

"Excellent," he said. "I am an admirer of your articles too, by the way. That one you wrote for us last month on the willful ignorance of the aristocracy to the plight of the poor on their doorsteps in the capital was eye-opening and very well researched. It certainly made me think."

"Thank you, Sir William." If she died and went to heaven right this second, she would go happily. Being praised for one of her essays by the great Sir William Stowe was a magnificent achievement in itself. She would have been cock-a-hoop with just the knowledge that he had read one!

"Call me William," he said as he disappeared through another door, expecting her to follow. "It's only a matter of time before the powers that be take that silly knighthood away, and we don't do airs and graces here at *Equitas* because we are all in this together." A throwaway comment that was music to her ears. He was every bit as wonderful and egalitarian in person as he was in print. A true man of the people. "Let me show you around."

Portia followed him into the most disorganized shambles she had ever seen in her life. She tried not to judge, but this was not how she pictured the flagship newspaper of the reform movement to look. There were piles of discarded correspondence and books tossed hither and thither; stacks of paper lined the crumbling walls and blocked the gangways, the lack of order making her head spin. The only area that wasn't filled with clutter was occupied by a giant printing press that looked so old it might have come off the ark.

"This is where all the magic happens." He swept his arm to encompass the chaos. "My apologies for the mess, but we had to move premises in a bit of a hurry to thwart a raid last month after your predecessor—that idiot firebrand Reynolds—got himself arrested. Although I knew that was only a matter of time the first moment I met him."

"Why?" Back in London, the recently imprisoned Matthew Reynolds was being heralded as a martyr to the cause. They were even going to send a brilliant but expensive London lawyer all the way to Bristol to defend him at his trial, so it was interesting that Sir William thought so ill of him.

"Because the fool forgot the first golden rule of life—the pen is always mightier than the sword!" Portia nodded like a woodpecker. "In his limited wisdom," continued her idol, "he thought violence would work more effectively than logic. Rather than use words to make people think differently, the fool tired of *Equitas* and abandoned us almost immediately to raise his own little army of like-minded troublemakers and then did his utmost to whip them into a frenzy." Sir William—just William—shook his head with disgust. "Even if our local member of Parliament is an arse—which he very much is—taking that mob to his house and threatening him with a gun is not the least bit acceptable."

"What on earth did he hope to achieve doing that?" Despite her revolutionary ideals, Portia had always believed that violence was the absolute last straw. But then her pen had always been her weapon of choice, as the perennial ink stains on her fingers were testament. The power of a well-chosen word was infinite. It could soothe, it could educate, it could banish indecision, it could highlight an injustice, it could elicit a smile or a laugh or a tear—and it could wound.

William shrugged. "Infamy is my best guess. He fancied himself a sort of George Washington character, without the common sense and intelligence necessary, of course, who would personally lead the revolution."

"That is not the narrative we heard at headquarters."

"I am not the least bit surprised." William huffed in exasperation. "The only thing Reynolds truly excelled at was twisting the facts to suit his purpose and blowing his own trumpet. I should imagine he has painted himself some sort of plaster saint in his frequent dispatches to London. Which, to be frank, was the only work he ever did here on the few occasions he graced us with his presence. The man was a waste of space and caused us more trouble than he was worth."

He gestured to the chaotic office. "Thanks to him, we were almost shut down for good so, in my less charitable moments, I am relieved that he is no longer *Equitas*'s problem."

William then raised a finger in the air as if addressing a crowd. "If we are ever going to create a fairer country for all, those in power need to see us as their intellectual equals with valid arguments that are worthy of consideration—not rampaging marauders. Nobody is going to willingly give the vote to a man wielding a pitchfork with murder in his eyes." He pinned Portia with his stare, his narrowed eyes magnified by the thick lenses of his spectacles. "You are not a pitchfork wielder, are you, Portia? Because I expressly requested that they send me an editor with some common sense and the ability to see reason this time."

"I'm a teacher by trade, not a marauder." Her revolutionary ideals had mellowed a great deal since the age of sixteen, thanks to a combination of education and maturity, so she was now of the firm belief that everyone would be better off if reform occurred without the need for a revolution. And certainly not the sort of bloody, arbitrary, and vengeful revolution like they had had across the Channel in France. Not everything here in Britain was broken, and throwing out the baby with the bathwater was never the answer. "I want equality and change to come from enlightenment and not down the threatening barrel of a gun."

"Excellent! We should get on famously then. Tea?"

She already held Sir William Stowe in the highest esteem, but he went up in her estimation by several notches when he didn't expect her to make that tea. Better still, he continued to make no mention of the fact that she was a woman at all. Nor did he make any concession for it as he explained what her role entailed over that tea. A role so complicated, Portia had to pull out her notebook to list all of it down.

"For obvious reasons, we are very cautious about security here," he said as he handed her a key. "The worst of the local constables has always had it in for us, but even more so since the Reynolds incident and the thwarted raid. So be sure to always come here by the most convoluted route possible and frequently check that you aren't being followed."

"I became quite adept at that in London." Being a reformer nowadays was as much about smoke and mirrors as it was about reforming. "Especially during daylight hours."

"Indeed. It is always easier to be clandestine at night." William toasted her with his teacup. "On that subject, we don't tend to keep regular hours here unless it's a Sunday when we go to print—then, of course, it is all hands on deck, so you've got a few days to unpack and get your bearings after your long journey. I take it you've already found lodging?"

"It's on my list of things to do, but for now I'm staying at an inn in town." One that, because this was Bath, was costing her an arm and a leg, but it had still seemed the more prudent option than staying at her mother's. As much as they loved one another, her mother absolutely did not approve of Portia's political endeavors at all. It had always been a sore topic that led to arguments, and so she was best avoided in the short term. Portia would only tell her the news that she was back home when she had proved herself worthy enough as the temporary assistant editor of *Equitas* to be made permanent.

"An inn here doesn't come cheap during the season," he said as if he read her mind.

"It doesn't." Just one week would make a huge dent in her savings. Two would likely decimate them entirely. "But once I know what my salary is, I can find a place that is more in line with my budget." She smiled, pleased at the subtle but direct way she had brought up money.

"Salary?" He blinked at her, confused.

"My wages, sir? For the position of assistant editor?"

William's stricken expression set alarm bells ringing. "Oh my dear girl, there aren't any. Everyone who works at *Equitas* gives their time gratis—myself included. Every last penny we make from sales of the paper is plowed back into keeping it going. Could headquarters afford to pay you a salary for the work you did for them in London?" Quite rightly, he appeared surprised by that.

"Well no . . . but . . ." Why the blazes hadn't she thought to ask this before she had thrown away her entire livelihood on an impassioned whim? But she knew the answer to that already. She had been so excited about the prospect of finally doing something truly meaningful for the cause that she had dropped everything without a single pause for thought. Dizziness swamped her as the reality of her situation hit, because nowhere in her ten-page essay that had helped her to make the decision to come had not earning a single farthing even been considered. "I assumed—"

"Never assume anything, Portia." William winced. "That's the second golden rule of life."

"It really should be the first." Her head fell into her hands while her mind reeled, and she wondered what the hell she was going to do now. Because Miss Prentice was right about one thing—principles were all well and good, but they didn't pay the bills.

Chapter
THREE

"I am sorry, Abigail, but I am putting my foot down." For some inexplicable reason, to underscore his frustration, Leo's booted foot came down with a decisive thud on the parquet, which made his sensitive giant mastiff whimper. He didn't like being the despotic big brother who laid down the law any more than poor Snifferson liked to hear his humans arguing but, frankly, his wayward sister had given him no choice of late. "My decision is final! You are all staying here in Bath for the rest of the season and that is the end of it." By which time he hoped his unsettlingly frayed nerves had repaired themselves and his headstrong sister would have the time and space to get over her worrying infatuation with the handsome, charming, and exceedingly dangerous Mr. Percival Digby.

Reading his mind, Abigail folded her arms, defiant. "If you think your being heavy-handed and keeping me here against my will for months on end is going to make me love Percy any less, you are wrong!" Good heavens above but she was being dramatic! "We shall pine for each other for the duration of my imprisonment because we are hopelessly in love. Not that I expect you to understand such an alien concept when all you seem to care about nowadays is yourself!"

He folded his own arms and, feeling wholly justified to have been heavy-handed, descended into sarcasm. "Ah yes . . . I am such a selfish, self-centered soul. I love being weighted down with the responsibility of a dukedom. Of managing all those thousands of acres that pay for your comfortable life. Of burning the midnight oil trying to juggle the unwieldy accounts of the estate and two households alongside the pressing matters of governance that we dukes get dragged into, whether we want to or not. Of wasting hours and hours—that I do not have—traveling backward and forward to London to accompany my ungrateful sisters to pointless balls which I have no interest in. Chatting to annoying, superficial, social-climbing people who have fluff for brains and live for naught but mindless gossip when I have so many more pressing things to do here. That is just *so* selfish of me."

He wagged his finger like a disappointed schoolmaster. "I especially love having to clean up the frequent messes that my spoiled sisters get themselves into! Because heaven only knows someone needs to have a care for your safety when you both have such little regard for it yourselves!" If Abigail thought being him was fun, then perhaps she could take a stint at being the 11th Duke of Debden, because Lord only knew that he was sick to the back teeth of it all.

Leo was only thirty, for goodness' sake, but felt more like sixty after just four years of ducal responsibility. It wouldn't be fair to blame his father for dying on him so young and leaving him to it all, because poor Papa had been a duke for twenty years before he had turned up his worn-out toes and floated off to heaven. But this last month, Leo repeatedly wished he'd had an older brother so he wouldn't have been destined to be a blasted duke in the first place and could just go off and be plain old Leopold Sloane instead.

He would have liked being the spare rather than the heir.

Spares could freely indulge in unburdened selfishness.

But instead, he had been cursed with sisters who had suddenly decided to gravitate toward trouble like moths to a flame. They were determined to think of him as the devil incarnate because he was the only thing keeping them from it.

He wanted to stamp his foot again but, for the sake of Snifferson's delicate nerves, settled for another finger wag. "So yes, Abigail, as the frustrated head of this family and entirely because of your utterly reckless deception, you gave me no choice but to drag you here to keep you safe from your blasted self!" Perhaps it had been a more extreme reaction than usual from him, but it had been instantaneous and visceral as well as entirely necessary, so he refused to regret it.

Abigail, who had more than a modicum of sense when she chose to remember, quickly changed tack. "How many times do I have to tell you that I just happened to be in the wrong place at the wrong time before you realize that you are overreacting? None of it was Percy's fault."

"Overreacting!" Leo pointed to the bandage still wrapped around his sister's head, queasy at the sight of it, and queasier still at all the what-ifs that had kept him awake this past week since she had acquired it. "If bloody Percy hadn't taken you to that protest rally in the first place, then you wouldn't have been hit in the face by the hilt of a soldier's bloody sword!"

The image of his sister being carried through the front door of his Berkeley Square town house by the scoundrel, barely conscious and bleeding profusely, was one that had haunted him ever since. "I forbade you to involve yourself with those radicals and he went behind my back and dragged you into danger! Are you aware that you could have been killed?" Because that was all he could bloody well think about. That she had almost died—again—while on his watch, and it had scared the life out of him. Enough that he kept being sucked into a spiral of blind panic as a result. Panic that left him breathless, tight in the chest, and was so overwhelming he could barely function.

"For the millionth time—" Abigail stamped her own foot in frustration and Snifferson whimpered again. "I didn't die and Percy did not convince me to go!" She fisted her arms at her sides and stuck out her chin, not in any way prepared to see reason. "If you must know, he begged me not to go to that rally because he sensed there would be trouble, but I disobeyed him too!" That he believed, because Abigail had always been as tenacious as she was stubborn and historically reckless in the extreme. But that defense only increased Leo's unease. "I joined that protest of my own accord!"

As his hair follicles bristled at that terrifying comment and his innards constricted, it only reinforced how right he had been about refusing to leave his headstrong sister in London. There was too much temptation there for her to indulge in her second grand passion after Percy—politics. Except rather than simply read about it or debate it over dinner like most did, she was one to rally behind a cause. What had started as the desire to knit socks for the poor, a perfectly hazard-free use of her time, had now morphed into the need to show her support more vocally. That hadn't been the first protest march she had gone on in recent months, and he sincerely doubted it would be the last, hence he had been forced to take this decisive action to stop her.

"In which case, Percy should have done the decent thing and immediately dragged you home where none of that"—Leo pointed to her wound again as the tight bands of panic that had decided to plague him since the incident twisted themselves around his throat like choking brambles—"would have happened and your stubborn, willful head wouldn't have been sliced open!"

"Why must you always exaggerate! It's naught but a graze and looked far worse than it actually was." She waved the injury away as if it were nothing. "The physician doubts it will even leave a noticeable scar."

"That *graze* was bad enough that it needed five stitches!" Stitches he had sat holding her hand for while sick to his stomach because he had never been any good with the sight of blood. Especially his sister's.

"And you had a concussion." That rare interjection of support, miraculously, came from his mother, who did not approve of Leo's hasty solution of removing them all to Bath either. "Your pretty new summer pelisse was ruined. Bloodstains are forever, darling." And that, in a nutshell, pretty much summed up his mother, who put a silly stain above personal safety and believed, catastrophically in his humble opinion, that his sisters needed to make their own mistakes. "I really don't understand what you were thinking, Abigail, to chant with a group of filthy rabble-rousing radicals in the center of Westminster like you did."

"Asking for an honest day's pay for an honest day's work hardly makes those poor factory workers radicals, Mama, and any rabble-rousing came from the unnecessarily heavy hand of the king's own soldiers. Soldiers, I might add, who were sent to quash a peaceful protest simply because they did not like what the protesters were protesting about." Abigail jabbed the air. "Just as they did at Peterloo two years ago. For heaven forbid they should tolerate any justified dissension in the lower ranks."

The mere mention of the infamous Peterloo Massacre, where eighteen had been slain and several hundred more were injured by overzealous soldiers, instantly made Leo's hair shoot vertical again. Just as it had that day when bloody Percy had carried her limp body home. In truth, the fear of history repeating itself while his sister was present was the main reason he'd brought her here where he could keep a constant eye on her.

"The army was only called in because it was an unauthorized protest!" As soon as those words left his lips, Leo knew he had given his outraged sister more ammunition.

"Of course it was unauthorized! The new laws against any form of protest are so Draconian and unreasonable, the only way to protest nowadays *is* illegally!"

As her point was valid, Leo quickly pivoted. "There are better ways to bring about reform, Abigail, than to align yourself to the radical cause. And reform will come." Bloodlessly. Or so he hoped. And without any further danger to his reckless sister. "The tide in Parliament is changing."

"At a speed slower than a snail over sand, Leo, which you would know if you attended there as often as you should!" A point he couldn't argue with either because the majority of the House of Lords still feared a bloody revolution that rivaled those that had happened in France and America, and therefore refused to concede an inch. They were so wedded to their outrage and entrenched in their ways that he had long given up trying to argue with them. Parliament gave him acid. Much like his sister was doing now. Unfortunately, he could only avoid one of those indigestible things, and it wasn't Abigail. "Meanwhile, while you ignore your duty, the people are still suffering."

Abigail huffed and, to further remind him of his unconscionable failings as a big brother, began to pace the Persian rug. Her limp was barely noticeable nowadays—but he noticed.

Leo always noticed because it was his fault she had it.

"It is a travesty how little the factory workers are paid, Leo, and you know it!"

Before this turned into a discussion on what was morally right and what was so plainly wrong, which he knew he couldn't win, he turned the topic back yet again to the safety of his womenfolk. "Until you marry, it is my sworn duty to protect you from harm. I promised Father—"

He was cut off by his sister's theatrical groan. "I might have known you'd link a small knock to my head with *the accident* and blow it out of all proportion." She rolled her eyes heavenward in a god-give-me-strength kind of way. The flippant gesture was mirrored by both his mother and his younger and sillier sister, Emilia, who all currently believed that he had mentally traveled back in time and was confusing Abigail's first wholly avoidable brush with death all those years ago with her most recent. Which was true, he supposed, in part.

Not that he would admit it aloud.

"Is that why you are more insufferable than normal? You are being an overbearing oaf because you feel guilty that I got a little knock to the head that you should have predicted and prevented, just as you believe you should have prevented me from climbing up that tree almost fifteen years ago?"

Of course it bloody well was!

She had fallen out of that tree as a child because he had failed to keep an eye on her that day, despite being tasked by his father to watch his sisters like a hawk. And she had got injured at last week's protest because he had failed to diligently protect her, yet again.

"Not at all." Both Abigail and his mother eyed him dubiously, so he continued undeterred. "I am being *insufferable* because one of us has to behave like a sensible adult and that clearly isn't going to be you."

Intercepting his sister's next interruption, Leo raised an imperious palm. "A bit of time and distance gives perspective, which you currently do not have, and a few months at home here in Bath will give us all time to reflect. Besides—we've not spent a season in Bath together in forever."

"For good reason," muttered his mother, "as it pales into insignificance against the London season because *nobody* is here."

"What nonsense! This city is a veritable hubbub of activity." To prove that he marched to the window to pull back the lace curtain, expecting to see the usual gaggle of tourists wandering along the Royal Crescent in awe and wonder at its architectural splendor, only to be confronted with a street as barren as the desert.

"Such a crush," said Abigail clutching her pearls before she rolled her eyes for the umpteenth time. "How are we to contain ourselves with so much pointless excitement going on all around us?"

"Bath is filled with nothing but old people and invalids." That came from Emilia, who had never liked being in their second home whenever there were leaves on the trees. "Here to take the waters in the hope that they will feel invigorated enough to be able to return to London where all the excitement actually is." Which was why she rarely came here anymore.

In fact, unlike Leo, none of his womenfolk had ventured here much since his father's passing. The ladies had visited only a handful of times in the last four years. Probably because there were reminders of the former duke everywhere and that made them all melancholy.

Leo, on the other hand, had no choice but to be here often. The bulk of his estate was made up of lands surrounding Bath, and it was impossible to manage it all from afar. However, what his sisters found boring, he found peaceful, and so this house had become his oasis. A place to escape all the noise and nonsense of London and simply . . . be.

"I have no friends here in Bath." Emilia was pouting now. "So I shall be bored to tears if I am incarcerated here all summer."

"Neither of us have any friends here." Abigail shot him a look that would curdle milk. "Which is precisely why our overprotective big brother has dragged us here. He wants us to be bored. Bored and dutiful because all that ruthless control makes his life so much easier."

"Actions have consequences, Abigail, and you have brought this on yourself." Leo gestured to his glaring sister's bandage again and instantly felt his pulse race. "As the head of this household, those consequences are mine to meter out." *Oh good grief, now he sounded like a bloody tyrant too and he loathed himself for it.* Loathed how out of control he felt. How unsettled and afraid he felt. Why couldn't his womenfolk see that he was doing this out of love? When he was saving them from themselves and keeping them from harm at the same time. Why did they have to keep pushing him and pushing him until the red mist descended and all his new and terrifying panic, which he still had no clue how to control, possessed him completely?

"Besides, I fail to see how a couple of months of blessed peace is too much to ask after all the worry you have caused?" As tempers were heightened enough already, he tried to be conciliatory. "All I am asking for is the summer—not eternity." Some time for them all to regroup and him especially. "And you will soon make friends here. I have a huge stack of invitations to all manner of things in my study and there is a ball at the Assembly Rooms twice a week, so there will be plenty for you to do."

Rather than be placated by that, Emilia looked stricken. "I do not see why I should be punished with the parochial society of Bath because of Abigail's mistake. I did nothing wrong."

"This week," he felt compelled to clarify. "But I think we can both agree that some of your decisions this season have left a lot to be desired. Especially those involving the opposite sex." He did not need to add that Emilia was damned lucky not to have been completely ruined a fortnight ago. If he hadn't accidentally interrupted her passionate kiss with a fortune-hunter soldier in the stables during Lady Bulphan's house party, all the other guests would have witnessed her up to no good when they had arrived mere moments later. What would have happened if he hadn't been there really did not bear thinking about. "Without someone sensible keeping an eye on you constantly, I shudder to think what will happen to you the next time you recklessly flirt with a man in uniform as you completely lose your head."

"How dare you imply that I am not sensible! I am quite capable of chaperoning my daughters," said his mother, annoyed. Although why she felt the right to be aggrieved was a mystery to him, when it was all thanks to her lackadaisical chaperoning that Emilia had been ravished and Abigail had snuck out to go on that hideously dangerous blasted march! "And have managed to do it well enough in your absence for most of the last two years!"

"Did you try to stop Abigail from absconding to that rally or do anything to prevent Emilia from sneaking off with that scoundrel at Lady Bulphan's? No, Mama, you did not. Worse, you did not even notice that either of them was missing until I pointed it out, so I rest my case." *Were none of them capable of seeing reason, for pity's sake?* Or of seeing the danger everywhere that kept him awake at night?

"Your sisters are adults, Leo, and need to follow their own paths.

That includes being allowed to learn from their mistakes rather than you suffocating them with your overbearing, I-know-best interference." His mother bristled, clearly missing the point that, where his sisters were concerned, he jolly well did know best! "Perhaps if you attempted to treat them like adults, they wouldn't feel so inclined to rebel like children whenever you are home!"

How typical that he would be blamed for their rebelliousness! "A convenient way of saying that you fail to even notice all of their shenanigans when I am not, Mother!"

"If there are shenanigans, you push them to it, Leo! With your controlling ways and doomsaying mentality, which frankly has increased a hundredfold since last week."

"If my sisters want to be treated like adults, they need to cease being so reckless! And we are all staying here for the summer as a consequence and that is that!"

"Well, I am not," said his mother, standing. "I have much better things to do with my time than waste it trying to sort out this epic, ham-fisted mess that you have decided to make, Leo! If you genuinely think that you know best and can do a better job of keeping a keen eye on this family than I can, then you can jolly well get on with it without my help! I am going on strike and heading back to Mayfair forthwith!"

"Then go with my blessing, Mama, as I am more than capable of properly chaperoning my sisters here without you. In fact, I suspect I shall do a much better job of it because they will have less chance of absconding without your *keen eye* on them."

"You seriously think yours will be keener?" His mother had the audacity to laugh. "You—who by his own admission does not possess enough hours in the day to deal with all your ducal responsibilities?" She laughed some more. In that annoying and sarcastic way that she did when she thought her only son an idiot. "Your aggrieved and willful sisters will run rings around you in my absence after what you have just done to them, mark my words."

"No they won't," he replied, suddenly doubting his own hubris.

"I wouldn't bank on that, big brother," said Abigail with such a bright light of defiance shimmering in her eyes that his already racing heartbeat decided to kick into a gallop. "You are going to have to find a dungeon to lock me in if you want me to behave like the adult you refuse to allow me to be."

"Me too." Emilia linked arms with her sister. "For be in no doubt, if I am being forced to stay here under duress, I shall need to do something to relieve the tedium. I do hope that there are plenty of soldiers here in Bath to alleviate our crushing boredom."

That below-the-belt threat made his incorrigible mother chuckle as she sailed out of the room. "Good luck being me too, Leo. You are certainly going to need it."

Chapter
FOUR

A week of desperately scouring the situations-vacant advertisements later, Portia found herself in the house of a duke on the prestigious and elitist Royal Crescent for an interview. About to bite her tongue in the vain hope of serving the aristocracy again when she had foolishly thought that all her subservient years were behind her.

However, she had made her bed and, for the good of the cause, she would jolly well lie in it—but the irony of this situation was not lost on her. Earning a wage from someone from the very upper echelons of the aristocracy was the only way that she could afford *not* to earn one at *Equitas*.

Assuming, that was, that she got this job over the other candidate sitting several feet away, who had been there when she had arrived and who was still doing her best to ignore her.

"Good afternoon." It felt churlish not to be polite despite them being rivals. Her interview for the temporary post of social secretary and chaperone was supposed to have started now, so they were both clearly stuck here until the poor timekeeper who was interviewing them deigned to see them. "I am Portia." She smiled her best let's-be-pleasant-because-we-are-in-the-same-boat smile because she harbored no malice whatsoever for the stern-faced older woman who was dressed head to toe in funereal black. "Portia Kendall."

"Good afternoon." Madam Sourpuss could not have made it plainer that she was only answering because manners dictated it. "I am Miss Strictland." A name that seemed to perfectly suit her as the woman clutched her austere black reticule closer to her body, almost as if she expected Portia to steal it from her at any moment, and turned back to stare at the wall. She probably also gargled vinegar to keep her judgmental frown in place constantly while she glared down her hook of a nose. As glares went, Miss Strictland's was quite impressive. It certainly let Portia know that she considered herself far superior in every way possible.

"Have you traveled far today?" As she had never been one for airs and graces, especially among those who had to serve their betters just like she did, she could not resist goading Miss Strictland into further conversation.

"Only from the *Circus*." Her rival gave her a slightly smug nod because anyone who knew Bath knew that the Circus was the only residential street in this city that came close to the Royal Crescent in grandeur. If the Crescent was the shimmering crown that sat atop the city's biggest hill, the Circus was its diamond choker. "Where I have been governess to the Marquess of Teignmouth's three daughters these past twenty years." Preempting Portia's next question, the woman wafted an imperious hand. "The youngest has recently come out, so she really has no need of a governess anymore. The family still want me to stay, of course." She wafted her hand again as if it held all the cards, which Portia did not believe for a minute when servants were always disposable as far as the aristocracy was concerned. "However, when they finally accepted that *I* was ready for a new challenge and that my skills and experience would be more beneficial to another grand family with exacting standards, they *personally* recommended me to the duke." That depressing piece of news was delivered with the semblance of a smile designed to inform Portia that she really did not stand a chance.

Which, if it were true, would not have meant that both of them were here for an interview, so Portia was going to give this her best shot regardless. Especially because this particular vacancy was ideal for her very particular requirements. The salary was decent and the advertisement had been clear that her hours would be confined to the daytime. Such regular hours meant that she would have every single evening free to fulfill her vital and extensive workload for the newspaper. As much as she loathed the idea of being an aristocrat's servant again, this position also came with a room and board and that would be a godsend in this expensive city.

The same clerk who had taken her dubious letters of recommendation when she had arrived reappeared and traced his finger down the worryingly long list in his hand. "Miss Strictland—his grace will see you now."

Well, well, well, Portia hadn't expected the illustrious duke to be the one conducting today's interviews. That was unusual. Men with grand titles usually had minions to deal with unpleasantries like their staff. At the very best, she had expected his duchess to put aside her urgent needlepoint to spare her five minutes, not the great man himself. In the normal order of things, he would be doing more important tasks like shooting his pheasants or drinking brandy in his club or tupping his mistress. But no! Today he was apparently going to honor those so far beneath him with an audience. This would be interesting.

Portia had seen the odd duke from afar, but she had never actually met a real one before and, because she disapproved of the breed and all that they stood for in general, wasn't overkeen to meet one now—but such was life.

She knew already what he would be like.

Gray-haired and supercilious.

Humorless and superior.

Primped like a peacock as he looked down his pompous, ducal nose at her with more gusto than the lowly Miss Strictland could ever manage, while never quite looking at her directly. Because, of course, the illustrious Duke of Debden would see her as more beneath him than her rival Sourpuss Strictland did—if he even bothered seeing her at all. Servants were somehow rendered invisible in the presence of those with blue blood coursing through their idle veins.

"His grace is running a little behind," said the harried clerk as he reappeared. "It has been a busy morning because he has had a lot of candidates to see."

"Precisely how many candidates is he interviewing?" Because with each one, Portia's odds of getting this job were reduced.

"Ten," said the clerk, rechecking his list. "You are the last—thank goodness."

Marvelous.

That meant that she had to somehow impress him more than the other nine preceding her had, including Miss Strictland with her personal recommendation from a marquess.

Left alone in the cavernous hallway once more, with only the ominous tick of the nearby grandfather clock to break the crushing silence, she took in her surroundings. It was always fascinating to witness how the other half lived and if this impressive hallway was any gauge, the Duke of Debden lived in the most glittering of gilded cages. She counted two Rembrandts, a Titian, and a Gainsborough on the walls of this luxurious marble hallway alone, never mind the impressive bespoke masterpiece gracing his grace's entire palatial ceiling. What sort of person had a mural of Mount Olympus piercing the fluffy white clouds of the sky, complete with every ancient-Greek god imaginable floating around it? The sort who believed they were on a par with the mighty Zeus, that's who! A man so full of his own piss and wind that she despised him already.

Sight unseen.

Another painful twenty minutes ticked by, which also did not bode well as clearly Miss Strictland was holding his interest, and Portia had pretty much given up all hope.

This was pointless.

A hiding to nothing.

A fool's errand.

A complete and utter waste of her time.

The most sensible course of action would be to quietly leave and thus save both herself and the pompous duke from the inevitable misery and disappointment of this pointless interview. She stared longingly at the front door the same moment a fluffy, white Persian cat wandered down the hallway toward her. It had mismatched eyes—one brown and one blue—and neither looked impressed as they stared at her in judgment. Portia held out her hand and made a kissing noise to attract it over to pet it, but the cat merely watched her efforts with disdain before it turned around, lifted its tail, and showed her its backside, which she supposed just said it all.

Then Miss Strictland reappeared with a smug grin. "That went *very* well. But then I knew that it would be impossible for his grace to ignore a *personal* recommendation from his good friend the Marquess of Teignmouth."

"Congratulations," said Portia, her stomach sinking, but she forced a polite smile regardless. "I take it he offered you the job?" Because if he had, then she had an urgent appointment with that front door as she had wasted enough time here already.

Her rival went back to looking down her nose. "Obviously he couldn't offer it to me on the spot as he has one last candidate to see." She flicked her finger dismissively Portia's way. "Good luck, Miss Pendle."

"It's Kendall. Portia Kendall," said Portia to the woman's retreating back and then, under her breath muttered, "you ungracious old hag."

It was, however, that ungraciousness that forced Portia to stay. She had never been good with being underestimated, and Miss Strictland's dismissive behavior, combined with that of the equally snooty cat, lit the familiar fire of rebellion in her belly. Nothing riled her more than being underestimated. Ready for battle and determined to be victorious, Portia sat straighter in her seat and waited for the clerk to return and take her to the duke.

Then she waited.

And waited.

When the grandfather clock chimed and signaled that she had now been waiting for another hour, it confirmed that she was on a hiding to nothing. Worse, the rude wretch hadn't even had the decency to send one of his minions out to tell her!

How dare he treat her as if she did not matter!

Because she mattered! And having inherited privilege and blue blood coursing through his veins was absolutely no excuse for being so rude!

Fuming, she stalked to the front door and was about to open it when a deep voice made her jump. "Miss Kendall?"

She spun a guilty circle and found herself confronted by a man.

A very handsome man.

With deep golden brows furrowed over the most startlingly deep blue eyes that she had ever seen.

He was flanked by two dogs who were both regarding her with interest too. One was a large and wrinkled mastiff with enormous brown paws, the other was a dainty ginger Cavalier spaniel.

"I am sorry to have kept you for so long." Those mesmerizing eyes flicked from her to the front door and back to her again as if he couldn't quite believe that she had had the nerve to try to leave. "Something urgent came up that I had to deal with. Can you still spare me a few more minutes of your time for an interview?" A question that was finished with a smile.

An amused, devastating smile that was bracketed by a pair of unexpected and totally disarming dimples.

"Y-yes, of course." She wasn't sure whether it was the dimples, the eyes, or his broad shoulders that were the cause, but her mouth seemed to suddenly be filled with wool. And her pulse . . .

Much to her complete disgust, it had ratcheted into a gallop.

For a bloody despicable duke!

A despicable, sandy-haired, handsome devil of a duke in his prime!

Oddly ill at ease in his own study for some inexplicable reason, Leo pretended to reread Miss Kendall's letter of application while his thoughts went to war. He had been convinced that Miss Strictland was the ideal candidate to chaperone his exasperating sisters before they exasperated him some more. Hence, a full week after his mother had deserted him, battered and browbeaten and with his already frayed nerves practically shredded, he was forced to acknowledge that he had bitten off far more than he could chew and needed to hire a reinforcement.

Miss Strictland came so well recommended and seemed every bit as no-nonsense and exacting in person as he had been promised. *Formidable* was what his friend the Marquess of Teignmouth had called her, and she was. She had the presence, age, and all the experience necessary to take on what was arguably the worst job in the whole world. Yet there was something about the final candidate sitting before him that gave him pause for thought.

Miss Kendall was, despite her stiff posture and icy glare, undeniably far too young to be taken seriously by his sisters. She couldn't be more than three or four years older than Abigail, so he could not possibly imagine she would be a more effective protector of his wayward siblings than he currently was. Not only was she too young to be a chaperone, but she was also far too pretty to be one. With her near jet-black hair, shimmering dark brown eyes, and trim, womanly figure, Miss Kendall would have to beat the men off with a stick every single time she left the house. By her stern expression, if she'd had a stick handy, he also did not doubt that she would currently use it to beat him with—but that did not lesson her attractiveness one jot.

The absolute last thing his sisters needed was more honey to entice the flies to hover. And hover they had this past week while Abigail and Emilia had dragged him from pillar to post. He had endured endless days of shopping and strolling through the parks for fresh air while they took every attempt to lose him. And of course, to further punish him for the egregious sin of being the brother to two wayward sisters, one of whom was obsessed with soldiers, the First Somerset regiment had mustered in Bath for a month of bloody training maneuvers!

Not that his evenings were much better—but at least in a ballroom or a dining room or a theater, his infuriating siblings were contained. But even so, after being run ragged from eleven in the morning to eleven at night, he had had to resort to burning the midnight oil to get any of his actual work done. Leo was so sleep deprived (doubtless precisely as his evil sisters intended) that he wasn't quite sure which way was up anymore.

A situation that was, frankly, too terrifying to be allowed to continue.

Sensing Miss Kendall was staring at him while his aged spaniel Captain Barkington stared up at her suspiciously from directly beside her chair, Leo lifted his gaze from her letter and tried not to notice how damned attractive the woman was. "You are much younger than I expected, Miss Kendall. Perhaps a bit too young, truth be told."

Two very dark brows kissed in consternation. "Your advertisement failed to stipulate that you required someone of a more matronly age. If it had, I wouldn't have wasted my time applying." She gestured to the paper beneath his hand. "Although my age is clearly stated in my application, your grace. Writ plain as day in the first paragraph."

She made no secret of the fact that she was peeved that he had kept her waiting so long, despite his heartfelt apology. Understandable, he supposed, when he had delayed her for almost an hour. It was hardly her fault that his troublesome sisters had forced him into another stand-up argument because they wanted to go out and he had had to forbid it until he had concluded his business here first.

Miss Kendall had been in the process of leaving when he had fetched her. And bugger, but that had impressed him. People did not usually storm out on a duke. Nor did they pull one up on what they had failed to put in an advertisement or completely missed in a letter. Miss Kendall clearly had some gumption, and whoever had the great misfortune to chaperone his sisters this summer would need that in spades.

"You are quite right, Miss Kendall. I should have stated on the advertisement that I wanted a more mature and experienced chaperone for my sisters, so that is my mistake. I can also see now that your age is clearly in the introductory paragraph too just as you've said." He hoped eating some humble pie might make her glare soften some. It didn't. "You are four-and-twenty." Nowhere near old enough to effectively deal with the two hellions currently plotting against him in the drawing room.

Although he realized why he had missed it in the seven or eight times that he had read her letter yesterday before his curiosity had compelled him to call her in. Because Miss Kendall's application had not been a letter at all, but a thoroughly convincing essay outlining all the reasons why he would be a fool not to employ her.

Leo had never read an application that had started with a question and covered six pages before but, and all credit to her, that method had certainly got his attention. The prickly minx had a way with words. Enough that she was still here despite being the least experienced of all the other nine candidates he had just put through their paces. She was also the first candidate in the history of ever not to sycophantically blow smoke up his arse because of his title. And bugger him but he admired that about her too. Miss Kendall did not suffer fools gladly. Even those with the word "Duke" before their name.

"I see that you have been exclusively a governess these last three years."

"That is correct." She looked him straight in the eye with far more boldness and confidence than all the other nine candidates put together, and answered somewhat begrudgingly in clipped tones. "After graduating from Miss Prentice's School for Young Ladies, I did a year with Sir Cloudsley-Shovlar followed by two years with Lord and Lady Warley."

Leo Knew about Miss Prentice's school because its sterling reputation in Mayfair preceded it. He also, sadly, knew Lord Warley. The fellow was an arse. "I have collided with Lord Warley a time or two in Parliament." From very opposite sides of the house. "His daughters are still quite young, I believe."

"Twelve and fourteen." Good gracious but her level gaze was unwavering.

Miss Kendall was a woman supremely comfortable in her own skin. He envied that. For some inexplicable reason, his currently did not feel like it fitted his frame properly.

Her fault. Something about Miss Kendall unnerved him. Possibly the outright hostility that positively radiated from her. Like his sisters, she made no secret of the fact that she was now here under duress, and yet, still some devil inside him screamed that she was precisely what he needed.

Why the blazes was that?

Determined to prove that screaming voice wrong—because she was plainly wrong in every conceivable way—he decided to probe deeper. Expose all her weaknesses and give himself the evidence he needed to silence the irrational voice in his head and send this hostile, confident minx packing.

"Did you like working for Lord Warley?" He pinned her with his own level stare to test her mettle. She might well be fearless, and he might well need someone who was utterly fearless, but he also needed honest and trustworthy.

She didn't even blink before she answered. "I very much enjoyed being the governess to his two daughters."

"That is a very clever and diplomatic answer, Miss Kendall." He offered her a begrudging smile because she had, inadvertently, passed his first test, drat her. Only an idiot could enjoy working for that nitpicking and obnoxious peer. "But if you enjoyed being the Warleys' governess so much, why did you leave their employ?"

"Because . . ." For the first time her gaze dipped to the hands clasped in her lap and her voice lost its sharp edge. "My mother lives here in Somerset and . . ." She sighed. "She isn't getting any younger." She stared for a while at her suddenly twiddling fingers before her lovely eyes lifted to his again. Still confident but definitely less confrontational. "London is two hundred miles away from where I presently need to be."

"I see." And he did. Leo knew the bond with your own flesh and blood was too strong to ignore. He understood, all too well, how harrowing it was to be worried about a loved one's health. You felt powerless. Hopeless. The guilt ate at you constantly from within. If her mother was ill, then that was the very best reason that there was for leaving Lord Warley, so he quickly changed tack. "I also see that all your experience seems to be as a governess of young girls, whereas I need a social secretary and chaperone for two young ladies. They are very different roles."

"Are they?" She frowned as if she thought that he was stupid to think so. "There are more similarities in the role of a governess and a chaperone than there are differences."

"How so?" Leo found himself leaning closer. She was so animated when she spoke and so assured and . . . spirited. Like his nosy spaniel, he could barely take his eyes off her.

And, heaven help him but he liked that she wasn't a shrinking violet too.

"A good governess has to have excellent organizational skills, your grace . . ." Perhaps it was his imagination, but he was sure her generous lips curled a bit at *your grace*. "She needs to know precisely what is going on at any given time to ensure that she is one step ahead of it. Preferably two because children are unpredictable creatures. I did say as much in my application." She flicked a finger toward it. "She has to find the delicate balance between the social interactions of her charges and their schooling, which can be a challenge when one is fun and the other feels like a chore. Lord and Lady Warley's daughters received many invitations, and it was my responsibility to respond appropriately to all, only accept the right ones, and ensure that they got there without incident. I often had to supervise them while they were there. Then, of course, I had to get them safely home again, which can be quite a challenge when they are overexcited from their visit and full of cake."

Cake! If only the lone reason for his sisters' frequent overexcitement was something quite so innocuous. "But Lord Warley's daughters are children and my sisters are adults. Stubborn and often headstrong adults." Leo had lost count of how many times he had been tempted to wring Abigail and Emilia's necks this week. He had come bloody close to actually doing it an hour ago when he had discovered they were trying to sneak out of the back gate for their afternoon stroll without him while he was occupied with interviews. "Adults who both feel that they do not need chaperoning and, despite neither being of age, should still be able to do as they please."

"Few react well to being told what to do—especially by an overbearing brother." Apparently, on top of all the hostility, Miss Kendall was now insulting him. He was about to defend himself, because the last thing he needed was a bloody chaperone who wasn't on his side either, when she huffed. "Assuming that they see you as the overbearing brother, that is."

"At the moment, they do see me as the enemy, Miss Kendall, but I will not apologize for thinking only of their safety. Especially when . . ." He had no clue why he felt the overwhelming need to justify himself to this confounding woman, but he did. Probably because she had justified every single bold claim she had put in her bloody thorough letter! "There was a particular incident in London recently that necessitated that I bring them both here immediately." She didn't need to know the ins and outs of it. "And stay here they must until the dust settles. That is, if we all survive their outrage at my necessary decision."

"Few respond well to an edict either, your grace." Was that more barely veiled criticism? Her glare was so unyielding he could not tell if she possessed an objectionable character or if she was purposefully trying to be objectional. Or if she simply objected to him. "Laying down the law often leads to unhelpful belligerence. As the old adage says, you catch more flies with honey than vinegar, and I've always found that gentle correction and misdirection are more effective methods of getting my charges to do the right thing than laying down rules like a dictator."

Heaven only knew what he had done to this confrontational and unconventional woman to get her dander up. "I fear keeping my sisters on the path of propriety will take more than gentle correction, Miss Kendall." Abigail and Emilia were going to eat her alive if that was the best weapon in her arsenal. "They are here in Bath under duress and blame me for that, so I am being punished and, by default, any chaperone I appoint to them will also be punished. Their shenanigans of late would try the patience of a saint." Leo sat back, ready to terminate this interview, and she sat back too, her dark eyes suddenly amused by either him or his situation.

"I would still argue that makes your sisters easier to deal with than children." Because of course she was going to argue; that seemed to be the one thing she excelled at! Both on paper and in person! "As I mentioned before, your grace, children are unpredictable creatures."

"And I can assure you, Miss Kendall, so are my sisters." Honestly, the flippant confidence of this unusual woman was starting to grate.

"Yes—but there is a logic to the adult brain that is entirely missing in a child's. Children act often entirely on impulse with no rhyme or reason. With adults, there is always a reason. Once you have worked out what that reason is—and I think that it would be fairly safe to assume that their current reason is the overwhelming desire to rebel against you—a good chaperone would be more than two steps ahead of any shenanigans. If you can predict it, you can thwart it."

Her confidence really was astounding—but he liked it. He also liked that she had worked out the crux of the matter. They were rebelling against him. To such an extent that relations between Leo and his sisters had now been reduced to a stubborn battle of wills. A battle he was currently outnumbered in and losing. "My sisters are fast, Miss Kendall."

"One of the benefits of being so much younger than all your other *more mature* candidates is that I am fast too, your grace." She looked him dead in the eye and folded her arms. Then, despite the lack of paper and pen before her, gave him another well-argued paragraph on why he would be mad not to employ her. "I am also, in case you haven't noticed, wily, tenacious, determined, unflappable, unbelievably stubborn, and annoyingly clever. And, because I am a dreadful cynic by nature—as everyone who knows me will attest—I absolutely always expect the worst of people." From her expression, he was left in no doubt that also included him. "I can assure you that chaperoning your sisters will not faze me in the slightest—but I will definitely faze them."

Chapter FIVE

Portia still could not fathom why the duke had given her the job. Convinced that the interview had been a perfunctory waste of her time, while also irritated at her body's peculiar reaction to a man who was the antithesis of all that she stood for, she had been rude and combative throughout it. She had been so annoyed at him, his dimples, and his dismissive tone toward her that she hadn't held any of her feelings back. Irrespective her egalitarian ideals and dislike of the privileged aristocracy in general, she had never done that to someone of his ilk before. Only an idiot bit the hand that fed—but she had bit his, and hard.

Her jaw had hit the floor when he had asked her if there was any chance that she could start tomorrow, and she had been in a state of utter bafflement ever since.

Now here she was, not twenty-four hours later, once again sitting in the Duke of Debden's study, waiting for him to find the time to see her. He had said one sharp, and according to the big clock on his mantel it was already twenty-five past, but at least in this instance she was being paid to sit around waiting for him to learn how to tell the time.

"My apologies for being late once again." The duke strode through the open door, followed by his two incongruously matched loyal hounds and the disdainful cat, looking all windswept and disgustingly interesting. "I was unavoidably delayed in town with my sisters."

Portia stood and bobbed the expected curtsy, but made sure to put more effort into it today than she had yesterday. "Good afternoon, your grace."

"Let us hope it will be, Miss Kendall, because my morning with them has been horrendous." He gestured for her to retake her seat, then took his own. As soon as he did, the permanent additions of both his lumbering mastiff and the constantly staring spaniel settled on either side of his desk, while the cat jumped onto his lap and promptly curled up into a ball. "But I am hopeful that my life is about to improve exponentially now that you are here to help me with them." He smiled and his dimples briefly flashed. To her complete disgust, that was all it took for her pulse to quicken. "But before I throw you headfirst into the lions' den, I wondered if you have any more questions."

As he was being unexpectedly affable, it would have been churlish for her not to make some similar concessions. So she smiled, even though it hurt her a great deal to do so. "I have none at the moment, your grace."

His explanation yesterday had been quite thorough. With his mother unavoidably detained in London for the entire summer, her mornings would be taken up with the social secretary side of things, sorting through the invitations and passing over to him any for the evening soirees, which he would escort the ladies to. Or not, depending on what he decided the family should attend. Her purview was any daytime invitations or excursions, accompanying his sisters much like a lady's maid would. She was to be wary of any invitations where single men might be involved, especially those from the militia, and should pass them over to him to consider. Although, he then said that she should probably immediately burn any invitations from anyone who wore a uniform, because it would be a cold day in hell before he allowed his youngest sister anywhere near a soldier ever again. "Emilia," he had cautioned with worry in his eyes, "loses all sense if she comes within twenty feet of a redcoat."

Portia's afternoons were at his sisters' leisure, where again she would accompany them on *all* forays into the outside world. He had underscored the word "all" repeatedly as he clearly did not trust either of his sisters as far as he could throw them. Which was why, she supposed, he needed a proper chaperone for them, and why he had been at great pains to stipulate that in *all* circumstances, and again the emphasis had been on "all," the young ladies were never to be out of her sight.

Anything that Portia felt was untoward, she was to bring to his attention. She already suspected that meant he would want to know the ins and outs of everything, whether she felt it untoward or not, because he seemed like the sort who needed to be in control. It wasn't her place to tell him that that was undoubtedly why his sisters rebelled against him so much. She certainly would if she were in their shoes, because the Duke of Debden was obviously an autocratic nightmare to live with.

"Splendid," he said, removing the cat from his lap before sweeping his arm toward the door. "I shall introduce you to them both and then leave you to it. We have already been out today, and the weather has taken a nasty turn, so I am hopeful that your first afternoon should be quiet enough that you can find your feet here before you have to use them to run after them. Or at least one lives in hope that will be the case—but with my sisters, one always has to be on one's toes." Unlike the cat, he waited solicitously for her to pass through the door first, a gentlemanly courtesy that surprised her when he significantly outranked her. But as he then allowed his dogs to go through before him too, she decided not to read too much into the gesture. "I assume my housekeeper has already shown you your office and your quarters?"

"She has indeed, your grace." And very nice they both were too. "Thank you."

"I trust both met with your satisfaction."

"More than, your grace." Her small but pretty bedchamber overlooked the garden and the unspoiled acres of common land beyond. "This is a beautiful house." And it was. Even with the Rembrandts, Titians, and Gainsboroughs casually dotted about, there was a homely feel to this grand residence that had charmed her. One that suggested that this was a family home first and foremost rather than a mausoleum whose sole purpose was to impress others, as the Mayfair houses of her two previous aristocratic employers had been.

"Thank you." His dratted dimples returned again as he smiled before he glanced toward the drawing room somewhat warily, almost as if he dreaded going in. "I could show you around . . ."

"Your housekeeper has already done the honors." That came out a bit more clipped than she intended, but the last thing she wanted was to engage in any more chitchat with him than was necessary. Especially when everything about him unnerved her in a way that she wasn't pleased about.

She blamed those disarming dimples.

And his bright blue eyes.

And his shoulders.

A despicable, despotic duke had no right being so well put together when he had too many advantages already than was fair or equitable.

"Right then." By his flat tone he had heard her clipped one and wasn't impressed with it. "Let's get this over with." He strode to the big double doors of the drawing room and muttered something under his breath before he flung them open. She couldn't be sure, because he definitely hadn't meant it for her ears, but it sounded a great deal like "Abandon all hope all ye who enter here."

Portia followed him in and bobbed a deferential curtsy to the two young ladies who were sitting on opposite sides of a tea table, regarding her with the same unimpressed interest as the snooty white Persian cat was now doing from its new perch on the sofa. "Abigail, Emilia." He gestured to each in turn. "Allow me to introduce you to Miss Kendall, your new chaperone." Both ladies stood as politeness dictated, but neither made any effort to disguise their resentment as he turned back to her. "Miss Kendall, these are my sisters Lady Abigail and Lady Emilia."

Her presence was acknowledged by twin nods before Lady Abigail spoke. Pointedly to her brother rather than at Portia. "I'll confess, Leo, Miss Kendall is not at all what I expected our new jailer to be like."

"Miss Kendall is your chaperone, not your jailer." The duke's jaw clenched, and a nerve ticked in his cheek. "And you are being impolite."

"My humblest of apologies, Miss Kendall." Lady Abigail bobbed an insincere curtsy. "It is not fair of me to take out my many frustrations with my unreasonable brother on you. I hope that you can forgive any offense I might have caused."

"No offense was taken, my lady, I can assure you." Before the duke could say anything further that would put Portia firmly in the firing line, she decided to deflect. She had come here to earn what she needed to work for *Equitas*, not complicate her life further by becoming embroiled in a silly family war of the overbearing duke's making. So for an easier life, she smiled and glanced around the room for something more pleasant to talk about.

The first thing she noticed was the full-length portrait of the duke above the mantel. His painted blue eyes twinkling. His annoying dimples flashing and a different pair of loyal dogs guarding either side of his feet.

At least his dogs liked him, she supposed. From the twin hostile expressions on his sisters' faces, not even his own family did. Hardly a surprise when he was such an overbearing tyrant.

That said, he was almost as disarming in oils as he was in real life, but at least that portrait showed him more for who he actually was, so she would take comfort in that. It took a special sort of self-indulgent, arrogant vanity to hang yourself over your own fireplace! So obviously, Portia would not pander further to his inflated ego by mentioning it as she wrenched her eyes away.

"Which one of you is the artist?" Thank goodness there was an easel set up by the window with a half-finished watercolor resting upon it.

"I am." Lady Emilia offered her the ghost of a smile. "Although I think calling myself an artist is overestimating my abilities."

"Nonsense." Doubtless overstepping her boundaries, but acting on impulse, Portia wandered toward the picture and bent to closer inspect the details. "You have captured the vista outside this window very well." Which was true. It wasn't as compelling as the portrait of the duke, but it was still a decent piece of work. "I have always envied those with the talent to paint as it is one which I do not possess. Your brushes in these clumsy fingers"—she wiggled them—"would, at best, result in a childish daub. Did this take you long?"

"No more than an hour, although I'll confess that I lost interest in it before it was properly finished. I prefer painting my landscapes from life." Lady Emilia shot her brother a peeved glare. "But alas, that is difficult to do when we are confined for hours every day in here."

"Then we must take your easel and paints out as soon as the weather improves so that you can study some wildflowers in detail." The best way to get these young women to cease seeing her as their jailer was to let them know that she wasn't going to keep them inside like their brother. "There is a pretty stretch of riverbank less than twenty minutes west of here that is a carpet of buttercups and oxeye daisies at this time of year." She did not wait for agreement, or for the duke to lay down yet another set of constrictive rules for such an outing, and instead turned to Lady Abigail, who was still regarding her with suspicion. "Do you paint, Lady Abigail?"

The elder sister shook her head and likely would have left it at that if her brother hadn't stepped in to save them all from an awkward silence.

"Abigail likes to read." A lifeline!

"So do I!" Portia smiled at her. "What book are you currently enjoying?"

"I think enjoying would be overstating it." The duke chuckled and his sister simply glowered at him. "My sister prefers lengthy intellectual and philosophical tomes and never seems to read fictional escapism for pleasure."

Lady Abigail bristled at that. "As I prefer to broaden my mind, I am currently enjoying a biography of John Locke." She announced that with the arrogance of one who assumed that nobody else read anything of substance. Portia pitied her that arrogance. It was so typical of someone from the aristocracy to underestimate the educational level of someone who did not come from their ranks.

"Ah yes. The father of modern liberalism." The young woman's eyes widened in surprise. "He is indeed an interesting character, although not quite as progressive in the modern liberal sense nowadays as he was considered back in Tudor times." Then as an olive branch and because she could not resist quietly putting the young woman in her place: "I have a copy of his *Two Treatises of Government* if you would like to borrow it once you have finished your biography. The Old English language is a tad cumbersome and the spelling bizarre, but it is easier to read than Latin and fascinating to hear his opinions straight from the horse's mouth. Even if some of those opinions have not traveled well."

Lady Abigail was all astonishment but did her best to politely cover it. "I would indeed, Miss Kendall."

"Excellent." Then, because she had no intentions of staying longer and creating any more opportunities for the overbearing duke to cause friction now she had made some inroads in disarming these two ladies, Portia took the lead again. "Then I shall let you get back to your tea in peace. Do let me know if you need me at all later. I shall only be down the hall."

"The only place that we would like to go later is to Lady Southgate's reading salon." That came from the bookworm Lady Abigail.

"But alas, our unreasonable brother has decreed that we must all stay in tonight after dinner as he claims to have better things to do than accompany us. So we must suffer an evening of tedium incarcerated here as a result."

The duke's mouth flattened at that barb. "One evening at home while I catch up on all the important work which I have been forced to neglect to cater to your selfish whims is hardly the end of the world, Abigail."

Portia acknowledged both comments with a suitably nondescript, almost-sympathetic nod and then wisely left the three battling siblings to it. They all knew that it was not her place to offer to attend the reading salon with them in his stead because that would be impossible. Servants weren't welcome in aristocratic parlors under any circumstances. Never mind that her working hours here ended at six and she had absolutely no intentions of ever outstaying that. The moment you gave the aristocracy an inch, they always took a mile. Besides, she also had a mountain of her own work to do at *Equitas* and that was far more important than whatever nonsense three spoiled aristocrats got up to in the evenings.

Chapter SIX

Her charges had remained in the drawing room all afternoon thanks to the rain that had poured constantly. They were now safely ensconced in their bedchambers to rest before they changed for dinner. Why the pair of them needed to lie down when they hadn't moved a muscle all afternoon was beyond Portia, but such were the quirks of the idle aristocracy. With all the invitations sorted and ready for the Duke of Dimples's approval and with nothing else to do, she tidied up her marvelous new office before she headed up to her own room to change at six on the dot. Eager, now that her working day here was done, to get to the newspaper ready to get stuck into something she was excited to do rather than something she was forced to do to pay the bills.

The first edition of *Equitas* that she would have a direct hand in would go to print on Sunday. It was usually a weekly publication, but thanks to her predecessor's reckless run-in with the law that had forced the paper to move offices, they had to skip the last few editions. Rather than be angry at that, William had been circumspect. The gap allowed them to pause, reflect, regroup, and put a fresh spin on things. "Change, like circumstances," he had said over one of their copious cups of tea, "should always be embraced because it always provides new opportunities."

One of those changes was going to be her own unique slant on the opinion piece that, in her humble opinion, had become rather stale and repetitive of late. She wanted it to be more relevant and reasoned than the-world-is-unfair-and-that-is-a-travesty stance it had taken in the last six months. Although she didn't criticize that uninspiring slant too much to William, because she knew he had been doing all the work while his former assistant editor had been absent without leave and causing trouble. But being the brilliant and insightful man that he was, he had wholeheartedly agreed that the column needed an overhaul.

Except so far, the perfect first subject for her debut column had eluded her.

Determined to find it tonight, she undressed out of her sensible, buttoned-up chaperone's gown to don a more comfortable garment to spend the next few hours writing meaningful words in. She was about to head out when she heard laughter coming from the garden below.

Laughter that sounded a great deal like it belonged to Lady Emilia.

Curious, Portia wandered to the window and saw, to her horror, both young ladies dressed for an outing and running up the path toward the back gate giggling like two naughty little girls.

As if they knew she would be watching, both paused to briefly glance back at the house before they hurried out of the gate to the mews.

They were, of course, escaping as an act of rebellion and to test Portia's mettle. How thoroughly childish of the pair of them to do that now that her paid hours were finished, and how typically thoughtless of them to do such a petulant thing to a servant! Did they not realize that their selfish actions wouldn't only affect the duke? Or did they not care that their petty behavior could lose Portia her job?

No. Of course they didn't.

Lady Abigail and Lady Emilia had always received everything on a plate and had never had to worry about things like money, food, or a roof over their silly, spoiled heads. Instead, all they cared about was not getting their own way. It gave her some sympathy for the duke if this was how the pair always carried on.

Some, but not much.

If his spoiled sisters expected her to chase them, then they all had another thing coming. They were his responsibility after six o'clock and that was written in her contract. Stipulated in black-and-white and signed by both parties.

Except she also knew that that the duke wasn't in. He had left the house for a meeting at four and she had no clue when he was due to return.

But that wasn't her problem. She was only paid to pander to those two idiots between the hours of eight and six and it was ten minutes after that!

Not her problem.

Very definitely *not* her problem.

Except that it felt very much like it was, seeing this was her first day and, whichever way she looked at it, she had already lost her charges.

With a groan, Portia dashed out of her bedchamber and hurried out to the garden. By the time she reached the mews, there was no sign of the girls, but as the only place to head that was of any interest was down the hill toward the fun of the town, that is precisely where she headed.

Now that the rain had finally stopped, the wet streets were busy. All the crowds and carriages made it difficult to spot two young ladies among them, so Portia had no choice but to dodge the puddles while she weaved in and out of all the pedestrians filling the Circus until she broke free of the melee on Cay Street.

She stood on a water trough to get a better view all the way down the steep street and, while she saw countless similar straw bonnets to the two those brats were wearing, there was still no sign of either Abigail or Emilia beneath them.

Now what?

She could admit defeat, head back to the house, and raise the alarm, but she didn't fancy her chances of keeping this job if she did. Or she could try to find them. In a sprawling city filled with people and copious streets, squares, and narrow lanes to hide in.

Where the devil would two spoiled young blue bloods intent on rebellion head?

Think Portia. Think!

The tearooms and the shops were all either closed or closing at this time of the evening, so the ladies were unlikely to head to the High Street or the surrounding environs—unless they wanted to waste this reckless break for freedom on gazing aimlessly at the merchants' window displays. That really was the most pathetic act of rebellion imaginable. They also weren't dressed appropriately for a night of dancing or cards at the Assembly Rooms. The rules of etiquette had always been strictly upheld there and even the sisters of a duke would struggle to gain entry without proper evening dress and a respectable chaperone.

That severely limited the girls' options. With the exception of the taverns, the bulk of Bath was shutting down for the night, and it wasn't as if two gently bred young debutantes would venture into a public house alone.

Or would they?

All of a sudden, Portia realized that those silly, spoiled girls were so furious at their overbearing brother that she wouldn't put it past them. Visiting somewhere forbidden, like a common taproom, was precisely the sort of thing that would make the controlling duke explode.

The only problem was that there were at least twenty raucous local taverns that the ladies could visit, and it would take Portia hours to search them all. Hours that she did not have if she hoped to rectify this problem before anyone realized that they were missing.

She had a better chance of finding a needle in a haystack.

Despondent, she jumped off the water trough and, because she had been too distracted by the problem at hand, straight into a deep puddle. Water leaked under the tops of her half boots and immediately soaked her feet.

Marvelous.

This evening just kept getting better and better

She was stamping on the pavement to force as much of the liquid out of her shoes as she could when a group of soldiers sauntered past. No doubt off to the Saracen's Head in the center of town because that was where the off-duty militia men always headed when they were here.

In a flash, Portia had an epiphany.

If the duke believed that Lady Emilia lost all sense around a redcoat, then what better way for the sisters to punish him than to expressly seek the soldiers out?

Acting purely on instinct and in the absence of a better plan, Portia decided to dash to the Saracen's Head. Something easier said than done with her sopping feet slipping inside her shoes. To irritate her further, when she arrived, the inn was teeming with soldiers. So many red-coated young officers that they spilled out of the tavern's doors and took over a huge swath of the pavement.

Not caring that she was a woman alone, because she pitied whichever fool dared to attempt anything untoward in her current foul mood, she pushed her way past the dense group of revelers outside and headed into the bar. The scene inside was every bit the duke's worst nightmare as groups of the militia, all in varying states of inebriation, sang bawdy songs, told bawdy tales, or cheered each other on as they played questionable drinking games.

As she scanned the crowd, a lieutenant swayed toward her. "Has anyone ever told you that you are the most beautiful creature in the world?"

"Has anyone ever told you that death is final?" She elbowed past him, but he followed her out the door.

"Do you believe in love at first sight? Because I swear that I have just been shot through the heart by Cupid's arrow." Beer sloshed out of his tankard and onto her skirts as he clutched at his chest as if smitten.

Portia rolled her eyes at that tired old line and tried to march away, but he flung himself in front of her. "Marry me, fair maiden." He dropped to one knee. Something that did not go well for him because he was so deep in his cups that he immediately lost his balance and tumbled forward, sending the rest of the beer in his glass all over the pale bodice of her dress.

"Oh for goodness—" As she flicked as much of the liquid off her front as she could, Portia left and caught a glimpse of a straw bonnet poking out from behind one of the buttresses of St. Michael's church next door. It darted back in again straightaway, almost as if it had realized it had been seen.

That had to mean that those petty, spoiled girls had been following her while she hunted for them! Sending her on a wild-goose chase for their own selfish amusement!

She started toward them, ready to give the childish pair of time-wasters a piece of her mind, when the lovestruck soldier, who was still near prostrate on the pavement, caught Portia's hand and tried to kiss it, momentarily distracting her. She yanked it away and sidestepped his next lunge, then spied those infuriating straw bonnets running across the road into Green Street.

Portia gave chase. As the duke had promised, they were fast—even Lady Abigail despite her slight limp. Faster than she was in her slippery stockings and boots. They shot up Milsom Street, then darted left onto George Street, where she briefly lost them again, before she spied them heading up Gay Street back toward the Circus.

Portia's lungs were burning by the time she reached there but, once again, Lady Abigail and Lady Emilia had disappeared. It was less than a five-minute walk now back to the house, three if they ran, but somehow, she knew those girls would not do the decent thing and go home unless she forced their hand. Therefore, instead of dashing left around the Circus, Portia went right and was rewarded by the sight of those bonnets about to flee into Bennett Street. Where, no doubt, they planned to find another route back down the hill to the town to continue this stupid game of cat and mouse in perpetuity.

As Portia would now rather die than let them beat her, she found the strength from nowhere for one last push. Hoisting up her wet skirts, she pumped her legs so fast that it was a wonder she did not take off, yelling at anyone who dared get in her way.

She was feet away from the runaways when she screeched at them like a banshee to stop. Her scream was so primal that it shocked the sisters into doing just that, and they gaped at her like two hooked trout from the opposite pavement. "Get here now!" Incensed and with her finger wagging, Portia marched forward and then instantly stepped back when a carriage whizzed past.

So close that she felt rocked by the draft it created.

So close that she was immediately showered with a tidal wave of mud and muck as its wheels churned through all the standing rainwater caught in the curb.

Barkington, the most diligent but smallest guard dog in the world, leaped from his sleeping position beneath Leo's desk and gave his customary three woofs to alert that somebody had just entered the house. Then both he and Snifferson bounded off to investigate, so Leo followed.

He sincerely hoped that it was Miss Kendall, who had been missing all evening after, if his housekeeper was to be believed, a collision with a puddle that had left her in the highest of dudgeons as she had frog-marched his sisters back into the house. He was keen to check that she was all right after her first day with them. He had worried all day that just one afternoon alone with his scheming sisters might have been enough to send her running for the hills.

He was keener still to know that Miss Kendall was home safe.

While he appreciated that her evenings were her own to do with as she pleased and that she probably spent them with her ailing mother, it was late. He did not like the idea of any woman out alone at eleven at night. The streets of Bath might be marginally safer than the streets of London, but it still was a long way from being a crime-free paradise, as he knew only too well. Now that she lived under his roof, he felt as responsible for her safety as he did for his sisters and would never forgive himself if something happened to a young woman alone on his watch.

Thankfully, Miss Kendall was in her office. She had her back to him and was unpacking papers from a satchel that she was stuffing into the drawers of her desk. So oblivious of his presence that he felt obligated to cough to alert her to it rather than frighten the life out of her.

"A-hem."

She jumped out of her skin anyway and spun around with wide eyes. "Y-your grace." She briskly tossed her satchel onto the chair behind her desk and bobbed a respectful curtsy that really did not suit her. "I wasn't expecting anyone to be up this late. I apologize if I disturbed you."

"You didn't." He waved in the vague direction of his study. "I was working. My apologies for startling you though—I should have made more noise as I approached."

"You are surprisingly stealthy for a big man." And she did not look happy about it, or perhaps she was just generally unhappy about his presence on the planet. She was such a prickly minx, it was difficult to tell. But he was determined to hold out an olive branch in an attempt to improve diplomatic relations between them now that they were technically on the same side. Just the two of them versus Abigail and Emilia and the vast enormity of their outrage. "I wondered how your first day went?"

His sisters had claimed, over yet another stilted and resentful dinner, that it had been uneventful, but he did not believe that for a second. Especially after his housekeeper had told him that his sisters had returned with quite the spring in their steps while their new chaperone looked like she had been dragged through a hedge backward.

She didn't now, of course. She looked . . . lovely. Her attire this evening more like that of any young lady about town than the uniform of a sensible chaperone. The pale pink walking ensemble suited her so much better than the sensible gray or brown serge outfits that he had only thus far seen her in and, for some reason, she had several ink stains on her elegant fingers.

His question instantly made her expression wary. "Do you have any cause to believe it did not go well?"

"Not at all." Bloody hell but she was crotchety! "I just wanted to check that it had been as uneventful as my exasperating sisters have claimed."

She forced the wariness away, but he could tell it was an effort. "It was indeed uneventful."

"Aside from you coming home soaked, I assume." And just like that her guard came up again.

"That was all my fault, your grace. I was so busy watching out for your sisters that I forgot to look where I was going and got splashed by a carriage as a result."

"Ah," he said, not sure quite what to say to that. "So long as it was an accident."

"It was."

"Splendid." Leo's toes began to curl awkwardly inside his boots and he found himself rocking on his heels like an admiral inspecting the fleet. "Splendid."

Oblivious of the peculiar atmosphere, which Leo was convinced he could actually cut with a knife if he had one to hand, Snifferson decided to sniff. First Miss Kendall's shoes, then her skirts, and then finally, not caring that he was being impertinent, the cumbersome mastiff wandered to her chair to thoroughly smell her satchel. She snatched it up so fast that Leo felt compelled to apologize.

"Snifferson is called Snifferson because he has always been nosy. There is no reason to what he finds interesting but as you are new here, you are a new smell to him." That sounded wrong. "Not that I am suggesting that you smell in the literal sense, Miss Kendall. In fact, your perfume is rather lovely. What is not to like about the scent of orange blossoms in full bloom?" And now he was just vomiting words. Nervous words because something about her always seemed to unsettle him. "My labored point is that dogs tend to explore and understand the world via their noses. Snifferson especially because I suspect his eyesight is shocking and he doesn't possess any respect for boundaries."

To prove that, his ill-mannered dog pushed his impertinent black nose into Miss Kendall's right thigh and sniffed all the way down it to her knee. But rather than take offense at it, she smiled at the dog. Not one of her forced smiles of sufferance that she only ever bestowed upon Leo, but a real one that fair took his breath away. "I am pleased to make your acquaintance, Snifferson." She tickled the mastiff's floppy ears and, like the shameless tart that he was, Snifferson rolled onto his back and lapped up all the attention she gave to his exposed belly.

Jealous, the spaniel decided to butt in to receive the worship that he felt was his due and Miss Kendall happily obliged. Crouching down to his level, she dropped her satchel on the floor so that she could use her other hand to pet him. It was clearly her writing hand if the ink stains on her fingers were any gauge. "And who might you be, you handsome devil?"

"That is Captain Barkington."

"Named literally, no doubt, because he barks?" She asked still smiling.

"Only commands. Hence, he is *Captain* Barkington. Because he is in charge. At least of me and Snifferson." Because his cat had now deigned to join them, he gestured to her as she regarded the dogs with her usual feline disgust. "M'Lady Whiskers—my imperious Persian cat—is an ill-tempered law unto herself."

Miss Kendall shot a smile his way and, for once, it wasn't forced. "The name suits her. She is a beautiful cat."

"She is—but alas it is only skin deep. If I dropped dead on this floor this very instant, while my faithful hounds howled their devastation at my passing, M'Lady would immediately feed on my carcass."

Miss Kendall laughed as she stood. Somehow, the shift in her position also shifted the atmosphere between them. It became a little awkward again—not hostile thankfully—but it was strange. Or, more to the point, strained.

"I . . . um . . ." She reached for a stack of invitations piled neatly on her desk. "Sorted through everything." The stack was divided into two piles tied with string. One considerably bigger than the other. She handed him the thickest bunch first. "These are all evening invitations. If you let me know which you want to attend, I shall reply to the senders accordingly." Her ink-stained fingers briefly brushed his as he took them and something very peculiar happened to the nerves beneath his skin. "And these are the dubious bunch which I should like your opinion on." Was it his imagination or did she take extra care not to accidentally touch him again as she passed over the second pile? "I included one from Colonel Radcliffe inviting you and your sisters to the regimental ball next month, even though I doubt you'll want to attend seeing as it is going to be filled with soldiers."

"I think that can safely be thrown on the fire, Miss Kendall."

She smiled again. Shyly this time as she struggled to meet his gaze. "I shall be sure to send your polite regrets before I do that, your grace."

"Thank you—but don't go to any trouble."

"It is no trouble, your grace, I can assure you. I love nothing more than to write." She held up her hand and wiggled the fingers with the stains as proof. "Even if it is only polite regrets." Before he could ask what sort of things she loved to write, she smiled as she bobbed a curtsy. "Good night, your grace."

As he had clearly run out of excuses to linger, he smiled back.

"Good night, Miss Kendall." He turned then and would have walked away but some devil inside him made him look back. "How is your mother?"

Her eyelids fluttered in confusion for a moment before she glanced down at her hands. "Well . . . thank you for asking."

"Does she live in Bath?" It was none of his business, but he wanted to know.

"Just outside of it. In Newton St. Loe."

An answer that made the roots of his hair twitch and his throat tight. "That is a good hour's walk away."

"But it is a pleasant walk."

"Not at this time of night it isn't, Miss Kendall, and I am not comfortable with you doing it again this late alone." The dangers did not bear thinking about but he was already thinking them. "Next time you visit her I shall send my—"

She held up both hands. "I did not walk back, your grace." Noticing her raised hands she dropped them and stared at her suddenly busy fingers. "A neighbor always drops me back into town, so you do not need to worry."

"That is a relief." And it was. Not that his twitching scalp and clammy palms had realized that yet. "That road is a well-known haunt for footpads in the dark—especially during the season." Just the thought of her colliding with anyone like that after sunset was the stuff of Leo's nightmares, but he breathed through it to keep himself reasonable. "A pair were brought before me only today."

Her brows furrowed again. "Why would footpads be brought before you?"

"Because, for my sins, I am one of the local magistrates."

Her lovely eyes widened to the size of saucers. "I had no clue that you were a magistrate."

"As the only local duke, I was press-ganged into it. It is a thankless task, but my father instilled in me an annoying sense of responsibility, and somebody has to uphold the law."

"And who better than a duke to navigate the fine line between what is right and what is wrong?" She said that with a half smile but such cold eyes that it sounded almost like a chastisement. "After all, if our present legal system was good enough for the Norman conquerors, it is surely still good enough for us today."

"Well I wouldn't . . ." He did not get to finish that sentence because Miss Kendall had grabbed her satchel and was bobbing another curtsy.

"Good night, your grace."

She barely gave him the time to bid her a good one back before she disappeared out of the door.

Chapter SEVEN

Portia had worked for the duke for almost a week before she had her first day off. She had insisted on every Sunday when she had taken the job because that would always coincide with *Equitas* going to print. To say that she was looking forward to a whole day of not supervising his spoiled sisters was the understatement of the century. They had proved to be every bit as rebellious and reckless as he had promised. Every day so far without fail, they had found some way to punish her for being their supposed "jailer." Whether that be trying to slip away unnoticed, which they hadn't managed to do for more than a couple of tense minutes since that fateful first day, thank goodness, or treating her as an invisible inconvenience to whom they refused to talk, they made it plain that it was them against her.

Portia was thoroughly exhausted by their constant petty shenanigans so was very much looking forward to this entire day away from them. For very different reasons, she was also looking forward to a whole day away from *him*.

She made sure that she and the dratted Duke of Dimples rarely collided. When they did, it was only to hand over the most recent invitations and to give him the brief and heavily censored synopsis of the day that he insisted upon. She hadn't liked him to begin with, but now that she knew that he was a magistrate, she felt even more unsettled around him. Hardly surprising when he was the law and she was, according to all the current unfair legislation, technically breaking it by willfully printing what he and his fellow peers would see as sedition. Although she rather liked the irony that he had, inadvertently, given her the perfect seditious topic for her first opinion piece for *Equitas*. An article that she double-checked was safely in her satchel before she left the house.

She walked all the way down to the river, stopping and checking regularly that she wasn't being watched by any prying eyes. When she was certain the coast was absolutely clear, she slipped into the warehouse, which was a hive of activity.

While the rest of Bath made their way to whichever of the city's churches they chose to worship at before they enjoyed their day of rest, today was their busiest day here at the newspaper. As soon as her editorial was typeset, she, Sir William, and their skeleton crew of volunteers would begin the labor-intensive and time-consuming task of printing the two thousand copies of *Equitas* that would leave via the River Avon tonight. By midnight, almost every single-paged broadsheet not destined to remain here in the West Country would be wrapped and loaded on a barge bound for London. If their precious cargo made it all the way along various rivers, canals, and locks to the capital, then it became somebody else's problem to distribute it. However, it was their problem until then, so Portia expected to be here for the long haul today.

"There you are!" William spied her first. He was already covered in grime and ink because their ancient printing press was temperamental. "Were you followed?"

"Of course not." She tossed her bonnet to the side and stripped off her lightweight summer spencer and hung it on a hook. She had worn an old dress on purpose, but still intended to put a capacious apron over it. The last thing she needed was anyone asking questions if they spotted her when she arrived back at the Royal Crescent covered in the same level of dirt as William. She gestured to his oily hands. "Have you and Bessie had a fight again?" Bessie was the name he lovingly called the machine because she apparently reminded him of his mother—forthright, formidable, and prone to temper tantrums.

"Print day wouldn't be print day without Bessie and I having a tiny disagreement." He grinned. "But I think we have reached an accord." He jerked his fluffy gray head toward the machine and the pair of legs currently sticking out of it. "Jim is putting her back together."

"Morning, Jim." Jim was a laborer by trade, and it showed because he was huge. "Are you winning?"

"Not yet, Portia, although I remain hopeful that we'll emerge victorious in the end."

He was a gentle, thoughtful, and resourceful soul, despite his bulging muscles and towering height, who could neither read nor write, but helped out with all the manual work, which he excelled at. His lack of literacy was, sadly, not uncommon. Few from his lowborn station were ever taught their letters or numbers because their impoverished families could not afford the luxury of schooling. They instead needed their offspring to earn their keep in the fields or the factories or shoved up chimneys or down mine shafts from a young age.

She turned back to William. "Will we be ready to go when Bessie is?" They had been nine-tenths of the way there when she had left here last night.

"Edgar is finishing the typesetting as we speak."

The last member of their motley crew was Edgar, a solicitor's clerk who wore the thickest spectacles Portia had ever seen but who, ironically, had the most meticulous eye for detail. He was also one of the sourest individuals she had ever met. While the others had all cheerily greeted her, Edgar merely lifted his brow in acknowledgment when she offered him a smiling hello, his attention never wavering from the tiny metal letters he was arranging neatly in the block.

"Here is my article, Edgar. I am sorry it is so late." It was the last one to arrive and so there was a lone empty space right at the top of the front page waiting for it. "My piece is under five hundred words—exactly as specified."

While adhering to Edgar's imperious instruction chafed, space was tight in *Equitas*. To keep printing costs to a minimum and to avoid having to pay the ridiculous stamp duty imposed by the government on any political newspaper printed at least monthly on two sheets or more, the entirety of *Equitas* had to fit on just one side of a large piece of paper. That meant that every article in it had to be succinct, and difficult editorial decisions had to be made. As she had been the one making them alongside William, she did appreciate the need for brevity in her own article. It had made it harder to write, but it was sharper as a result, and she was proud of it.

Immensely proud.

Edgar finished the last word in the sentence he was constructing before he deigned to glance at the piece of paper she had put beside him. "Better late than never, I suppose."

He had taken an instant dislike to her when she had arrived, probably because he did not like being outranked by a woman. Not that she had used that rank over him yet when she was trying her best to fit in among the loyal few here who were instrumental in getting the finished newspaper out.

"I wanted my first column to be perfect." She owed that to the cause.

Edgar grunted as he picked it up, no doubt ready to find some fault with it, as he did with anything she gave him.

He scanned it and frowned. "Have you gone quite mad?" Edgar immediately turned to William. "This topic is grossly inappropriate in the current climate." He tossed her article across the desk to their approaching editor in chief as if it carried some hideous infection. "I do not wish to be difficult, William." *Yes, he jolly well did!* "But in my humble opinion"—which Edgar considered vastly superior to all others—"I think it highly likely that Portia's column is only going to rile up the local law enforcement, who, I am sure that I do not need to remind you, are looking for any excuse to shut us down." He jabbed at her words. "This incendiary article is daring them to raid us, and Portia is playing with fire!"

William shot Portia a quick he'll-come-around placating look, and took the sheet. "'*Is the worst form of injustice pretended justice?*'" Then he chuckled. "What an attention-grabbing headline, Portia."

"An unnecessarily provocative headline," interrupted Edgar like a crotchety wild dog with a bone.

"Nonsense!" William waved that way. "The powers that be all think that we are naught but uneducated oiks who wouldn't know their ancient Greek from their Roman, so a well-chosen quote from a learned tome like Plato's *Republic* will bring up short those who are taught the classics from the cradle." He tapped her article. "This is excellent work, Portia, and an excellent and *timely* choice of topic—in *my* humble opinion." Then he winked at her as he gave her nemesis a comradely pat on the shoulder before he turned away. "Get it set, Edgar, so that we can go to print."

"But this article calls the entire justice system 'flawed and fundamentally rotten to the core!' That's a direct quote." Edgar wasn't one to take defeat graciously. "Might I remind you that Portia has already increased our risk of scrutiny from the authorities by taking a job in the house of one of the local magistrates, so attacking our legal system in this way is a reckless and unnecessary gamble."

"Is your employer aware of your involvement in *Equitas*, Edgar?" She tried to say that sweetly but there was bite in her tone. "Or do you, like me, keep your political leanings discreet while you earn your living because you know that they are bound to lose you your job otherwise?" She took satisfaction in the way his thin lips flattened at that irrefutable logic. "Before I came here, I worked for three years at the League's headquarters while also juggling my responsibilities as a governess for an active anti-reformist member of the House of Lords, and not once did I do anything that jeopardized the cause." And he could stick that in his sanctimonious pipe and smoke it!

"Constable Nolley is already after our blood! Baiting him with this"—Edgar slapped her article with the back of his hand as he followed William back to the printing press—"will bring trouble to our door." Once again, he spoke about her as if she weren't there. "Portia is playing with fire—but it is all of us who will get burned by this recklessness."

William sighed. "Constable Nolley would still be after our blood whether we printed Portia's article or not. But we cannot live in fear. We must print the truth, Edgar, because only the miserable, sorry truth will help our cause. That is what we do. It is what we have always done, irrespective of the risks." Sir William deposited the article back in the now-ranting typesetter's hand, signaling that the matter was closed. "We print and be damned!" Their editor in chief wagged a righteous finger in the air as he walked off. "That is *my* final decision."

"Then expect me to say I told you so when all our property is smashed to smithereens and we're all locked in the clink." The muttering Edgar took that decision with all the belligerence Portia expected of him, snatching up her article and scrutinizing it again now that Sir William wasn't in direct earshot. "Why is this signed in a different name to yours? Are you so ashamed of what you write that you have to hide behind a pseudonym?"

Portia offered the man her best go-to-hell smile. "As you've already pointed out, I work for a local magistrate and don't want to give him any reason to bring trouble to our door." As much as she wished she could print her real name and be damned, she liked the irony of calling herself Pendle after her rival for the position in the duke's house, Miss Strictland, had called her that to put her in her place.

Irony in all its forms always amused her.

"William has already approved that pseudonym, Edgar, but do check with him *again* if you don't believe me."

He muttered something under his breath as she sailed away but she didn't give the childish pedant the satisfaction of responding. If he had a problem with a woman being second-in-command here, that was entirely his problem to contend with because she wasn't going anywhere.

Or so she hoped.

A hope that was swiftly dashed not more than five minutes later.

"I meant to tell you, Portia," said William after he and Jim finally got Bessie going again. "Headquarters are sending us another reinforcement! An upstanding and up-and-coming young chap, by all accounts, who has impressed the top brass no end. He expressly asked to work with us too and seems to have all the skills we need. I am reliably informed that he has a way with words, just like you do, and isn't a pitchfork wielder, so I have high hopes for him."

Her heart sank.

So much for her proving herself here. How was she supposed to do that after helping to edit just one edition if they were already sending her replacement?

"That is good news." She managed to smile rather than stamp her feet like she wanted to. "What role do you envisage him taking?" She hoped that was a subtle enough way of asking if she was already out of the job without throwing a justified tantrum on the blatant unfairness rife within the United League for Reform as well as in the country.

"He's quite an adaptable and affable sort, or so I'm assured, so I am sure he can turn his hand to most things. I'll leave you to put him through his paces to see where he best fits though."

"Me?" She hadn't expected that. Nor fully understood what that meant.

"Of course," said Sir William. "Seeing as I have already had to pull rank today, the power has quite gone to my head, as power always does, so I feel inclined to delegate." He grinned before he wandered back to the printing press while flicking a dismissive hand. "I do not want the bother of teaching him the ropes. Especially as he'll be your assistant, Portia." He inserted a blank page into Bessie to test that they were ready to go, and then heaved the platen down. "Although if I were you, the first job I would give him is sorting out this office. Your expressive face does a very poor job of hiding how much all the disorganized clutter annoys you."

Chapter
EIGHT

Constable Nolley was an angry fellow at the best of times, but this evening he was positively incandescent with rage. So red and seething that it was a wonder he wasn't already foaming at the mouth.

Oblivious of little Barkington, who, as an impeccable judge of character, was growling at him in warning, Nolley practically screamed, "They have gone too far this time!" His hands were balled into tight fists, and it was only a matter of time before one of those fists punched Leo's desk. "We cannot allow those dangerous radicals to continue to publish treason in our city!" Sensing an imminent display of violence too, Snifferson, who hated a raised voice almost as much as Barkington hated the constable, immediately sought refuge beneath the desk, not caring that he had to roughly barge past Leo's legs to do it.

"This isn't treason, Constable Nolley." Leo glanced down at the newspaper that was rapidly becoming the bane of his life. Despite its month of silence, *Equitas* had clearly come back with a bang. Quite a bold and defiant bang if its opinion piece was any gauge. "Treason has quite specific parameters in law. It has to be committed in deed, not just words. And this—" As he had predicted, the fist came down on the desktop before Leo could finish his sentence.

"If it's not treason then it's a slanderous pack of lies! It's a libelous defamation of all our good characters! It's a clear-cut case of sedition!"

It was none of those things either but trying to get this unpleasant and wholly unreasonable man to see that was likely a complete waste of Leo's breath. But waste it he must or, like a cocked pistol, the constable was likely to go off and do untold and unhelpful damage. "Please sit, sir." He gestured to the chair opposite his desk that the constable had recently shot up from like an incensed firework. "So that we can discuss this calmly." Although he also knew there was fat chance of that happening after reading "the pack of lies" that had riled up the constable.

Not that they were lies either.

Leo took issue with several of the broad accusations in that well-written column—because they were generalizations that did not apply to every court in the land—but he could not argue with the crux of the piece. The worst form of justice really was pretended justice, exactly as Plato had said two thousand years ago, and the entire legal system *was* flawed, well past its prime and in urgent need of the sort of reforms suggested in this article.

"I'll be calm when I get my warrant, your grace!" Nolley dropped back into the chair with a thud, his arms immediately folding as he glared like a petulant child. "I would have it already if I reported to Lord Corston!"

Leo did not doubt that for a second because Corston was almost as unreasonable an arse as Constable Nolley was. The only difference between their hang 'em and flog 'em outlooks was in the diligence with which they pursued that quest. Being paid to do the job, Nolley was a royal pain in the neck every single day of the week, whereas Lord Corston rarely turned up at the petty sessions because he nearly always had better things to do with his time than sit on the magistrates' bench. Things that usually involved drink, women, or feathering his own nest either socially or financially. But he'd happily string anyone up if he felt they deserved it—and with little regard for the particular circumstances or, indeed, the necessary proof that the accused were actually guilty.

"But you don't report to Lord Corston, you report to me, Constable Nolley, and so you will plead your case for a warrant calmly and in line with the letter of the law, or I will not grant it." Sometimes, and much to Leo's chagrin, the only way to get the constable to see reason was to remind him who paid his wages.

Lord Corston hadn't fought tooth and nail to have all the local constables that he oversaw paid. That libertine was content to give the roles to any corrupt individual with a pulse, so long as it did not affect him in any way, and would happily abdicate all responsibility for a constable's actions. Whereas Leo believed in holding them to account. It was one of the reasons he *had* fought tooth and nail for those who served the city to be paid, although Nolley had not been his choice. He had inherited him because of proximity. In Leo's absence, Nolley could report to anyone, and gratefully grasped any opportunity to do so.

"We have a civic and moral responsibility to the citizens of Bath to do things properly. And a legal responsibility to maintain an accurate and watertight public record so that it can withstand any and all scrutiny if challenged. On what grounds do you want a warrant issued regarding *Equitas*?" Leo picked up a pen so that he could pretend to make a record because he knew the man would have nothing solid. "And what tangible evidence do you have to justify it?"

"Isn't that treasonous rag evidence enough?" Typically, Nolley jabbed a finger toward the newspaper as if its mere existence rendered it guilty as charged. "It is direct contradiction of the Blasphemous and Seditious Libels Act."

"How?"

"They have called me a pathetic minion and you a biased, privileged, and unreliable mouthpiece of the government."

Leo wanted to smack his head against his desk, but didn't. "Neither you nor I were named in this article, so it cannot be construed as libelous."

Constable Nolley crossed his arms again and stuck out his chin. "As that article was written within the confines of this city and that newspaper is printed somewhere within it, then the libel toward all those of us here who uphold the law is implied by default."

"There is no mention of Bath in this piece either. As I read it, this questions why we continue with a legal system struggling under the weight of its increasing burdens when the world has moved on since the medieval monarchs created it seven hundred years ago."

Instantly that reminded him of Miss Kendall's thinly veiled and sarcastic criticism that if their legal system was good enough for William the Conqueror, then surely it was good enough for us? A bizarre coincidence that made Leo's mind wander back to her, something he apparently needed no excuse to do seeing as it had wandered to her more times than he could count today alone. He had no clue why, beyond that something about her got under his skin.

As much as he would have preferred to ponder the pretty but vexing Miss Kendall some more, he forced his attention back to the nuisance that was Nolley. "Personally, and I am sure that you will agree with me, seeing as you are one of the few paid and professional constables outside of Bow Street in London . . ." It might help to flatter the man's ego a little. "I believe that our legal system does need to be run by professionals in both root and branch. Paid experts in their field who are all held accountable to the same robust set of standards. Judges, magistrates, and constables alike." Because god only knew how happily Leo would hand the poisoned chalice over to somebody salaried who actually knew what they were doing.

Never mind all the other nonsense that magistrates got roped into on top of crime. Like the collection of overdue local taxes or the funding of roads or poor relief or trying to figure out ways to stop people dying from whatever epidemic next decided to kill the inhabitants of a town in droves. And do not get him started on the stupid disputes between neighbors that he was supposed to adjudicate on. "They probably shouldn't be members of the peerage either as that only seems to rub the ordinary people the wrong way."

Obviously, his impassioned and reasoned speech fell on Nolley's deaf ears. "I'm sure I'll find plenty of libelous sedition if you'd just grant me a blasted warrant to search their premises. Or at the very least issue one for the immediate arrest of that rabble-rouser Sir William Stowe. I'd love to put him and that bloody Pendle fellow"—he jabbed a finger at the offending article again—"on the next bloody boat to Botany Bay!"

"For what crime, Constable Nolley?"

"Incitement to riot!"

Leo stood because, frankly, he was about to have a conniption of his own. "Nowhere in this publication does it ask the masses to arm themselves and lay siege to anywhere or anyone, Constable Nolley, or to actively disobey the laws of the land. When it does, come back and see me and I shall happily issue you with a warrant. Until then—" He stalked to his study door. "You will just have to suffer the fact that *Equitas* and you have very different opinions, which to the best of my limited legal knowledge has not *yet* been deemed a crime." He flung the door open and blinked in surprise at the sight of Miss Kendall on the other side.

While Nolley had risen from his chair, his feet remained planted firmly in Leo's office. "These people are dangerous criminals, and we need to make an example of them!"

"Then bring me some actual evidence, sir." Leo swept his arm forcefully toward the hallway. "I am afraid that I am going to have to leave you to show yourself out, Constable Nolley, as I am already late for my next appointment." Then for effect, he did some theatrical groveling to the stunned-looking stunner waiting to tell him that she was finished for the day. "My humblest apologies for keeping you waiting, Miss Kendall. Please do come in."

Sensing tension, Miss Kendall quickly scurried into his study, lowering her head and not making eye contact as she passed the still-incandescent constable as he reluctantly exited the room.

Leo had never been so glad to close the door on someone in his life and leaned against it to breathe. "Sorry about that—but as you can plainly see, the constable's dander is well and truly up."

She acknowledged that with a nod, her dark brows furrowed. "Would it be impertinent to ask why?"

"That," he said, pointing to the newspaper on his desk, "is his archnemesis."

As soon as she clocked it, her brows instantly shot skyward before she wrestled them back under control. "He does not approve of a newspaper?"

"More that he does not approve of that particular publication." She was now staring at the newspaper as if it were something offensive too. "Are you familiar with *Equitas*?"

She shook her head. "I cannot say that I have ever heard of it, your grace. Is it a scandalous local rag?"

"If only it was, Miss Kendall, then my life would be so much easier."

"How does this newspaper make your life difficult?"

"Because its very existence outrages the constable, and he then makes my life difficult." He sighed at the never-ending cycle that they were locked in. "Constable Nolley would have everyone who has a hand in it clapped in irons and sent to the Tower if he had his way. He holds me personally responsible for stopping him."

Confusion pulled at her features. "Why do you stop him if your life without that newspaper would be easier?"

"Because I take my unenviable and interminable responsibilities as a magistrate seriously and insist that he proves to me that *Equitas* is breaking the law—which so far, he hasn't. What it prints might be unpopular with some, but it doesn't lie, and it doesn't, despite the constable's constant assertions, print anything overtly seditious. Besides, and this really bothers him, I happen to believe in the freedom of speech."

Her mouth hung momentarily slack. "You do?"

"History is peppered with grave examples of what can happen when anyone tries to suppress it. You only have to look across the channel to France or across the Atlantic to America to see the dire consequences of burying your head in the sand and hoping that everything will come out in the wash when the people aren't happy." She was properly befuddled now and he couldn't blame her. She had come here to fill him in on her day and not listen to him vent about things that did not concern her. "But I digress." It was well after six thanks to Nolley's unexpected interruption and her day was finished. "What pointless delights do you have for me today, Miss Kendall?" He held out his hand for the small pile of invitations she had brought him. Just like she had every evening at six since she had started working here. Her unsubtle daily reminder that his troublesome sisters were now all his problem again until the morning.

Still looking a bit perplexed, she tore her eyes from the newspaper and began using the businesslike tone that he had also come to expect whenever they collided. "A ball at Lord and Lady Denby's house on Saturday next and three invitations to dinner, although I am fairly certain that you will not want to attend two of them because the families concerned are only visiting Bath for a few weeks and both state that they would be delighted to *make your acquaintance*."

Leo rolled his eyes, grateful that she had quickly worked out that every Tom, Dick, or Harry wanted the gravitas of hobnobbing with a duke, and he wasn't the least bit interested in engaging. He always found social climbers awkward to be around and had little patience for fawners or fakery. "You are right, Miss Kendall. Dinners with actual acquaintances are quite tiresome enough."

She smiled at that. "Then I shall send your polite regards to them both before I decline."

"Don't be too polite. It might give them the awful idea of suggesting alternative dates."

"If they do, then I shall politely decline again without bothering you." She stood then, her business with him clearly concluded. "Have a pleasant evening, your grace."

"I sincerely doubt it as I am being dragged to the theater." He pulled a face, trying once again to engage her when she clearly didn't want to be engaged. "For *Macbeth*. The most depressing play ever written. Two hours of misery in a cramped and stuffy box await me—which is doubtless why my sisters are dragging me to it. They know that I am not a fan of the theater. They also know that I prefer a comedy over a tragedy, so this is another flagrant and unsubtle attempt to punish me for keeping them here."

"What is the old saying, your grace? Like all things, this too shall pass."

"Just not soon enough."

She merely offered him a sympathetic smile before she bobbed one of her lackluster curtsies. "Good night, your grace?"

She had worked for him for over a week and, try as he might, he was still struggling to have any sort of extended conversation with her. She liked to keep things businesslike and was always out of his office as quickly as possible. He wasn't sure why she did that and, for the life of him, could not comprehend why he cared. But he did. So before she could leave his study again, some devil inside him called her back. "Do you prefer Shakespeare's tragedies or his comedies, Miss Kendall?"

She paused, her expressive brows drawn together once more in confusion. Or perhaps irritation that he was delaying her. "I—"

A bloodcurdling scream pulled them both up short.

"That was Emilia!" His heart in his mouth, Leo was out of the door like a shot, heading in the direction of his baby sister's continued screams. The closer he got to the drawing room the more those screams merged with the sounds of some sort of commotion going on inside.

There was a bang.

A crash.

The unmistakable sounds of glass breaking.

He flung open the door in time to see Abigail fling herself face forward onto the sofa as she tried to wrestle something into submission. As Miss Kendall skidded unceremoniously into the back of him, his sister growled while something beneath her did as well. "Well don't just stand there, Leo! Come and help with your horrid cat!"

"M'Lady Whiskers has brought in a bird!" shrieked Emilia from the corner she was cowering in. "And the poor thing is still alive!"

Leo went to assist Abigail, who was still sprawled on the sofa, but clearly fighting a losing battle as the Persian had managed to free one paw and was using it indiscriminately on his sister's shoulder. The cat's bared claws were unsheathed like tiny but lethal daggers as she slashed and hissed and fought for freedom. As he tried to grab the feral menace from beneath her, no mean feat now that both Snifferson and Barkington had joined the fray, one of those claws caught Abigail's cheek and she yelped.

To his sister's credit, she barely recoiled an inch at the onslaught, but that was all M'Lady needed to break free. She scrambled up the back of the sofa, a substantial and still squawking blackbird clamped in her jaws, and made a bolt for the door with both dogs hot on her heels.

Miss Kendall made a valiant stab at throwing her body at the door to slam it before she got there, but M'Lady was a cat on a mission, and that mission was to escape the lot of them with the poor blackbird at speed.

However, despite his advanced age, Barkington wasn't having that, and somehow managed to get in front of her before she could shoot upstairs with her flapping prey. The cat growled at the little dog in warning, her paw raised ready to take a swipe at him too, but Barkington stood his ground. He barked back at her and guarded those stairs with his life while the rest of them, Snifferson included, fanned out behind her to block every other conceivable exit.

Leo carefully shrugged out of his coat, trying not to do anything to distract the cat from hissing at the spaniel, who was doing his level best to keep her attention. He knew from bitter experience that the only way to prise anything out of M'Lady Whiskers's evil fangs was to ensure that the hissing devil was properly restrained first. And the only way to effectively restrain her, as he knew to his cost, was to wrap her up tight like a blasted Egyptian mummy.

He held his coat up like a net and lunged, miraculously managing to engulf the hissing Persian in the fabric, but she was having none of it. She wriggled and bucked like a thrashing salmon as he tried to bundle her up in it. Then, in a blaze of fluffy white and flapping black feathers, she emerged and decided to use her claws and the back of his scalp to haul herself out.

As he cried out in pain, Miss Kendall grabbed the cat's back legs. "I've got her!" And clearly she had because M'Lady protested by sinking her front claws even further into his skull. "Can somebody try to prise her mouth open?"

Of course that somebody was Abigail, because Emilia, who was always about as much use as a chocolate teapot during a crisis, was still screaming.

The altercation now happening directly on top of him, Leo had to reach up behind himself and try to blindly unhook each individual claw from his skin, but no sooner had he freed one paw and started on the other, then in the claws went again.

"Let go, you wicked animal!" He had no clue what his sister was doing to the cat but whatever it was, it was done with tremendous exertion. "Release your damn jaws or—*Urgh!*"

Blessedly, the claws finally retracted from his scalp just as Miss Kendall hugged the cat to her chest with such speed that M'Lady's grip on the blackbird lessened enough for it to escape. Panicked and afraid, it flew directly into Emilia's screaming face as it made its own bolt for freedom, then straight into a window. It flapped disorientated above their heads for a few moments before it flew a haphazard course down the hall.

The cat, of course, took umbrage at that and greater umbrage at Miss Kendall, who was still hugging the hissing demon for all she was worth, despite the flailing claws that were slashing out now with a vengeance. Somehow, the darned cat twisted and hooked one of its paws into her hair. Then, as if M'Lady knew how to inflict maximum pain, she used Miss Kendall's no-longer-neat chignon for purchase, arched upward, and tried to bite her chin. Yet still, with commendable bravery, his newest employee tried to keep the cat imprisoned—but she was fighting a losing battle.

Within seconds, M'Lady had broken free again and followed the blackbird down the hall in hot pursuit, nowhere near ready to give up her prize.

Both dogs then chased after her, closely followed by Miss Kendall and Abigail, while Emilia finally found the wherewithal to do something useful and helped Leo up from his prostrate position on the floor.

By the time Leo caught up with them, the terrified blackbird had sought refuge in his study. It flapped a squawking, warning circle around the ceiling while the cat menacingly scaled his bookshelf to get to it, both his dogs barked for all they were worth, and his poor wounded scalp throbbed like the devil.

"ENOUGH!" As he bellowed that at nobody in particular, the bird, with perfect timing, whizzed above his head and deposited a well-aimed and doubtless nervous splatter of droppings directly on his shoulder.

Chapter
NINE

Enough!" Clearly at the end of his tether, and despite the sticky white mess now decorating his green silk waistcoat, the duke pointed a quaking finger at both of his dogs in turn. "Out!"

They immediately stopped barking and skulked out of the room.

Then he pointed at Portia and his sisters. "One of you go and get a blasted blanket so we can get the bloody cat out of here!"

Lady Emilia happily did that, and Portia closed the door behind her so that the blackbird couldn't escape. Her hand shook slightly because her nerves were in absolute tatters.

She could not completely blame this debacle with the cat for that.

They had been in tatters since she had accidentally collided with the constable outside this very room mere minutes ago. Now, alongside the damning copy of *Equitas* that had incensed him so still staring up at her in accusation from the duke's desk, there was a distressed bird flying hither and thither and a disdainful Persian with murder in its different-colored eyes.

"Perhaps once the cat is removed, the poor bird might settle so that we can rescue it?" The duke rubbed the back of his head and then huffed his disgust at the noxious deposit on his shoulder before he balked when he noticed the blood smudged on his fingertips. "I hate blood," he said, turning almost as green as his waistcoat.

Lady Abigail rolled her eyes. "Pull yourself together, Leo! And if you cannot do that, try to at least put off fainting until the poor bird is out of danger." She tossed him her handkerchief, and he took a deep breath before he used it to wipe all trace of the blood from his hands.

Then he glared at M'Lady Whiskers, who was trying to figure out a way to catch the bird from her precarious position hanging from the top of his bookshelf. "I hope you are proud of yourself, madam! Get down this second." Unlike his loyal dogs, the cat was impervious to both his angry tone and his command and merely used her claws to scoot herself sideways along the book spines while her focus never left the bird.

Lady Emilia returned and squeezed herself through the thinnest possible crack in the door. She was about to throw the shawl she had brought back to her sister when Lady Abigail threw up her hands.

"Well don't just stand there, Emilia, wrap the menace in it!"

Now it was Lady Emilia's turn to balk. "Not on your life! That cat is vicious!"

"Oh for goodness' sake!" Lady Abigail snatched the shawl back. "Heaven forbid you be of any use!" She half limped, half stomped over to where the cat still hung and without a moment's hesitation, used the shawl to pin the animal to the bookshelf. The duke went to help and while he peeled M'Lady Whiskers off a couple of hefty encyclopedias, his sister bound the Persian's fluffy white body tight in the fabric. "Can you at least open the doors, Emilia, so that I can shut Leo's vile cat in the kitchen?"

Her wary gaze never leaving the hissing animal, Lady Emilia did exactly that, making sure to close the door behind them as they left, leaving Portia alone with the duke and the bird.

As it seemed like the most sensible thing to do, she opened the sash window as far as it would go, hoping that the blackbird would just fly out. When it didn't, the duke tried his best to shoo it out, but all that succeeded in doing was sending the poor thing into hiding. It pushed into the very top corner of the bookshelf that the cat had just been removed from, wedging itself into a tiny gap between the wood and the ceiling.

"Splendid," said the duke. "Now what?"

He was tall but the high ceiling was much taller.

"Do you have a ladder?"

He looked at Portia as if she had gone mad as he gestured wildly around his study. "Why the blazes would I have a ladder, Miss Kendall?" Which she supposed was a valid point. Men like him paid people to bring a ladder if a ladder was required.

"Perhaps you could reach it if you stood on a chair?"

He did a quick gauge of the distance and shook his head. "I might be able to do it if I stood on my desk."

In tacit agreement, they both grabbed opposite ends and heaved the heavy oak desk to the bookshelf. The duke clambered atop it and stretched as far as he could while she was forced to watch from a position just below his bottom—a firm, fine object of irritating beauty which, thanks to his lack of coat, was practically staring her in the face.

"It's still too high . . . but perhaps if I climbed . . ." His thigh muscles and buttocks flexed beneath the tight fabric of his buff breeches as he lifted one booted foot onto a bookshelf, and much to her chagrin, Portia's greedy eyes thoroughly enjoyed the spectacle. He grabbed the top of the highest bookshelf and, to unsettle her further, the same thing happened to the muscles in his arms and shoulders as he heaved himself upward. He brought his standing foot up to join the other one balanced precariously on the edge of the shelf.

Instantly, that shelf gave an ominous creak, and he immediately jumped back down. When he turned, her wayward eyes went straight to his crotch. Thankfully, he was too busy gazing around the room and trying to work out his next move to notice.

She just managed to wrench her gaze back to his face a split second before he said, "I need a bit more height, so pass me a chair." He pointed to the small, hardwood chair his visitors sat on rather than at the enormous leather and oak beast he used.

Portia hoisted it up, then tried not to appreciate what happened to all his muscles again as he climbed on it. He let go of the backrest but as he tried to straighten, the chair wobbled. Instinctively she grabbed his ankles to steady them, and they both let out a relieved sigh as he finally found his balance.

"I'm going to gently grab the bird and pass it to you—will that be all right?" He was watching her warily, as if she were going to have a touch of the vapors at the prospect of handling a creature just like his youngest sister had.

"I have just gone into battle with a deranged Persian, your grace, so I think I can manage a blackbird with no problem."

He smiled at that, then turned toward the huddled bird. "All right, little fellow, let's get you out." With Portia still steadying his feet on the chair, he reached out with both hands, rummaged in the gap, and then pulled them out cradling the bird. "Gently does it, Miss Kendall." He crouched a little and offered it to her. The only way to take it was to let go of his ankles and cup her hands around his—which was most disconcerting after her close encounter with his bottom and crotch—while he eased his out from beneath her fingers.

The frightened bird twitched within her palms, its tiny heart racing as its whole body shook. But at least it was alive and, miraculously when one considered it had been impaled between M'Lady's sharp fangs, did not seem to be bleeding. The same could not be said for the duke, who had a tiny trickle of blood going down his neck, which she decided was best not to apprise him of, seeing as the mere sight of the stuff clearly bothered him.

She carried the blackbird carefully to the window and gently placed it on the sill. It blinked back at her for a few moments as if it could not quite believe that its ordeal was over, then without further ado, swooped out into the garden and over the trees.

"We did it." She turned, smiling at the duke, and he smiled back, and suddenly she was off-kilter.

She had no clue if it was his dratted dimples that sent her pulse aflutter, his deep blue eyes, the lingering effects of his touch, his intriguing muscles, or his annoyingly perfect backside, but it really was most peculiar. She felt a little giddy and slightly breathless and wasn't the least bit happy about any of it.

"We did, Miss Kendall." He went to step down from the chair and without her stabilizing him, it wobbled. He grabbed the molded top of the bookshelf at the same moment she lunged for his ankles again, but unfortunately neither of their efforts helped. The chair slid sideways beneath him just as the bookshelf began to tip ominously toward them, and he fell to the floor, taking her with him.

He hit the floor first with an almighty thud, twisting slightly so that his body broke her fall, then he rolled to cover her as most of the books from the upper shelves rained down upon them. Portia felt every single buffered blow through his chest, which was flattened against hers. Every pained whoosh of his breath against her cheek as he absorbed each hit. Then they both held their breath while they waited for the heavy oak bookcase to follow—but it didn't. The equally hefty oak desk had saved the day and had only shifted slightly as the bookcase had toppled, but it did cast a looming shadow over them as the shelf leaned upon it.

The duke levered himself up on his elbows and stared down at her wide-eyed. "Are you all right?"

No she jolly well wasn't!

Having his face mere inches from hers had given her palpitations. Having her breasts flattened against the solid wall of his chest had given them improper ideas they had no place having and his thigh wedged right between the apex of hers was as thrilling as it was scandalous.

"I am just a bit winded, your grace." Although she feared that the sudden impact was only responsible for half of her breathlessness. "You?"

He stared down at her for several long seconds before her words registered. "Er . . ." He shifted off her and immediately winced as he sat. "I fear my ankle and my knee took the brunt."

Bizarrely, Portia instantly missed the contact, but scrambled to sit too, supremely conscious of the fact that he was hurt because he had selflessly saved her from harm. She wasn't sure what she felt about that noble gesture, beyond grateful but bothered by it, so put that dilemma to one side to tend to him instead.

By the tenseness in his perfectly proportioned features, he was in some pain as he bent to massage his lower leg.

"Do you think you've broken something?"

He gritted his teeth as he shook his head. "All the bones feel intact. It's probably just a sprain. Nothing some ice won't fix." He went to stand and grunted.

Portia stood and kicked several fallen books out of the way to clear a safe path before she braced herself to hoist him up. He grabbed her hand, took a deep breath, and then heaved himself upright. The moment he tried to put any weight on his leg he faltered, forcing her to grab his solid bicep to stop him from hitting the floor once more.

"Let's get you to your chair and—"

"It's carnage in here. Help me to the drawing room." He looped an arm around her shoulders, leaning on her heavily and giving her no choice but to slide her arm around his waist as they made slow progress out of the study.

All of the commotion had brought the housekeeper and the footman running.

"Your grace!" The housekeeper's hands flew to her face before one of them pointed to his. "You're bleeding!"

"Am I?" He instinctively touched the trickle, took one look at the blood on his fingertips, and immediately began to sway. "I hate blood," he repeated quite unnecessarily as the burly footman rushed forward to help Portia support the duke's weight. Together, they got him to the sofa in the drawing room while the housekeeper dashed off to fetch some ice and send someone for the physician.

With Portia's help, the duke heaved his leg onto the sofa. She didn't know much about nursing but she knew that if his ankle was swelling, then the sooner she got his boot off the better. He winced as she tugged it, biting down on his lip when it finally began to give and she gently eased it off.

It shouldn't have surprised her that a man who was so well put together would also have decent-looking feet, but they galled nevertheless. Was there nothing about him that wasn't perfect? His ankle, however, was practically purple and was swelling like a balloon. There was also a large and vivid bruise marring the annoyingly golden skin of his calf and knee. Without thinking, she smoothed her palm over his lower leg to check that nothing was amiss beneath his marred flesh and immediately regretted it. It felt too familiar. Somehow more familiar than lying prostrate beneath him had just a few minutes ago.

Portia sat back on her heels in case her errant hands went wandering again. "I don't think anything is broken but I don't think you'll be dancing for a while."

"Every cloud," he said through green gills and gritted teeth. "I hate dancing. Almost as much as I hate blood."

That was when Lady Emilia burst through the door. "Oh my god!" She quickly took in the scene and the state of her brother. "Leo!" Then, because apparently all she was good for was screaming, she began screaming for her sister. "Abigail! Leo is injured!"

The older sister arrived shortly afterward, looking as worse for wear after her run-in with the mad cat as Portia suspected she did. "Has somebody sent for the physician?"

"The housekeeper has." Portia shuffled back a bit as his sister fussed, examining the duke's leg with more confidence and doubtless with fewer palpitations than she had managed.

She shook her head at the state of him. "Dare I ask how this happened?"

"I fell off the chair that I had foolishly put on my desk to rescue the bird, and then the bookcase promptly fell on us."

"Us?" Lady Abigail's head swiveled to Portia and there was genuine concern in her eyes. "Are you injured too, Miss Kendall?"

"No." And that was all down to him. "His grace was very noble and used himself to save me." An instinctive and totally selfless act that forced her to reevaluate her harsh opinion of him somewhat. A truly self-absorbed and selfish aristocrat would have thought only of themselves in a crisis and probably used her as a shield, whereas he had, despite his irrational fear of blood, sacrificed himself rather than see her hurt.

He had also, staggeringly, stuck up for *Equitas* with the constable and that also did not fit well with the unflattering narrative that she had constructed around him, which was both enlightening and irritating in equal measure.

Perhaps there was such a thing as a decent duke after all? She would have to write an essay on the topic later, just to properly sort her jumbled thoughts out. "Thank you, your grace." She smiled at him and, to her surprise, realized that she meant it. "But now I feel dreadful that only you are injured."

He waved that away. "Better me than you." Which was a rather lovely thing for him to say too. "It was my cat that caused all the chaos, after all, so it is only fitting that I suffer the consequences. Besides, as my mother and my sisters are so fond of telling me, I have a ridiculously thick head, so I knew it would take more than a few encyclopedias to do it any real damage." He grinned and his dimples flashed and Portia's pulse quickened once more, but for once she just enjoyed it rather than castigate herself for her weakness toward one of the enemy. Because something deep down told her that he wasn't the enemy now, and she didn't know what to do with that new knowledge other than take it away and ponder it on paper later too.

"He does have a ridiculously thick head," said Lady Abigail squeezing his hand and inadvertently displaying, for the first time, how much she loved her brother. "But for once I am actually grateful for it."

And so, bizarrely, was Portia.

Chapter
TEN

Leo didn't know which was worse—the constant throb in his lower leg or the hunger pangs clawing in his stomach. What he did know, however, was that he wasn't going to get a wink of sleep while they both plagued him simultaneously.

He was also sick to the back teeth of his bed, which he had been confined to since yesterday thanks to Abigail and his housekeeper. They had taken to heart all the advice from the overcautious physician who had been adamant that Leo needed to keep the weight off the bad sprain for at least a week. Therefore, they had both decided to treat him like he was knocking on death's door. That meant bed rest and plenty of what his housekeeper called "a fortifying convalescence diet" to get his strength up. A diet that basically consisted of thin, tasteless soup, awful dry rolls baked with bird seeds and served without butter, and pints of a foul herbal tea that were brought to him in an invalid's cup with a bloody spout.

So instead of doing as he was told and ringing the bell if he needed something, he decided that he was all done wasting away on gruel and penance bread. He would treat himself to a clandestine midnight feast in the deserted kitchen instead.

He shuffled to the edge of the mattress to throw his legs over and tentatively stood. His ankle protested and he almost reached for the cane that the physician had insisted that he use until the swelling went down, but rebelled again. He despised the old-man's cane as much as he did the child's drinking cup, and was thoroughly convinced that he didn't need either. Instead, he used the furniture to support himself while he wriggled himself into some breeches and a shirt, then used the walls to assist him as he part shuffled, part hopped out of his bedchamber.

Barkington and Snifferson immediately rose from their usual sleeping position directly outside of his door and, still yawning, loyally followed him as he hobbled and hopped his way to the stairs.

Three painfully slow stairs down and Leo realized that he might be expecting too much from his battered ankle. It had really begun to hurt with a vengeance now, but as it would be a cold day in hell before he hollered for help and was inevitably chastised for not following doctor's orders, he decided to sit himself down and shuffle down them on his arse instead. A solution that, although undignified, worked a treat.

In no time at all, he was hopping along the narrow corridor to the kitchen where the promise of some real food lured him like a siren.

He was almost there when Barkington hurried forward and gave his traditional three yaps to signal a change in the wind.

"Shhhh, boy." Miss Kendall's soft whisper floated from the kitchen. "Remember our deal. We don't want to wake the whole house up, so you only get a treat if you stay quiet."

The word "treat" was all it took to excite Snifferson, who clean forgot his solemn duty to protect Leo with his life and barreled past him to get to her, forcing Leo to limp the last few yards unaccompanied while he listened to his disloyal hounds being made a fuss of.

She was crouched on the floor, tickling both of their bellies by the time he got to the door and clearly, thanks to the excited dogs, hadn't heard his approach, so he took a moment to take in the scene. Or more specifically her. Because he had been thinking about her all day. Or more specifically, how intimately intertwined they had been yesterday and how the womanly feel of her soft body pressed against his seemed to be indelibly printed in his mind.

He was so busy drinking her in that it took several seconds before he noticed that she was still in her coat and bonnet. Which coincided with the exact moment that she lifted her gaze and gasped as she spotted him.

"Your grace!" Her eyes were wide as she shot up. The soft light from the only lit lamp in the kitchen made copper flecks dance in her dark irises. "You made me jump!"

"My apologies." He used the wall to edge closer. "You are back late, Miss Kendall." And that really bothered him. "I trust your mother's neighbor still dropped you home?"

She blinked and then nodded. "Of course, your grace." Then she frowned. "What on earth are you doing out of bed? You are supposed to be keeping off your ankle."

"I am dying of hunger thanks to being put on starvation rations, so I am on the hunt for food."

"Should I ring for someone?"

"Only if you have no pity in your soul, Miss Kendall. The staff are all under strict instructions to only feed me gruel and I am in urgent need of some real food—hence this clandestine forage to the kitchen."

She smiled at that while untying her bonnet, then turned to place it on the side. "I saw your supper being prepared and it did look grim."

"It was beyond grim." Leo pulled a face. "It was foul."

"Poor you." She smiled. "Would you like me to make you something? My culinary skills are severely limited, but I can manage a sandwich, or if you would like something hot, I can also make toast."

The thought of a couple of thick slabs of toast slathered in butter made him salivate. The way she shrugged out of her pelisse to reveal the tight bodice of a pretty, short-sleeved summer dress made him salivate some more. She had always cut a pleasing figure in her dark and sensible chaperone's gowns, but this simple, embroidered muslin did something wonderful. The scooped neckline showcased the merest glimpse of the upper swells of her breasts and the utter perfection of her English rose complexion against her dark hair. Reminding him, in no uncertain terms, that she was a young woman in her prime. And a beautiful woman to boot. With undulating curves in all the right places and a bottom that reminded him of a peach. A juicy one that—

She turned back for his response to her offer, and he only just managed to wrench his gaze from her arse in the nick of time.

"Toast sounds like the nectar of the gods, Miss Kendall, so long as it is made with proper bread made from real flour and not the stuff the cook has been scraping up from the stable floor. Nobody should have to suffer those grim invalid cannonballs she bakes to complement my tasteless sickroom gruel. Although why the blazes they have decided to treat my stomach when I am as right as ninepence everywhere except from below my left knee is anyone's guess."

She laughed. It was a warm, earthy, seductive sound that he liked a great deal. "That does seem a little harsh."

"Harsh is an understatement. I doubt they even serve anything that bad to the prisoners in Newgate."

"I sincerely doubt that, your grace. Conditions in Newgate are purported to be horrendous. I read a troubling article about it recently that was the stuff of nightmares." Despite her habitual need to put him in his place, she must have noticed that he was struggling to stand as she pulled out a chair at the table, then rushed over to grab his elbow so that he could hop to it. It was a kind and almost motherly gesture, so he felt slightly ashamed that his body thoroughly enjoyed the gentle press of her bosom against his bicep as she steadied him while he sat.

She left him to fetch another chair but the alluring scent of her still lingered in his nostrils. Orange blossom merged with the fresh night air from outside in a heady mix that, although delicate, somehow suited her.

When she returned, she placed the chair in front of him, topped it with a cushion and then bent to help him heave his bad leg onto it, inadvertently giving him a splendid view right down her cleavage in the process.

Instantly, his groin tightened.

"Would you like some ice, your grace?"

"P-please." What the blazes was the matter with him? He wasn't usually the sort to ogle. And he definitely had never been the sort to think improper thoughts about a woman in his employ. That went against all his upstanding gentlemanly principles and those of his father before him. Clearly the hunger had stopped him thinking straight. Except it wasn't just food that he craved now. "If it's not too much trouble." That she was finally warming to him after a week of standoffishness wasn't helping him either.

"It's really no trouble at all." She disappeared to fetch it and that gave him a bit of time to regroup and give himself—and his groin—a stiff talking-to.

Miss Kendall worked for him. That meant that she was out of bounds. Which meant no looking and definitely no wayward thoughts of touching!

And certainly no inappropriate stirrings!

To reinforce that, he readjusted his breeches as he huffed at himself in disgust, then caught Snifferson staring at him intently as if he could see all the way inside Leo's filthy mind. "I know! I'll repent by stuffing some of the ice down my bloody waistband!"

"What did you say?" Because of course the competent Miss Kendall had returned with the ice already.

"I was just letting Snifferson know that I would remind you that you promised him a treat." Both dogs stared at him in disappointment then, and he didn't blame them. If he could find some excuse to dash away so that he could flagellate himself for all his improper thoughts, he would. But he knew that if he tried to escape, she would come to assist him and that wouldn't help the twitch in his breeches one bit.

"I did, didn't I?" She handed him the wrapped ice and turned to the dogs. "What a naughty Portia I am."

The absolute last thing Leo needed to hear were the words "naughty" and "Portia" in the same sentence because both gave him ideas, so he gritted his teeth and focused on placing the icy bundle on his ankle rather than watch her caress Barkington's ears.

All the while silently wishing she was caressing his instead.

The world had clearly gone quite mad as Portia was making toast for a duke and—this really flummoxed her—she had offered to.

She wanted to blame that solely on how unsettled his question about her mother's imaginary neighbor escorting her back had made her because she didn't want to keep lying to him. She preferred never to outright lie to anyone—which was why she was still avoiding her mother like the plague—so that wasn't unique to the duke. But after the way he had selflessly saved her yesterday, she felt bad about all the necessary fibs she had to tell.

The duke was, she realized now, not quite the archetypal aristocratic villain that she had been keen to paint him. Despite his galling title and his overbearingness, he actually seemed to be quite a decent man.

He was an affable, reasonable sort who was trying to do his best under the most challenging of circumstances. Two weeks into her employment and she realized that he was not one of the idle rich because he had neither the time nor the patience for their usual pursuits. Instead, he worked hard managing his estates and fulfilling his duties as a magistrate while being the best brother that he could be.

It could not be easy to juggle all that he did with the added responsibilities of two rebellious sisters, who she now knew firsthand were quite the challenge. So yes, he was a bit of a controlling tyrant where they were concerned, but it wasn't entirely without cause.

She lifted the hot toasting forks from the edge of the fire and deposited the two steaming slices on a plate that she set before him. They were lopsided and not pretty, but they did at least smell divine. "Here you are, your grace." As she had already put the butter dish and a pot of strawberry jam on the table, she offered him another surprisingly genuine smile. "Don't stay up too late." Then she spun on her heel, ready to escape.

"You're not having any?" Of all the things she expected him to say, that wasn't it.

"Well . . . I . . ."

He picked up one of the slices. "Only thanks to your rather cavalier way with the bread knife, these are two gargantuan pieces of toast, Miss Kendall." Then he smiled but there was a vulnerability in his expression that tugged at her heart. "And I cannot deny that I would appreciate the company after being imprisoned in my bed and forced to stare at the same four walls all day." Then his dimples worked their usual magic as he grinned. "Besides, as I have been starved all day too, despite the ridiculous thickness of these slices, I still might need you to make a second round. We don't want me wasting away now, do we?"

As there seemed no way of getting out of that without appearing churlish, she sat in the chair opposite him and tried not to wonder what sort of a state her hair was in after her brisk walk home across the city all the way from the newspaper in the dark.

The duke spread a generous layer of butter on a slice and passed it to her before he set about buttering the other for himself, apparently oblivious to the fact that men of his station did not generally prepare or share their food with someone of hers. "I suppose I need to ask you if you would be kind enough to cancel all my social engagements for the next few days?" He tried and failed to look disappointed at that prospect. "Which obviously devastates me." He covered the threatening grin with a huge bite of his toast.

"That is already done."

"That was very proactive of you, Miss Kendall, but thank you."

"It was your sister's idea actually." She pulled a tiny corner of her crust off for appearance's sake. Not because she didn't want to eat the toast—quite the contrary as she was hungry too—but because good manners dictated that she eat it like a lady. He was a duke after all and, uncharacteristically, she was self-conscious about eating in front of one despite the informality of the setting. "Lady Abigail told me to cancel everything until Friday straight after the physician left yesterday."

"Did she?" He seemed surprised by that as he chewed thoughtfully. "I wonder how long this armistice will last?"

"Just enjoy it while it does." Portia popped the tiny crumb into her mouth, and he paused chewing to stare at her, incredulous.

"Oh please don't tell me that you are one of those women who pretends to eat like a bird? Because such restraint really doesn't suit you, Miss Kendall. You've always struck me as a grab-the-bull-by-the-horns, I-do-not-care-what-anybody-else-thinks sort and if I can sit here proudly with butter all over my chin, so can you." He took another huge bite, his blue eyes lit with challenge. "Or does my lofty title intimidate you so much that you are suddenly rendered meek?"

Could he read her like a book? "Nothing intimidates me, your grace, and especially not your title." And to prove that, she stared him dead in the eye as she lifted the whole slice to her mouth and took a hearty crunch out of it.

"There she is! That is the Miss Kendall I employed."

"I've often wondered why you did employ me. Especially when I cannot believe that I was as experienced as the other candidates."

"You weren't—but you came across as fearless and that clinched it. My sisters need fearless. They also need a chaperone who is wily, tenacious, determined, unflappable, unbelievably stubborn, and annoyingly clever."

Portia felt a blush infuse her cheeks at him quoting back her own arrogant words but made no effort to hide it. "Oh please don't remind me of all that I said in that interview as it was not my finest hour."

He had such a lovely smile. The sort that utterly charmed. "Whyever not? You were magnificent in that interview. Unconventional, yes. Overconfident—perhaps a tad." He held his thumb and index finger an inch apart. "Borderline rude too—most definitely. But still impressive." His deep chuckle drizzled over her like the melted butter on her toast. "I've honestly never seen anything like it."

"Any other duke would have thrown me out for my impertinence."

"I like to think that I am not like any other duke—but I know that I am merely flattering myself on that score. Unfortunately, I am simply a replica of my father in every way possible. Everybody says so," he said, swiping crumbs from his lips. "We even have the same sized feet and identical dimples." He smiled broadly just so that he could poke his finger in one.

"Really?"

"Well you tell me—you must have seen the portrait? The enormous one hanging above the fireplace in the drawing room."

Portia gaped at him, so shocked by that unexpected revelation that she forgot herself. "I thought that was you!"

"See," he said shaking his golden head in amusement. "My point is proved. There is absolutely nothing original about me. I am my father's son through and through. Not that I am complaining because my father was—" Then he frowned. "Wait . . ." His blue eyes narrowed. "You thought that I was so vain that I actually hung a giant portrait of myself above my own fireplace?"

"I . . . um . . ."

"Oh I see!" He sat back in his chair and folded his arms, those mesmerizing cornflower eyes twinkling. Looking utterly disarming thanks to his pillow-mussed hair and the day-old, burnished-gold stubble on his chin. "Now it all begins to make sense why you didn't like me. You had me pegged as vain and self-absorbed."

"I . . . um . . . wouldn't say that . . ." But as he was laughing, she couldn't help sniggering too, seeing as he didn't seem to have taken the slightest bit of offense at her assumption. "Perhaps I did form some opinions of you that weren't correct on the back of that interview."

"Ah-ha!" He pointed at her. "Didn't anyone ever tell you not to judge a book by its cover, Miss Kendall?" His cover now, thanks to just the thin, untucked linen shirt and breeches, was about as unducal as it was possible to be, and heaven help her but it suited him. Somehow more than the well-tailored coats and silk waistcoats those garments were usually covered by.

"In my defense—you did keep me waiting for almost an hour and you did as good as offer Miss Strictland the job beforehand, so I thought you were wasting my time."

He leaned on his propped hand across the table, staring deep into her eyes with such hypnotic intensity that, for a moment, she clean forgot he was a duke. "What changed your mind about me?"

"What makes you think that I have?"

"You are talking to me, Miss Kendall, rather than glaring. And . . ." He flicked a finger in the direction of her face. "Your smiles aren't false anymore."

"Yesterday," she said honestly. "With the cat, the bird, the fall, the books, and . . ." In for a penny, in for a pound. "In the way you dealt with the constable."

"Constable Nolley would try the patience of a saint."

"Everything about yesterday's debacle would try the patience of a saint, but you managed to deal with it all—with the exception of your pathetic swooning at the blood—with remarkably good grace." Then, because the irony amused her, she added, "Your grace."

"Ah yes . . ." He winced. "I am *pathetically* not good with blood after a bad experience with it. Try not to judge me for it."

"We all have an Achilles' heel."

"What is yours, Miss Kendall?"

Currently, it was clearly a delightfully rumpled, blue-eyed, dimpled duke who refused to fit the mold, whose company she was enjoying more than she ever would have thought possible. "By all,

I obviously didn't mean me, your grace. I am too wily, tenacious, determined, unflappable, unbelievably stubborn, annoyingly clever, and fearless to have any sort of weakness. And even if I did, I am too proud to admit to one."

"They say pride comes before a fall, Miss Kendall, and I have always thought dignity is overrated."

"Maybe so, but I shall cling to mine regardless."

"Spoilsport."

"What bad experience?" The question popped out unbidden because she not only wanted to move the subject away from her, but because she was curious. "If it isn't too impertinent to ask, of course?"

"Abigail fell out of a tree and broke her leg as a child. Badly. There was blood everywhere. All my fault. I was a stupid, distracted sixteen-year-old and I took my eyes off her and she nearly died as a result. Haven't been able to abide the sight of it since." His nose wrinkled and he dropped the last crust of his toast before he pushed his plate away. "Not my finest hour." She wanted to ask for more details of that accident, especially why he blamed himself for it, but didn't because his gaze now looked haunted enough just by the memory.

"I suppose that explains why you are so protective of your sisters now."

"That combined with their uncanny ability to dive headfirst into trouble. They are both much too reckless and always act before they think." Then he pinned her with his stare. "You are a girl, Miss Kendall, so you will know the answer. At what age will they grow out of it?"

"I suppose that depends very much on the person. I daresay some will always be reckless if they believe it is right to be." Much like herself. Portia knew all the risks associated with her involvement in the newspaper, knew how harsh the consequences could be if she ever fell foul of the law, yet took the gamble anyway.

He folded his arms, drawing her attention to the tanned skin of his forearms. "That is not the reassuring answer that I was hoping for."

"If you had specified that my answer was meant to make you feel better, I wouldn't have answered honestly, your grace. I shall try harder next time you ask me for my opinion to only say what you want to hear."

"Urgh." He huffed. "Please don't. I get enough of that from everyone else. Aside from my sisters, of course, or my mother." He pulled a face when he said the word "mother" as if she were somehow more of an irritation to him than his rebellious sisters were. "Have you any idea how frustrating it is to be constantly fawned over and flattered? Or worse, constantly lied to by pretty much everyone who swears the oath in court to tell the truth and nothing but the truth then does nothing of the sort. Trust me, Miss Kendall, when you are burdened with the titles of both duke and magistrate, genuine honesty is a rare gift indeed. So I beg you, even if I do not like it, continue to always be completely and refreshingly honest with me."

Guilt and shame swamped her because she could never be completely honest with him and had lied to him more times than she cared to count already. "That won't be hard as I am apparently very opinionated, your grace." That "your grace" instantly reminded her that, despite how affable and easy he was to be around, he was still both a duke and a magistrate so she probably should keep her often controversial opinions to herself. And as such, it would not do to ever be too cozy in his company. No matter how much she was enjoying it.

"It's late so, I'd best hide away all this evidence of your clandestine foraging before someone discovers it. Then I shall take you to bed." That last bit sounded like an invitation, but before Portia could correct the end of her sentence with "I shall help you back up to your bed" she was sure his gaze heated for a moment. But then the yearning that she thought she saw—perhaps wanted to believe she saw—was gone. And he was standing.

"I can take myself, Miss Kendall, as I have importuned you enough already this evening."

"Let me help you." She stood too. "You *are* supposed to be keeping your weight off your leg." No matter how much he had left her off-kilter, and how much more off-kilter she would be if he had to wrap his arm around her again, she did not want him to do more damage.

"No need." He stayed her advance with a raised hand. "I managed to get down by myself, so I daresay I'll manage to get back up myself in much the same way. It's hideously undignified so for the sake of my manly pride, I would prefer to shuffle back up on my backside in private, Miss Kendall."

"I thought you just said that dignity was overrated, and that pride always comes before a fall?"

"When I said that, I obviously wasn't talking about *my* dignity or *my* pride, Miss Kendall, so I shall cling to both regardless, if you don't mind." His smile was ironic. And perhaps a little wistful, as if he too knew that the pair of them really shouldn't be enjoying one another's company quite as much as they currently were. "Please take your time following me up the stairs, and thank you for feeding me."

Portia wasn't sure if she was relieved by that reprieve or disappointed. "It was my pleasure."

And, rather bizarrely, it was.

Chapter
ELEVEN

Miss Kendall looked thoroughly miserable from her desolate position in the middle of the otherwise empty wallflower chairs, and that filled Leo with guilt. He had cajoled her into coming to this fundraising ball tonight to help him out because ten days on from his accident he was still hobbling around. But, being one of the patrons of the local hospital this event was raising funds for, he felt duty bound to attend. Fearing that his sisters might use his incapacity against him despite their uneasy armistice, he wanted some assistance nearby in case they attempted to rebel. Especially as he was in no fit state to chase after them.

However, two hours in and, likely because as it was tipping it down outside, neither Abigail nor Emilia had tried to escape the ballroom once. Emilia was enjoying being one of the only young ladies present with a full dance card. Abigail, who was undoubtedly the most aggrieved with him, had been ensconced in a serious-looking conversation with a bunch of her new academically minded acquaintances and showed no signs of tiring of it anytime soon.

In short, it was eleven o'clock and all was well. If that blessed miracle continued until midnight when this blasted ball finished, then he had definitely dragged poor Miss Kendall here under false pretenses.

"Allow me to introduce you to Mr. Joshua Marshall, a businessman who has recently moved to our great city from Bristol. Mr. Marshall has generously donated twenty guineas to our cause." Lord Teignmouth, Leo's friend and the organizer of this evening's fundraiser, brought their next victim over because clearly Mr. Marshall had a great deal more money than his twenty-guinea contribution suggested. As the resident duke and therefore precisely the sort of connection that the increasing Bath contingent of new money craved, it was his job to encourage this man to part with more.

"It is a pleasure to meet you, Mr. Marshall." Leo tore his gaze from Miss Kendall to stick out his hand with what he hoped was convincing enthusiasm. "What line of business are you in?"

He spent the next ten minutes asking all the right questions that guaranteed Mr. Marshall talked about himself and his success, which made the man feel good, and by default guaranteed Mr. Marshall would reopen his purse. All the while Leo's gaze frequently drifted to Miss Kendall, who was doing a splendid job of being his eyes as far as his sisters were concerned. Despite her diligence, he still sensed her unease at being in this ballroom and fought the urge to wander her way to make her feel good about herself too.

She seemed self-conscious, for some reason, although he could not fathom why. Even in her simple coral evening gown, which she filled to perfection, she outshone every other woman in the room.

There was something about her that drew the eye and, from the appreciative glances he kept noticing from plenty of the other men here, not just his. She had a natural glow that out-shimmered all the expensive jewelry glittering beneath the ballroom's chandeliers. An effortless allure that did not require all the additional adornments worn by every other lady present. Who knew that a few ink stains held the power to draw the eye better than a diamond? Although he suspected that really did depend on who was sporting the stains.

Conscious that he was staring, Leo forced himself to focus on Mr. Marshall while he inwardly gave himself a stern talking-to. All his staring and the peculiar yearning that he had developed for his sisters' chaperone was as improper as it was impertinent. She was his employee, for goodness' sake.

His *employee*!

And he was certainly not the sort of employer who would ever try to take advantage of someone who worked for him. He had always deplored those who did.

Leo had principles. Rigid principles that were set in stone. Principles that dictated that he always treated every member of his staff with the utmost respect.

As was only fair and proper.

Because he was a gentleman.

Perhaps if he said that often enough, he might stop thinking of her as an attractive and intriguing woman who appealed to him far too much.

He blamed the new change in their relationship. Their lack of the proper formalities, which they both seemed to have dropped since his accident, had made him stop thinking of her as an employee and more like a . . . well . . . friend of sorts. Just with some unrequited, ungentlemanly lust and longing thrown into the mix to further complicate things.

While Mr. Marshall droned on, a handsome gent sidled up beside Miss Kendall and began to flirt with her; the urge to go to her increased tenfold. But when the silver-tongued devil sat down Leo was compelled—viscerally propelled—to act upon it.

He excused himself politely and picked his way around the edge of the crowded dance floor. As soon as she spied him, Miss Kendall said something to her new companion that made him quickly stand and then, to Leo's absolute disgust, the scoundrel kissed her hand before he beat a hasty retreat.

He covered the hot flash of jealousy with a smile. "You will be pleased to know that there is less than an hour of this torture left."

"Thank goodness for that." The relief on her lovely face was palpable. "And thank you for saving me from that chancer." She offered him a resigned half smile. "I presume you noticed that he was being a pest and that is why you hobbled all the way over here to save me?"

"He did seem a little persistent." Suddenly self-conscious of both his haste to get to her and the old-man's cane that he needed to lean on to do that, when her robust admirer had no such impediment, Leo lowered himself into a chair.

"Opportunists always are." She pulled a face. One that said that she was used to men trying to seduce her and that did nothing to ease his irrational jealousy any. "Have you had a successful evening convincing the rich to part with their money?"

"The coffers of St. John's Hospital are significantly fuller, so yes."

"You seem to have a knack for fundraising." Sometimes, when she looked at him, he could see the cogs of her clever mind turning as if she were trying to figure him out just as much as he was trying to figure her out. He had no clue whether that was a good or bad thing but still foolishly hoped for the former. "I have never seen so many people so happy to have their pockets picked."

Did that mean that she had been surreptitiously watching him too? A prospect that warmed him more than it should. "Being a duke has its advantages."

"I suspect that is part of it, for sure, but a greater part is you. You are quite the charmer on the sly, aren't you?" He tried to wave that compliment away, but she wouldn't let him. "Being able to turn people to your way of thinking so effortlessly is a rare talent indeed. One that I wish that I possessed. But alas, I am too cynical, prone to lecture and can frequently be too . . ." Her brows kissed as she sought the right word.

"Prickly?"

Her bark of not-so-outraged laughter made him want to puff up with pride because, reluctantly, even if she did not lust after him in the way he did her, she was definitely warming to him. "I was going to say acerbic, but I suppose prickly fits just as well."

"I admire that you do not suffer fools gladly, even when you thought me one of those fools."

She smiled but didn't deny it. "You have grown on me since then, your grace."

"I apologize for that—because I appreciate how painful it must be to have to admit that."

"Thank you." Her lips twitched but she held her amusement in. "There is nothing a cynic loathes more than their lowly expectations being surpassed."

"That is not it at all. You just hate being proved wrong."

Her caged smile broke free. "There is that too."

"But now that I have gone up in your estimation, I am curious, Miss Kendall—what was it in particular about me that you initially took the most umbrage about?"

For a moment, he didn't think that she would answer honestly, but she sighed. "To be frank . . ." She swept her arm around the room. "This. I find it difficult to feel any compassion for those who have only ever existed among all this privilege and yet are so oblivious to it."

Leo frowned, unsure whether to be offended by her sweeping generalization. "Surely none of us can help what we were born into?"

"Of course we can't—but we can decide how we choose to treat people." Her smile now was resigned. "I will wager that it would never occur to most of the people in this grand ballroom to share their toast with an employee or, for that matter, to use themselves to stop a heavy shower of books from raining down on one either. In fact, I'll wager most do not even see their employees. Just as most have flatly refused to see me this evening. If they have, with the exception of that chancer just now who was on the prowl for a willing woman, they look down their aristocratic noses at me—just like those two ladies are currently doing." She flicked her eyes briefly toward the exact same pair of debutantes who had simpered over him not an hour ago, who were undeniably shooting daggers her way. "They are positively outraged that a duke would waste his precious time talking to someone as insignificant as me."

He scoffed. "They are more likely outraged that you are the most beautiful woman in the room, Miss Kendall." *Oh good heavens above he had actually said that aloud!*

Before he could find some way to claw that unintentional confession back, it was her turn to scoff. "You do not need to use your well-practiced charm to make me feel better about their disdain, your grace, for I am well used to being glared at down an aristocratic nose. Almost as much as I am to being rendered invisible by them. We are disposable and too easily replaced to even feature in their thoughts. That is the unique curse of a servant. To always be underestimated simply because we weren't born to privilege and to always be judged solely by our humble exteriors."

Then she grinned. "But be assured that while I am outwardly demure and seemingly oblivious to their scorn, as is expected from someone from my lowly station, internally I am judging them just as harshly as they are currently judging me. Perhaps even more so because I am such a prickly cynic. What pathetic creatures those two ladies must be to feel threatened by me? Even if I am currently talking to the most eligible peer in the ballroom." There was a twinkle of mischief back in her fine eyes now. "How does that feel, by the way? To be coveted by every single young lady present who is in want of the most titled husband?"

"Awkward," he said truthfully. "Annoying. But . . ." He nudged her playfully with his elbow. "That is the unique curse of us dukes. To always be underestimated simply because we were born with a silver spoon in our mouths and always be judged solely on our impressive title and even more impressive ducal exteriors." Then he winked. Purely to get her reaction. Or perhaps to flirt. He really wasn't sure which.

"Again, your practiced charm is wasted on me, your grace, as I have always tried to judge a man on his measure and not a lofty title that he inherited purely out of happenstance."

"Dare I ask how I measure up?" He was in grave danger of genuinely flirting now as he fished for more compliments, and thought he might have gone too far because he felt her stiffen beside him until he realized that she had instead stiffened because they had impending company.

"Debden! It's good to see you!"

Leo resisted the urge to groan aloud and pasted on a smile as he reluctantly held out his hand. "Corston." *Lord but he loathed this man!* "I would stand but . . ." He tapped his leg as an excuse, even though he could easily stand on it if he chose to.

"Yes—I heard you'd had an accident." Then the old letch ogled Miss Kendall. "But it least it gives you a decent excuse to sit out the dancing, eh? Who is this attractive filly?" Because surely every woman must be thrilled to be compared to a horse.

"My social secretary." Leo left it at that. Because sometimes the only way to get rid of someone that you didn't want to talk to was to leave an awkward silence dangling.

Corston's smarmy chuckle filled it, and it was as grating as the man. "Then I shall leave you and . . ." The letch swept his eyes the full length of Miss Kendall. "Your *delicious* social secretary to it."

They watched him walk away. Leo was on the cusp of apologizing for Corston's inappropriate innuendo when she leaned closer. "Would it be impertinent to ask why you dislike Lord Corston so?"

"Who says that I dislike him?"

"Your face. Your tone." Her gaze flicked to his mouth. "That snarl."

He scrunched his face to banish it. "I shall only tell you if you solemnly promise to keep it to yourself." He slanted her a glance and she nodded in mock seriousness, holding up one palm as if swearing an oath. "My dislike is twofold. Firstly, as a magistrate, he is part of the local hang 'em and flog 'em brigade that still believes that ruling by fear is the best way to tackle the soaring problem our towns and cities now have with crime. And secondly . . ." Leo shrugged, somehow knowing that he could trust her with his honesty. "I find his character utterly objectionable. He's a lazy, entitled, self-absorbed, philandering, hedonistic, and odious snake whose principles jar completely with pretty much all of mine."

"That is a damning assessment of the man indeed."

"And what is your assessment of him, Miss Kendall? Because . . ." He twisted slightly to watch her reaction. "You must have an opinion of the man if you grew up on his doorstep. The village of Newton St. Loe where your mother lives is but a stone's throw from Corston Park, is it not?"

She offered him a begrudging smile. "I might have one or two, your grace."

He wanted to ask her to call him Leo—but that probably was as improper as Corston's vile ogling when she was his employee.

His EMPLOYEE!

Something he struggled with when she leaned closer. "Sadly, my assessment of Lord Corston is just as damning as yours. He isn't liked by those who are unfortunate enough to have to work for him. Or those who have to rent from him. Or even those who only have to coexist close to him. I am not the least bit surprised that he is as dire a magistrate as he is a person."

Leo could not argue with that. "He is a dire magistrate. The direst in fact. I pity whichever poor soul comes up in front of him. Fortunately, he is not a very diligent magistrate, so we are spared his particular brand of justice for the majority of the sessions."

"The local hang 'em and flog 'em brigade are not substantial here then?"

"There are twelve of us serving Bath and its environs and only four of us are disparagingly called liberals. Five more hover somewhere in between, although which way they will go often depends entirely on the wind. Which leaves the permanently outraged three who believe fervently in throwing the full weight of the book at whoever is in the dock. It makes my job all the more . . ." Leo sighed because this was a topic too depressing for this suddenly lovely evening.

"Important?"

"I was actually going to say tiresome, but I suppose you are right too. Not that it stops me from ruing the day that I agreed to take my father's seat on the bench any less. Being a magistrate is a thankless task. One I would happily wash my hands of if I could find some other upstanding fool misguided enough to take the awful job on."

"Hmm." Her dark brows furrowed as she stared straight ahead, and he realized that she wasn't impressed with that answer.

"Remember that you can always be forthright with me, Miss Kendall, so do feel free to say all that you are clearly holding back. What is it about what I just said that you take issue with?"

"Your own oblivious sense of entitlement, your grace." A response that surprised him because he had never thought of himself as entitled. "You see your role as a magistrate as a chore—and while I do not doubt that it often is—you seem unaware of the phenomenal privilege that it is too. *You* have a say in what happens." She punctuated that with a point. "Frankly, a disproportionate say too when you, as someone who owns more than forty shillings' worth of land, are one of the rare few who are considered worthy enough to get the vote as well. Only three percent of the population are privileged enough to put a member of Parliament in the house to represent them."

"That is quite a specific number, Miss Kendall."

"It is quite a specific privilege, your grace. But as *peer* of the realm, you do not only get the vote and a seat on the magistrates' bench, but you also get a coveted seat in the House of Lords as well, which is where we all know the true power resides. So you technically have thrice the say of any less blue-blooded member of that select three percent. You, *your grace*, are one of the significantly less than one percent of this country's population who hold all the cards. You are a unicorn. *The* needle in the haystack. *The* pig that flies. Oh how I wish I had just a fraction of your power!" She finished her sermon with a good-natured glare. "But I daresay pigs will actually have to learn to fly before any of that three percent of entitled wealthy men ever consider giving women the vote—even if they are lucky enough to own forty shillings' worth of land."

"Well that well-argued lecture has put me firmly in my place."

"Good," she said with a smile. "Then my work here is done." Then as an aside, she added, "You did instruct me to always be completely honest with you when you knew that I was prickly. But I am also curious—who else here do you loathe as much as Lord Corston?"

Chapter
TWELVE

Despite her unexpected collision with the horrid peer who had plunged her and her mother into poverty all those years ago, and despite the miserable first two hours of the ball, Portia had actually had a rather lovely evening by the end of it. And all thanks to a duke too! Because they had spent the last hour chatting, laughing, and (unbelievably) enjoying one another's company. Which she never would have thought possible just a few short weeks ago when she had still been convinced that she despised all dukes purely on principle.

But the Duke of Debden was not like all dukes. In truth, she could not imagine him being like any other duke on the planet, so she was prepared to cut herself some slack for liking him so much.

She—Portia Kendall, cynic extraordinaire and passionate reformer—liked a duke!

And a great deal more than was prudent.

An irony that was not lost on her as she found herself smiling ever-so-slightly soppily at him as he helped her out of the carriage.

"Thank you for tonight." His big hand enveloped hers as his sisters disappeared inside the house. "I am indebted to you."

"You are very welcome, your grace." He was still holding her hand, and it was playing havoc with her senses. Proof that she more than liked him—she was attracted to him too. Enough that her flesh was heating and her pulse felt erratic. "But I can assure you, no debt is owed. You did save me from all those books, after all."

Was it wrong that she did not feel inclined to remove her fingers from his? Or that she was in no hurry either to follow his sisters up the porch steps and into the house because something about this moment excited her?

He excited her.

His gaze briefly flicked to her lips and that was when she realized that she wasn't the only one affected by the peculiarly charged atmosphere that suddenly engulfed them. To further confirm it, they both seemed content to linger.

His blue eyes darkened with what she sincerely hoped was evidence of his matching desire for her before they dropped to where their hands joined. "I . . ." His sigh was soft and so close that his warm breath whispered over her face. "I . . . um . . ." He leaned closer, his gaze dropping to her lips and the wayward, wanton, reckless part of her willed him to just kiss her and put them both out of their misery. "I would appreciate you passing on my apologies to your mother for stealing you this evening when I am aware that she likely needed you more."

Nothing killed a wholly futile, totally inappropriate romantic moment quite like guilt. "Of course." But for some inexplicable reason, and despite all the shocking lies she had told him about her robust mother's health, she still did not step away.

"At least she has you for the whole day tomorrow instead." His eyes flicked briefly to her mouth again before he smiled, and his dratted dimples appeared. But while they still made her inwardly sigh, they also served to make her feel more wretched.

He had generously offered her the Saturday off as well as Sunday for the inconvenience of this evening. She had so much work to do at *Equitas* before the next edition imminently went to print, she had grabbed his offer with both hands. At the time, she had seen the extra day off as a godsend. A chance to focus on the important work that she had come to Bath to do.

But now the duke's generosity only served to make her feel awful about her decision. It was all well and good doing something for the greater good, but it no longer sat right with her that she was, technically, taking advantage of a very decent man while doing it. And lying to him too. Not to mention that she was also technically lying to her mother, who, thanks to Portia's weekly letters sent by route of Kitty back in London, still thought that she was a governess in Mayfair.

As a lover of the written word, one particularly apt literary quote that she had read somewhere pricked at her conscience in warning.

Oh what a tangled web we weave, when first we practice to deceive.

A stark reminder of all the good reasons why she should have kept him at arm's length. Worse, rather than thinking of new ways to put some distance between them, she had not moments ago been open to stepping into those arms. Irrespective of the irrefutable fact that those arms not only belonged to a duke—but also to a magistrate.

She was, as the terminal doomsayer Edgar had warned, playing with fire, and it was time that she reinstated some of the barriers that had become blurred. She should probably go straight to her room and write an essay debating all the reasons why she couldn't allow herself to get waylaid by a charming, dimpled duke and keep it constantly on her person as a reminder whenever she felt herself slipping again.

And she would get cracking on it just as soon as she found the wherewithal to tug her fingers from his.

"Leo!" It was the duke who severed the contact by jumping back at the unfamiliar feminine shout, then he winced as an older woman bounded down the front steps, her arms outstretched. "I came back as soon as I heard about your terrible accident!" She smothered him in a hug. "You might not be my favorite person at the moment, and I might still want to wring your stubborn, supercilious neck—but you are still my son!" Then she wagged an irritated finger in his face. "I shouldn't have had to rely on Abigail to tell me about your accident via letter. You jolly well should have told me yourself that you were injured! And by express!"

"It is just a sprain, Mother. There was no reason to bother you."

"No reason?" She shook him by the shoulders. "You might well be thirty, Leo, and think that you always know best, but to me you will always be my baby!" She smothered him with some more love that he did not seem to appreciate. "If you were a parent, which of course you would need to find time in your busy schedule to marry to achieve becoming, then you would know that when one's child is seriously hurt, any good parent would move heaven and earth to get to them. So obviously that is what I did, darling." She threw up her palms, then used them to squish his cheeks. "I'll soon have you back on your feet again."

"I am on my feet." He pointed to them. "One just limps a bit."

"A limp almost killed your sister!" His mother was about to shake him again when she suddenly noticed Portia doing her best to melt into night. "And who is this lovely young lady, Leo?" She gave Portia a thorough, smiling appraisal. "And why the blazes haven't you yet thought to introduce us?"

"Yes . . . um . . ." He shuffled slightly, like a naughty schoolboy. His eyes lifted awkwardly to Portia's. "This is obviously my mother, the Duchess of Debden. Mother—this is Miss Kendall."

The older woman's eyes widened. "You are the chaperone?" Her gaze swept Portia again, somewhat incredulous. "*You?*"

"Yes, your grace." She dipped into a proper curtsy this time, hideously aware of the woman's stare the whole time because she had just witnessed one of the help apparently hand in hand with her titled son.

"Well," said his mother. "Well . . . you are *a surprise*." Then her eyes skewered the duke. "Interesting. Wholly unexpected but very . . . *very* . . . interesting."

The next morning, she was so early that she was the first person to arrive at *Equitas* and that suited Portia just fine. After a fitful night of self-recrimination, irrational regret, and reevaluation, she had decided that she had to trust that fate had stepped in yesterday for good reason.

She had allowed herself to get too close to the duke and, for the sake of *Equitas* and herself, it was undoubtedly for the best that her time in his employ had come to its natural conclusion now that his mother had returned. She would soon find another job to pay her bills; she would also find another place to live where she would never have to run the risk of ever colliding with the constable, and she would channel all her focus back on the newspaper where it belonged.

It was sad but it had always been inevitable. Her position as a chaperone in his house had only ever been temporary and, despite the odd ache in her heart, she had never been foolish enough to believe that there could be anything between her and the duke beyond passion. She was not, and never had been, mistress material and she certainly wasn't wife material, let alone duchess material, so whatever that odd moment had been between them last night, she was grateful that it had been nipped firmly in the bud.

Supremely grateful.

Perhaps if she told herself that often enough then the odd ache in her heart would disappear. While she waited for that to happen, she decided that some tea was the answer and set about making it before the rest of their merry crew arrived.

"Good morning!" William was next through the door. "Were you followed?"

"Of course not! In fact, I walked at least a mile out of my way en route here."

"Excellent. We can't be too careful with the constable after our blood." He finished his customary doomsaying lecture with a beaming smile when he saw that she was already preparing the cups. "Thank goodness you have your priorities right."

"I know that you do not function without at least three pints of Darjeeling in your system." She handed him a steaming mug. "Did I miss anything important last night?"

"Only Bessie having another conniption." He rolled his eyes. "And Edgar sent his apologies that he will not be joining us here today and tomorrow as he feels a little under the weather."

"Is he really under the weather or is he sulking because I am still here?" Relations between Portia and their onery typesetter had deteriorated even further in the last two weeks. "For heaven forbid our crusade for equality be extended to include a woman, irrespective of how good at her job she is."

"I actually suspect he is avoiding me to prove just how invaluable he is." William chuckled. "Which I suspect will backfire when you and your new assistant manage to complete all the typesetting to the highest possible standard in his petulant and contrived absence."

They both froze at the knock on the door, until Sir William checked his pocket watch. "And speaking of your new assistant, I'll wager that's him now."

Portia pasted on a smile as William went to the door, and she prayed that the new recruit had more respect for women than their woman-hating typesetter did. A handsome, smiling fellow in his very early twenties came in and immediately stuck out his hand.

"Miss Kendall—it is such an honor to officially meet you. I have always loved your articles. And the speeches that we all know you had more than a hand in back at headquarters."

"Officially? Have we collided before?"

He nodded. "Twice, although I am not the least bit offended that you cannot place me as I have been a mere dogsbody in the organization up until now." A comment that he immediately apologized for. "I know that I am still a dogsbody here, of course, and quite rightly as I still have so much to learn, but it feels like a massive promotion to even be allowed inside the hallowed walls of *Equitas*." He gestured to those tatty walls with such reverence Portia decided there and then that he would do very nicely.

"Portia is going to show you the ropes as you will be working for her." William seemed keen to hand him over. "I do hope you learn quickly, young man. We have a great deal to do over the next two days if we are going to get a paper out tomorrow."

She gave him a quick tour, then sat him beside her at Edgar's desk so that they could muddle through all the typesetting together.

"I very much enjoyed your last column on the state of the British justice system," he said after they had worked in companionable silence for an hour. "Probably because I have experienced the overly heavy hand of the law."

"Really?"

"I attended the Westminster workers' protest last month which didn't end well."

Portia had been about to leave London for Bath then and hadn't attended, but it had been all over the papers. "They sent in the army, didn't they? Were you arrested?"

"I wasn't, thankfully but my fiancée was injured in the fray and needed stitches."

"You are engaged to be married! Congratulations!"

"It is still unofficial because her family do not approve, so we have to wait until she turns twenty-one in a few months before we can do the deed, although we'll still probably have to run away to Gretna to do it."

"What don't they approve of?" She now knew that Percy was an independently wealthy third son of a viscount, so it couldn't be either his connections or his fortune.

"My involvement in the cause. Campaigning for change is not the done thing in Mayfair."

"Ah . . . Yes. Mayfair can be like that. I take it she's one of the ton too?"

He nodded. "But she isn't like most debutantes. She's clever and liberal and believes as passionately in reform as I do and . . ." Percy's expression turned slightly soppy. "Obviously, she is also the most beautiful woman in the world."

"Obviously." Despite her cynical nature and her current futile attraction to one of the aristocracy, Portia had a great deal of sympathy for the young man's plight even if she could never imagine herself feeling that deeply about anyone. "Love apparently always finds a way, so I am sure things will work out for you and your beloved in the end."

"They will," he said with utter certainty. "Because she is my soulmate, and we are meant to be."

She wanted to scoff at that but didn't, because in the last year, two of her friends had said much the same thing before they had hastily, and in Portia's humble opinion recklessly, wed their husbands after barely weeks of knowing them. Almost as if they could not wait to start their lives with them. Neither Georgie or Lottie were sentimentalists like Kitty, but both had quickly fallen head over heels in love with the unlikeliest of men and were now deliriously happy with them, so perhaps love did sometimes find a way?

"Do you have someone special in your life, Portia?"

"Good heavens no," she said emphatically—but oddly not without some regret. "I am wedded to the cause." Which was true and always had been. She liked men. Had experienced both attraction and desire, and wasn't averse to indulging in some harmless flirtation if the mood struck, as it clearly had last night, but she had never seen herself as a man's wife. Never wanted to be one, truth be told. Being a wife, in the eyes of the law, meant being a chattel and that had always put her off the idea of marriage. Her independence and her freedom to follow her own path was something she valued. Too much to ever want to give it away.

Jim arrived then, his expression grave. "I've just heard that they have moved Reynolds's trial forward a month to next Thursday—from the local Bristol assizes to Winchester. It was posted on the court schedule last night apparently and has caught even him by surprise."

"Can't he appeal?" asked Percy. "It will take at least a week to get his lawyer down from London to be able to represent him."

"Apparently he already has." Jim shrugged his beefy shoulders. "And was flatly turned down."

"They don't want his lawyer there." That came from William. "Having a barrister there would make it harder for them to throw the book at him when they are so desperate to make an example of him. That's also why they've moved him from Bristol to Winchester. He'll get less sympathy from a jury almost a hundred miles away than he will from one just up the road."

"But that is grossly unfair!" Poor Percy clearly still did have a lot to learn if he thought that everyone got a fair trial. "Surely they cannot do that? Not on trumped-up charges when all Mr. Reynolds is guilty of is working here!"

"Irrespective of how trumped-up the charges—and I can assure you that in that fool's case he is a guilty of them as sin—not only can the courts do that, it is also much more common practice than it should be." William sat heavily. "Headquarters should have anticipated this and appointed that idiot Reynolds a more local lawyer in the first place."

"I'll send an express to headquarters." Portia grabbed her coat. "If I hurry it might still catch the morning post and, if a miracle occurs, they might still get their lawyer to him in time."

"That is all we can do." William's tone and his expression said that he didn't hold out much hope. "Reynolds's fate is in the jury's hands now."

Poor blue-blooded Percy was still open-mouthed. "But what the authorities have done is tantamount to perverting the course of justice. Surely that is against the law?"

"They are the law," said Portia with a resigned shrug. "That is the problem. As William just said, this sort of thing isn't uncommon, and headquarters really should have anticipated a last-minute change of trial location."

"And we are just supposed to blithely accept that outrage as the way of things?"

"All we can do is keep pointing out why it is an outrage so that others can be outraged too." Something positive Portia could at least do in this week's opinion piece. "Only momentum changes laws."

"Speaking of outrage . . ." Jim's tone suggested that he was the harbinger of more bad news. "Mr. Reynolds's merry band of agitators ain't happy about the switch. They are having a meeting tonight."

"That means trouble is brewing here in Bath that we'll inevitably get linked to." Even William looked concerned at that. "So we all need to be extra careful and extra vigilant. It also goes without saying that if and when trouble erupts, we all need to be as demonstrably far away from it as is humanly possible or the constable will have us up in front of the beak too. And in our case, on whatever trumped-up charges he sees fit."

Chapter THIRTEEN

Leo stared down at the scandal sheet his mother had gleefully brought him earlier and huffed. Because of course a duke's hour-long chat with his undeniably pretty employee at the fundraising ball made excellent fodder for the gossips. The outrageous speculation in this article—titled *Doting Duke Captivated by Chaperone*—was yet another awkward thing he would have to apologize to Miss Kendall for, as apparently the innuendo-laden reaction of his marriage-obsessed mother wasn't quite enough. Never mind all his lingering while he held her hand hostage on the pavement beforehand.

He hadn't seen Miss Kendall since she had scurried back into the house two nights ago, and that bothered him. As it was now half past midnight and she still hadn't returned after her two days off, that bothered him more.

For the umpteenth time, he stared out of his open study window and willed her to be wending her way down the darkened path, but alas, it was as silent as the grave.

Or at least it was until both his dogs suddenly leaped up from their sleeping positions next to his desk and began to bark with excitement.

Her!

Finally!

The time to prostrate himself on the altar of dignity and apologize for his inappropriate behavior had finally come.

As he limped out of his study, both dogs flew past him to the kitchen. As there seemed little point in prolonging the agony, Leo released them into the garden and followed them outside. He expected to meet Miss Kendall midway, but he was almost at the end of the lawn when he heard her whisper.

"Shhh, dogs. I'll be down in a moment." An odd thing to say but not quite as odd as the sight of her straddling the top of the eight-foot wall at the end of his property. Her bonnet askew, her skirts ruched and twisted around her knees and her expression vexed as she tried to unhook the back of her clothing from one of the fleur-de-lis spikes that protected the top of the brickwork. At least it was vexed until she noticed him and she winced. "Good evening, your grace."

"What the blazes are you doing up there, Miss Kendall?"

"Somebody decided to move the key to the back gate from its usual hiding place, so I couldn't get back in. Rather than disturb anyone's slumber, I decided to just climb over the wall instead."

"Was your plan just to throw yourself from the top and hope for the best?" Because it was a long drop.

"It was actually to use these spikes to gently lower myself to the ground. If I manage to ever untangle myself from them." Her smile was sheepish. "I did rather misjudge the width between them and the width of myself." She reached behind her and wrestled with the fabric some more. She gave a final yank, then grinned triumphantly while she quickly used the freed fabric to cover her exposed calves. "That's better."

That all depended on your point of view, and he had much preferred the view of those shapely calves than not, but he smiled regardless as he lifted his arms. "If you swing your other leg over, I shall catch you."

She eyed his outstretched hands dubiously, then shook her head.

"If it's all the same to you, your grace, I'd much prefer to do this myself."

"I can assure you that I will not drop you, Miss Kendall." His manly pride was slightly offended that she doubted his abilities. "My ankle might still be a bit tender but there is nothing wrong with my arms." Would it be wrong to flex one and try to impress her with his muscles?

Probably.

"It's more your eyes that worry me, your grace, and the fact that my descent isn't likely to be pretty." She pulled a face and he laughed.

"I thought we had already agreed that dignity is overrated."

"And yet I would still prefer to cling on to mine regardless, if you don't mind."

"It wouldn't be gentlemanly to abandon a damsel in obvious distress and I'd never forgive myself if you ended up hurt when I could have prevented it." He folded his arms and vainly flexed his muscles regardless in the pathetic hope that she would notice them. "So I am staying and you will just have to swallow your pride on this occasion."

"Can you at least turn around while I do the worst of the maneuvers? Only, as a gentleman, I am sure that you appreciate that a skirt is an unforgiving garment during any physical challenge."

He had never seen her all missish and it amused him. "Very well." He turned. "Let me know when you need me."

"*If* I need you, your grace—which I can assure you that I won't, so don't you dare even think of turning around unless I personally request it. I am not the damsel in distress type." He could hear the exertion in her voice as she changed position behind him. "In actual fact, if you want to know my honest opinion, I disapprove of the very concept of a damsel in distress because women are just as capable as men. What we might lack in upper body strength"—she paused to grunt—"we make up for in intelligence and resilience."

"Do you indeed?"

"We do." More grunting. "It will be a cold day in hell before I ever need a man to save me. I am in charge of my own destiny and quite capable of saving myself, thank you very much." Then there was an ominous *oof* followed by the sound of ripping fabric. Then a beat of silence. "Um . . . unfortunately, I think I might have spoken too soon."

"Am I allowed to turn around, Miss Kendall?"

"Only if you promise not to laugh."

He turned, blinked, then roared because Miss Kendall now dangled like a marionette facing him. The top of her coat from her shoulders to her elbow was caught on the spikes leaving her feet suspended several feet from the ground. "You look like you've been hung up to dry on a washing line!"

Her lips twitched. "Rather than just standing there and stating the obvious, your grace, I would be much obliged if you would do the gentlemanly thing and help me down."

"Oh the irony!" Leo bent double he was laughing so hard. "There must be a blizzard currently raging in hell because you—*you*!" He pointed at her between guffaws. "Suddenly need a man's help!"

"I am sure I will appreciate the irony too . . . eventually." Her half-trapped arms pleaded. "But in the meantime, this thoroughly disgusted damsel needs rescuing."

"Yes . . . right . . ." Leo pulled himself together and scratched his head. How the blazes to best do that? "Maybe if I lifted you up a bit you might be able to dislodge the trapped fabric?" Which of course meant touching her. And quite inappropriately because her upper thighs were level with his eyes. "Do you mind if I . . ." He wiggled his hands a couple of inches shy of either side of her hips. "Only I am afraid this might involve some manhandling."

"Just do what you need to do, your grace."

"Right," he said, stepping forward while suddenly feeling totally self-conscious. "Brace yourself." Then he grabbed her hips and tried to heave her upward but she was too much of a deadweight for that to have much effect. "I think I am going to need a bit more purchase." Cringing, he slipped his hands lower and around her bottom and tried his best to be gentlemanly and not notice how delightful those two plump cheeks felt in his grasp. Or how the side of his head was now resting on her midriff as he tried to use his entire body against hers for leverage.

He managed to hoist her a couple of inches but nowhere near enough.

"Perhaps if you bend at the knees a little and lift me from lower down?"

"Right," he said, adjusting his position and hugging her thighs this time, trying not to think that the side of his face was now level with her crotch. He knew already that this unseemly debacle was going to haunt his dreams for the foreseeable future. Miss Kendall had haunted them enough already since he had fallen on top of her in his study, so he really did not need to know what her bottom felt like beneath his palms, or her thighs. Or that all he had to do was turn his head and he was within kissing distance of the absolute most intimate place she possessed. "Ready?"

"As I will ever be."

Leo craned his neck as far right as it would go so as his face wasn't completely buried between her legs, then heaved with all his might. He managed to raise her at least a foot higher. While he held on tight, she began to wriggle her upper body to try to free the trapped fabric. That, inevitably, caused the bottom half of her body to jiggle too and her hip—and worse—kept making contact with his cheek.

Dear god, he hoped this was over soon!

"I just need a couple of inches." Words that sounded too much like an invitation and went straight to his cock.

"I'll try." From somewhere he found the strength to push her higher but the only way to keep her at that height was to use his entire upper body to pin her to the wall—including his head. Which meant his ear now occupied all the space in the crevice where the tops of her legs met her womanhood.

As she wriggled this time, he felt all her intimate lower muscles clench with the effort it took. But Leo gritted his teeth some more and did his best not to hear her make the same sorts of breathy sounds that a woman in the throes of passion would make in the bedchamber.

"Yes . . . I'm almost there . . . so close . . . can you push a little harder?" Leo had never wished for death before, but he wished for it now. On the swiftest wings possible. "Yes!" She bucked against the side of his face and then groaned. "It isn't working. But we might get a bit more height if I pushed my knees against your shoulders—"

He jumped back then as if a snake had bitten him because the absolute last thing he needed was to have his entire face buried between her legs. The moment he let go, she dropped back into her dangling position like a sack of potatoes with a grunt. "I would have appreciated a little warning there, your grace."

He raked a frustrated hand through his hair. "We need a better plan!" One that wasn't the stuff of his erotic fantasies. "It's your coat that's stuck, so perhaps if you unbutton it, I can catch you once you are free of it?"

"An excellent plan that I can assure you I would have already tried if . . ." She wiggled her wrists to remind him that both her arms were pinned to the wall. "You'll have to unbutton it for me."

Things were going from bad to worse! "Right," he said, not feeling the least bit right about having to undress her. "Right . . ." He stepped nearer again to reach up and found himself staring directly at her breasts jutting above him. Breasts that the damned line of buttons ran straight between.

Leo tried his best not to contemplate the twin temptations that lay either side of the buttons as he tackled them. He had enough problems with gravity and his ridiculously clumsy fingers working against him. Miraculously, he successfully undid the first two buttons after he was forced to wrap one arm back around her bottom so that he could lift her slightly again. There were only two more and both were in the area that, as a gentleman, he wasn't supposed to think about. The only way he could to do that was to focus on something unpleasant. And frankly, he could think of nothing more unpleasant than immediately tackling his cringe-inducing apology.

"While I've got you here . . ." His chuckle was about as false as his toes were cramped as they curled inside his boots. "I . . . um . . . wanted to apologize for the other night." *Don't shilly-shally. This will be less painful if you just lance the boil and get it over with man!* "I had an odd moment when I helped you out of the carriage . . ." Although not anywhere near as odd a moment as he was having now. "And I fear that was probably a little too familiar and might have caused offense." The button directly between her breasts refused to budge, so he focused on that rather than gaze up at her to gauge her reaction. "I am thoroughly ashamed of myself."

She was so silent that he risked glancing up and saw her face turned away as if she couldn't even bear to look at him. Then, utterly mortified and because the backs of his knuckles kept grazing her bosom and giving him more improper ideas, his patience snapped a little as he wrestled with the fastening in the hope that the heavens would take pity on him and end this torture. "Who the blazes sewed these buttonholes?"

Her silence stretched some more, until she huffed. "You didn't offend me. It was an odd moment all round which we both got too caught up in, so do not blame yourself solely for it."

She'd been caught up in the moment too? Caught up in him?

What was he supposed to say or do about that?

Rejoice or let sleeping dogs lie?

Before his addled brain worked through that conundrum, she spoke, gesturing stiffly to the sky with her restricted mobility as best she could. "Let us blame the moonlight after an unexpectedly pleasant evening and never mention it again."

"Yes. Good idea." Except it didn't feel particularly good. "We'll pretend it never happened."

"Not that anything particular did actually happen, your grace."

"I suppose not." A disappointment that he blamed entirely on the untimely arrival of his blasted mother. "But you should also know that we somehow made the scandal sheets regardless, for which I am also dreadfully sorry." He winced. Partly at having to admit that inconvenient truth and partly because the damn button between her distracting breasts still would not budge.

"What did they say?" She did not sound pleased.

"Doting duke captivated by chaperone—although they were careful not to name either of us."

"Where there any other dukes at that fundraising ball?"

"Sadly, no." He had to bounce her a little in his arm to readjust his grip on her backside in case he dropped her again. "I fear the whole of Bath knows that the offending duke was me."

"Oh dear."

"Sorry." And he was. Because in being so captivated by her he had, inadvertently, brought her unfairly under public scrutiny. "While I am apologizing, I should probably also say sorry for my mother as well. She put two and two together when she caught us on the pavement having that odd moment and, because she revels in any sort of scandal, she assumed that we were . . . um . . ."

"About to be scandalous?"

"I am truly sorry, Miss Kendall." The dratted button still would not budge and so, figuring that her coat was ruined by the spikes it was impaled on, he decided to take some of his many current frustrations out on the fabric, gave up on the buttonholes, and tried to rip her coat apart instead. "Both for giving her that impression and for the merciless grilling you will doubtless get about it the first moment she can collar you alone."

Rather than be rightly peeved at all the trouble he had caused her, she smiled. It was a wry and worryingly wistful smile. "All things considered, it is probably for the best then that my tenure as your social secretary has come to its natural conclusion, though I shall be sorry to leave here."

That made him stop fighting with her coat to frown up at her. "There is no need for you to leave." And he certainly did not want her to. "All this gossip nonsense will blow over as gossip always does."

"It's not so much the gossip—more that my services are somewhat redundant now that your mother is back to resume the chaperoning duties."

"Ah . . . yes . . ." Embarrassed, Leo went back to war with the buttons. "About that. I fear I wasn't entirely honest with you when I first offered you the job. You see the thing is . . ." *Bloody hell, they should make armor out of whatever fabric this damned coat was constructed with, it is so unyielding!* "You know how my sisters are punishing me because I am keeping them here in Bath? Well, my mother is too because I might have, in the heat of the moment, said some things about her parenting that offended her, and so my dear mama is punishing me by going on strike."

"Gracious." He could hear the amusement in her tone. "What on earth did you say to make her withdraw her labor?"

"That she is a very lackadaisical chaperone. Which, in my stubborn defense, she is. Everything bad that has happened this season happened on her watch. Although I'll concede that I shouldn't have said that quite so bluntly nor claimed I could do a better job."

"That is very noble of you." She was laughing at him now and he couldn't blame her. "I hope you have apologized. Hell hath no fury like a mother scorned."

"I did—but alas, even after I admitted that I didn't manage to do any better a job than she had without your help, she's still spitting feathers about it. Enough that she made a special point of telling me yesterday that she was still on strike as far as chaperoning the girls goes, because I apparently need to learn a valuable lesson. Hence you are very much still needed as my sisters, as you know, are a nightmare."

"As mortified as I am by this"—she gestured to her predicament with a smile—"I am supremely grateful that it was you that found me tonight and not one of them. Your sisters would have definitely left me hanging."

"Then you will take pity on me and stay?"

Before she could answer, one of the stubborn buttons chose that moment to finally give in. With only the final one remaining in the very center of her cleavage, Miss Kendall suddenly jerked downward causing that last bastion to pop too.

As her arms slipped rapidly out of the still impaled sleeves, she lurched forward, effectively smothering him with her breasts, and Leo staggered backward, trying to support her whole weight without falling. "I've got you." Which was true, albeit in the most ungainly fashion, because she was practically bent over his shoulder now and was gripping on to the back of his waistcoat for grim death.

He grunted and shifted position so that he could, with a great deal of exertion, attempt to lower her feet to the ground before they collapsed in a giggling heap against the wall.

"If I am staying, for the sake of our mutually dented pride and shattered dignity, let us never speak of this again, either, your grace."

"Agreed. This whole debacle never happened."

But, heaven help him, her lush body was still pressed against his.

Her arms were still looped around his shoulders and she was gazing up at him with amusement in her lovely eyes, so it seemed like the most natural thing in the world to close the scant distance between them and give in to the overwhelming urge to kiss her.

It was a soft kiss.

A much too short one.

A test.

One that she responded to by looping her arms tighter around his neck so that she could pull his lips immediately back to hers.

When she kissed him back, he gathered her closer and did the only thing that he was capable of—he reveled in her. Her taste, her touch, her obvious passion.

He had no clue which of them deepened the kiss, but his whole body responded when her tongue tangled with his. It hit him like lightning. He had never experienced such a swift and fevered desire to possess a woman in his life. It was as if a wildfire suddenly blazed through him, out of control, and what was left of his restraint evaporated because his need for her was so complete. He certainly lost all track of time as he lost himself in her.

Her fingers threaded through his hair to anchor him in place as she feasted on his mouth. Leo filled his hands with her bottom and she arched her hips against his, moaning against his lips in encouragement before her palms explored his chest over his waistcoat.

Then under it.

As her hands had gone wandering, his did too. One burrowed beneath her skirt to find the soft skin of her outer thighs above her stocking tops while the other found her breast. Her moan was deliciously carnal as she pushed it into his palm; her leg hooking around his so that she could press her hips tighter against his erection.

He fisted his hands in her skirts and raised them while her fingers found the buttons on his falls.

"Leo!" His mother's shout had them both jumping apart. "Do something to stop your stupid dogs barking!" It took a moment for him to realize that both his dogs were barking—at him and the rumpled woman blinking at him in shock—and that his mother's voice had come from a window above. "It is the middle of the night, for pity's sake! Some of us are trying to sleep!"

"Barkington! Snifferson!" Leo clicked his fingers. "Get back in the house now." The spaniel was about to protest, so he clicked them again. "I said now!"

As the chastened dogs skulked back down the path, Miss Kendall's lovely eyes were wide. "Do you think she saw us?"

He shook his head. "It's too dark." Then he pointed to his mother's bedchamber window in time for them to witness the curtains snap back closed. "Besides, she'd be halfway out here if she had." For some reason, awkwardness had descended like a shroud and he couldn't understand why, when mere moments ago she had seemed as invested in and unraveled by their kiss as he had been and just as ready for more. "Do I need to apologize again?" *Please say no.*

She shook her head, and his foolish heart soared. "It was just another odd moment."

"We seem to keep having them." Too frequently to be able to ignore them. Not that he wanted to now. However, any hope he had for them was swiftly killed stone dead by her next words.

"But . . . that one really has to be our last."

"Why?" He took a step closer so that his fingers could graze her cheek, but she pulled back. "If you like me, Portia, and I clearly like you and we are both unattached but well matched, I see no earthly reason why we cannot—" He found himself staring at her raised hand.

"Because you are a duke."

"And?" He shook his head, hoping to convey by his baffled smile that he honestly could not give two figs about the difference in their stations. "I am mostly just Leo actually. Especially here at home. The duke thing is a mantle I have to put on when dealing with certain responsibilities."

"I cannot be with a duke." She seemed appalled by the very idea and that hurt.

"What is so awful about being with a duke?" Until it occurred to him that she might think his intentions weren't honorable. That he was the sort who used and abused people, as so many of the aristocracy did. "I am not looking for a mistress, Portia, if that is your concern. I am my father's son, remember, and therefore a hopeless romantic at heart, so I could not be able to do anything other than take what seems to be blossoming between us as seriously as it deserves." It was the truth and for the first time in his life, and totally, unexpectedly out of the blue, he had the overwhelming feeling that he had found the one. "I've honestly never met anyone like you before. You call to my soul, Portia." He touched his heart, suddenly so full of emotion that he had to let some of it out. "In a way that transcends the obvious desire I have for you and . . ." Her lovely eyes widened in panic and she began to shake her head so violently that it made him pause his heartfelt declaration.

"Please do not say any more, your grace, I beg of you."

"I think, after what we just shared, you should call me Leo." Perhaps then she would stop thinking of all the duke nonsense as a barrier? "Just Leo."

He took another step forward and she took a decisive step back. Not in disgust, which would have been bad enough when he had just bared his heart, but in fear. But fear of what?

Him?

Them?

"For both of our sakes, let us pretend that this"—she flapped her hand in the vicinity of their mouths—"did not happen either and never, ever speak of it again, your grace."

"What if I can't?" Now that he had let those feelings out, he didn't want to put them back in. "What if I want you too much to pretend that I don't anymore? What if we were meant to be, Portia? What if—"

She shook her head. "Trust me, your grace. Nothing good ever comes of playing with fire and I truly don't want you to get burned."

Then, before he could get to the bottom of that cryptic comment, she picked up her skirts and dashed after the dogs back into the house.

Almost as if her life depended on it.

Chapter FOURTEEN

While Portia's body still hummed with need almost an hour later, her head was spinning like a top. She still couldn't quite believe what had just happened, or how significant and perfect it had felt. Or where it would have gone if they had not been interrupted again.

But she did, however, know that kissing the duke had been a massive mistake.

For so many reasons she didn't quite know what to do about it all—other than never see him ever again. A prospect that filled her with such sadness it caused a physical ache in her chest in the vicinity of her heart that she didn't know what to do about either. The ache had begun the moment he had confessed that she called to his soul. Likely because he called to hers too. So much, she couldn't stand it.

How on earth could she have been so stupid to develop feelings for a duke?

And not just a duke, but a magistrate to boot? One who had clearly also, unbelievably, developed some feelings for her too.

Or at least for the woman he thought that she was.

Oh what a tangled web we weave, when first we practice to deceive!

For the umpteenth time, she picked up her pen to try to make sense of all her conflicting feelings on paper, but instead paced to her bedchamber window because, for the first time in her life, she was unable to write a single word. Then she stared out, wishing she could just blame the moonlight for what had happened. At some point in the last week the duke had crawled under her skin and mined all her defenses and . . .

That heady moonlight suddenly cast a human-shaped shadow on the lawn. One that was moving at speed toward the end of the garden.

It was Lady Abigail, and by the dark cloak that she wore and the furtive glances behind her back toward the house, it was obvious that the duke's sister was up to no good.

Portia didn't pause to think; for Leo's sake, she just went after her.

The rest of the house was as silent as the grave, which was odd when nothing usually got past the dogs. It was only when she reached the kitchen and saw both hounds munching on a juicy bone that she realized why they were so quiet. They were so engrossed, they barely looked her way as she hurried out of the back door.

There was no sign of the duke's sister at the end of the garden, but the gate that had been very much locked when Portia had arrived back from the newspaper was now wide open. There was no sign of her in the quiet mews either, so Portia turned right, assuming that Lady Abigail would head toward town, but some sixth sense made her glance left. That was when she saw two shadowy figures in the darkness hurrying hand in hand toward the desolate parkland.

The closer Portia got, the more apparent it was that Lady Abigail was having a tryst with a man, because once the pair of them started embracing, they didn't seem to want to stop. She empathized. If the duke's mother hadn't interrupted their passionate embrace earlier, she would have offered him everything because she had been so caught up in it all—so caught up in him. She had wanted him that much.

Still did, truth be told.

"Lady Abigail . . ." Just as Portia and the duke had done, the pair jumped guiltily apart at the sound of her voice and blinked at her in the darkness. The only problem was that the man looked worryingly familiar.

"Percy?" She stalked closer to double-check. "Percy! What the . . . ?"

"Portia!" He looked as surprised to see her as she was him. "What are you doing here?"

That was when Lady Abigail's hands went to her hips. "I cannot wait to hear how you two know each other." For some inexplicable reason the girl was jealous as well as resentful. "Or when you gave her leave to use your Christian name, *Percy*."

"Because Portia . . . I mean Miss Kendall . . . is my superior at the newspaper." Unaware that he had just announced Portia's deepest, darkest secret to the sister of both her employer and a local magistrate who could shut *Equitas* down, Percy stuttered some more. "I am her assistant." Then, in case Portia had not been able to work out the scale of the monumental catastrophe she had just uncovered, he decided to introduce them. "Miss Portia Kendall, this is Lady Abigail Sloane—" His chest puffed with pride. "My fiancée."

Dizziness swamped her. "Oh good grief—this cannot be happening." Just when Portia thought that her situation couldn't become more complicated, life went and poured paraffin over it and then set it ablaze.

"*You* work at the newspaper?" As she, at least, realized the gravity of the situation, Lady Abigail's question came out in a squeak.

"She does more than work at it, Abigail, she is the second-in-command. And she's a brilliant writer. You must have read her work as she has had many articles published in *Equitas* over the years. And she now writes the weekly opinion piece too. Although if you haven't read her work, I'll guarantee that you have heard it because she used to write many of the *League of Reform's* speeches too and . . ." Percy stopped gushing to stare at them. "What am I missing?"

"Miss Kendall is my chaperone, Percy." There was vitriol in the younger woman's tone now. "She is paid handsomely by my brother to ensure that I have nothing whatsoever to do with you."

"Oh," he managed to stutter in between gaping at Portia like a fish. "Oh."

"And be in no doubt that she is about to inform on us to Leo just as soon as she can!"

That was indeed what Portia was paid to do. And doubtless what she should do under all normal circumstances—except these circumstances weren't normal. Now that the cat was out of the bag regarding her involvement with *Equitas*, and now that she had developed some unexpected feelings for the duke—the magistrate—her situation was precarious indeed.

"Portia is not our enemy." That came from Percy. "You *can* trust her to keep our secret, Abigail." Then he turned to Portia. "That's right, isn't it?"

"I . . . er . . ." She had never felt so torn in her life. Between the duke who had apparently stolen her heart when she hadn't been looking and the cause that had always been her first love. Now, whichever she chose would mean betraying the other.

She stared at the two star-crossed lovers again. Their hands entwined. Their eyes hopeful. Whoever had first said that ignorance was bliss knew what they were talking about. If she could turn back time, she would ignore the shadow in the garden and blithely carry on none the wiser because her other dilemma between her heart and her head was big enough already.

But in the end, prudence dictated that she had only one choice. "I am paid to be Lady Abigail's chaperone between the hours of eight and six. What happens outside of those hours is not my concern." Feeling utterly wretched, she spun on her heel and repeated the cowardly phrase that seemed to be her new mantra rather than face up to the consequences. "Let us pretend that this hasn't happened and never speak of any of it again."

Portia barely slept and spent most of the night trying to work through all her multiplying problems on paper. By the time she ventured downstairs early the next morning, she felt wrung out like an old dishrag but at least had a solution. One that she knew was ultimately for the best.

For the duke. For the cause. And for *Equitas*.

That it made her utterly miserable was by the by. She had made this bed, and she would lie in it. Then perhaps, in a month or two, with her life significantly less complicated and if she buried herself in her important work at the newspaper, he would feel less important to her.

His study door was ajar as she approached it, which was normally a sign that this unconventional, informal duke was happy for anyone to come in and bother him. But still she knocked. She needed to make this formal. It really was the only way she could get through it.

"Come in." He sounded distracted and not quite himself, and she knew that was all her fault too.

"Your grace." She breezed in and bobbed a curtsy. Determined to pretend that nothing monumental had shifted between them last night and to absolutely not speak of it, in the hope that he wouldn't either. A hope that was quickly dashed when she witnessed the longing in his deep blue eyes.

"Portia . . ." He stood. Went to rush to her and then thought better of it. Uncomfortable, he shuffled awkwardly from foot to foot while his gaze searched for any clues that she was as unsettled by everything as he plainly was. "Can we talk? Only, I appreciate that you are a little bit overwhelmed by all the duke nonsense, and I wanted to reassure you that I don't care that—"

She cut him off. She had to. All the longing and concern in his eyes was quickly smashing through her resolve. "I came to give you this, your grace." She held out the letter that she had wept over while writing not an hour ago.

He stared at it in trepidation, clearly sensing he wasn't going to like what it said. "What is this?"

"It is my resignation. If it is all right with you, I should like to leave straightaway."

He swallowed and raked a frustrated hand through his hair. "Of course it's not bloody well all right with me!" Then he began to pace, his movements stiff and jerky as he did his best to keep all his emotions contained. "I don't want you to go! Especially after last night."

"But I must." It was the only way to unweave some of the tangled web that she had created. "And most especially after last night."

"Why? Because you want to get away from me or because you want to run away from us?"

"Both," she admitted honestly, and to underscore it, she placed her letter of resignation on his desk. "There can never be an us. Even if we tried, I can assure you that it wouldn't end well. Oil and water were never meant to mix, your grace."

"It's Leo, goddammit!" His angry eyes turned molten as he stalked toward her. "Is that really so hard to say when you've had your hands all over my body?"

"Your grace, I—"

"You kissed the man, not the duke, Portia." His hands reached for her upper arms and she felt his touch everywhere. "Say my name. Make this personal—because it *is* personal and you know it! Stop trying to put distance between us that doesn't need to be there."

She eased herself from his grasp. "I have to, your grace."

"You don't *have to*, Portia—you want to! I just don't bloody understand why?" His arms folded. "So tell me why you cannot *be* with a duke? What is so vastly different in the composition of my human body and yours that we cannot possibly mix?"

With her customary impeccable timing, that was when his mother arrived. But this time, Portia was grateful for it. "Leo!" She burst through the door without knocking, blinked at them both and then smiled. "I am so sorry to interrupt—but there is a horrid little red-faced man here who is causing quite the commotion on the doorstep. He absolutely insists on having an immediate audience with you."

The duke's furious gaze refused to leave Portia's. "Not now, Mother."

His mother was not the least bit fazed by his icy tone. "I've told him that you are convalescing, but he won't have it. A Mr. Nilly or Nally something. Anyway, he wants a warrant apparently, although why I have no clue. He is ranting so much it's difficult to make head nor tail of what he wants."

That was when the constable stalked in and slammed the latest copy of *Equitas* on the desk.

"Now they are accusing us of perverting the cause of justice!" Clearly it was Portia's latest opinion piece that had incensed him so. The one she had written on the back of the authorities moving Reynolds's trial from Bristol to Winchester to ensure a conviction, seeing as that had seemed quite a timely and topical subject.

Nolley jabbed his finger at the headline. "*State-Sanctioned Meddling Most Foul: How the law legally perverts the course of justice.*" She regretted that provocative headline too now that she was stood barely two feet from a man who wanted her hung, drawn, and quartered just for writing it. "If that is not seditious and blasphemous libel then I do not know what is! So I want that warrant today, your grace!" He slapped the article hard enough that Barkington began to growl at him. "And I am not leaving until I get it!"

The duke's temper snapped. "I am clearly in the middle of another important meeting, Constable Nolley." He pointed to the door. "So you will wait outside until it is concluded!"

Nolley banged the desk with his fist, causing Snifferson, who was hiding underneath it, to whimper. "With respect, your grace, nothing could be as important as this!" He glared at Portia. "Your fancy woman can wait!"

"Why don't Miss Kendall and I leave you to it, dear?" The duchess grabbed Portia's elbow and tugged her toward the door.

"I want this Pendle fellow's head on a pike." The constable was repeatedly slapping the table now as if he imagined it was her head, so Portia was only too happy to be dragged to wherever the duchess wanted to drag her to. "And I want every bit of wherever they print that treasonous, slanderous rag razed to the ground!"

The duchess closed the door and pulled a face. "Well, that was unpleasant." Portia nodded. Too shaken by all this morning's unpleasantness to know what else to say.

The door reopened and the duke was framed in it. His handsome face now a barely contained mask of fury. "*Miss* Kendall." He had never sounded so clipped and cold. "As you are so determined to escape me at your earliest possible convenience, know that it is not convenient for me for you to do so. If you consult your contract, you will see that you are required to give me a month's notice. Be assured that this duke expects you to *be* here for all of it!"

Then the walls shook from the force with which he slammed the door.

Chapter
FIFTEEN

"Have you seen this?" An irate Abigail slapped today's copy of *The Bath Chronicle* on his desk, reminding him of just how sick and tired he was lately of people shoving unpleasant pieces of paper at him. "Your lot have moved the trial of a reformer to Winchester simply to get an undeserved guilty verdict!"

There was so much to take issue with in that accusatory sentence, he didn't quite know where to start. But because he had been in a foul mood for days and wanted to take someone to task for the wretched way he was feeling, he started with the most offensive. "By 'your lot' I presume you mean every unfortunate soul here in Somerset who has taken on the thankless responsibility of upholding the law?" Which was about as fair as assuming that just because he had to be born a duke meant that he couldn't possibly have genuine feelings for a blasted chaperone, or vice versa.

"I specifically meant the magistrates' bench, as they are the idiots that had to sanction this. Please, tell me that you did not have a hand in this travesty, Leo?"

"I did not. This was decided in my absence after you decided to put me on enforced bed rest for a trivial sprained ankle."

"Did you not like your freedoms being curtailed on the back of a minor injury, big brother?" She pulled a sarcastic sad face. "At least yours were only taken from you for a week, whereas mine have been stolen for the entire summer. But I digress." She folded her arms and glared. "Now that you are no longer on enforced bed rest, what are you going to do about this travesty?"

"Nothing," he said folding his arms too. "The decision was made by a quorum of magistrates, and I cannot overturn it. Nor will I even try to."

"Even if an innocent man is convicted?"

"Matthew Reynolds is not an innocent man, Abigail. He's a rabble-rousing thug."

"His only crime is being a reformer! But apparently that is all one needs to be guilty of nowadays to get charged with incitement to riot and clapped in irons!"

"He might well be a reformer, but that isn't why they clapped him in irons!" Bloody hell, did nobody ever consider all of the facts before they jumped to unfair conclusions? "He took a gang of armed men to the home of our local member of Parliament, had him and his wife tied up, dragged them out of their house in their nightclothes, and then he stuck a gun in the man's face. So your holier-than-thou Mr. Reynolds isn't up on trumped-up charges of incitement to riot like it suits him and his violent gang of followers to have everyone believe—he is up for attempted murder." Seeing as everyone else seemed to do it, he bashed his own desk. "And frankly, so he jolly well should be!"

"Don't you think that him *allegedly* having a gun could be a convenient lie that is being spread by those who unjustly arrested him for protesting? It certainly justifies their heavy-handed actions. I'll wager every witness they have to corroborate that falsehood was paid handsomely by the authorities for their statements."

"I can assure you that the authorities really do not have the funds to pay off the thirty-two neighbors and random passersby who stepped forward." Suddenly the sheer bloody futility of trying and failing to be the voice of reason weighed him down. After the last few days, he was sick to the back teeth of being both a magistrate and a duke, when both titles apparently made him the enemy. "Not that I expect you to believe me on that score. Why let the truth get in the way of a convenient pack of lies and your own blind prejudice?"

Sadly, it did not surprise him that his sister wasn't the slightest bit convinced. "I would believe that were it not for the fact that Matthew Reynolds was also the assistant editor at *Equitas* and your constable has a personal vendetta against that noble publication. If anyone has a prejudiced view here, it is he. Surely you can see that, Leo?"

"Don't let the door hit you on the way out, Abigail."

"Here are today's invitations, your grace." It was cowardly, but in the three days since she had handed in her notice, Portia had done her best to avoid the duke and so had begun to hand over her day's work to his mother at six o'clock instead. Although today, because William had expressly instructed it, she had made sure to work late so it was now closer to seven. Nobody was to go anywhere near the newspaper today. Or the center of Bath. If trouble did erupt on the back of Matthew Reynolds's hastily relocated trial, then everyone involved in *Equitas* had to be as distanced from it as possible. Preferably ensuring they were around enough independent witnesses that they had a rock-solid alibi. "It has been a quiet day." And long may that continue.

"It has indeed been a blessedly quiet *afternoon*, Miss Kendall." The duchess smiled wryly. "The least said about all this morning's dreadful commotion, the better."

Portia gave a sympathetic nod because the whole of the Crescent must have heard the argument between the duke and his sister just after breakfast. Both had stormed off in different directions at the end of it with him slamming out of the front door and Lady Abigail stomping up the stairs.

She felt for him because his sister had completely the wrong end of the stick when it came to Matthew Reynolds. Something she almost ventured up to Lady Abigail's room to tell her earlier but had resisted. Even if she had, she suspected any well-meant interference would have fallen on deaf ears. Since the fateful night Portia had discovered the younger woman's secret engagement to Percy, Lady Abigail had avoided her like the plague. She hadn't left the house during daylight hours since, and if they happened to collide in the hallway, she glared at Portia with hostility and outright suspicion.

Perhaps that was because Portia could expose her secret, but she got the distinct impression it was more out of Lady Abigail's loyalty to her brother. She now knew that Portia had lied to him repeatedly about what she got up to in her spare time and she plainly did not like it. An irony that wasn't lost on her when his hypocritical sister had been barefaced lying to him too.

"Tell me about yourself, Miss Kendall." The duchess motioned for Portia to sit, then immediately set about pouring her a cup of tea too. Something Portia would have rather avoided despite needing an alibi, but what could she do? If a duchess tells a servant to sit, then sit they must.

"There is really not much to tell, your grace. I grew up close to here but left at sixteen to train at Miss Prentice's School for Young Ladies in Mayfair and I have been a governess ever since."

"And who are your family?"

"My father was a gamekeeper."

"Was?"

"He died. A long time ago." Anticipating further questions on that score, Portia gave the abridged version. "In an accident. It took my mother and I quite by surprise. Her more than me, I suspect, as I was too young to really understand how final death actually is."

The duchess frowned. "Oh I am sorry. It is especially hard to lose someone before their time." She glanced wistfully up at the portrait of her husband, the former duke, with obvious affection in her eyes. A portrait that was so staggering in its likeness to Leo that Portia couldn't look at it without regret. "We lost Rafe far too soon too. One day he was as fit as a fiddle and the next, he was gone."

She tapped her chest. "The doctor said it was his heart that gave in and perhaps it did. It was such a big heart and he probably overworked it. Rafe was all about family. Loved us all to distraction with every fiber of his being and always tried to do what was right by those he cared about. Both Leo and Abigail follow him in that, albeit from very different angles. My son does it by taking on a misguided responsibility for everything and everyone near and dear to him. That can, on occasion, become suffocating when he is being particularly zealous. Which he has been for weeks now. While my eldest daughter has taken to marching and putting herself in danger in a frequently misguided knee-jerk way to save the rest of the world. So obviously, they clash, and I frequently fight the overwhelming urge to knock their heads together." The duchess huffed. "Do you have siblings that you drive your poor mother to distraction with, Miss Kendall?"

"Sadly not. I am an only child. But I do have good friends with whom I frequently fall out when I am being annoyingly overzealous, so I appreciate how frustrating you must find it."

"I do not think anyone can fully appreciate a parent's frustrations until they become a parent themselves." The duchess sipped her tea, so Portia did the same and almost spat it out when she said, "How many children would you like to have, Miss Kendall?"

"Er . . . none, your grace."

"None?" The older woman's teacup clattered in her saucer. "Whyever not?"

"Because to have children, society dictates that I would need a husband, and I have never wanted one of those."

"None of us do, dear, until love rears its head." The duchess smiled as she wiggled her brows. "Then all good sense and past resolutions evaporate like steam."

"Mine won't. I like my independence too much to ever relinquish it."

"Poppycock." The duchess laughed at her certainty. "You will change your mind once you meet the right man and decide that you cannot possibly live without him. Or perhaps you have met him already and just haven't realized it yet?" She pinned Portia with a knowing stare. "Is there someone who inexplicably unsettles you? Or vexes you or confuses you? As that is usually the first sign."

Portia gulped because this woman's son did all of those things. "Of course not."

"And outright denial is usually the second, Miss Kendall. But the eyes never lie. Even when we deny the truth to ourselves, the yearning and indecision always thrive there for all to see." The duchess's gaze flicked to the portrait. "He is so like Leo, isn't he?"

Before Portia could respond, Lady Emilia wandered in frowning. "Have either of you seen Abigail? Only she's not in her room."

"She can't have gone far," said her mother with an impatient flick of her wrist because she did not want any distraction from her inquisition. "Knowing Abigail, she is reading something dull in the library."

"I've checked the library, Mama. And the dining room, Leo's study, and now here." The furrow between the younger daughter's brows deepened. "The last I saw her was after luncheon when she asked if she could borrow my paints."

"Since when has Abigail painted anything but placards?" The duchess's flippant comment set alarm bells ringing in Portia's mind. "She is an atrocious artist."

"Perhaps she was bored," said Lady Emilia. "But she did not look bored when she stalked into my room. She looked ready to have someone's guts for garters." Then she pulled a face. "You won't need three guesses to work out who that someone was."

"Did she say anything else when she borrowed the paints?" Because Portia's unease was growing. "Like what she wanted them for."

"To be frank, Miss Kendall, she was in such high dudgeon I

didn't dare ask. She was too busy ranting about Leo abdicating all responsibility for what was morally right."

"Why don't I have a proper hunt for her?" Worried and yet still grateful for any excuse to escape the duchess's prying questions, Portia did not wait for permission. Instead, she hurried out of the door and went straight up the stairs, silently praying that the duke's headstrong but misguided sister hadn't done something that they would both live to regret.

She knocked on Lady Abigail's door and when there was no answer, she slipped inside. The paints were discarded on the dressing table and the wardrobe door was wide open, but other than that, nothing seemed to be amiss. Portia was about to leave when she spotted several sizable screwed up balls of paper sat atop the unlit fire. Fearing the worst, she retrieved them all. Then, like a jigsaw, she pieced together all the torn pieces, and her heart sank at the damning words daubed large in black that screamed back at her.

BATH—THE CITY OF CROOKED COURTS AND CORRUPT CONSTABLES!

Chapter SIXTEEN

It was nearly nine when Leo finally arrived back home, still in a horrible mood as he marched up the garden despite the long hours he had put in on his estate to try to shake it. He hoped a decent soak in a hot bath might help him feel less aggrieved before bed, although didn't hold out much hope. He was just too angry and too hurt to do anything other than fester.

I cannot be with a duke! What the blazes did that even mean?

He could understand and accept that she didn't want him—as that was her right, but he could not bloody well understand what his blasted title had to do with anything. Because if her only objection was that he was a duke, that was unreasonable. He couldn't help being born a duke any more than she could help being born into her station.

Bloody woman!

In fact, he would even go as far today to say bloody wo*men* because every single one that he cared about seemed hell-bent on making his life a misery!

His dogs met him at the kitchen door, and he tried to be thankful that they did not hate him. However, even they were oddly subdued as they followed him. Snifferson especially had the drooped ears and sad eyes he only wore when he was upset.

He heard his mother in the hallway and seriously considered sneaking all the way up to his bedchamber via the servants' stairs to avoid her before he decided to bite the bullet. If he allowed her to lecture him en route about his latest argument with his infuriating sister, then it not only got that inevitability over and done with, it put a short and sweet time limit on how long she could lambast him. Then, with any luck, he would be left alone to fester in private.

"Leo!" Instead of instantly castigating him, his mother ran toward him, her eyes red and her demeanor agitated. "Thank god you are home! Abigail is missing!"

And just like that, all his self-pity evaporated and was replaced by panic. "Missing! Since when?"

"Nobody has seen her since this afternoon."

"Did she take a horse?" Because if she had, she could be bloody miles away by now.

His mother shook her head. "Wherever she went, it had to have initially been on foot. I was in the drawing room all afternoon and would have seen if a carriage pulled up outside." His mother tugged at his sleeve. "But she has been gone so long and was so angry, I fear she could have decided to take the afternoon post back to London."

"What does Emilia know?" Because he wouldn't put it past either of his sisters to do something like this to punish him.

"Nothing—she raised the alarm at seven when she failed to locate Abigail." That was two hours ago. A person could go a great distance and find a great deal of trouble in two hours. More if she had been gone since earlier in the afternoon.

Leo tried to calm his racing mind by running through all the sensible next steps in his head. "Have you sent someone into town to investigate?" If they could retrace her route, it might give them a clue where Abigail was headed.

"I sent the footman and the stable lad to do that over an hour ago but neither have returned yet."

"Have you made inquiries with some of her new friends? And have you called the constable?" As much as Leo loathed Nolley, the man knew the city well and had a sizable group of watchmen at his disposal who could all help.

"I did not realize that she was missing when the constable called for you earlier and by the time that I did, it seemed prudent to wait for you before I escalated this and potentially dragged her good name into disrepute unnecessarily." His mother's voice cracked. "I had hoped that she would have had the good sense to return home before dark. Or to at least have the decency to send us a message to reassure us that she was safe." Her eyes refilled with tears. "Aside from the fact that making us worry so much is unforgivable, she is a woman on her own in the dark, for pity's sake. Clearly, she has no care whatsoever for her own safety!"

Finally, his mother now realized what he had known for months. "I think we've passed the point of trying to avoid a scandal." Their top priority now had to be getting Abigail home safe. He wished Portia was here so that she could help him. She had a level head on her shoulders and also knew the city well, but he knew she had likely already gone to her mother's before Abigail's disappearance had come to light. "If you call on her friends, I'll alert the constable."

He was about to dash back out to the stable to do just that when somebody hammered on the front door. Leo didn't wait for a servant to come and answer it and flung it open himself. Then experienced a moment of sheer terror when he saw Constable Nolley's grave face.

"Your grace." The man had taken off his hat and was twisting the brim around in his fingers, and something about his demeanor made the roots of Leo's hair tingle ominously as if it knew something was very wrong. "I am afraid I come here on official business pertaining to your sister—"

Tight bands of panic constricted his throat as he instantly spiraled into thinking the worst. "Is she dead?" All Leo needed were the particulars, not the preamble, when a thousand terrible scenarios were already whizzing through his head. "Is she hurt?" *Please god let her not be dead!*

The constable shook his head. "She is neither—" The breath he had been holding whooshed out of Leo's lungs in relief. "But if the woman who is currently claiming to be Lady Abigail Sloane is indeed your sister, then I have to inform you that she is currently under arrest."

"What the . . ." Of all the awful things he had expected the constable to say, it certainly wasn't that! "What the hell has she been arrested for?" Fresh panic swamped him, but he tried to beat it back. At least until he fixed whatever needed fixing.

"There has been some trouble in town with those radical agitators, your grace." Nolley said that with more glee than was necessary. "And your sister was among them."

"What sort of trouble?" Although after their heated words this morning, he had a nasty suspicion he knew what was coming.

"An illegal protest for that traitor Matthew Reynolds which turned violent."

"Did it turn violent before or *after* the militia were sent in to quash it?" He feared he knew the answer to that question too.

"They needed to be cleared," said the constable, unrepentant, "because that chanting rabble were amassed in direct contradiction to the Seditious Meetings Act of 1819, among various other statutes which were willfully broken by most of those in attendance. We've arrested forty-three of the blighters so far." A number which obviously delighted him. "We've mustered as many of the magistrates as we can to hear all their charges as swiftly as possible and issue warrants for further arrests, but there are a lot of them to get through. I came to summon you earlier to assist, but your mother informed me that she had no clue where you were. But now that your sister is implicated, I realize that it wouldn't be proper for you to serve on the bench tonight."

Bloody Abigail! Trust her to rebel against him by joining another illegal protest! "What charge is my sister held on?"

"On top of attending an unlawful meeting, she is charged with a breach of the peace, resisting arrest, and seditious and blasphemous libel." Serious charges indeed. "But if the woman we have in custody is actually your sister as she claims to be, then the other justices have agreed that as a mark of respect to you, they will let her off with a warning and release her to your care to deal with privately—what with you being a peer of the realm and a sitting magistrate and all." Leniency that the constable's expression screamed he did not approve of.

"Lady Abigail Sloane *is* my sister, Constable Nolley, as I am sure you already know seeing as you've met her on several occasions."

"Still," said the man, enjoying putting Leo in his place for a change. "As you are so fond of telling me, we must follow the proper procedures and, for the sake of the official records, I will need you to formally identify her as such, in person, before we can release her, your grace. We have, as you have repeated often, a civic and moral responsibility to the citizens of Bath to do things properly, after all."

It was galling to be quoted back by a man who would happily ride roughshod over the law at the slightest provocation—but they were Leo's words so he could hardly argue with them. "Where is she?"

"The city jail on Grove Street with all the other rioters."

Of all the things Portia had considered she might, one day, be arrested for, trying to save the rebellious sister of a duke wasn't one of them. Yet here she was, manacled at the wrists, bruised and battered and jammed into a cramped and airless, filthy cell with the stupid girl alongside twenty other prisoners who were all, rather worryingly, men.

At least half of those men were not ones she recognized from the protest, so that meant that she and Lady Abigail had been placed into this cell alongside a great many regular criminals. A couple of whom were sending them lecherous glances as they sat huddled together on the floor in the corner

"Why haven't they released me yet?" The duke's sister was becoming increasingly agitated and that, in turn, made the timbre of her voice higher pitched. "Don't they know that they have no right to keep me? Don't they know who my brother is? Are they not aware that Leo is a duke as well as a magistrate?"

A shifty-looking fellow instantly glared at the word "magistrate," but her companion seemed oblivious that was a dirty word in a prison. Before the spoiled fool got them both beaten, Portia jabbed her in the ribs and hissed. "Keep your voice down, Abigail, and for pity's sake, watch what you say!"

The duke's troublesome sister bristled. "Who are you to speak to me like that?"

That entitled outburst was the last straw. "Who am I? Only the person who risked life and limb to try and extricate you from that protest before the army rampaged in. The person who was arrested alongside you because you refused to leave when I begged you to! I am also the person who might well end up with a criminal record because of your misguided stupidity! Which could well mean, that thanks entirely to you, I could be unemployable as your lot tend not to look favorably on someone who has had a brush with the law, no matter whose fault it actually was." Portia jabbed her finger between them. "I am also, currently, the only person in this putrid cell who has a modicum of sympathy for you—although I have to warn you that that is presently wearing very thin—and I am the only thing standing between you and real physical harm. Or did it not occur to you that some of these men in here might have an axe to grind with your brother, you self-indulgent, selfish, and stupid idiot!"

Lady Abigail recoiled as if she had been slapped. "I . . . I . . ." Finally, she dropped her voice to a whisper. "I was just trying to stand up for what was right." Her bottom lip quivered and that only irritated Portia more. "I thought you of all people would appreciate that—especially as Matthew Reynolds is one of *us*."

"Then do the rest of *us* a favor and get your facts straight before you go on a half-cocked and dangerous crusade, Abigail! Matthew Reynolds isn't innocent. He isn't some martyr to the cause. He is a reckless, ambitious, and dangerous firebrand. A loose cannon who was never 'one of *us*' really." Portia checked around her for any eavesdroppers before she lent to whisper in her misguided cell-mate's ear.

"He never did anything for *Equitas* beyond bring trouble to its door. Nobody at the newspaper had seen hide nor hair of him in months because he was too busy raising his own little band of ruffians to wreak havoc with. Havoc, I might add that was never sanctioned by anyone in the reform movement except himself." Then, because someone had to say it, she added, "Your brother was right about everything he said about the man. Nobody lied. He's not on trial on trumped-up charges. He threatened to murder a bound man shivering in his underwear in cold blood and, as far as I and the rest of *us* are concerned, he jolly deserves whatever punishment they give him! And I cannot believe that Percy, who I thought was sensible, was stupid enough to have told you any different!"

The silence hung for several seconds while Abigail digested that, then in a small voice she said. "Percy didn't. I haven't seen him since you caught us together the other day."

"Then who did?"

"I received a letter from a friend in London."

"Did it not occur to you to corroborate that unreliable hearsay from two hundred miles away with anyone here in Bath who might just know the actual facts? Oh wait—you did." Sarcasm dripped from Portia's lips. "You asked your brother and then called him an idiot because he told you the unpalatable truth." She let every bit of her disgust show as she shook her head. "If anyone is the fool in this instance, it is you, Abigail, not Leo. But all of a sudden, I cannot help but noticing that your brother isn't the enemy anymore because you need his help, which I daresay makes you a hypocrite too, doesn't it? Because you are apparently only a crusading reformer when it suits you to be, but an entitled aristocrat who deserves to be above the law when it doesn't!"

The younger woman blanched. "I do not think that I am above the law, Miss Kendall, I just assumed . . ." Abigail sighed her contrition and finally had the decency to look thoroughly ashamed of herself. "You are right. I am scared and I am panicking but that is no excuse for assuming that I should get special dispensation for my foolhardy actions simply because of who my brother is."

"And yet the irony is that you doubtless will just as soon as he gets here. Privilege of Peerage is only supposed to cover members who serve in Parliament, yet, with a nod and wink, few blue bloods ever stand trial. No matter how heinous their offense, so take comfort in that."

Portia had meant that to ease Abigail's mind, but instead it made her frown. "That is very wrong, isn't it? The law should apply to everyone with an even hand without prejudice."

"It should—but it doesn't." As Portia was presently only too aware. She did not possess any blue-blooded or well-connected relatives who could make this disappear. And if they managed to link her to *Equitas*, she was done for.

"LADY ABIGAIL SLOANE!" As the prison guard approached the bars with rattling keys and a lantern, all the inmates rushed to the front of the cell shouting abuse. "SHOW YOURSELF, WOMAN!"

The angry crowd booed and leered as Portia and Abigail scrambled to their feet. As they tried to push their way through, they were helped on their way by several pairs of unsubtly groping hands. One pair snaked around Portia's waist and dragged her back unceremoniously against a smelly inmate's crotch.

"Leaving so soon, darlin'? I was so hoping we could get better acquainted before you left."

She brought the heel of her boot down hard on the groper's foot and broke free just in time for him to respond with a growl and a violent push. One that forced her hard against the bars. As she struggled to get her breath, she found herself staring directly into a familiar pair of utterly stunned blue eyes on the other side.

Chapter
SEVENTEEN

"Just get in the damned carriage, Abigail!" Leo was so angry and disappointed, and so bloody terrified he could barely think straight. "You can say your piece once I have sorted out your latest bloody mess and not before!" He slammed the door behind her and sent the driver on his way because at least that was one problem dealt with.

Now all he had to do was sort out Portia before any of the scoundrels she was still incarcerated with did anything further to hurt her—which he was convinced they would if he didn't get her out of there fast.

He stalked back into the jail to find Nolley, who was enjoying lording it over him in petty revenge for all the times Leo had thwarted him from trying to bend the law to suit his own ends.

He found him manhandling a group of shackled prisoners toward one of the back rooms where his fellow magistrates were holding the emergency sessions with more aggression than the task deserved. "We need to talk."

"Not if it's about that woman on your payroll, we don't." Nolley disappeared into the makeshift courtroom, forcing Leo to pace outside it until he reappeared alone.

"I am sure this is all a mistake. A classic case of someone being in the wrong place at the wrong time. Miss Kendall is a chaperone, not an insurrectionist." Or at least he hoped she was at this stage. After the bizarre night he'd had so far, nothing seemed out of the realm of the impossible.

Nolley had the nerve to roll his eyes. "As I've already explained to you, your grace, Miss Kendall was caught red-handed in possession of a seditious banner and then tried to resist arrest. She is not your kin, nor is she related to anyone of any import, so does not qualify for any special dispensation on any grounds. She is being charged for her crimes and that is that."

That was clearly his next battle and if the constable was determined to be unreasonable, Leo would have to have it with someone else. But, he needed to ensure that Portia was safe before he spiraled into an illogical, ranting mess who would be no use to anyone. "But she is a woman alone in a cell full of men, Constable Nolley, and I must insist that she be held in a separate place as it is dangerous for her in there."

"We've arrested nearly fifty rioters so far and they are still coming in, so we've nowhere else to put her. Once she's been charged, I'm sure they'll move her somewhere more appropriate."

"And if something inappropriate happens to her while we wait?" Because that didn't bear thinking about. "Surely you don't want that on your conscience?"

"She should have thought of that before she decided to spread sedition, your grace. And frankly, you should focus on getting your own house in order rather than criticize this one."

"She is a woman on her own in a cell full of randy men! One of whom we both witnessed drooling over her before he assaulted her!" A sight that had made Leo's hair literally stand on end.

The constable's face contorted into an ugly snarl. "To my mind, that slanderous bitch deserves whatever she's got coming! But I'm not the one shagging her."

Leo's temper snapped then and he slammed Nolley against the

wall. “Watch your dirty mouth!” He resisted the overwhelming temptation to allow the red mist of panic to blind him so that he could pummel the constable to a pulp and settled for growling in his face for Portia’s sake. “I do not care how you do it—but get her out of there now! That is an order!”

The insufferable man simply stuck out his chin. “I am not sure that you can give me an order pertaining to any detainee when you have a personal interest in their case, your grace. Is it not custom for a magistrate whose objectivity might be compromised to step aside in such cases? Or do you expect us to make an exception to your usually rigid legal principles this evening just because it suits you?”

The bastard had him there, so Leo stalked into the chamber, not caring that he was interrupting the magistrates in session because he urgently needed their help. Unfortunately, rather than find at least one friendly face, he was confronted by the entire hang ’em and flog ’em brigade.

“Debden?” It was Lord Corston who spotted him first. “Have you finally come to join the fun?” Because of course the arrogant fool was relishing in his power tonight just as Nolley was.

“I have a problem.” There was no point beating about the bush when every minute Portia remained in that cell she was in grave danger. “One that I need to discuss with the bench urgently.”

“But I thought we sorted your problem.” Corston tapped his nose and winked in the most unsubtle manner, without a care for the poor souls in the dock who weren’t lucky enough to be related to a duke.

“I’m afraid that I have another.” For the first time in his life, Leo had to abandon all his rigid principles to ride roughshod over the law. “And it is pressing.”

Constable Nolley came to personally collect Portia from the cell and seemed to take an inordinate amount of pleasure in manhandling her through the prison corridors. All the while trying to goad her into anger, no doubt as a way to give him an excuse to be more violent toward her. "It'll take more than your *doting duke* to get you off this charge, whore—it'll take a miracle!" His breath was hot and rancid against her cheek; his nails digging into her upper arms like talons. "He might be blinded by your wiles, but I'm not! Nor will the other justices be. They'll all know a wrong'un when they meet one. Especially when they see all the evidence we have against you. That'll teach you to accuse me of being corrupt!"

She wanted to speak up and fight back with every sinew of her body, but knew that was precisely what he wanted, and clamped her jaws shut. The constable had recognized her from the second she had been brought to the jail, just as he had recognized Lady Abigail, and he clearly had an axe to grind. One that he was unlikely to be able to grind with a duke's sister. With Abigail already released, Portia knew that she was Nolley's only hope at getting some petty revenge against Leo. Only when they reached the closed door of their destination did the constable stop goading her. By the time the clerk opened the door, he looked every inch the calm, but put upon, law enforcer rather than the spiteful bully that he had been since her arrest.

Portia was led to stand in front of a long table where three magistrates were seated. She knew that they were magistrates because one of them was the odious Lord Corston, but it was another who spoke first.

"State your name for the record."

"Portia Elizabeth Kendall." She thought she could sense the duke behind her but did not turn to confirm it because Nolley was watching her like a hawk for any confirmation that she was indeed his mistress as he had repeatedly accused her of being.

"On what charge is this woman brought before this bench?"

"*Charges*, my lord," corrected the constable, "for there are several."

The sour-faced magistrate nodded in acknowledgment and Nolley continued. "This prisoner is charged with attending the seditious meeting that took place on the High Street here in Bath in direct contradiction of the Seditious Meetings Act of 1819. As a consequence of her actions during this meeting, she is also charged with breaking the peace and resisting arrest."

"Do you have witnesses to these offenses, constable?"

"The militiaman responsible for arresting her at the scene has provided a statement and has offered to bear witness at any criminal trial, my lord." Nolley handed several pieces of paper to the clerk. "Two other witness statements attest that they saw the prisoner at the meeting. All of them saw her violently resisting arrest." He paused while the magistrates scanned the statements. "Furthermore, she is charged with composing and publishing seditious libel in accordance with the Blasphemous and Seditious Libels Act of 1819." Before he was asked for it, he opened Lady Abigail's hand-painted placard so that they could all see the damning words daubed across it. Every single magistrate frowned as the clerk delivered *BATH—THE CITY OF CROOKED COURTS AND CORRUPT CONSTABLES!* to the bench.

Lord Corston seemed particularly aggrieved by it. "Did you write those words, Miss Kendall?"

"I did not, my lord."

"She's got black ink stains all over her fingers that say different and she certainly held those words aloft," said the constable lying through his yellowed teeth. "I personally witnessed her doing so."

"Ah . . ." Lord Corston's eyes shot to the back of the room before Portia could argue. "That complicates things, I'm afraid."

"This is the prisoner's first offense." Leo's confident and commanding voice gave her some hope that she wasn't doomed to swing for a crime she did not commit. "And I have already personally vouched for her good character."

"That may be so, but she has called into question the good characters of everyone here present with that seditious placard, and that egregious insult cannot be ignored." Lord Corston had decided to take great umbrage that anyone would call his good name into question, which was irony in its purest form as there was nothing good in him. "How do you plead to these charges, Miss Kendall?"

"Not guilty, my lord." Portia left it at that because she knew arguing that all those charges were tenuous at best and outright fabrication at worst would not do her any good in this hostile room. Despite her having nothing to do with that stupid placard, beyond trying to snatch it out of Lady Abigail's hands as she tried to drag her out of harm's way, it was the unwritten rule of the reform movement that you did not incriminate another reformer under any circumstances. Even one who was a blithering and ill-informed idiot.

"Then this case will have to go to trial." Lord Corston shrugged. "Unless the constable agrees to drop the charges."

"I do not." Nolley stuck out his chin, defiant. "We set a dangerous precedent if we do not punish an agitator simply because they happen to work for a duke. Especially when we have already dropped all charges against one of his kin as a favor."

"Now, now constable . . ." Lord Corston wagged an unconvincing finger at him. "That was no favor. We have already ascertained that his grace's sister happened to be at the wrong place at the wrong time and had nothing whatsoever to do with that illegal protest." Then he turned to the recording clerk. "You will strike anything that suggests different from the record."

Nolley's eyes narrowed. "I have witness testimony that puts Miss Kendall right in the very center of that protest."

"If those witness statements that you have are from other members of the militia who were sent in to stop a peaceful protest, we all know that a jury is unlikely to convict Miss Kendall of any of this." Leo finally stepped into Portia's eyeline as he approached the bench. "We would only be wasting the court's time."

"She called me corrupt!" Nolley bashed the table. "And that placard and those damning ink stains prove it!"

"Then . . ." Leo's gaze flicked to hers and he winced. "Leave the seditious libel charge to stand, but drop all the others. If Miss Kendall pleads guilty to that one lesser charge, then you have the power to fine her here and now and discharge her to me."

Portia glared at him. "But I am not guilty of *any* of these trumped-up charges! The constable is lying! He knows damn well that I had nothing to do with that placard and he certainly never saw me with it. The first time we collided was here at this jail—well after my arrest!"

It was the wrong thing to say as far as the constable was concerned. "Do you hear that? You all just witnessed her calling me a liar to my face, didn't you?" The entire bench nodded. "She's accusing me of corruption aloud in this court now! That's more seditious libel right there and I want it added to the charges!"

"Can I have a moment to speak to Miss Kendall in private?" Leo asked the bench, who all looked at one another and nodded.

"A moment," said the sour-faced one who had initially asked her name. "But keep it brief."

Leo stalked to a side door and jerked his head toward it to get her to follow. Portia did and as soon as it closed behind them, she let rip. "This is an outrage, Leo, and Nolley is lying just to get back at you through me!"

"And if he is, you basically played right into his hands with that outburst."

"But he's lying!"

"And you just called the man corrupt to his face in front of a room of eminent witnesses. That is all the proof he needs!" He was angry and frustrated, and for some reason at her. "Why couldn't you just keep your mouth shut for once and let me help you?"

"Because this is wrong." She grabbed his hand. "The constable's account is not at all what happened and your sister can corroborate—" He yanked his hand away to pace, clearly in no mood to listen.

"After her atrocious behavior today, Abigail would not be viewed as a reliable witness."

"So we don't even try to give the truth a chance? We just give up? Roll over? Plead guilty to an offense that I absolutely did not commit?" Could he not see how morally wrong that was? How appallingly unfair? "I will not do it, Leo! Under any circumstances."

He grabbed her shoulders. "Don't you see! If you plead guilty to the lesser libel charge, then Nolley will be appeased! And you get to walk out of here tonight with the rest of those more serious charges dropped. If you don't, they are going to throw you back into that cell with all those leering men and you *will* get hurt. Do you hear me?" He let go of her to rake his hand through his hair in agitation as he resumed pacing the tiny anteroom like a caged lion. "There is nowhere safe that they can keep you until they send you to wherever they see fit for you to stand trial, whenever they decide to send you there, and there will be nobody around to ensure that those men will leave you be."

That brought her up short. "But if I plead guilty, I will have a criminal record!" One that, if she was ever unlucky enough to be arrested again for producing and publishing seditious libel—a very real possibility when she worked for *Equitas*—would guarantee her a one-way trip to Botany Bay!

He threw up his palms. "Which no one need ever know about, so long as the bloody fine is paid! I can beg another favor and keep it from the newspapers and then this all ends here!"

"But the blot on my record stays here! Indelibly written on an official document that could be used against me at any time!" Portia threw up her own manacled palms, wishing she could tell him exactly why the stakes were suddenly so high. "And correct me if I am wrong, but under the conditions set out in that outrageous piece of legislation called the Blasphemous and Seditious Libels Act that your corrupt bully of a constable is so fond of quoting, if I am found guilty of a second offense of such libel—no matter how similarly unjust that charge might be—the punishment is automatically fourteen years transportation!" A punishment that made her throat constrict with fear. "I cannot and will not take that risk!"

"Risk?" Leo grabbed her hands. "You are covered in ink, Portia!"

"But I am always covered in ink!"

"They don't know that!" He pointed to the door. "And the whole court just heard you call Nolley a liar—on that alone I guarantee that any chance of risk has been replaced by certainty as he now has three magistrates as witnesses. Do you know what impact that will have on a jury? Be in no doubt, if they uphold Nolley's testimony, you *will* be convicted of seditious libel if this goes to trial and it will be on your record anyway. The only difference is that this way you won't end up imprisoned *and* molested as well as fined! That is the only real risk that you should be concerning yourself with now!"

"But I am innocent and, given time, I could prove that!"

"If you are . . ." That damning *if* cut through her like a knife. "And if you can get proof, then I can get that blot on your record bloody well erased! In the meantime, seeing as you are so fond on divvying up everything and everyone behind nonsensical battle lines, this is my world and not yours. So trust me and just do as I say!"

Chapter
EIGHTEEN

"Portia Elizabeth Kendall, you are charged with composing and publishing seditious libel on this day in the city of Bath in accordance with the Blasphemous and Seditious Libels Act of 1819. How do you plead?"

As Corston read out the charges, Leo hoped fervently that she would do as he had asked but still wasn't sure that she would. They had argued like cat and dog right up until the last moment when the clerk of court had come to fetch her. She had been adamant, but he hoped that she understood how limited her options currently were. If this was wrong, he had given her his word that he would make it right. In truth, even if she was as guilty as sin as the evidence suggested she was, he would single-handedly charge against a rampaging army if it kept her out of harm's way.

That's what a man did for the woman he suspected he was already more than half in love with—even if she had an adamant and nonsensical reason why she wouldn't allow herself to attempt to love him back.

A sudden epiphany he would have to digest properly and deal with once this crisis was over.

"How do you plead, Miss Kendall?" Lord Corston was as frustrated with her silence as Leo was.

Portia squared her shoulders and stuck out her chin and Leo's gut clenched in fear. Her expression was defiant as she flicked her gaze his way and he willed her to see sense.

Please, Portia! Trust me!

She looked away and stared at the floor, releasing an audible sigh as she seemed to deflate in the makeshift dock. "Guilty." Her voice was small and defeated and he hated it. Hated seeing this fearsome, formidable woman who always radiated such fire reduced to a browbeaten shell of self-loathing.

He wanted to go to her. Wrap her tight in his arms and tell her that it was all going to be all right, but he knew that wouldn't go down well with the court, who already suspected that she meant more to him than an employee should. Instead, he had to settle for being supremely grateful that she was safe and everything else could wait until tomorrow.

They left her manacled as the clerk took down all her particulars, treating her like a common criminal, and that galled. But he sat on his hands and waited quietly, counting every excruciating second until they deigned to release her into his care.

"Place of birth?" asked the clerk.

"Newton St. Loe."

Corston's ears pricked up. "My neck of the woods, eh? I knew a Kendall way back—a Terence Kendall. He was a gardener, or maybe a groom, on my estate for a while, I believe. Is he any relation?"

There was no imagining the venom in Portia's tone as she replied. "He was my father and he was your gamekeeper for fifteen years." *Why the blazes hadn't she told him that? And what else didn't he know about her?*

"Whatever he was, he was a good man. One who knew his place." Corston could not have been more patronizing. "You would do well to follow his example, Miss Kendall, and learn yours."

Her lovely eyes narrowed at that dismissive chastisement and for a moment, Leo was sure she was about to tear Corston off a strip, but she didn't. She clenched her jaw instead and only spoke again when spoken to, and only to answer questions for the record.

At Nolley's insistence, the fine was a hefty one, but Leo paid it without comment, then waited while the constable finally produced the keys to unlock the humiliating shackles. "She's all yours again, your grace." The innuendo in the vile little man's tone chafed, but not as much as the way Nolley shoved Portia toward him. "And you are welcome to her."

It took all Leo had just to nod as he maneuvered her to the door. He would deal with the constable in due course. Right now, his only priority was getting Portia home.

He helped her into the waiting carriage where she sat stiffly opposite, staring out of the window rather than look at him.

"I know that you are angry, Portia."

Two molten brown eyes skewered him. "Angry doesn't even begin to describe how I am feeling, *your grace*." He was back to being "your grace" again and that didn't bode well. She jabbed the air between them. "How would you feel if you had just been beaten into submission by your employer after being made a scapegoat by a liar? Oh . . . but that would never happen to you, would it? Because you are of *noble* birth so none of those unfair laws ever apply to you, and nobody gets to tell you to do as you are told or to know your place!"

She was right of course. "If we can find proof that the constable lied, you have my word that I will appeal this conviction and get it struck from your record."

She scoffed in disbelief. "And how long will that take?" She folded her arms. They were bare because at some point she must have been separated from her coat. Finger-sized bruises marred her upper arms, and her wrists were ringed with red where the manacles had been attached too tight. Nolley would pay for both of those things as soon as Leo got his hands on him. "One year? Two? Never—because I am not important? I pleaded guilty, after all, and apparently of my own free will." Her expression now was one of complete disgust and it was him that she was disgusted with. “Because as you so rightly pointed out, I was done for anyway. I never stood a chance.”

“But at least you are safe now.”

“For how long?”

“I am going to look after you, Portia, I promise.” He moved to sit beside her and wrapped a comforting arm around her, leaning his forehead against hers, needing the contact. “We can put all this behind us and . . .” Rather than blurt out how he felt about her when his emotions were all over the place, he placed a soft kiss on her lips. “I swear on my life that I won’t let anyone or anything hurt you ever again.”

Rather than be relieved by that heartfelt reassurance, she pushed him away as she shook her head, her voice catching while she proudly held back her tears. “Can you not see that every single bit of that was wrong? From the overreaction to the protest to the arbitrary arrests by the authorities, to your blue-blooded sister’s release without charge to the constable’s bloody lies to charge me for her offenses. And the court’s readiness to do favors for a duke irrespective of the truth—just because he has the privilege of being a duke. And their keenness to find me guilty until proven innocent just because I had the audacity to be lowborn.” She turned toward the window again as if she couldn’t stand the sight of him. “But thank goodness that I know my place, kept my mouth shut, and did as I was told by one of my betters, *your grace*. For heaven forbid that I dare to expect the basic courtesy of either the benefit of the doubt or a fair trial in a country that is so unjust, unequal, and institutionally unfair to people—like me—who do not matter that it is rotten to its very core!”

Unsurprisingly, Portia barely slept despite her physical and emotional exhaustion. She was too infuriated, too hurt, and too disgusted by her shocking treatment from the authorities and her disappointment at Leo’s awful solution that she could do nothing other than rage at the unfairness of it all. She gave up trying before dawn and headed to the newspaper. She didn't care that it wasn't her day off or that she was supposed to be working her notice for the duke. Now that she had a criminal record thanks entirely to him and his stupid sister, she no longer felt obligated to fulfill her contract no matter how hurt and conflicted her feelings for the wretch were. Frankly, the sooner she left his house, the better. However much her heart would ache for him, she was all done playing with fire and now that the constable had it in for her, only an idiot would remain working for the magistrate that paid that crook's wages.

She also needed to vent some of her frustration at yesterday's travesty, and the only way that she could make any sense of it all was to write it all down. Thankfully, the newspaper office was as silent as the quay outside, so she locked herself inside, pulled out a piece of paper, and dipped her pen in some ink.

BATH—THE CITY OF CROOKED COURTS AND CORRUPT CONSTABLES!

By K Pendle

Ironically, Lady Abigail's placard gave Portia the perfect headline for a piece that she knew was going to be too incendiary to ever print, but that she needed to write regardless. One which didn't need a question that required debating, because there was nothing to debate.

The usually calm city of Bath was marred by unspeakable violence last night when the heavy-handed and heavily armed militia were sent in to quash a protest. While that protest was undoubtedly ill-informed, it certainly did not warrant the force or the state-sanctioned malevolence that was unleashed upon it. Bloodthirsty soldiers cut through the crowd indiscriminately, using fists, bayonets, and rifle butts to wound everyone in their path. Once down, the abused were beaten into submission before they were dragged to the goal where, sadly, the real crimes of last night were committed. In the name of the law and with the abominable statutes of suppression not on their side, the accused were paraded one by one before a mockery of a court and were charged with whatever fabricated offenses vomited out of Constable William Gabriel Nolley's lying mouth.

The lucky ones—and by lucky, I mean those with blue blood coursing through their veins and connections powerful enough to warrant special dispensation for the heinous crime of having an opinion—were released without charge irrespective of the evidence against them. Those not lucky enough to be related to the persuasively dimpled Duke of Debden—or born into any rotten branch of our despicable and dishonorable ruling class for that matter—had the book thrown at them. And it was thrown indiscriminately by a bunch of privileged and entitled blue-blooded idiots who have the effrontery to call themselves justices of the peace.

However, I can assure you that not one of those morally moribund men metered out any justice last night.

Hang 'em or flog 'em is the Bath magistrates' motto.

Oppression is their sole purpose.

So rather than scrutinize the evidence and search for the truth they pretend to stand for, they gleefully listened to the constable's lies and then casually ruined the lives of all those poor lowborn individuals stood before them with a callous swipe of their sanctimonious pens.

Everyone charged had to be punished whether guilty or not. As it serves the nefarious purpose of the few who rule us to use whatever unscrupulous means they have to repress or force to confess the disposable many rather than making any attempt to fight for any actual justice for them!

"Portia?" William's voice made her jump. "Why are you here so early?" But before she could answer, he frowned. "And did you make doubly sure that you weren't followed? Only there was apparently a great deal of trouble in town last night and the constable would love nothing more than to be able to arrest one of us for it."

"Of course I wasn't followed but—" Before she could finish her sentence, the floodgates opened and she burst into tears, and the whole sorry tale of the dreadful night before spilled out.

Chapter
NINETEEN

Portia was nowhere to be found when Leo got up. Her things were still in her room so he assumed she was coming back, but nobody knew where she was or had seen her leave and that bothered him. He bitterly regretted giving her some space to calm down while he read Abigail the riot act. And he wished he had begged Portia to speak to him after she had barricaded herself in her bedchamber. He was already second-guessing himself over the way he had dealt with the situation last night. Especially now that he had dragged the whole truth out of his troublesome sister, who had corroborated every single bit of Portia's story. He now knew that he could have and should have handled it all better if only he hadn't allowed his panic to overwhelm him. Portia had been rightly furious at being pushed into pleading guilty to a crime that he had known in his heart that she did not commit.

And as he had spiraled into contemplating apocalyptic what-ifs, he *had* pushed her.

Instead, he probably should have guarded her all night rather than harangue her into seeing his panicked version of sense in her hour of need. Or sent in a couple of burly guards to protect her while he interrogated every single witness himself. Used his privileged position as a magistrate to put the fear of god into those soldiers who were lying for the constable. Found other witnesses. Put Abigail on the stand rather than try to keep his foolish sister out of further trouble. Then used his extensive knowledge of the law to blow holes in the rest of Nolley's flimsy arguments and call the man a liar and a perjurer in that court too. Worse than that! A petty, vengeful, morally corrupt bully, who was only using Portia as a way to get back at him.

Powerless to do anything other than worry about her while he waited for her to return, he fired off a message to the constable to report to him as soon as he received it. That had been hours and hours ago and there was still no sign of either of them. While relieving Nolley of his duties could wait a few more hours, making amends with Portia couldn't. Her obvious disappointment in him was eating him from the inside. He needed her to understand that she mattered—especially to him. That he would always be on her side. And that he was going to do his very best to move mountains for her and clear her good name if it was the last thing he ever did.

Hence he was here.

Riding into Newton St. Loe.

Hoping that Portia had run home to her mother so he could beg her forgiveness and start to make those amends.

Leo checked the address the local postmaster had given him again and frowned. He hadn't expected her ailing mother to live above a shop. He searched down the side alley for a separate entrance and when he couldn't find one, went into the draper's shop to inquire. He was instantly greeted by a handsome, smiling dark-haired woman in her middle years.

"Can I help you, sir?" She returned a heavy bolt of fabric to the shelf before approaching him.

"I am looking for a Mrs. Kendall."

"Are you indeed? Now there is a name that I haven't heard in a few years."

"Then she doesn't live here?"

"She does—I just go by Mrs. Byrne nowadays to please my husband."

This could not be Portia's mother despite the more-than-passing resemblance. Portia's mother wasn't well and needed looking after, while this woman looked to be as fit as a fiddle. She was probably a relation of some sort. An aunt or some such because Portia's mother was all on her own. Far too old to be on the right side of fifty like this woman with Portia's exact dark brown eyes. "I don't suppose you have a relative called Portia, do you, Mrs. Byrne?"

"I do, as it happens." Friendliness turned slightly into wariness. "Portia is my daughter. Why do you ask?" Wariness instantly gave way to worry. "She's not gone and got herself into any trouble, has she? As I wouldn't put it past her. I've warned her time and time again that her opinions are dangerous but she's a headstrong girl. Always has been."

"She's not in any trouble." It wasn't his place to tell her mother about last night. "I was just passing and urgently needed to talk to her." As that comment made a pair of dark eyebrows as expressive as Portia's shoot skyward with alarm, he tried to ignore his twitching scalp and introduced himself. "I am Leopold Sloane." When she still blinked at him blankly, he was forced to use the title Portia hated. "The Duke of Debden."

"Oh good heavens above! My humblest apologies for my informality, your grace." Mrs. Byrne, who was apparently neither a widow, an invalid, nor a Kendall, bobbed a surprisingly spry curtsy. "I would be happy to send whatever word to Portia that you need me to—although I cannot fathom why on earth you would need to speak to her." The eyes went back to suspicious again. "But if you apprise me and I deem it important enough, I will give you her address in Mayfair if you would prefer to write to her yourself."

The hairs began to prickle on Leo's neck. "Mayfair?"

"That is where she works, your grace." Portia's mother smiled proudly. "She's been the governess to Lord and Lady Warley's daughters for the past two years."

The plot thickened. "I take it that you haven't recently seen her then?"

"Not since Christmas, your grace, when she came home for her last visit."

What the blazes was Portia up to? Whatever it was, there were alarm bells ringing in Leo's head now. Big, clanging, and insistent alarm bells. Because the woman he suspected he loved was clearly a liar as well as a conundrum—but by the end of today he was now doubly determined to get to the truth.

Mrs. Byrne's dark brows kissed exactly like her daughter's did. "Might I inquire how you know my daughter?"

"We are friends," he answered not entirely sure what they were anymore. "We met in Mayfair . . . recently."

"She's never mentioned any sort of acquaintance with a duke in any of her recent letters, your grace. To be frank, that she is surprises me given her visceral dislike of the aristocracy in general." Portia's mother now looked perplexed, which mirrored his own feelings because none of this made any sense. "Not that I am insinuating that she dislikes you, your grace." A blush bloomed on Mrs. Byrne's unbelievably healthy face as she backtracked. "You must be a very fine duke indeed for Portia to even consider calling you a friend."

What the blazes did that mean? "She is clearly a woman who keeps her cards close to her chest." The duplicitous minx! "On the subject of which, I'll confess, I believed you to be a widow, Mrs. Byrne." One knocking loudly on death's door.

"I am—or I was. Portia's father has been dead over a decade. But I remarried two years ago." She gestured around her shop. "So I am now Mrs. Byrne, the draper's wife."

"She neglected to tell me that, despite our many conversations." That and a whole host of other important things!

"She excels in neglecting to tell things, your grace. Especially if she knows that you will heartily disapprove of them." Her lips pursed briefly before she smiled, uncomfortable, her eyes wary again but also apologetic. "But what can you do? A daughter will only let you mother her for so long, and Portia is used to doing as she pleases nowadays.

She's always been headstrong like that, truth be told, which I am sure, as her friend, you would know." Eyes, so like Portia's, narrowed in challenge.

"I do indeed," he agreed, chuckling as if he did while his head spun. If she didn't spend every single evening and all of every Sunday here, where the blazes did Portia go until silly o'clock every night? And why the bloody hell would she constantly lie about it? "I've often been at the sharp end of one of her lectures."

"Oh good heavens above, that girl! Only she would be brazen enough to lecture a duke!" Mrs. Byrne shook her head. "But she can be intractably single-minded about causes when she has a particular bee in her bonnet." *Causes?* "I take it that's how you met her?" At his blank expression, she elaborated. "At the United League for Reform?"

Didn't I tell you that you were playing with fire!" It was hardly a surprise that Edgar had little sympathy for her predicament as Portia shared her awful news with everyone, but the venom in his tone was particularly vicious. "You weren't satisfied with dallying with the magistrate and now the bloody constable has a personal vendetta against you!" The spiteful typesetter immediately turned to William. "She's put us all in enough danger, I say we send her packing back to London and lie low for a while."

"This isn't Portia's fault." That came from Percy, who was still as white as a sheet at discovering that his beloved fiancée had been arrested too. "She had no choice but to go after Abigail—it is her job."

"None of us were supposed to go anywhere near that protest!" Edgar glared at her with malice. "And you should have done a better job of handling your woman, Percy, else this wouldn't have happened!" But of course, he didn't expect William to send Percy packing back to London.

"Pointing fingers isn't helpful." Gentle Jim tried to pour oil on troubled waters. "What's important now is keeping everyone here safe and most especially Portia, who is in the most danger."

"Agreed." William was his usual circumspect and supportive self as he patted her hand. "We need to get you out of the duke's house today. Can you stay with your mother until we can find you another job and less exposed lodging?"

"Of course." She knew that she couldn't risk staying at the Crescent anymore, but it still hurt to have to do it. Leaving Leo and never seeing him again, irrespective of how angry she was at him, would be a wrench. She had too many complicated feelings for him even if they were all as foolhardy as they were futile.

"Will your Abigail tell her brother anything that we do not want him to know?" William asked that of Percy.

"Not if I tell her not to. I could try and see her tonight and—"

William stopped him mid-sentence. "Out of the question. You cannot go anywhere near the duke's house in this current climate—or his sister. We cannot risk anyone making any links between us and *Equitas*. The law will be gunning for this newspaper after last night and so we must all be extra vigilant and extra cautious. Write her a note and Portia can slip it to her before she leaves."

Percy nodded even though it was obvious he was desperate to see Abigail. He couldn't believe that she had been so stupid and had apologized to Portia twice already for her ill-informed zeal.

"Excellent," said William. "Then we have a plan."

"A stupid one!" Edgar shot up from his chair like a firework. "Am I the only person here who can see that *she* is a poisoned chalice?" He pointed his finger so close to her face that Portia had to clench her fist to stop herself from slapping it away. "Her card is marked! What if Nolley has her followed? And what if she leads him here?"

"Then we cross that bridge when we come to it." It was Jim who pushed Edgar out of her way. "And we stick together—because we are all in this together and we have all always known the risks of what we do here. If this was you in trouble, Edgar, you'd expect us all to rally around you as a mark of loyalty for all you do for us, and to move heaven and earth to try and get you out of it. If you can't do the same for *all* of the rest of us, then perhaps it's you that should be sent packing?"

"Nobody is being sent packing." William glared at Edgar too before he smiled kindly at Portia. "You have had enough of an ordeal. Get yourself home and packed, dear girl. We can all regroup tomorrow and decide if we think it's prudent to still go to print this week or not."

"It's not!" Edgar was shouting now. "You don't prod a bear when it's angry!"

"And you don't roll over and play dead either because you still get eaten regardless!" She was sick to the back teeth of Edgar, but even more sick of being told what to do.

"We can decide on that tomorrow when we are all calmer." William pleaded with her with his eyes. "Our first priority is getting you out of the constable's way. So get yourself to your mother's with all haste and then get a good night's sleep. I hope it is not being unkind to say that you look thoroughly exhausted and if we do go to print this week, *Equitas* and everyone who relies on it to tell them the truth will need you to be at your very best."

He was right. She knew he was right. But leaving here meant also leaving Leo and she was trying to put that inevitability off. "I shall see you tomorrow. Bright and early."

"Bring your pen." It was William's way of telling her that he was keen to print and be damned, and she was grateful. There were so many things that needed saying now and the only way she could realistically fight back was to say them in her column.

"I'll bring two."

She gathered her coat and bonnet and trudged her weary way out. She was so tired, disappointed, and so utterly wretched that she failed to notice the man watching her from the shadowy doorway farther along the quay.

Chapter
TWENTY

Leo flung the drawing room door open and stalked toward his sister, not caring that fear had whipped him into an irrational frenzy. "Tell me everything that you know now, Abigail, or so help me I will not be responsible for my actions!"

His sister briefly winced, a telltale sign that she knew precisely what he was talking about even if his mother and Emilia didn't. "I told you everything I knew last night, Leo. I went to a protest, Miss Kendall followed and tried to drag me away from it, and then the pair of us got arrested."

"And?" He loomed over her, ready to shake the rest out of her if necessary, he was so bloody angry. "Let us not pretend that she isn't a committed and rampant reformer just like you are because I've just had tea with her mother!"

Abigail shrugged, trying and failing not to look alarmed. "So we share some political views? What else do you want me to say?"

"I want you to tell me where she is, goddammit! And what the hell she has been doing!" He had galloped home like a bat out of hell he was so desperate for answers.

"For pity's sake Leo, stop shouting!" His mother yanked his arm. "Miss Kendall is upstairs! She is packing her bags and frankly I do not blame her after all the trouble you two unreasonable idiots have caused her!"

"How bloody convenient!" He tugged himself from his mother's grip and marched to the stairs. He was halfway up them when somebody had the audacity to hammer on his front door.

"It's the constable! Open up!" He was going to bloody strangle Nolley—but not before he had some bloody answers from Portia. Like where she went every single evening and with whom she went there! Or how the blazes she got home! Because nothing she had told him so far was anywhere close to the truth!

The footman hovered at the door and looked up to him for some guidance and Leo shook his head. "He can wait!"

"Open up or I'll break this door down!" Nolley just kept hammering. "I have a warrant!" Words that turned Leo's blood to ice and made him hurry all the way back down.

He opened the front door himself, making sure his body blocked it, and was greeted by the ominous sight of the constable flanked by two others, and several militia men who were all armed. "What sort of warrant?"

"A warrant to search these premises and for the arrest of Miss Portia Elizabeth Kendall."

"On what grounds?"

"Composing and publishing seditious material in direct contravention of the Blasphemous and Seditious Libels Act of 1819."

"You cannot charge anyone with the same offense twice, Nolley—especially when she has already pleaded guilty!" Leo grabbed the man by the lapels and snarled in his face. "That is the law. Not that you have any regard for it!"

"This isn't for the placard." Nolley pulled himself away and held up a rolled-up newspaper that he slapped in Leo's chest. "It's for this!" Then with a click of his fingers the militia charged forward and Leo was pushed unceremoniously to the side. "Turns out that your fancy woman is one of the ringleaders of that treasonous rag that incited last night's riot. Writes her poison under the unimaginative pseudonym of K Pendle because she thinks we're all idiots. Funny that the only idiot that she fooled was you though, isn't it, your grace? Thank goodness the rest of us weren't taken in by her sultry wiles, though, ay? But at least you got your cock wet."

The punch was instinctive and totally out of character but for once Leo enjoyed the sight of blood as the bastard flew backward onto the pavement, his nose bleeding profusely.

For the second time in less than twenty-four hours, Portia was huddled in the corner of the same airless, dingy cell in the Grove Street Jail—only this time she had it all to herself.

Or at least she did now that Nolley had gone.

For how long he would leave her all alone in the dark, she had no clue, but she hoped it was long enough to come up with a plan. Because if she didn't come up with something brilliant soon, she was doomed.

The rest of the cells were quiet, so she had no idea where the others were, but she knew that she wasn't the only one of them to have been arrested. Nolley had bragged that he had personally arrested three of her fellow traitors down at the quay and that one of them had informed on them during their interrogation, so she dreaded to think what the authorities knew or how brutal the other interrogations had been. She had painful bruises everywhere after being shoved unceremoniously wherever Nolley had decided she needed to be shoved. He had seemed to take particular satisfaction in pushing her so hard into the cell that she had ended up falling to the floor before he snuffed out the only lantern down here in the bowels of the building.

It did not take a genius to realize that he was keeping her in the dark—both figuratively and literally—because he wanted her absolutely quaking in her boots by the time she was brought before the magistrates in the morning.

But the man was a fool if he thought taking the paltry single candle away and bellowing directly into her face would put the fear of god into her. The very real fear of a trip to Botany Bay had already done that the second she had been arrested, and she was now so terrified she didn't even have the capacity to cry.

She heard footsteps coming down the stairs and braced herself for more verbal abuse. Then slumped in relief when she saw the unmistakable outline of Leo emerge from the darkness—although he wasn't alone. For some reason, alongside a prison guard and a complete stranger, he had also brought his mother and Lord Teignmouth along.

They all held back while he approached the bars. "There's not much time," he said in a hushed whisper as soon as she made it to them. "You are being taken directly to Bristol assizes at dawn where you will stand trial. The court sits the day after tomorrow and they plan to rush this through, Portia. All the magistrates are in agreement. What with it being your second offense." She could see the guilt etched into his handsome face for his part in that. "And with them having more than enough evidence to convict you."

"What evidence?" Nolley hadn't told her any of this.

"A watchman who saw you leaving the warehouse where you keep the printing press shortly before they arrested the others there, red-handed. Every single column that you have written, including the one you left out on your desk in your handwriting that has the exact same headline as the placard the constable is still adamant he saw you waving at the protest. Several more half-finished articles that he found in your things at my house." Now he appeared guiltier still despite his clipped but matter-of-fact tone. "They had a search warrant and I couldn't stop them. And one of your fellow conspirators—an Edgar somebody—has named you as K Pendle, the assistant editor of *Equitas* and author of the opinion piece." Of course Edgar would be the one to feed her to the wolves. "It's all pretty damning, Portia."

"Oh god." She felt sick and the room began to spin. "I don't stand a chance, do I?"

He shook his head. "Not in a courtroom. I've racked my brain, and you only have one option left to stop them throwing the book at you."

"I am not going to incriminate the others to save myself!" She wouldn't be able to live with herself if she sold William or Jim or Percy down the river. "I will not make a deal with the devil for immunity!"

He reached through the bars to cup her cheek; his fingers gentle despite all the anger in his eyes. "They are all first offenders who will leave here with a fine at worst, so they won't bother asking you to." Leo's expression was grave and frustrated and furious all at the same time. "Especially as they intend to put you on the next convict ship that leaves Bristol harbor. And be in no doubt that they can do that to Miss Portia Elizabeth Kendall." He paused. Gulped. Steeled himself. "But they will have to pardon the Duchess of Debden."

"What?" *Surely she hadn't heard that right?* "I can't marry you!"

"You are going to bloody well have to if you don't wish to live out the rest of your days in a penal colony on the other side of the world!" He had never sounded so angry or so bitter. The sunny, funny man that she knew was now replaced by a stranger. "Trust me—after all the lies you've spewed, I don't want to do this anymore than you do!" He practically spat that. "But I feel a misguided sense of responsibility for convincing you to plead guilty yesterday, despite all your calculated machinations!" His expression more than conveyed his reluctance, and yet he didn't pull his hand away from her face. "But I've bribed a guard and brought the bishop of Bath and Wells with a special license. Dragged along two upstanding witnesses, and I've bought you about fifteen minutes until Nolley realizes that he's been sent on a wild-goose chase and comes back here and puts a stop to this. Therefore, you need to choose immediately which awful fate you would prefer. Fourteen years of brutal incarceration, which you likely won't survive, or the unpalatable chore of being shackled to a duke!"

Chapter
TWENTY-ONE

"Welcome home, your grace." Mrs. Rumpole, the housekeeper, dipped into a curtsy as soon as Portia walked through the front door. The woman looked shocked to be doing it, but she could not possibly be as shocked and stunned by it all as Portia was. "I have had the maids run a bath for you." She then dipped a curtsy toward Portia's new mother-in-law. "As requested, your grace, I have also sent up all the medical supplies you asked for."

"Thank you, Mrs. Rumpole." It was the duchess—now the dowager duchess—who answered because Portia had no words. Neither, apparently, did her new husband, who hadn't uttered a single one to her since they had hastily mumbled vows to one another in that fetid prison cell several hours ago. That he chose to stalk straight to his study and slam the door rather than linger in her company any longer now that they were finally back in the Royal Crescent did, however, speak volumes. "Could you have some breakfast sent up on a tray shortly too? Our new duchess has had quite the ordeal overnight and desperately needs some rest."

On leaden feet, she followed Leo's mother up the stairs and was about to continue up the next flight when the other woman stopped her with a gentle hand and a smile. "I hope you do not mind, but I sent word ahead while we were waiting for everything to be sorted to have all your things moved to your new bedchamber on the family floor. I couldn't allow you to see the mess that horrid constable made of your things. Some, I fear, are now beyond repair and they confiscated so much but . . ." She brushed that violation away. "We'll sort all that out in due course. Let's get you cleaned up first."

"Thank you." Portia forced a smile even though she felt dead inside because this woman had been nothing but kind to her over the last few turbulent hours. Why she wasn't as angry as her son was that he had married someone like her, she couldn't fathom, but she was grateful for at least one friendly face on the worst day of her life.

She was led to an enormous bedchamber painted in soothing soft green. It was a feminine room, but not overtly so. Like everything in this house, it was decorated and furnished more for comfort than to make a statement, yet it made a statement anyway. A beautiful, canopied bed was draped in expensive, crisp linens that had been delicately embroidered with trailing ivy and wildflowers. A thick, luxurious rug covered almost all of the highly polished wood floor. Gossamer lace billowed gently in the summer breeze floating through the open window and just before it was a fancy enamel bathtub. Inviting steam wafted from the frothy bubbles, which reached all the way to the top of the bath. As much as Portia wanted to sink into it, it still felt wrong.

"This is too much, your grace. There was nothing wrong with my old room and I will be perfectly content to remain—"

"Nonsense." The duchess—the dowager now—bustled over and began to unlace the back of Portia's gown. "You are the new mistress of this house, and this is the mistress's room."

"Your room, you mean?"

"My darling girl, it was never my room. I always slept in there." She flicked her hand toward a side door that Portia hadn't noticed. "With my husband." Which likely meant that *her husband* now slept in there and knowing that they weren't even separated by a solid wall unsettled Portia instantly. "It has much better views of the garden and I always slept more soundly next to Rafe." As the laces loosened and back of Portia's dress gaped, the duchess helped her step out of it before she kicked it out of the way. "I fear the only way to clean that is to burn it. That cell was positively filthy. Inhumanely so. Thank goodness Leo managed to get you out of it."

By selflessly sacrificing himself. "He hates me now, doesn't he?" He had uttered every vow curtly; staring straight ahead. So obviously hurt and angry at her betrayal that he couldn't bear to look at her. Hardly a girl's dream wedding scenario. Not that she had ever wanted one, but now that she had, it had been the stuff of nightmares.

"He's hurting, dear girl. Hardly a surprise after all the lies you've told him."

"I didn't want to. I . . ." Her voice trailed off. "I should have left this house the second that I realized that he was a magistrate. I know that now and bitterly regret that I didn't but . . ."

"It is him you need to purge yourself to, not me. He deserves the truth after all he has done for you, doesn't he?"

Portia nodded, feeling utterly wretched. "I'll go and talk to him."

"Leave him be for a while. Like my Rafe used to, Leo needs to pickle in his own juices for a while before he'll be in any mood to listen." The duchess smiled kindly as her gaze swept the length of Portia, who was now standing in nothing but her shift. "You are covered in bruises, you poor thing. Is that all the work of that vile constable or did somebody else do the dirty for him?"

"It is all his. He enjoyed pushing me around."

"Undoubtedly. Bullies like him enjoy taking their revenge out on the helpless and I daresay that the weaselly coward felt obligated to take it out on you after Leo gave him a well-deserved pasting right on our doorstep."

"He did?"

"Punched the snake on the nose and sent him flying onto his backside when he came to arrest you. Of course, the soldiers restrained him then as we all knew that Leo had only just started, and you know what happened next because they came to fetch you. But it was all rather unpleasant and unnecessary." The duchess frowned as she took a closer look at Portia's face and then stroked her cheek. "Did the violence only involve pushing, my dear, or were you subjected to worse?"

"Only pushing." Thank goodness.

"I shouldn't be relieved to hear that as a man who uses any violence on a woman is abhorrent enough—but external injuries do at least heal. Do you think you need to see the physician?" Portia shook her head. "Very well. You enjoy a nice long soak in the bath in peace and I'll come back and put some iodine on all your bruises once you're done."

"Thank you, your grace."

"It's either Mama now, seeing as we are family, or Letitia. I really do not mind which."

Her mother-in-law closed the door behind her as she left, leaving Portia all alone with her tangled thoughts. She gingerly removed her chemise and wandered to the long mirror in the corner to assess the damage for herself. She ached so much because she did indeed have bruises everywhere. There were grazes on her hands and knees from where she had landed on the cold flagstones of the cell floor. Her hair was a rat's nest and her hands and face were filthy. But it could be worse. She could still be there. But entirely thanks to Leo she wasn't.

Once she was clean and when he was ready to see her, she would have to thank him, but until then the bath called. She carefully eased her battered bones into it, sighing as the warm water enveloped her in its comforting embrace.

For the longest time, all Portia did was soak as she stared up at the ceiling, too overwhelmed to do anything else. She knew she had to think and regroup and find a way to deal with her strange new reality, but didn't have the energy to do that yet. Her bath had started to cool before she even thought about scrubbing the dirt from her skin and, conscious that the dowager was doubtless waiting patiently for her to finish, she forced herself to set about it with some purpose.

Her hair was full of soap and bubbles when the main door suddenly opened a crack. "Just a moment, your grace! I'm not decent!"

But instead of the duchess returning as she expected, it was M'Lady Whiskers who swung in, her whole fluffy white body hanging from the doorknob by her claws. The cat dropped silently to the floor, took one disdainful look at Portia, and hissed her disapproval. Then she sauntered over, lifted her tail, and swiveled to show her bottom. That cutting feline insult delivered, she hopped up on the bed and began to paw at it for at least half a minute until she settled herself on the pretty comforter, making sure to thoroughly ignore Portia while she licked her snow-white paws.

Bizarrely, that small, unfriendly bit of familiarity made Portia smile. "If you can open doors, M'Lady, basic good manners dictate that you should learn to close them too. Especially when somebody is in the bath."

Sadly, with the door to the landing still ajar to the width of one spoiled Persian and Portia as naked as the day she was born, she could no longer afford to linger in that lovely bath, so she quickly dunked her head under the water to rinse away the soap in her hair.

"Is your plan to ignore your new wife forever?" His mother walked into Leo's study with her arms folded. "Because if it is, somebody should tell the poor thing. She is just staring into space with no clue what to do next."

"That makes two of us." After the most fraught and shocking night of his life, and now that so many of her lies had been exposed, he couldn't bring himself to so much as look at the duplicitous minx, let alone speak to her. If publishing sedition wasn't enough, she had also been in cahoots with Percival Bloody Digby, and that was a betrayal too far. Now, his poor, battered heart was bleeding and he felt like the world's biggest fool. "I am currently mulling the benefits of immediately sending her as far away as possible and pretending none of this ever happened."

"It's too late for that, Leo." To add insult to injury, his mother tossed today's *Bath Chronicle* onto his desk. The headline *Doting Duke Makes Seditious Chaperone His Duchess* glaring up at him in cruel mockery. "Somebody at the prison must have leaked it because your wedding made the front page."

Of course it had! What fabulous gossip the whole sorry tale made for everyone else. Never mind that he had ended up heartbroken!

"But if I send her away at least I shall be free of her!" What a joke this all was, albeit an unfunny one. What a bloody joke he was now too. "She is nothing but a lying, scheming, backstabbing radical who used me abominably to serve her own ends!" One he had as good as plighted his troth to after just one kiss because she had tied him in so many blasted knots.

Probably on purpose.

Because nothing was as blind or as stupid as a besotted man, and he had certainly been all of those things. "It can hardly be viewed as a coincidence that she came to work here. What better way to keep one step ahead of the authorities than being a spy in a magistrate's bloody house! And do not get me started on how she conspired with Abigail. I paid that damned woman to protect my sister, not to provide her with every clandestine opportunity to meet with that scoundrel Digby while they all plotted the downfall of society behind my back!" He could picture how funny she must have found that. How laughably pathetic she must have found him. "In fact, the more I think on it, the more I realize that it was no coincidence that she was arrested alongside my sister at that protest. It was Portia who encouraged Abigail to go! Portia who gave her that damn placard, and then the scheming witch shamelessly used her connections to my title to get herself released!"

"Abigail swears that isn't the truth, Leo. You would know that if you deigned to talk to her rather than shoot silent daggers at her each time you stomp away."

"Of course she does!" His fist erupted with pain as he slammed it onto his desk. "And I've got nothing to say to bloody Abigail either while she's still under Digby and his fellow conspirators' toxic bloody spell! She's obviously been coerced and conditioned by the radicals who have their claws in her." He tapped his forehead. "She's been turned. Twisted to their way of thinking and doesn't recognize the truth anymore!"

"Your sister is too clever and too headstrong for that, and you know it. She's too stubborn herself, just like her supercilious, I-know-best older brother. Just as you also know, when you aren't being irrational, that a coincidence is sometimes just a coincidence."

"All I know is that I brought a Trojan horse into this house and in a moment of sheer madness, I married it!" In case his mother needed any proof of the full extent of Portia's betrayal, he slid over the damning article that had been found at the offices of *Equitas*. Written in her unmistakable hand. An article that she had personally insulted him in too! And to think he had found the constant ink stains on her fingers charming! What an absolute besotted buffoon he had been!

"Can I make an observation, Leo?"

"Will anything I say or do stop you?"

"You could have left her to face the music by herself last night." She slipped into the seat opposite him, a sure sign this unwelcome lecture was destined to be long. "Nobody would have judged you for it when there was so much evidence of her guilt—none of it that you were aware of until yesterday. But you didn't. You still wanted to save her. Even with all that damning proof."

"I felt beholden!"

"You didn't look beholden to me, my darling. You looked terrified. As if you couldn't face the prospect of never seeing her again. So you moved heaven and earth to keep her with you."

He loathed that his mother was right, but denied it anyway. "Actually, I could not care less if I never see her again."

"Why? Because just looking at her hurts?" His mother's expression was one of pity. "It is impossible to feel as betrayed as you so obviously do and not to have invested your heart."

"My heart has never been attached to her!" Perhaps if he said that often enough, the dratted organ would stop bleeding.

"I've seen how you look at her, Leo. From the first moment I witnessed the pair of you on the pavement, it was obvious to me that you wanted her."

"She is an attractive woman and I am not blind, Mother, but I have certainly never been stupid either." Which was why the constant ache in his chest was so acute. "She is dead to me!"

"That's not how love works, Leo." She reached over and squeezed his hand. "I am sure you will figure that out eventually once you've calmed down, put aside your pride, and realized that all this love you feel for her is worth fighting for. In the meantime, there is a grateful but terrified young woman upstairs who desperately needs to hear you tell her that everything is going to be all right—even if it isn't. One pretty much covered from head to toe in bruises that were given to her by that horrid constable of yours. Given, no doubt, as punishment because you punched him."

That cancerous dollop of fresh guilt delivered, his mother sailed out and left him to fester. Except it was Portia's bruises now and not her treachery that filled his mind.

With a frustrated growl at his own misguided sense of moral obligation, he took the stairs two at a time and stalked to the bedchamber next to his where his interfering mother had put the duplicitous witch. He went to knock, but when he saw the door was open, just marched on in, then stopped dead.

Because his new wife was standing naked in the bath.

Chapter TWENTY-TWO

Portia squealed as she snatched up the towel to cover her modesty and he quickly spun around like a gentleman—but he had already seen pretty much everything and there was no way his mind was ever going to allow him to forget it.

"My apologies . . . the door was open so I thought . . ."

"The cat opened it." Water sloshed out of the tub as she clambered out. "And you should have knocked!"

"I should have. I'm sorry. I . . ." He huffed. "I needed to see for myself all that Nolley had done to you."

"Well you've certainly seen it all now!"

"I certainly have but . . ." He sighed, wishing that he couldn't instantly picture the water droplets cascading down her perfect, pert breasts and dripping off her dark puckered nipples. Or the sublime curve where her trim waist flared at her hips. Or the neat triangle of wet, almost jet-black hair that nestled between her alabaster thighs. But he turned around wincing anyway. "I'm sorry." He flicked a wary finger toward the purple and brown patches that marred her arms poking out of her wrapped towel. "Those bruises are all my fault." He pushed all his desire aside to scan her bare arms and legs, taking them all in with horrified disgust. "If I hadn't have hit him, he wouldn't have hit you."

"He didn't hit me, so do not blame yourself. These bruises came from his manhandling, which he thoroughly enjoyed."

The fury was instant and all-encompassing. "I promise you that he will pay for every bruise!"

"They are only bruises."

He walked toward her, his focus now solely on the state of her hands, which suggested the bastard had done more than manhandle her. He gently reached for them and turned them palms up. "I'm going to call the physician."

"Please don't. Nothing is broken and nothing needs stitching." Her lovely chestnut eyes were sad. Contrite. Riddled with guilt too. "And I've caused you enough trouble, your grace."

"It's Leo," he said, tugging his fingers away sharply as he suddenly remembered that he was also furious at her. "For better or for worse, we are married now."

"We shouldn't be," she shook her head, her lip quivering slightly. "I never should have allowed you to make that sacrifice. But I am supremely thankful for it, even if I never saw myself as a wife." Her words were tumbling out as she hugged herself. He knew that she was overwhelmed, but that didn't make them easier to hear. "I never wanted to be a man's chattel, and I certainly never saw myself as a duchess. I have always been proudly one of the people and an outspoken critic of the privileged elite. And now . . ." Her pretty face contorted into a horrified scowl as she stared at the ring he had put on her outstretched finger, and it wounded. "This . . ." She gestured around the room still frowning. "Is the antithesis of the purposeful life I had planned for myself."

"I never saw myself shackled for all eternity to a duplicitous liar in a loveless marriage, my reputation as an honest and principled man in absolute tatters, so I suppose both of us will have to lower our expectations of what we thought our futures might hold from hereon in!"

She absorbed that like a blow. "I suppose I deserved that."

"You definitely did. You've done nothing but lie through your teeth to me since the first day we met! You never even told me that your father worked for Corston—even when the opportune moment presented itself! I had to find out that dangerous *state secret* in a bloody courtroom!"

She nodded with quiet dignity at his bitter sarcasm. "I don't know why I didn't tell you. I suppose I somehow thought the less you knew about me, the better it would be for both of us. I knew I had inadvertently placed you in an untenable position by coming to work here, but I swear to you that I never would have taken this job if I had known in advance that you were a magistrate. I did try to leave when things started to change between us—you know that." He did. Just as he knew that he had done everything in his power to selfishly keep her with him, just as his mother had accused him of. "With hindsight, I should have left that day irrespective of what my contract said because if I had, none of this would have happened, and for that I am truly sorry."

"Sorry that you got caught, you mean." He desperately wanted to pace. "But not as sorry as I am for falling for all of your rot."

"I never meant to hurt you, I swear." She touched his arm, and he retracted as if he'd been bitten because he couldn't bear how much he pathetically needed that paltry bit of disingenuous affection.

Trust him to fall head over heels for a liar!

"Yet you did. You have. So much that I wouldn't dare trust you now as far as I can throw you! But lucky me, I am still stuck with you—even though I cannot stand to look at you!"

She didn't balk despite his vitriol. "You don't have to be. You could divorce me. You could probably even get this marriage annulled if you do it straightaway. I certainly would if I were you." That sliced like a knife. "Claim you didn't know the half of it until after we had said our vows."

"I didn't know the half of it!" Yet even though he knew she was right, and that he probably did have ample grounds for an immediate annulment, he still couldn't bring himself to do it even if she would and, apparently, do it gladly. The very thought made his hair stand on end and his bludgeoned heart hammer in panic. Because he was clearly a blithering idiot. A hopeless glutton for punishment. A blasted fool in love with a woman who was more of a stranger to him now than she had ever been. *God help him!* "I suspect I still don't—but now that we are married—" He paused to choke out the next bit. "While we are married, I insist that at the very least, there are no more secrets between us."

"That strikes me as fair." She stared levelly as she sat primly on the mattress, even though she looked as far from prim as it was possible to be wrapped in just a towel and with her wet hair tumbling seductively down her back. "What would you like to know?"

He wanted to ask if she had any feelings for him, but didn't. If any of what he had thought was blossoming between them had ever been real? If she was prepared to muddle through and give them a go despite the inauspicious start to their union? "You can start by telling me how long you've been involved with that seditious rag." But, of course, wounded petulance won.

"You don't believe that it is seditious, Leo, even in temper." She looked him dead in the eye. "You believe in freedom of speech and fairness, and you've done nothing but defend it up to now, despite all the trouble it's caused you."

Her wistful smile as she read him like a book wasn't the least bit patronizing. "But to answer your question, I joined *Equitas* a week before I joined you. Before that, I am not ashamed to admit that I have been an active member of the United League for Reform since I turned sixteen. I blame Mary Wollstonecraft because it was her essays that lit a fire in me and started me writing, but Lord Corston's abominable treatment of my mother after my father's death also played its part, as he had been the first one to highlight to me how grossly unfair our society is." Thanks to Portia's mother, Leo now knew that her father had been killed when one of Corston's guns backfired while he had been preparing it for a grouse shoot. Instead of helping the family the way basic humanity, let alone duty, dictated he should have, Corston evicted them and swindled them out of most of the pension that should have been owed. Something that beggared belief but that sadly did not surprise him because it was so typically and selfishly Corston.

"I have always had a talent for writing, and well-argued essays, as you saw in my letter of application, are my speciality. For the last few years, I put together most of the League's pamphlets. More recently, I wrote several of the major speeches—which were all gallingly delivered by men who had no hand in them, for heaven forbid a woman actually speak out." She rolled her eyes at the injustice, reminding him so much of her off-the-cuff lecture to him about his privilege that he realized her strong sense of inequality was so intrinsically a part of her that she couldn't hide it, even when she tried to. That gave him some consolation; she wasn't a complete stranger to him now. He knew parts of her—her essence—and that was something to cling to.

"*Equitas* was my first opportunity to do something truly meaningful for the cause. I was Matthew Reynolds's replacement, not that that egotistical agitator ever really worked for the newspaper. However, before I took over editing it, I had contributed many articles over the years. All in my real name because I was proud of them and still am." There was that bold stare again that had originally intrigued him so. It irritated that he could not help admiring her unapologetic pride in what she was and what she stood for. "K Pendle only came about, reluctantly, when I discovered that I was working for a magistrate and because we all knew that the constable had it in for the paper."

It also annoyed Leo that he found all that plausible, so he turned to something that was already making the roots of his hair twitch. "There was no neighbor who brought you home every night, was there?" She shook her head. "Dare I ask how you did get home?"

"I walked."

Panic wrapped its tentacles around his innards. "From the bloody quay! In the dark! On your own!" He knew that awful truth would keep him up at night as his brain worked through every possible dangerous scenario that she could have encountered.

She winced. "I always carry a pebble in my reticule."

Was she serious? "You think a pebble would stop a gun or a blade or the sort of predator who hides in the shadows on the hunt for a woman?" His heart was racing so fast it was a wonder it didn't bounce up his throat. "You actually thought a pebble would keep you safe?"

She stared down at her clasped hands rather than his wildly waving ones. "I've never had cause to test it."

"More by luck than judgment!" The potential consequences of that reckless choice made him lightheaded. "And what of Mr. Percival Digby and the protest?" Rather than sit beside her on the mattress as he wanted, he folded his waving arms and loomed instead, hoping he at least looked in some sort of control even though his emotions were currently running riot and any grasp he had left on his control was tenuous. "Are you seriously going to deny influencing and aiding Abigail on that score now that we both know that you are a passionate reformer as well as a compulsive liar?"

She sighed. "When Percy arrived at *Equitas* a couple of weeks ago, I had no clue that his fiancée was Abigail."

"What?" How the top of his head didn't explode was a bloody miracle, the anger was so swift and so ferocious. "They are engaged!" His arms unfolded and waved in the air of their own accord again. "Over my dead body will she marry that dangerous libertine!" He was going to wring his sister's bloody neck!

She grimaced. "Sorry. . . . That was clumsy of me. I thought you knew."

"I knew about them! Which is obviously why I tried to put a stop to it—but I did not know that things had escalated so far in their relationship that he had bloody well proposed, and she had accepted!" His hair did stand on end then and, typically, the red mist descended ensuring all he saw was danger. "Not that she can accept without my permission and not that it will bloody well happen—but still!"

He began to pace to reassure himself that the ground was still solid under his feet, because for so many hours now it hadn't been. "How dare he! How *dare* he!"

"He loves her," said their treacherous, backstabbing enabler with a shrug, "and, for what it is worth, I know that he is a good man."

"He's a bloody revolutionary!"

"He's a reformer, just like me. One who wants necessary change but who doesn't want to take up arms to achieve it. But at least unlike me, he comes from your world and, for what it's worth, I think that it is obvious that Abigail loves him too. I know that they are both perhaps too young, but if literature and history are to be believed, there is no force as powerful or as determined as two star-crossed lovers whose love is forbidden. Perhaps if it wasn't, they wouldn't be in such a hurry to dive headlong into forever together?"

He pointed a quaking finger at his treacherous new wife rather than hear any of her unwelcome counsel. "I paid you to chaperone her, not to lecture me on my responsibilities or to provide her with clandestine opportunities to meet with the man I brought her here to avoid! And you—" He jabbed the air between them. "You betrayed me!" And that hurt so much he felt eviscerated.

She nodded, her bare, slim shoulders deflating. "I did—but not easily. The first I knew that Abigail and Percy were together was that fateful night after I got locked out and we . . ." She couldn't look at him then, and he didn't know exactly how to interpret that flash of shyness from a woman who was usually so confident. "I couldn't sleep and saw her sneaking out of the garden, so I followed her as any good chaperone would. I was doing the job you paid me for, right up until Abigail discovered what I did for the newspaper."

"Are you trying to excuse your neglectful behavior by suggesting that my sister blackmailed you into silence?" Inexplicably, as furious at her as he was, a part of him wanted to be able to blame Abigail for Portia's silence. As if that would somehow make it more bearable.

More excusable.

What a bloody pathetic fool he was!

"She didn't. Although it put me in such a terrible and impossible position that I resigned the next morning. I hated lying to you. About everything." There was pain in her lovely eyes. Pain he wanted to believe meant more than just guilt. "But once a lie is out there and it is believed as fact, it is a difficult thing to unravel without dire consequences and, despite all the reasons why I shouldn't have worked here, I liked being here too much to want to leave." Her dark eyes locked with his, pleading. "I swear on my life that neither I nor Percy had any clue that Abigail planned to attend that protest. I will not deny that I have attended plenty of protests in my time and made and waved more homemade placards than I care to count, but I had no sympathy with that one. Nobody at *Equitas* had a hand in what Reynolds did, nor condoned it. We were all warned to go nowhere near it, so I planned to stay here all evening where I had witnesses who could provide me with an ironclad alibi. I only went to fetch your sister once I realized where she had gone, and you know all that happened next."

"Yes, I got to read about it in your scathing article that sealed your fate."

"With hindsight again, I know I shouldn't have printed that. If I hadn't, then perhaps Nolley wouldn't have followed me down to the quay the next day." Regret was etched into her features and his fingers itched to smooth it away. "But I was angry at you for talking me into pleading guilty because I knew the consequences of what would happen if ever my involvement with *Equitas* made its way to the authorities—like it did. Now here we are." She looked miserable and he sympathized. Leo had never felt so damned wretched in his life.

"Here we are." He sunk onto the mattress beside her and wished he did not want to tug her into his arms and just hold her tight and tell her everything was going to be all right—even if it wasn't. But he wasn't ready to forgive her yet. He needed more answers. More proof that his irrational desire to forgive her for everything wasn't just a feckless leap of faith.

"You really shouldn't have married me because the truth is I knew the risks of what I was doing and did them anyway, knowing full well that one day I would have to answer for them in a court of law." Her expression was resigned now but oddly stoic. "Now that I am calmer, more rational, and less petrified, I am fully prepared to face those consequences. I made my bed and I will lie in it, so I will not try to fight the annulment. You married a liar and a criminal when you really shouldn't have. You need to go to London immediately and get this marriage declared null and void, your grace, for your own sake."

Fresh and irrational fury swamped him, only this time tinged with panic. "My first priority is to somehow sort out the enormous mess you have made of everything in the quickest way possible! Until I decide how best to do that . . ." Leo backed away, needing to put as much distance between them as he could until his foolish heart stopped bleeding. "I expect you to fight your overwhelming tendency to lie about everything while trying to behave in a manner more befitting that of the Duchess of Debden—*your grace*!"

Chapter
TWENTY-THREE

She hadn't seen Leo since she had confessed all to him yesterday. Largely because she hadn't plucked up the courage to leave this bedchamber and face the world as a duchess just yet. However, she had, at least, seen the newspaper. It had magically arrived along with the breakfast tray that she had not requested, because, despite her hunger, she could not bring herself to ring the bell. Summoning a servant was something a duchess would do, and that mantle felt as uncomfortable as a pair of stiff shoes that were ten sizes too small.

While the bulk of the news consisted of speculation as to why an eligible duke would marry a rabble-rousing radical revolutionary rather than see her transported (a question she wouldn't mind a proper answer to herself), it did briefly mention what else had happened. It gave her a great deal of relief to know that William and Percy had been released with only a fine. Edgar had too, but she was too angry at him to feel any satisfaction. There was, however, no mention of Jim and nothing about the fate of *Equitas* beyond the news that it had been raided. She suspected it had been raided because of her and that was a bitter pill to swallow. Almost as bitter as the enormous sacrifice her new husband had made for her when she knew she did not deserve it.

However, he had asked her to try to behave like the Duchess of Debden for as long as she remained it, and that was the least she could do while she waited for him to come to his senses and offload her like the local newspaper seemed convinced he would. Rather than ring that privileged bell, which sat in convenient reach of her bedside, she washed in the cold water left on her sumptuous new nightstand and did what she had always done.

She dressed herself.

She had hidden in this bedchamber long enough and it was time to face the music, whatever that music was destined to be. The only thing that was certain was it was completely out of her hands now. She had lost the legal right to have any say in her own future the moment she had accepted Leo's hand.

She took a deep breath and ventured downstairs, colliding with the dowager and her two daughters in the hallway, all wearing their finery. "Good morning, dear—you look much better."

As both Emilia, and especially Abigail, were smiling at her shyly, Portia smiled back. "I might look better but you all look splendid. Where are you off to?"

"To wherever we shall be seen the most." The dowager poked a hatpin to secure the tall, feathered confection that somehow made her look even more imperious. "The only way to deal with a scandal is to own it with unapologetic bravado. Want to come with us?"

"Absolutely not." It was bad enough being a duchess, albeit temporarily, let alone parading around trying to act like one.

"I thought as much." Her new mother-in-law grinned. "It will be far better if you make your debut as a Sloane after we have *duchess-ified* you. The modiste is arriving at five, by the way, to make a start on that, but we shall be back well before then."

"I really do not require the services of a modiste, your grace. Especially as I doubt I shall be here long enough to ever wear anything that she makes." Fine silk and lace wouldn't last five minutes on a convict ship and if Leo did decide to go for an annulment as basic common sense dictated he should, she had no doubt that she would be formally charged with seditious libel yet again and sent to trial.

"Poppycock," said the older woman with a wink. "Leo will never let you go, mark my words. Just like his father, once his heart has picked *the one*, nothing will deter him from that decision." Before Portia could argue that nothing could be further from the truth in their case, Letitia chivvied her daughters with open arms toward the door as if herding sheep. "We must carry on as normal, girls! Backs straight, eyes forward, smile as if you know a great secret that the rest of Bath doesn't, girls, and remember that we are *Sloanes*. And Sloanes do not care one jot what people think of us. Let us have a *very* long and sedate walk all the way around town to prove that."

"We would pass everything and everyone if we walked all the way down to the barracks and back," said Emilia. "That is a particularly long walk."

A comment that earned her a stern glare from Letitia. "Really, Emilia? Our family is in the midst of an epic crisis and all that silly head of yours can think about is soldiers?"

"Well you did say that we were supposed to carry on as normal," said Emilia with an unrepentant shrug. "And I was only trying to be helpful."

"It would be more helpful if you were less trying, dear," said her mother with a roll of her eyes. And with that, the footman flung open the door and they sailed out into the Royal Crescent with their heads held high.

Now what?

"A letter arrived for you this morning, your grace," said the footman awkwardly as he turned to her. She couldn't blame him because up until yesterday they had been in the same boat.

"I am still just Portia to you, Adam."

"That really wouldn't be proper." But his smile was much friendlier as he handed her the missive. "This came by messenger."

She recognized William's spidery handwriting straightaway and quickly took herself into her former office to read it in private. It was brief and to the point. Everyone was safe and they were all gathering at the warehouse at noon to assess the damage and hatch a plan forward. He would be delighted to see her today, but perfectly understood if she wasn't able to come.

She was glad he understood because not being able to go was a pain that was visceral. As painful as discovering that the authorities had taken away all her papers when they had ransacked her bedchamber. How on earth was she supposed to carry on and not be an integral part of the cause she had devoted the last eight years to?

But she owed it to Leo to behave in a manner more befitting the Duchess of Debden for as long as she was the duchess, after all he had sacrificed for her. Just as she owed him his freedom back. "Is his grace at home?"

"He's in his study." The footman pulled a face. "And still in the highest of dudgeons."

"Thanks for the warning."

Leo's door was open as she approached and she could see him bent over a pile of papers, leaning heavily on one hand as he read them with the deepest furrow between his brows that she had ever seen. Rather than sail in like a duchess would undoubtedly do, she knocked.

He jumped, took one look at her, and hastily covered whatever it was that had absorbed his attention so with a ledger. Annulment papers? If they were, she couldn't blame him. The quicker he applied, the more likely it was that one would be granted. "Portia." He didn't look the least bit happy to see her. "How can I help you?"

"By telling me what I am supposed to do, your . . . um . . . Leo."

"About what?"

"About everything." She gestured around her before she bent to acknowledge the dogs who were expecting their customary tickles. "I have no clue how to behave in a manner befitting the Duchess of Debden and would appreciate a steer."

His golden brows furrowed afresh, anger positively shimmering in his deep blue eyes. "Do whatever you want, madam, for I certainly do not care."

"I want to visit *Equitas* today to see the full extent of the damage that I wreaked upon it and check that my friends are as all right as they claim, but I daresay you'd care about that." In the spirit of gratefulness and honesty, she decided to rise above his petulant tone and tossed William's missive onto his desk, noticing the merest dog-eared edge of a copy of *Equitas* poking out from under the ledger. She also recognized that now was probably not the time to ask why Leo was suddenly reading it even if she was itching to know. "In the absence of anything else to do, I would be grateful if you could suggest something that I can do to fill all my new free time instead as I am not the idle, embroidering sort and am used to being busy."

As he glanced at the letter, a myriad of unfathomable emotions skittered across his handsome features before he lifted his wary gaze to her. "You can visit so long as I accompany you."

Portia hadn't expected him to say that in a month of Sundays and her expression doubtless screamed that because she had to haul her gaping jaw back up. "Really?"

"You are not the only one who would like to see the place that you lied so extensively to keep secret, madam."

She didn't know what to think about that and probably should have declined for the safety of her friends and to avoid any further trouble, or simply because she objected to the way he now kept referring to her as "madam," but her gut told her not to. Leo might still be sulking, and frankly he had every right to, but he wasn't the malicious sort. He could get the address easily enough from the authorities who had raided it and visit without her if he chose to, and everyone, barring Jim, had already been charged and couldn't be recharged unless a second offense was committed. "Then I shall be ready to leave whenever is convenient." *Good grief but she hated this new formality between them.* The gaping chasm that had opened up and killed the easiness they'd shared.

"There is no time like the present." He stood and stalked past her. "I'll send for the carriage."

Twenty minutes later, he was sitting opposite her in it as they sped through town. His jaw tight. His lips flattened and his brows still resolutely furrowed deeper than a freshly plowed potato field, making her realize just how much she missed his dimples too. She hadn't seen either of them since the morning she had handed in her notice, and his uncharacteristic silence was deafening.

"If Nolley has been as thorough at the warehouse as he was with my things, I doubt there will be much left to see." Portia spoke her thoughts aloud to break the awkward tension he seemed so determined to maintain.

"What, precisely, did he take of yours?" His question was abrupt and his expression stony, letting her know in no uncertain terms that he resented the interruption.

"Only my words." Which were everything. "Every single essay I have written since I was sixteen." She tried to shrug as if it didn't matter, but it did. "Every decent one at least."

"If it's evidence of sedition, then it is probably best gone."

"I do not just write sedition, Leo—not that I see the necessary need to argue for reform as sedition. There was a great deal of personal correspondence to myself among all those stolen papers too."

One golden brow broke rank and arched, spoiling the impenetrable mask of disappointed disinterest he had chosen to wear in her presence. "You write letters to yourself?"

"I write essays to myself, actually. Whenever I have a conundrum or a crisis or even if I am upset or out of sorts, I ask myself a question and debate it thoroughly on paper. It helps me organize my thoughts and find the right path forward. The sort that are so intensely personal and cringeworthy that I'd probably rather die than let anyone ever read. But now Nolley has." And that made her feel queasy. "He's stolen my little chest filled with eight years' of mortifying soul-searching and youthful overdramatics as well as the bigger one containing all my life's work. It is all gone. Every single thing that I have ever written." Which felt like a piece of her was missing. "He even took my pens, for pity's sake. Because clearly, if they are mine, they are poison pens that have no right existing. Although I do appreciate the irony of my particular old, overused nib being seen as such a powerful weapon when I have always believed that the pen is mightier than the sword."

He almost smiled. "You do have a way with words, madam, I will give you credit for that."

Purely to vex him, she smiled back, despite feeling utterly broken inside. "It's Portia, Leo, and not "madam." Unless you want to go back to being called your grace, *your grace*."

His blue eyes narrowed slightly, but only with feigned irritation. "Just take the compliment without the lecture, woman, as I can assure you they will be thin on the ground in the future." Then his gaze hardened as the carriage turned onto the quay. "I see we have arrived at the scene of the crime."

Despite his determination to remain angry at her, he still helped her solicitously out of the carriage, even if he did treat her hand like a snake that he was quick to let go of. Then he quietly followed her down the overgrown path to the back of the warehouse.

The first thing Portia noticed was the state of the door; the old wood splintered as if somebody had gone at it with an axe. She could hear movement inside and so as not to alarm anyone, announced her arrival as she pushed what was left of the door open. "Hello."

"Portia!" It was William's voice. "Thank goodness you are safe!" He came to greet her, then stopped dead when he saw Leo. "And I see that you have brought your new husband along. It is a pleasure to meet Portia's rescuer, you grace. I am William Stowe, Sir William for my sins although we don't bother with all that here." He held out his hand and, to her surprise, her new husband took it and shook it.

"I didn't exactly give her a choice not to bring me, sir."

"Is this official business then, your grace?"

Leo shook his head and left it at that, so an awkward silence descended until Portia filled it. "How bad is it?"

William ushered them both in. "Come see for yourself, dear girl, but I'll warn you it's not a pretty sight."

And it wasn't.

If the offices of *Equitas* had looked shambolic before the constable had arrived, it looked like a rampaging Viking army had pillaged it after. Thousands of sheets of the large blank paper they printed the newspaper on covered every inch of the floor, as the wrapped bundles they were usually stacked in had been torn open. Every single tiny typesetting block was scattered like seed. All their research books had been yanked from the shelves, ripped to pieces, and trampled all over. Every desk was smashed. Every chair shattered and poor Bessie the printing press was reduced to a pile of mangled parts on the floor. To add insult to injury, Nolley's men had poured all their printing ink over everything to ensure nothing could be reused.

Jim, who had been rifling through Bessie's twisted metal for bits that could be salvaged, paused to give her a smile.

"I'm glad you're safe, Portia. I thought you were done for."

"So did I." She still might be, but that wasn't a conversation for now. Any more than asking how he had managed to evade capture was when a magistrate was standing not six feet away, albeit one of the good ones. "I'm glad you're safe too, Jim." She gestured to Bessie's remains. "Can she be fixed?"

"I'll do my best." But even with his skill as a mechanic, they both knew that the ancient heart of *Equitas* would likely never beat again. "But be prepared for the worst."

Leo's eyes were everywhere. The only indication of any emotion was his intensely furrowed brows, but if they were from disgust at this wanton destruction or for the newspaper or for her involvement in it, she could not decipher.

"The constable kept us here to watch while they did this," said William. "He went for Bessie with the sledgehammer himself, but had to hand it over to his men because she put up quite the fight."

"We should have offered him a bribe." That came from a disgusted Jim, who was staring levelly at Leo, not caring if he was friend or foe. "Word is he's partial to one."

"Only if your face fits," added William. "We could have offered him a king's ransom and he still would have done this to us."

"Ay, and pocketed the money regardless." Jim folded his beefy arms. "He's an upstanding fellow, our constable."

If their plan was to bait Leo, he took it all in with silent indifference.

Portia gestured to the mess. "If this is what they left, what did they take?"

"Everything with anything written on it," said William in resignation. "Every letter, every note, every single piece of correspondence. Our entire archive of back issues. Basically, anything and everything that they thought might be incriminating. But we are all resolute—*Equitas* will continue." Now it was William who stared at Leo, defiant. "It will rise like a phoenix from these ashes and come back stronger. Just as soon as we can secure new premises and beg, borrow, or steal a new printing press. The truth needs to be told and all of us here and in the wider reform movement are committed to telling it."

Portia had to ask. "Including Edgar?"

"That backstabbing Judas hasn't yet shown his face," said Jim with a snarl. "Just as well, because I am determined to rearrange it for him."

"You will have to stand in line after me." That came from William. "If the blabbermouth coward has any sense, he will realize that he is no longer welcome here after the way he hung you out to dry. There was no excuse to implicate you when you weren't even here when they raided! His malicious treachery is unforgivable."

It was, but after a great deal of soul-searching, she understood Edgar's motives even if she did not condone them. "We all know that *Equitas* was raided because of me." She wasn't afraid to say what they were all too kind to. She had brought this dreadful calamity straight to their door. Because she had played with fire with the handsome duke who had tempted her so much that she hadn't been able to muster the willpower to resist. "I cannot tell you how sorry I am about that. I should have known that the constable would have me followed after my first arrest. But instead, I came straight here the very next day and this is the result." Tears of guilt and shame pricked her eyes. "I played with fire, just as Edgar warned, and you all got burned."

"My dear girl," said William wrapping a comforting arm around her. "My name features in our seditious rag every single week and always has, so who says he didn't follow me here? Or Percy or Jim or Edgar himself?"

"Because it is too much of a coincidence." She swiped her self-pitying tears away with impatience. "I should have gone back to London after my first arrest just as he wanted and, selfishly, I didn't." Of their own accord her eyes flicked to Leo and his locked with hers, curious, until she tore them away. "I loathe myself for it."

Percy arrived then, dragging a large crate behind him through the door. "I found this. It might be useful to put anything worth saving in so we can move it to wherever we end up." He saw her and beamed as he rushed toward her. "Thank god you are all right, Portia, I've been worried sick." He was about to hug her when he spotted Leo and froze, all the color draining instantly from his face as he inclined his head. "Your grace."

"Mr. Digby." Never had two words conveyed such malice. If looks could kill, poor Percy would now be as dead as a doornail. For several tense moments, Leo stared at him while they all held their breath. "I'll wait for you in the carriage, madam." With that, he spun on his heel and stalked out.

Percy looked absolutely terrified, so she squeezed his hand. "He's angry but he can be very reasonable and sensible when he isn't in a temper, so he'll come around. I am sure of it." Or at least she hoped he would for Percy's sake. There was a slim chance of him extending the same to her. "If it is any consolation, the majority of his fury is directed at me. He only thinks that he hates you. He now absolutely loathes me with every fiber of his being."

"But he still made you his duchess," said Jim with a sympathetic smile. "So maybe his loathing is only temporary."

"It is more likely that me being his duchess is only temporary." With Leo out of earshot, there seemed little point in not telling them how precarious her position still was. "Let's face it, he knows that he has more than enough grounds to have our hasty marriage declared null and void, then who knows what will happen? I could still be charged. Still tried and found guilty." But as much as her uncertain future scared her, she put a brave face on. "But I daresay they need reformers more in the new world than they do even here, so every cloud."

"He won't throw you to the wolves, Portia, nor divorce you." It was Percy's turn to squeeze her hand. "Abigail suspects he has strong feelings for you."

"Oh he does—just all of them are negative."

"He can't be all bad if he's allowed you to come back here," said William.

"Accompanied by him is what he actually said. He has also made it plain that while I live under his roof, I need to behave in a manner more befitting the Duchess of Debden."

"And?" He seemed amused. "You do not strike me as the sort of woman who would pay any attention to a hasty vow to obey your husband, especially one who isn't likely to remain your husband for very long."

"For now, I fear that I owe it to him to. He has just saved me from a fate worse than death, after all." Surely that meant that she was morally obligated to retire her pen and behave in a manner more befitting the Duchess of Debden for however long she remained his duchess? An eye for an eye and a sacrifice for a sacrifice?

Even if the sacrifice he expected her to make currently felt like a fate worse than death too.

Chapter
TWENTY-FOUR

"Your grace!" All the color drained from Nolley's face at the sight of Leo on his doorstep.

"Mr. Nolley." He used the "Mr." on purpose because the man wasn't fit to carry the title constable. He never had been, truth be told, but the events of the last few days had cemented the need to relieve the man of his post with all haste. Not just because of all the egregious things he had done to Portia, although those factored the highest among Leo's reasons for being here this morning, but because his heavy hands had no place being linked to the law. "Can I come in?"

Nolley looked decidedly shifty and uncomfortable as he shook his head, almost as if he knew this meeting wasn't going to end well. "I'm pressed for time at the moment, your grace, and need to take some statements from witnesses to the protest before the ringleaders stand trial next week."

"I have transferred responsibility for that to *Constable* Richardson." A reasonable man with a strong civic conscience who had voluntarily served Bath well as an occasional watchman for many years and who, at the very least, seemed to have a good grasp on what was right and what was wrong.

Nolley's eyes narrowed as he began to put two and two together. "Since when has Richardson been a constable?"

"Since I offered him your job an hour ago." As there seemed little point in beating around the bush, Leo delivered his final blow for now. "I no longer have any faith in your abilities, Mr. Nolley, and refuse to employ a man who thinks using force on a woman is acceptable."

Instantly Nolley's temper exploded. "That liar's got your knackers in a vise if she's convinced you of that! I didn't punch her!" He dared to shake his fists, so a split second later he found himself pushed up against his porch; his short legs fighting for purchase on the ground because Leo had hoisted the little shit upward by his lapels so he could snarl directly in his obnoxious face.

"But you pushed her, didn't you, Nolley? You enjoyed inflicting bruises on a scared and manacled woman who couldn't fight back, all to get back at me, didn't you, you pathetic, bloody coward?" He took great satisfaction at the way the man's eyes bulged in fear in his reddened face. "So now it's my turn to repay that favor!"

Nolley winced as if expecting a physical blow, but Leo wanted a more fitting revenge. A more lasting one. He let go of his former constable and wiped his hands as if he had handled something nasty, which he undeniably had. "You are dismissed, Mr. Nolley. Effective immediately."

"Suits me!" Nolley bellowed at Leo's retreating back. "I'll go to work for Lord Corston instead, you pious, sanctimonious, lily-livered, pedantic *liberal*!" He spat that last word as if it were somehow an insult. "He'll employ me as a constable."

Over Leo's dead body would that ever happen, but Leo didn't bother turning around because he was all done with Nolley—for now at least.

Once Leo had all the evidence he needed against him, Nolley would get his full just deserts. But for now, this would have to do. "I wish you well prising any wages out of him. It is only us lily-livered liberals who believe in paying their constables—or providing them with comfortable cottages to live in rent-free." But he couldn't resist twisting to deliver his last, killer line. "Be sure to have your corrupt and sadistic arse out of this one precisely one week from today or I shall take great pleasure in tossing you out on it!"

Several hours later, Leo found himself staring at Portia's little chest on his study floor. He had requested it from the clerk of court on the off chance, convinced all the private papers that seemed to mean so much to her would have been destroyed by the vengeful Nolley just as everything else that she had written had been. But the clerk had miraculously found the battered marquetry box among a mountain of other confiscated items pertaining to the protest that had just been left at the prison.

Obviously, Leo was going to return it to his wife. That went without saying because not only was it the right thing to do, but it was the kind thing to do too. She had lost her independence, her beloved *Equitas*, and what she had wistfully called her life's work all in one fell swoop, and he wanted to at least give something back to her. Something precious to her that might banish the stoic sadness that had taken permanent residence in her lovely eyes since he had married her.

But should he take a peek inside first? That was his quandary.

On the one hand, inspecting the contents was obviously a gross invasion of her privacy. Especially when he knew that these were her personal, soul-searching essays to herself. On the other, he was desperate to learn as much about the woman who now bore his name as possible in the hope that it would guide him in what to do about her next. Because currently, he had no bloody idea, and avoiding her like the plague, which had been his strategy for the last few days, wasn't a long-term solution. He had barely slept a wink. Every single time he closed his eyes, he was either swamped with hurt at all her lies, filled with fury at himself for falling for them, or consumed with guilt at his part in her downfall. All that was mixed with an enormous dollop of lust, thanks to the wholly unwelcome but indelible memory of how blasted good she had looked in her birthday suit!

Not that his waking hours were any less painful when the minx now utterly consumed him. If he wasn't mulling over her, he was frantically trying to find any diversion that might stop him mulling, so far with minimal success. Not even his dogged quest to find the evidence to get her first conviction quashed, as he had solemnly promised her, diverted his attention that far from Portia, because ultimately it was her he was doing all that digging for. Her he was seeking justice and retribution for. Like a man possessed. Or obsessed. Or just pathetic.

Or likely all three.

Frankly, for the sake of his sanity, something tangible had to shift his dilemma one way or another, or he was going to go bloody stark staring mad. Because he needed a valid reason to either forgive her or forget her. To want her or want her gone. To love her or loathe her. Where his tumultuous feelings for Portia were concerned, there really couldn't be an in-between.

Which all rather suggested that just a quick, cursory glance into this battered and well-loved box was the answer. And was invading her privacy a little a crime when she had told him such a pack of lies that he didn't know which, if any, of her words he could actually trust?

Because Barkington and Snifferson were currently staring at him with the same intensity as he was staring at her box, he deferred to them. "What do I do, boys?" He tapped the offending wood with his toe. "Should I open it or not?"

Snifferson sniffed it, then resumed staring at Leo, perplexed, but when Barkington barked that felt like a permission. Before remorse set in as it inevitably would, he lifted the chest onto his desk, winced at the enormous rush of guilt that flooded him, but still flipped the lid.

He only gave the contents a cursory glance, simply to ascertain that they were indeed hers and that they were still in there. That wasn't a violation of her privacy, was it? It was diligence.

Surely?

He leaned over, ensuring his hands were firmly clamped behind his back in case looking became touching, when touching crossed the line.

Inside was, unsurprisingly, stuffed with papers all written in Portia's bold and flamboyant hand. Essays that smelled unsettlingly of her perfume; each folded into a neat rectangle so none of her precious arguments became separated but making them impossible to surreptitiously read.

Apart from one that he noticed had been stuffed down the side. The only one that wasn't folded closed.

He twisted his head to attempt to read it and that was when he saw the underlined question at the top: *Is it just the dimples or is it more?*

Bloody hell! She'd written an essay about him! Leo knew that without a shadow of a doubt as he was now a bit of an expert on her distinctive writing style after he had spent hours and hours since their nuptials poring through every back issue of that damned newspaper that he could get his hands on. Whether she was the incognito K Pendle the editor or the P Kendall who had been a bold and brazen regular contributor over the last few years, she still wrote with a clever combination of pith and wit. Always starting with a question and then answering it with Portia-esque aplomb. Her arguments well researched, reasoned, and flawlessly convincing—just as they were when she vocalized them.

But what conclusions had his clever wife come to about him?

Rightly or wrongly—most definitely wrongly—he had to know and snatched the essay up.

Two weeks ago, if you would have asked me if there could possibly be anything redeeming about a duke, even a particularly handsome one, I would have emphatically said no. For dukes, as a breed, are an entitled and privileged lot who are so out of touch with those beneath them that it would be practically impossible for someone with such strong reforming ideals as mine to even find anything to like, let alone admire. That, of course, was before I collided with the Duke of Dimples. A charming, liberal-minded man with such an easy manner, twinkling blue eyes, and the most disarming smile that I have ever seen. But is it just his dimples that have turned my usually sensible head, or is there more to him that calls to me than his obvious attractiveness?

To answer that properly, I must first and most reluctantly discuss those distracting dimples . . .

The light knock on the door had him guiltily jumping out of his skin.

"Leo?" The sound of Portia's voice made him stuff her essay back into the box and shut the lid. "Sorry to disturb you but you have a visitor."

He flung himself into his chair, pushed the box to the furthest edge of his desk and yanked open a ledger in a pathetic attempt to look consumed with something other than her. "What visitor?"

She swung the door open to reveal M'Lady Whiskers hanging from the doorknob and smiled. "Her worshipfulness couldn't get in."

He smiled too, widely, so that his distracting dimples showed, as the imperious Persian dropped to the floor and sauntered in as if she owned the place. She gave Barkington her customary hiss, leaped up onto his desk, then promptly curled into a ball right on the ledger he had pretended to be reading.

"Don't mind me, M'Lady. I was only working. Your sleep is so much more important."

"Good luck moving her now." In the spirit of the awkward truce they had fallen into, Portia did not cross the threshold of his study and instead leaned against the doorframe. "She's pretty much taken over my bed and if I try to reclaim any more than the sliver of the mattress she has deigned to leave me, she can be quite rude about it."

"To be fair to M'Lady, she had declared that room hers long before you moved into it and if she's granted you a sliver then she has clearly agreed to tolerate you—which is a rare honor indeed. Trust me, Emilia isn't allowed anywhere on the sofa if the cat is on it, and she despises Abigail so much since the incident with the bird that she's taken to hissing at her whenever they collide. But M'Lady adores me." To prove that, he scratched the spot under the Persian's ears and she immediately vibrated loudly as she purred. "I think it's because she cannot resist a man with dimples." Like the pathetic fool he was, he then grinned some more in the vain hope that they still worked their magic on his reluctant wife.

"Or maybe it's just because you are a man and your cat dislikes all women? Perhaps she sees us all as rivals for your affection? Or perhaps she's just nasty to everyone, irrespective of their sex, and it is only you that she tolerates?" She pushed herself from the frame. "I shall leave you to . . ." That was when she noticed the box on his desk and blinked, first in disbelief and then in wariness. "Is that my . . ."

"It is."

She rushed forward, went to touch it, and then stopped herself. "Can I . . . ?"

"Of course. It is yours, after all."

The beaming smile she offered him then took his breath away. "Did you get it back for me?"

He gave her a noncommittal shrug, not wanting to admit that he had, but also still wanting her to be pleased that he had at the same time. Because he was pathetic. "I knew how much it meant to you."

"Oh Leo." That came out as a sigh. "Thank you." Then she frowned. "Are the contents still in it or has everything been confiscated?"

He shrugged again and focused on stroking the cat rather than lie to her hopeful face. "You'd have to check inside to see as it certainly wasn't my place to." *How the blazes had she lied so effortlessly when just this tiny fib was making his buttocks clench?*

She lifted the lid and a delighted bubble of laughter escaped.

"They left all my papers!" Then she rummaged to the bottom and giggled as she pulled out an old friend. "And my poison pen!" She hugged the pen to her chest and gazed at him as if he were suddenly her hero. "Thank you. I cannot tell you how much this means to me."

"You are very welcome." Then, because he rather liked being her hero, he added, "You should also know that I did some digging and discovered that it wasn't your fault that the authorities found *Equitas*. It was actually Sir William who was followed." He retrieved the watchman's statement from the drawer in his desk that he had liberated from the official files and slid it over to her. "Nolley got a warrant to do so from Lord Corston."

She quickly read it and a bit more of the sadness in her eyes dissipated. "That is a huge weight off my mind. I've barely slept worrying about this. I am surprised I haven't kept you awake too with all my fevered pacing from dawn to dusk next door."

He had heard her pacing while he had stared listlessly up at his ceiling endlessly mulling all his own worries. He'd lost count of how many times he had wanted to just fling open that flimsy door that connected their rooms to try to sort everything out between them. "You didn't disturb me. I've slept like a log." His buttocks clenched some more. "But you can rest easy now." If only the causes of his insomnia could be banished with the arrival of a box! Hurt, lust, and unrequited love combined made deep sleep impossible.

She stared at the watchman's statement some more. "Can we keep this between us, Leo?" Her eyes lifted to his sheepishly. "Only, William has always been particular about security and would be devastated to learn that he had compromised it with an uncharacteristic bit of carelessness. *Equitas* is his life."

"As you wish."

"And thank you again. For everything." There was something different swirling in her expressive dark eyes now. Something tender and affectionate that filled his aching, wounded heart with hope. "You have been so—"

"Leo!" His mother's shrill shout effectively spoiled what was promising to be another nice moment. "You've just received an express!" She burst through the door waving a letter. "From the king!"

"What?" He held out his hand in disbelief, convinced his mother had got it wrong, but the second he saw the enormous Royal Seal he realized that she hadn't.

"Open it!" His mother bounced with excitement. "Open it this second!"

"I would, Mother, if you would actually give it to me."

She handed it over and he cracked the wax. Then almost groaned aloud. "We've been summoned to London."

"We?" All the delight on Portia's pretty face had now melted into horror as his mother snatched the missive back. "Surely you mean you?"

"No, it clearly states the both of you." His mother squealed with glee before she read. "His Majesty King George IV and her Royal Highness Princess Sophia request that the Duke of Debden present the new Duchess of Debden to the court of St. James's on Wednesday the twenty-seventh day of June." Then she frowned. "That is cutting it a bit fine! It gives us just ten days, half of which will be taken up with travel and preparation, and Portia's new gowns aren't even back from the modiste yet! But if I send her a message now with the good news, I am sure that she can rush some to us before you have to leave. And of course, she is going to have to make a court dress!" Then she clapped her hands. "Oh my goodness, this is so exciting!"

His mother hugged her, completely oblivious to the fact that Portia's stunned expression was the exact opposite of excited. "I'll also send for the hairdresser immediately. And get the staff to start making all the necessary arrangements and . . ." She squealed again. "There is so much to do and not enough hours left of today to do it all in!"

They both watched her practically sprint out before Portia finally spoke. "Can't you politely decline?"

"I might well be a privileged duke, but I am nowhere near important enough to refuse the monarch. This is a summons, not an invitation." He didn't like it any more than she did, but a royal summons was a royal summons. "We are going to have to leave first thing on Sunday morning if we stand any chance of getting all the way to Mayfair in time."

"But Leo . . ." Fear mixed with her panic. "We cannot pretend to be a happily married couple in front of the king if we aren't likely to remain a couple for very long. Surely it would make getting an annulment so much more difficult?"

Clearly, he had pathetically misread her gratefulness as affection if she still preferred the idea of an annulment over staying married to him. "I cannot ignore the king's summons and neither can you."

She opened her mouth to argue but his mother came back. "When I said that there was a lot to do, Portia, I did not mean that only I had to do it. This is all about you, so come along, dear, and stop dawdling!"

Then she grabbed his reluctant wife's arm and dragged her away.

Chapter
TWENTY-FIVE

Portia had gone from twiddling her thumbs with nothing to do to not having a single moment to herself. If she wasn't being poked and tugged by the modiste while she endured fitting after fitting, she had to suffer what Letitia called "duchess training."

Duchess training consisted of being accomplished in a series of nonsensical behaviors that were only apparently needed in a royal court. One of those things was a court curtsy, which was vastly different to the sorts she had been bobbing her entire life and basically involved contortionism at a veritable snail's pace. Her weight on her right foot, she was supposed to gracefully circle the toes of her left foot to rest directly behind it, then somehow, without losing her precarious balance, dip all the way down until her left knee practically hit the floor. All without bending at the waist or using her hands, which had to hold a pointless fan just so, while the other subtly held her skirts to stop her falling over. Then, after a respectful incline of her head, she had to rise effortlessly "like steam," according to the dowager, which was absolute torture on the thigh and calf muscles.

Yesterday, after a whole afternoon of relentless tutoring, Portia had thought that she had mastered it—but apparently not. Now that she had grasped the basics, she was having to learn it all again in the makeshift court garments that the dowager had brought to the drawing room to torture her some more with this evening. Because the appropriate ladies' court attire was even more ridiculous than the painful court curtsy, consisting of a long and heavy train (which presently was a blanket tied around her waist) and a headdress that consisted of at least seven tall, snow-white ostrich feathers, which made contorting herself into that curtsy practically impossible! Not that she was currently sporting ostrich feathers as all their court feathers lived in Mayfair. Instead, Letitia had strapped an arrangement of dried flowers to Portia's head using several yards of ribbon and at least three million hairpins. This particular arrangement was chosen because it was filled with fluffy, waving meadow grasses that were, apparently, the exact right height. Which, frankly, beggared belief when they were well over a foot long.

"That's almost it," said her tormentor, as Portia dipped all the way down to the floor for the thousandth time. "But you are still sprinkling dried petals on the carpet, a sure sign that you are juddering on your descent. We want one fluid and graceful movement on the way down and one on the way up." The dowager wafted her hand regally up and down in demonstration as if this impossible task was simple. "So gentle that all those petals stay on the stems."

Portia bit her tongue and tried again, only to be sprinkled with more confetti the second she inclined her head. She pulled a scratchy clump from her cleavage and tossed them in frustration. "These stupid flowers are dead, so of course I am sprinkling petals everywhere!" And the combination of the spikey stalks and the heavy hairpins digging into her scalp were starting to give her a headache.

"You need to extend your neck a tiny bit more and hold your head as steady as one of the lanterns on top of the sturdy lampposts outside. Then incline it more slowly as yours is starting to resemble a nod, and a nod has no place being seen at the palace."

"In case it has escaped your notice, neither do I!" As Portia shot her mother-in-law a glare, Abigail came to her rescue and tossed aside the book she had been pretending to read while she thoroughly enjoyed the entertainment.

"Before one of you kills the other and the poor maids have to get blood as well as all those trodden-in petals out of the carpet, why don't we all take a short break for tea?"

"An excellent idea." Before the pain in her left thigh turned fully into a cramp, Portia rubbed it as she staggered to the sofa. "Can you put some fortifying brandy in mine? Better still, just pour me a stiff brandy and dispense with the tea!"

She ignored M'Lady Whiskers's warning hiss and raised hackles to flop onto the sofa next to her. "Go ahead, devil cat—scratch me. Because today I can assure you that I will scratch you back!" The cat glared out of her different-colored eyes while she decided whether or not to attack and then clearly saw that Portia was in no mood to be trifled with, so readjusted her sleeping position and ignored her instead.

While Abigail rang for the tea and Emilia tried her best not to laugh as she hid behind her easel while pretending to paint, Portia's fingers went to the knotted ribbons under her chin.

"Leave that on," said Letitia, admonishing her yet again. "It will do you good to learn how to hold yourself in your court headdress as you'll likely have to wear it for a couple of hours after your presentation."

Portia huffed, well aware that she was being petulant but entirely comfortable with it. "I never thought I'd ever wish to be back in that prison cell, but suddenly it doesn't seem so bad. This is all ridiculous." She pointed to the contraption on her head. "I am ridiculous. The court rules are especially ridiculous. Will somebody really count the feathers on my headdress to check that there are at least seven?"

"Oh it's all very formal, dear." Letitia sunk into a chair, an amused but sympathetic expression on her face. "But at least George IV has dispensed with his mother's more stringent requirements. Queen Charlotte preferred the fashions of her youth to be worn, so up until a few years ago, a lady's court dress resembled something Marie Antoinette would wear. As I know to my cost, that involved a stiff, unyielding bodice, a corset laced so tight you couldn't breathe, and an enormous pannier and hoops that were so wide at the hips that the only way to enter the chamber was sideways. And we still had to wear the feathers. How I didn't pass out when I was presented at court was a miracle. A woman in her seventh month of pregnancy isn't supposed to wear a corset but no allowances were made for that."

"Are you saying that I am getting off lightly?"

"I would have killed for soft stays and just seven ostrich feathers, dear. I had swollen up and was swooning so much by the end of it, Rafe had to slice me out of my gown in the carriage. But even so, it was such an exciting day that I look back at it fondly. You will too."

"I sincerely doubt that. Even if I master the curtsy and the headdress, I am still a walking scandal, remember? And a commoner. In fact, I am fairly certain that I am the most unlikely and unsuitable duchess in the history of duchesses and everyone will hate me."

Letitia threw back her head and laughed. "So was I and that was part of the fun! I made a game out of counting all the disapproving looks before I stopped and engaged with every single one, which forced them to curtsy to me. Because I realized that being one of the few duchesses in the realm meant that I suddenly outranked all those snobs, which really outraged them. Trust me, there is nothing more rewarding than being on the receiving end of a begrudging curtsy."

"Mama was never supposed to be a duchess either," explained Emilia from behind her easel. "Her father was a merchant, not an aristocrat. They caused quite the scandal but the story is *sooooo* romantic." The hopelessly romantic Emilia then sighed as she clutched her brush to her heart. "Because their forbidden love conquered all."

"Really?" That was news to Portia. "But you are so . . ." She searched for the right words and couldn't find the right one. "Duchess-like."

"I shall tell you a secret," said Letitia leaning closer. "Being a duchess is a state of mind, one that it is handy to employ when required and best ignored at all other times."

"How did a merchant's daughter end up a duchess?"

"Against all the odds." Letitia grinned. "Rafe's family did not approve of me in the slightest and forbade him to have anything to do with me. They had him earmarked for some marquess's daughter, I believe. But when a Sloane man decides he has met the one, nothing will stand in his way. We met for the first time at the May fayre here in Bath at the tender age of fifteen. Obviously, I hated him on sight but he was tenacious and we plighted our troths just two months later. It was all very intense and romantic as first loves are prone to be—but we were inseparable from that moment on. Obviously, because I was so far beneath him, we had to meet in secret for years—which was thrilling, as the forbidden always is. Then as soon as we both turned one-and-twenty, which conveniently happened within weeks of one another, we ran away to Gretna Green to tie the knot."

Emilia giggled. "They had to."

"The plot thickens." It had staggered Portia how quickly these three women had accepted her as part of the family. Since the night of the protest, Abigail especially had softened toward her. Whereas Leo's mother had been nothing but kind and accepting of her from the outset. She had even been a willing witness at their wedding when most aristocrats' mothers would have tried to talk their sons out of such a travesty. "Do tell?" She already knew enough about this mischievous woman to know that few topics were ever off-limits.

The older woman chuckled at the memory. "It was a close-run thing, I can tell you, as I had the devil of the job disguising my fat belly under my skirts until my birthday. We got married on the day of it and Leo popped out three months later. I cannot tell you what a scandal it all was and, because Rafe was the heir to a dukedom, it was all over the papers for months."

That explained so much about why his mother had never judged her for where she had come from. "So it is all Leo's fault that you almost passed out at the palace?

"Why do I hear my name said in vain?" he asked as he strode through the door looking all windswept and handsome. Then he stopped dead, smiled, and dazzled Portia with his dimples. "And why the blazes do you have a haystack on your head?"

"It's a floral arrangement actually." She was proud that she managed to say that with a completely straight face despite the blush that instantly heated her cheeks. "Which is standing in for an ostrich."

"Of course it is." He helped himself to a biscuit as the maid carrying the tea tray passed him. "Because a giant bird makes so much more sense."

"We are practicing Portia's court curtsy," said his mother.

"Which has to be performed with a minimum of seven tall ostrich plumes sprouting from my cranium or society will apparently crumble."

"Who knew it was only ostrich feathers that held it up?" His blue eyes danced, making her realize how much she had missed them. They had been so politely formal to one another since their wedding that she longed for the easiness they had once shared before she had gone and made him hate her. "Then I have to walk out of the room backward without tripping over the ludicrous train that I also have to wear because I am reliably informed that it isn't the done thing to turn your downturned gaze or your back to the monarch. Which is a shame as I was hoping to prostrate myself on the floor at his royal feet after tugging my forelock as someone who is as unworthy as me undoubtedly should."

"Portia is chafing against some of our ancient traditions, Leo," said Abigail with a smile. "And if you want my opinion, big brother—"

"Which I don't."

"—I do not think your wife has much respect for our king."

"That makes two of us." Leo offered her another brief smile before he chomped on his biscuit. "But what can you do?" Portia bit back the "oust him and replace him with a republic" that almost popped out of her mouth, but by the light of challenge in his gaze, he still expected it.

"What have you been doing all day?" His mother poured the tea. "Only that's the fourth day in a row now that you've missed breakfast. We've hardly seen you."

"I've been busy."

"Doing what? I thought you had told the bench that you were recusing yourself from the chore of it for a few weeks." That was also news to Portia. Especially as he had seemed so determined to make the constable pay for pushing her around.

"Important ducal things, Mama," he said cryptically. "I won't bore you with the details."

Letitia immediately gave Portia a peeved look. "That was exactly what his father used to say when he didn't want to tell me what he'd been up to." Then she skewered her son with her glare. "Just so long as your important ducal things are done for the day as we are *all* going to the Assembly Rooms tonight for Portia's debut as a duchess. A debut which she cannot possibly make without her woefully absent husband."

"I got that message loud and clear the first three hundred times you reminded me, Mother. Hence, I am home early, ready to be bedecked in all my finery, exactly as instructed." He slanted Portia a mischievous glance this time that did outrageous things to certain parts of her. "Although I might have to rethink my choice of waistcoat as I fear the one I've had pressed is going to clash with your magnificent haystack."

Chapter

TWENTY-SIX

Leo had been right by her side all night acting like the solicitous husband, but was so politely detached that he might as well not have been. Portia wished she knew what was going on in his handsome head, but to do that they would actually have to have a more than superficial conversation. She was dreading their long journey to London almost as much as she was dreading meeting the king, as that was bound to be as awkward and painful as tonight was.

Unfortunately, it wasn't only Portia who had noticed his standoffishness, because by the way she was staring at her son, his mother had too. The pair of them had exchanged several hushed words over the last hour and each set had Letitia rolling her eyes. Now that they had finally finished exchanging pleasantries with everyone in the Assembly Rooms, the three of them were stood together near the refreshment table. Sipping weak glasses of punch while watching the dance floor and pretending to be having as nice a time as the social butterfly Emilia was on it.

The country dance came to an end and suddenly the volume in the crowded ballroom increased as all the young ladies in the ballroom chattered in excitement while they searched over their fluttering fans for their next partners.

"It's the waltz," said Letitia with a pointed look toward her son. "The dance of love." Then she nudged him hard. "So unless you want to see more scathing speculation in the newspapers, I suggest you go dance with your wife."

He huffed, which wasn't a particularly flattering response, and then begrudgingly held out his hand. "If we must."

Portia wanted to tell the rude swine to stick his begrudging hand where the sun didn't shine but slapped hers in it and allowed him to lead her to the floor. Conscious of absolutely everyone's eyes on them, she pasted on a smile as he twirled her into his arms and waited for the music to start.

His gaze, of course, was resolutely over her shoulder and his jaw was locked as tight as a miser's purse. "Is your plan to punish me with indifference until you can escape this mockery of a marriage?" That got his attention, and his eyes snapped to hers. "Or do I need to remind you that it was your idea, not mine?"

"Why do you always do that? Why do you take every available opportunity to remind me that you want an annulment?"

"Don't you?"

His gaze flicked away again. "I've been busy."

What the hell did that mean? "Time is ticking and the longer you leave it, the harder it will be to achieve." A nerve in his jaw twitched. "If you feel any misguided sense of obligation about the authorities charging me again, you really shouldn't. I made my bed and I certainly do not expect you to lie in it with me."

His eyes locked with hers again and shimmered with frustration. "I wouldn't be able to live with myself if they did that and sent you away."

"They would not be able to do that if you were able to get my first conviction quashed as you promised."

Leo, of course, reacted badly to that. "I am a man of my word and do not need reminding of anything I promise!" The quick flash of temper morphed back into frustration. "What the hell do you think I've been doing all week? After I sacked Nolley I've spent every spare hour pulling all the records apart to hunt for any proof that he was a liar who fabricates evidence. I've even interviewed the soldiers who arrested you to try and get them to admit that their statements are false."

That double bolt out of the blue knocked her sideways. "You dismissed Nolley?"

"Of course I did! Did you honestly think I would allow him to keep his post after what he did to you?" The ferociousness of that protective declaration staggered her. "Nobody gets to treat one of mine like that and get away without paying!"

One of mine? It shocked her how much that phrase thrilled her. "And now you are investigating him? Why didn't you tell me any of this?"

"Do you confide in me?" It was a toothless barb as beneath her palms, his solid shoulders slumped. "I didn't want to build your hopes up. Especially as those soldiers aren't stupid enough to admit to perjury. I think I might have found another avenue to pursue but the files are huge, there are a lot to wade through, and interviews take time. I have to do them covertly to avoid tipping Nolley off that I am investigating him in case he covers his tracks."

"I could help. . . . I am excellent at researching and two heads are always better than one. Please let me." She watched his expression shutter and knew he was going to say no. He was the man of the house. He knew best. "Please Leo. I'm going slowly mad with nothing meaningful to do and this does involve me, after all."

He said nothing for the longest time while an odd battle played out on his face. "All right," he finally said, refusing to look at her. "We'll discuss it more tomorrow." It was clear he didn't want to talk about it now. Or perhaps ever. He had become such an uncharacteristically closed book since their marriage it could go either way.

"You never know, we might actually work well together." Rather than resort to nagging him, she tried a different tack. "I am phenomenally clever, and you seem to be of above-average intelligence—for a duke."

As she had hoped, that brought amusement back into his eyes. "You are a supremely irritating pain in the neck, Portia. Do you know that?"

"Does it make me odd that I take that as a compliment?" She fluttered her lashes to force him to flash his dimples. "But be careful as such a pretty one might convince me to stay married to you."

"Heaven forbid." But he tugged her closer as he spun her around, and the solid heat of his body against hers did more than turn her head.

It made it want.

Leo did not care that he was being rude or that he had been absent from the ball for over an hour; after Portia's latest bombshell, he still needed the air outside.

It had not occurred to him that in seeking proof of Nolley's guilt—he would pay for all the bruises he had placed on Portia's skin—Leo was also giving her a clear and easy path out of their marriage. One free of any threat of transportation to the other side of the world. He had been investigating the constable because he wanted to wipe the floor with the scoundrel and because he had promised her that he would get that first blot on her record erased. That blot that had been all his fault. That the evidence of the man's guilt was also exactly the sort of evidence that would expediate an annulment had not once crossed his mind.

But now she was not only delighted at the prospect, but she wanted to help him do it, and he did not doubt that his reluctant but clever wife would manage to do that in record time, when time was rapidly becoming his enemy.

Leo could not keep stalling and hope that the sorry state of relations between them would somehow miraculously fix themselves. Nor could he keep her as his duchess against her will. That would not result in the sort of happy union he wanted with the exasperating woman he had fallen head over heels for.

"I had a feeling I would find you out here." Instead of the woman he desperately wanted to seek him out, his mother joined him on the stone bench outside the Assembly Rooms. "Hiding again."

"It is stuffy inside."

"Portia seems to be coping well. She's chatting with some of Abigail's new friends."

"I might have known she would gravitate toward the placard wavers."

"In the continued absence of her husband in her life, I am just glad that she has found some people who want to spend some time with her."

"If you came out here to lecture me, Mother, know that I am not in the mood."

"Your eyebrows gave that away, dear. They are just like your father's and become quite ferocious when you are in high dudgeon." Her sigh was wistful. "I wish he was here to help you through all this as Rafe would know precisely what to do."

"I wish he was here too, Mama." Because Leo was drowning and no longer knew which way was up. "Portia wants an annulment."

"I think that she *thinks* she does, because she thinks you do too. She is going to continue to believe that until you let her know otherwise."

There seemed little point in denying that when his mother had always had a canny knack of knowing exactly what her offspring were feeling. "I don't know what I want."

"Poppycock, Leo. You know. You've known from the moment you first clapped eyes on her. You are too much like your father not to know your own heart."

He only huffed in response, so she took his hand and held it tight. "We were all talking about him today. Reminiscing. And it reminded me of when your father and I first met. He rode his horse too fast through a puddle just as I arrived at the fayre and splattered my pretty new dress in mud." She got such a faraway look in her eyes whenever she spoke of him that Leo could not help wondering how she bore the loss when she had loved his father to distraction. His heart was in pieces at just the thought of Portia leaving. To lose her was not something he could imagine ever coping with.

"I told him off." His mother smiled because telling her husband off was something that she had done regularly with almost the same passion as she had loved him. "And he apologized but I would have none of it. He was just too cocky and handsome and charming." She sighed at the memory. "It was such an inauspicious start to an epic love story, but it would not have been one at all if your father hadn't been the stubborn, I-always-know-best fellow that he was. I was quite content to dislike him in perpetuity, but he got it into his thick skull that I was the only one for him, and thus he persisted. And oh my goodness did he persist! He pursued me relentlessly and wooed me shamelessly until I had completely run out of excuses to resist him. I never stopped wanting to strangle him though, because all the things I loved about him were also all the things that drove me mad."

"And your point is?"

"If you want the girl, Leo, go get her."

"In case it has escaped your notice, Mother, I already have her."

"Not the bit that you want though." She touched her heart and his bled some more.

"That part is already taken completely by the United League for Reform."

"Having a worthy rival with both feet already in the door is a tricky thing to be sure." She decided that was the perfect moment to stand. "But not insurmountable—unless you allow it to be."

Chapter
TWENTY-SEVEN

Portia had recognized William's writing on the front of the letter the second she spotted it in the housekeeper's hands with the rest of the morning post.

"I can deliver all those for you, Mrs. Rumpole."

"Well . . . if you do not mind, your grace . . ."

"It is still very much Portia to you and of course I do not mind."

She relieved her of the pile and found a quiet corner to read his missive. In typical William style, it was brief and to the point.

We have a new home and a printing press and we intend to go to print again this Sunday!

I sincerely hope that you will find a way to join us!

William

She had no clue how such a miracle had occurred so quickly but was delighted that it had. However, there was no way that she could join them at the new address scrawled at the bottom of the letter, even for a few minutes.

None at all.

Not while she was the Duchess of Debden.

Except, as she wandered around the house to distribute all the letters, it soon became apparent that she was doomed to suffer another pointless morning of doing nothing. Leo had left early to "borrow" some files from the clerk of court to show her. His mother and sisters intended to spend one final morning shopping to be sure that they had everything that they needed for the trip to the palace and Portia would rather stick pins in her eyes than do any more of that. She had had seen enough modistes, cobblers, milliners, and glovers this past week to last her a lifetime and had so many fancy new clothes upstairs now that there wasn't any space left in the wardrobe to put them in.

Was there really any harm in paying one last visit to *Equitas* to congratulate them on their good fortune? It would also give her a great deal of peace to know for certain that it would be able to continue without her. And she was headed to Mayfair tomorrow with no clue when she would be coming back, so this morning really was her only opportunity.

What to do?

Torn, she pleaded a headache to ponder it and guiltily hid in her room until the ladies left. Once the house was as silent as the grave, the urge to go to the newspaper overwhelmed her. Before she changed her mind again, she snuck out the back gate with Snifferson and Barkington attached to their leads so that she had a good excuse for venturing out alone if anyone happened to see her sneaking back in.

The new premises were still near the river, but this smaller and still ramshackle warehouse was tucked well out of sight behind a tannery. That meant that the air outside the building wasn't the most fragrant, but that was a small price to pay for the additional privacy. The inside was as neat as pin when she arrived. Neater, in fact, than she had ever seen *Equitas*.

After Nolley's senseless destruction, a mismatched collection of secondhand desks had been procured from somewhere that were begging for somebody to cover them in the clutter that only came from publishing the truth. Each was paired with an assortment of donated chairs and stools, and there was even a nearly new bookcase. Empty, but in dire want of knowledgeable books. The old kettle that filled William's copious cups of tea had been salvaged and was already steaming in anticipation of his next one on the tiny hearth. But the thing that really drew her eye was the much smaller, more modern, shiny black printing press that made the dearly departed Bessie look like a relic from the Dark Ages.

"It's a Stanhope press," said William caressing it lovingly. "Made by Robert Walker of Soho—one of the best makers in the country." Which Portia could see thanks to the shiny brass plaque. "Isn't she lovely?"

"She is. Does she have a name yet?"

"I'm toying with 'Helen' seeing as she is the most beautiful woman in the world. Or 'Verity,' in honor of the Roman goddess of truth Veritas."

"My vote goes to 'Verity' as that is less insulting to your long-suffering saint of a wife."

"A very good point Portia, thank you."

"How did Verity come to pass?"

William shrugged, his besotted gaze never leaving his wonderful new machine. "I wrote to headquarters to tell them the bad news and this arrived at the old place on the back of a cart yesterday."

"They stumped up for a brand spanking new printing press? Will wonders never cease?"

"Believe me, nobody was as surprised as I was, but I am relieved that they have finally invested in us as we've had to get by on next to nothing up till now."

Portia glanced around the barren walls where all their reams of paper were supposed to live. "It's a shame they couldn't have stumped up for some paper to print on too. Don't they realize how expensive that is?"

"I agree, but we've had more than one savior step up." William grinned as the kettle whistled. "We were flooded with donations from local supporters after our catastrophe. Enough that we could at least afford enough paper and ink to see us through the next two editions." Snifferson followed him as he headed toward the kettle, his inquisitive nose never leaving the floor. "And speaking of the next edition, I do hope you will be a part of it. Every issue after for that matter too. You are the best assistant editor I have ever had."

"I can't, William. Not yet at least." It was staggering how much those words cost her when her fingers itched to get cracking again. "But as soon as Leo gets his annulment, obviously I will be back here with a vengeance." She filled him in on Leo's plan to discredit Nolley and get her first conviction overturned so she no longer had to worry about being transported. "In the meantime, I am headed to London, to be presented to the king, so even if I was allowed to help, I still can't."

"When do you leave?"

"Tomorrow. First thing."

"Could you at least supply me with an opinion piece?" He clutched at her sleeve, his gaze beseeching. "Without both you and Edgar the Snake here to help we are dreadfully shorthanded."

"I know—but I owe it to Leo not to embarrass him while he is stuck with me, so both K Pendle and P Kendall are temporarily retired."

"What if we don't print either name? We could give you another one or just leave it blank? Nobody need ever know that it's you outside of these four walls."

"I really can't, William, as much as I want to. Leo—"

"Need never know either." Honestly, when Sir William Stowe wanted something, the rogue had sadder puppy eyes than Snifferson. "I desperately need your help, Portia. *Equitas* needs your help. Our cause needs your help or I wouldn't ask. Please."

The temptation to say yes was overpowering, but so was her need to do right by Leo. "I shall think on it, William, but please do not hold out much hope."

"I shall hold the column regardless until we go to press tomorrow—just in case you have a change of heart."

This is what I have found so far." Leo slid the two documents across his desk and tried not to notice how the copper in her hair shimmered in the lamplight or how his foolish heart yearned for her. "The first one is a list of every arrest made at the protest and the second is the list of all those who were charged at the jail. Notice anything different?"

"Only that the second one is shorter to the tune of six names and one of those missing is Abigail's."

"So if we assume that the other missing five names all had the charges dropped and were released just like Abigail was, it suggests that Constable Nolley had no proof of the guilt of those five and released them. Seeing as we already know he isn't averse to fabricating proof when he wants it, that strikes me as unlikely." Leo hoped he wasn't clutching at straws. "Or it suggests that the other five all came from a similar privileged background to my sister. Or something more sinister is afoot—like bribery."

"Why do I get the distinct impression that you believe it is the latter?" Portia's clever eyes were narrowed.

"Because I went to visit every single one of those people this morning and there is nothing aristocratic about any of them. They do all, however, possess fathers with reasonably successful local businesses. The sort who could pay our untrustworthy constable a decent amount to avoid their relatives getting a criminal record."

"You have proof he has taken bribes?" Her eyes lit up and he tried not to be upset by that. "Because if you do, then we have grounds to declare my first conviction unsound."

"In theory, yes. But in practice, no, because none of those five people or their fathers would admit to that when I spoke to them. They are all adamant the charges were dropped because they were arrested by mistake and are all the sort of upstanding citizens who would never dream of attending a protest. In other words, Nolley has obviously put the fear of god into them as well as pocketing their money."

She leaned on her chin with a huff. "They were also probably wary of admitting to a second crime to a local magistrate. Bribing an official is as much an offense to those making the bribe as it is to the constable for taking them. Doing anything to obstruct the administration of justice carries a death penalty."

"They are more likely to be transported nowadays—but I take your point. Thanks to Nolley, they do not trust the law and I am very much the public face of it here in Bath."

"And he worked for you."

"There is that too. Which leaves us with only two options. I either keep digging into his arrest records going way back to find someone who is brave enough to testify against him or I send you to talk to the five and use your talented way with a convincing argument to try to encourage them to tell the truth."

"Then let's get started!" She was up out of her chair like a shot, which he supposed would be the exact speed that she would leave this house and him if he granted her an annulment.

"It's almost midnight, Portia." Leo managed to catch her hand before she sprinted out the door. "Hammering on somebody's door at midnight, especially someone already scared, isn't going to achieve anything beyond scaring them further."

Instantly, she deflated. "But we leave first thing for London so there won't be time then."

"I know," he said as his thumb stroked her palm in sympathy. "This is going to have to wait until we get back. A couple of weeks isn't going to alter the facts or change the outcome. A bit of time and distance might even work in our favor as those five people are likely still reeling from both their arrests and my visits to them today. Besides, for all Nolley's faults, being a fool isn't one of them. Rushing into this might tip him off that we are on to him and we don't want him covering his tracks."

She opened her mouth to argue, then snapped it closed. "Much as it galls me to admit it, you are right." She rolled her eyes as if it really pained her and then gave a saucy smile. "But I take comfort that even a stopped clock is right sometimes." A comment that made him smile too until she spoiled it. "And I suppose I can cope with being a duchess for a few more weeks."

And there it was.

Another reminder, not that he needed one, that she could not wait to be shot of him. "That's jolly decent of you." Because he was still holding her hand like a lovesick fool, he dropped it and in doing so noticed her ink-stained fingers.

He grabbed them again and scowled. "Please tell me you are not writing sedition behind my back again!" It came out sharper than he intended, but his scalp had already started to itch and his throat constrict at the thought of her putting herself in danger again.

She yanked her hand away. "How unlike you to immediately think the worst of me!"

"Well, you do have form, madam, and it is hardly my fault that I do not trust a word you say!"

He spat that with such venom that her head snapped back, but before he could apologize, her chin tilted in that stoic, defiant way that it always did when she wanted to put him in his place. "I did not realize that I needed your express permission to write to my friends in London. As your legal chattel, I shall be sure to seek it next time I dare to put pen to paper." She spun on her heel and before he could find the right words to tell her that he was sorry without admitting that he had only lashed out because she had brought up the damned annulment again, she was gone.

Chapter TWENTY-EIGHT

"Your grace!" Kitty dipped into an exaggerated curtsy as soon as she spied her outside Gunther's on the corner of Berkeley Square. She had asked her friend to meet her here rather than Leo's town house just yards away, because she had wanted to be able to talk to her openly without Letitia, Abigail, Emilia, and, most especially, Leo, within earshot. "Now there are two words I never expected to say with regards to you!"

"That makes both of us." Portia hugged her friend tight, needing the comfort of familiarity in her suddenly topsy-turvy world. "Promise me that you will never use them again in my presence either because I hate them."

"Oh dear. Things are that bad, are they?"

"I've lost my purpose, my name, my independence, my legal right to make my own decisions, and my writing. I'm married to a nobleman—which bothers me immensely—but also a *noble* man, which bothers me more. Leo hides it well, but can no longer bear to be in the same room as me and has made it plain that he doesn't trust me. I have been forbidden to write anything that could be construed in any way as seditious and, to add insult to injury, I'm going to have to curtsy before our awful king tomorrow while I try and doubtless fail to act in a manner befitting a duchess. Never mind that Mary Wollstonecraft would be turning in her grave to see how much I have betrayed my reforming principles, so what do you think?"

"I think that you are very lucky not to be on a prison hulk bound for the Pacific." Kitty had never been one to mince her words. "So perhaps you need to start counting your blessings, Portia, rather than your sorrows, as you do sound rather ungrateful when that man saved your life."

"I am supremely grateful, that is the problem. I feel as beholden to him as he feels beholden to me for getting me my first criminal record. We are achingly polite to one another if we are forced to collide, but do our utmost to avoid one another otherwise. If we spend more than five minutes in one another's company all we do is argue. I've just spent five interminably long days in a carriage while he preferred to ride on his horse beside it, and it honestly felt like five months."

Thanks to the longer early summer evenings and even earlier mornings, they had made the journey from Bath to Mayfair in record time. Helped by the brevity of their rest stops and their cringingly awkward but blessedly short meals together watched by the rest of his family.

"Don't you even collide at nighttime?" asked Kitty in her customary open way as she slapped her hands together and wiggled her brows. "What with you being married and all?"

"*That* is not something we do."

"Recently or ever?" asked Kitty undeterred.

"Ever." While Portia had initially thought that she was relieved by that, seeing as any sort of physical relationship wouldn't have been wise if they were getting an annulment, she couldn't help seeing his lack of interest in her doing her wifely duty as a sign of how much he now loathed her.

"Gracious." Thankfully, Kitty didn't say anything else until after the waiter had seated them and left them alone with menus. "What happened to all that passion he had for you in the garden *that* night?"

Because of course her friend, who could never remember where she was supposed to be or what she was supposed to be doing most of the time, remembered every minute detail of every anguished letter that Portia had sent her.

"That died once he discovered that I wrote for the enemy."

"But still . . ." Her friend wasn't convinced. "It is quite possible to be furious at someone and still love them madly. Feelings do not change that quickly."

"His have. He is pleasant when we collide but not really himself most of the time. He's more guarded and less . . . Leo." Portia couldn't really define what that meant, even to herself, beyond that it wounded. "At least he's not the man I got to know before everything went to hell in a handcart. I see glimmers of the real him once in a while, but they quickly disappear as soon as he remembers what I did to him, and I can always see precisely when he remembers because his brows furrow a split second before the shutters slam back down again."

In truth, she hadn't seen any sign of the real Leo since their last altercation in his study after he had accused her of using her poison pen again. "I honestly think that if he could have stayed in a different inn to me every night this week too, he would have."

"He never once came to your room?"

"Never once even walked me to the door despite his room being on the same floor."

"And, let me guess, you never once ventured to his either?"

She had wanted to. Each time she heard his footsteps next door she had yearned to go to him and try to bridge the impasse between them but had stopped herself. "I know where I am not welcome and I am sick and tired of the arguments," Portia huffed as she threw up her palms. "So we are trapped in this horrible vicious cycle where neither of us are the least bit happy about any of it and we cover it up with politeness."

"Could it be that his pride is simply dented? You did rebuff him, after all, when he practically offered you his heart on a plate. Although how you could resist him when you claimed that his kisses are so intoxicating that they made you weak at the knees is beyond me."

"Do you know how to whisper?" Portia hissed as she hid her ferocious blush behind her menu. "The whole of Mayfair really doesn't need to know of the nonsense I wrote to you in a moment of sheer madness."

"Are you now claiming that his *clever* lips didn't make you swoon?" It galled now how much her friend was quoting Portia's own damning words back to her.

"I am simply trying to explain that he no longer wants me in *that* way. Or at all, in fact. If you must know, he's already in the process of gathering all the evidence he needs to get our marriage annulled without feeling responsible that I'll be transported to the Antipodes."

"So it really is a loveless marriage of convenience?" A reality that clearly distressed the romantic dreamer that was Kitty. "Are you sure that there is no hope for you both to live happily ever after together? No spark? No glimmer?"

Portia still felt sparks but Leo clearly didn't. "Not everyone gets to live happily ever after, Kitty. But he'll be happier once he is rid of me and I'll be happier when I get my old life back."

Her friend scoffed. "And again, I will remind you that feelings do not work like that. You might think you will be happier with your old life back, but it is as plain as the nose on your face to me that you will be devastated to lose him."

"I will not." Yes she would! "I will be a little sad, of course, because he has always been decent to me and Leo is an affable, likeable sort most of the time, despite his obnoxious title and despotic need to bend everyone to his stubborn will. But he is a duke, for pity's sake, and I am a reformer to my core and never the twain shall meet." Except when they had, it had been magical.

"There is such a thing as compromise, Portia. Perhaps if you find some middle ground, you will find a way to muddle through. Especially as you have clearly fallen in love with him."

"I have not!"

"You have too!" Kitty yanked Portia's menu down so that she could jab the air between them. "I have known you since we were both sixteen years old and I have never seen you so bothered by a man in all that time."

"Of course I am bothered by him. I am accidentally married to him and need not be! Both for my sake and Leo's."

"Are you aware that something peculiar happens to your face each time you say his name? Or of how gushing you were about him in your letters despite all your lofty claims of twains never meeting? Or how fondly you speak of him despite his despotic need to bend everyone to his will or how utterly wretched your expression becomes every single time you mention the word annulment?"

"I am not made of stone, Kitty. This is an awful situation and I do feel wretched about it."

"I think you are falling on your sword, Portia, because you think he wants to find a way out of the marriage, and you think you should want out of it because you have always been convinced that marriage wasn't for you."

"I value my independence and am, and always have been, wedded to the cause. I cannot pursue my political ambitions as some man's chattel—."

Kitty yawned loudly. "Oh for goodness' sake! People change, Portia, and what they want changes too. It is perfectly acceptable for a grown woman of four-and-twenty to reevaluate what she thought she wanted as a child of sixteen! You have grown up a lot since then and I sincerely doubt that you still believe that everything is as black-and-white as you did back then, do you?" Her friend did not even give her time to nod at that irrefutable logic. "Just as it is perfectly acceptable to be scared to dare to want different."

"I don't want different!" But perhaps she did and that really was a scary prospect. Especially with him.

"Methinks the lady doth protest too much," said Kitty, waggling her finger. "And, for the record, not every husband treats his wife like a chattel. Georgie's doesn't and neither does Lottie's, so if our friends can find happiness with a partner and still lead fulfilling lives why can't you? They are living proof that it *is* possible to have it all."

A part of her wanted to believe that, no matter how unlikely or practical it would be in her case. "Neither of them are married to dukes nor constricted by the strict societal confines of being a duchess."

"You are just making excuses now when you know that he didn't have to marry you but did anyway. Probably because he still has feelings for you just as you do him, so perhaps you would do better to consider that rather than using pathetic excuses to overcomplicate things."

"Things *are* complicated, Kitty. He married me in haste to get me out of trouble—not because he had a burning desire to spend eternity with me. There is nothing romantic in that."

"Are you sure? Because from where I am standing, his noble sacrifice sounds like the most romantic thing in the world." Kitty swept her hand in an arc as if painting the sky. "Duke tells a chaperone she calls to his soul, rushes to rescue her from prison—twice—then marries her to save her from transportation to a penal colony and perhaps certain death."

"It really wasn't like that." Although if viewed through a less cynical lens than Portia was prone to, perhaps it was. Leo had been the only one there for her. Jumped in front of a bullet for her. Put her safety over his own happiness and what was that if not hopelessly romantic?

Kitty must have seen her indecision because she reached across the table to squeeze Portia's wrists. "Nobody who loves you would judge you for deciding that you do not have to completely be the person that you chose to be at sixteen. You can still be an idealistic, lecturing, crusading pain in the backside and make a little room in your life for love."

Like Leo would let that happen! He practically hit the roof when he assumed she had been writing sedition again. "I would have no choice but to pick one or the other. If I remain his duchess, he has made it repeatedly plain that I cannot have both."

"I'll wager you could if you both stopped being such stubborn fools and gave love a chance. Especially when you clearly like him—so much in my humble opinion that it terrifies you—and he has made it plain that he liked you well before you married."

"Kitty—"

"Well, he did, didn't he? And you were not immune to his confession. In fact, if I remember it correctly, you wrote to me at the time that you wished he wasn't a duke because then you wouldn't have had to rebuff him."

"I was confused and—" Portia found herself talking at her friend's raised palm.

"I know you better than anyone and I can see that your martyring and oh-so-convenient belief that you couldn't possibly ever give up your precious independence for something as wonderful as love is wavering! If you forget for one moment that he is a duke, then he has obviously affected your heart enough that you are tempted to want more of him. And let us not forget that his kisses made you swoon—just as yours did him." Her incorrigible friend wiggled her brows. "All that pent-up lust between you isn't healthy you know. Nobody can think straight with all that complicating matters—so uncomplicate them and give your *love*, in all its splendid forms, a chance."

"Things are complicated enough without adding *that* into the mix, thank you very much, and we can hardly indulge in *that* anyway if we want an annulment." No matter how much her body and, heaven help her, perhaps even her heart, craved different.

"You do know that there are only three criteria in English law for an annulment to be granted, don't you? And the only one you stand any sort of chance with is fraud because the other two are incompetence and *impotence*." Thankfully Kitty made sure to whisper that last word. "If neither party is underage then the only way to prove incompetence is to have one of you declared insane by a physician and then they would have you locked up. A physician would also have to prove impotence, and the tests for that are extremely invasive. Your poor duke would have to physically display before witnesses that he is not *capable* of consummating your marriage, and from what you hinted at in your letter about your midnight tryst beneath the moonlight, he very much is."

A ferocious blush bloomed on Portia's cheeks but she did not doubt her friend because for all her chaotic flakiness and optimistic, overly romantic nature, Kitty's brother was training to be a lawyer, so the strange complexities of the English legal system was something she knew about. "So proving my fraud is our *only* hope?"

"Unless a couple of expert courtesans—or better still, you—can't stir something in the Duke of Debden's breeches in front of a doctor, it is." While Portia's jaw hung slack, her incorrigible friend gestured for the waiter and then grinned. "Therefore, even if the marriage is doomed not to last as you seem so stubbornly convinced that it has to be, it would be a crying shame for you both not to have enjoyed at least one of the benefits of it while it does."

"Why the devil aren't you wearing your court clothes, Leo?" The fanfare of feathers atop his mother's head quivered in outrage as much as they could within the confines of the carriage as he joined all the ladies in it. "Or did you not see that I had them expressly laid out on the bed for you?"

"I saw them and then expressly ignored them because they are hideous." It would be a cold day in hell before he ever donned those unflattering gold satin breeches and gaudy red satin and gold brocade coat again.

"But it is perfectly acceptable for me to look ridiculous?" That came from his wife who, to be fair to her, had to sit with her neck hunched to avoid damaging the veritable ostrich wing sprouting from her hair while the heavy cream and brocade gown that she was trussed up in like a ham caused her bosoms to be scrunched under her bent chin. "Thank you for the show of husbandly support."

"I am here, aren't I?" He had to lift her enormous train just to be able to sit next to her. "Besides, nobody is going to care what I am wearing when it is you they are all itching to see."

"Please don't remind me." Worry was etched in her expression. "Something that is impossible to do when this stupid headdress weighs a ton. I dread to contemplate the size of the bird they plucked these feathers from, but I will wager it was the biggest ostrich that ever lived."

She had a point. "They are rather tall."

"On purpose," said his mother who was doubtless responsible for the gargantuan avian confection. "We want her to stand out as it sends a defiant statement." She wafted a regal hand. "*We* are the *Sloanes* and Sloanes do not care one jot what anybody thinks of us."

"Easy for you to say," said his wife, trying and obviously failing to find any position that made her comfortable. "I am about to meet two hundred people who, if today's edition of *The Times* is any gauge, all already hate me."

"So some hack who thought that they were being witty called you the Delinquent Duchess of Debden—there are worse things to have levied at you." His mother reached over and squeezed her hand, which was one of the few parts of Portia not draped in brocade. "Remember, being a duchess is a state of mind, dear, so straighten your shoulders, keep your chin up no matter what, smile as if you know a secret that nobody else does and, whenever you feel a little intimidated by someone, imagine them on the commode and I promise you that you will instantly feel better."

"That is good because I currently feel sick." And she looked it.

"Or you could just be yourself and to hell with the lot of them." Without thinking, Leo covered her hand in his, then tried not to notice how his mother delighted in witnessing that rare show of spousal affection. "I will be right beside you at all times and if anyone tries to belittle or insult you in any way, they will have me to answer to."

Portia was clearly not herself because, to his mother's further delight, she laced her fingers gratefully through his and held tight. "How am I supposed to be myself when I am dressed like this?" She pointed to the feathers. "And I have to hold my silly matching feathered fan just so?" Then her eyes widened as she tugged her hand away and patted the seat around her. "I have forgotten my fan!" She went to rise and he stayed her.

"I'll go fetch it. Where is it?"

"Probably still on my bed."

He hopped out and jogged up the stairs to her room. For obvious reasons, he hadn't ventured inside any bedchamber that Portia happened to occupy since he'd accidentally caught her in the bath because he hadn't fully recovered from that mind-boggling experience. He suspected the image of her alabaster breasts glistening with water was one that would be remembered to his grave, so he did not need any more erotic images of his reluctant wife to join it. He had lost count of how many dreams those saucy, dark, puckered nipples had invaded since he had seen them, or how many times he had awoken hot and hard and desperate for her as a result.

Despite only occupying it for one night, the alluring scent of orange blossoms teased his nostrils as he entered her room. Her enormous ostrich fan was indeed on the bed and he grabbed it, turned to leave, and spied her battered old pen sitting in an inkpot on her dressing table next to an untidy little pile of paper. The top sheet was tantalizingly covered in her flamboyant handwriting.

Leo knew that he shouldn't read whatever it was after he had accused her of writing sedition last week, but it drew him like a magnet anyway.

Perhaps he would glance at just the first line?

Accidentally?

In passing?

He leaned closer and almost choked on his own tongue.

Is it possible that Kitty is correct and I have foolishly fallen in love?

As there was no way in hell he could leave it at that, he snatched up the paper and carried on.

It is undeniable that Leopold Sloane, the illustrious Duke of Debden, is not a typical duke. If one ignores that he is as handsome as sin, which is nigh on impossible if you happen to be a woman in possession of a pulse, he is also kind, funny, clever, charming, principled, and liberal. In fact, if it weren't for the fact that he was a duke with an annoying propensity for overbearingness, he would be exactly the sort of man I would willingly give my heart to if I were the sort to give it to anyone. But there is the rub. Am I actually the sort to give my heart to anyone or are all the odd and overwhelming feelings that I feel for him merely a classic case of pent-up lust caused by our enforced proximity to one another?

There is, undeniably, an element of forbidden fruit about our situation but . . .

Leo hastily turned the page.

. . . there is also

And on that unsatisfying cliff edge the essay ended.

He sunk to the mattress and went through it again trying to read between the scant lines to find the answer to her initial question. When he couldn't, he could only surmise that she was in two minds.

But two minds were certainly better than the indifference or abhorrence he had been convinced she felt for him. And if she was in two minds and needed a persuasive reason to decide one way or another, then surely he had to try to persuade her that being in love with him wasn't foolish at all?

Which also rather suggested, in no uncertain terms, that if he wanted her, then he should bloody well go and get her before it was too late. Do as his mother had claimed his excellent father before him had done and pursue the woman his heart wanted relentlessly. Perhaps this essay, this unwelcome trip to the capital, and Portia's forgotten fan were all signs from the universe that it was long past time that he stopped dithering in wounded indecision and set about shamelessly wooing his reluctant wife until she ran out of excuses to resist him?

Chapter
TWENTY-NINE

To Portia's complete disgust, Piccadilly was unusually clear for the time of day and the long line of carriages waiting to be admitted into St. James's Palace that she had prayed for were nonexistent. They arrived at the palace just five minutes after they left Berkeley Square.

Leo, sensing her anxiousness, held on to her hand the whole way and his solid presence meant the world. He helped his mother and sisters out of the carriage and, as if he knew she needed a moment to gather her nerve, sent them on ahead before he assisted her. Pathetically, her hand shook as he took it and he sighed. "Tell me something—do you have any regard for our king?"

"Not really."

"Or any respect for his privileged and entitled entourage either?"

She shook her head feeling miserable and out of her depth regardless.

"Then why do you suddenly care what they think?" He tipped up her downcast chin with a gentle finger, forcing her to meet his eyes. "What happened to the acerbic cynic who sat in that ballroom next to me last month and claimed to be judging everyone who dared to look down their aristocratic noses at her as harshly as they were judging her?"

"I didn't have to behave in a manner befitting the Duchess of Debden then."

"When I told you to be yourself just now, I meant it. The Duchess of Debden can be whoever you want her to be. In fact, for the record, I would prefer it if she was more Portia than not. And the Portia I know is wily, tenacious, determined, unflappable, unbelievably stubborn, annoyingly clever, and too fearless to show any sort of weakness—even in front of a king." Her words, some of the first she had ever said to him. "That Portia is a prickly minx who doesn't suffer fools gladly, and fools don't get more foolish than those that hover in there." He tilted his head toward the palace entrance.

"That Portia is also capable of being imperious when she wants to be and, from someone who has occasionally been at the receiving end of one of your disdainful looks, trust me, nobody glares down their pretty nose better than you do." He tapped it and smiled. "Furthermore, as we have both already agreed, I am not a typical duke, why the blazes would you even think that I would expect you to behave like a typical duchess?"

That got her attention. "You don't?"

"I just expect you to be you, Portia." An answer that both surprised and touched her. "So straighten your shoulders, keep your chin up no matter what, smile as if you know a secret that nobody else does, and do not allow them to beat you, or you will have me to personally answer to. Do you hear me?"

Portia felt her lips curve upward for the first time today. "Yes, Leo."

"That's my girl." Then, to her complete surprise he kissed her. It was much too brief but right on the mouth, so she felt it everywhere. She blinked back at him in shock until he grabbed her hand and dragged her forward. "Let us go put on a show, *your grace*, so we can hurry up and get the hell out of here."

Rather than allow her to take his arm like all the other couples in the receiving line, he kept her hand in his, refusing to let go even as they approached the throne.

"The Duke and Duchess of Debden," announced the page or equerry or butler or whatever he was when their turn came.

Thanks largely to Leo's steadying hold on her fingers, Portia managed to successfully survive the dreaded court curtsy without falling over. An achievement that stopped at least five of the ten thousand butterflies in her tummy from flapping as she smiled in forced politeness at the monarch.

The king looked a great deal unhealthier in person than any of his official portraits dared suggest, no doubt as a result of his well-documented hedonistic lifestyle. He had ruddy cheeks and bloodshot eyes that stared at Portia with interest as they swept the length of her before he spoke directly to her husband as if she weren't there. "I can see why you married her, Debden."

Leo inclined his head. "Thank you, Your Majesty."

"Although I am not happy that I had to find out about it from the newspaper."

"My apologies, Your Majesty." She knew enough about Leo already to know that from his short, almost curt, responses, he clearly did not hold this particular monarch in any regard either as his smile was as strained as hers had been.

The bloodshot eyes returned to her. "Are the rumors about your revolutionary tendencies true, madam?"

Portia was intimidated enough by the setting and the company to want to nod but didn't for two reasons. Firstly, she didn't trust the feathers to stay put if she did and, more importantly, simply because the conundrum of a man still holding her hand and scrambling her wits had told her that he wanted her to be herself. "It is true that I am a campaigner for reform, Your Majesty, but would prefer to see that happen without the need for a revolution."

"Ah," said the king with an unimpressed scowl before he turned back to Leo. "Then I shall have to trust you to keep her in check, Debden."

"Noted, Your Majesty." Leo inclined his head again and left it at that. Apparently, content to let the silence stretch, which took some guts here with two hundred pairs of eyes staring at them and one of those pairs belonging to the crown.

"We've not seen you here in forever, Debden." The king wafted his hand and all Portia could think of was his fingers resembled sausages. The pale and raw sort that hung in a butcher's window. "Remind me, when was the last time you graced us with your presence?"

"Just after my father passed, Your Majesty."

The king made an odd noise that was neither a grunt nor a word but a strange amalgamation of both. "As I recall, your father was very lax about his court duties too."

"The Debden estates are very far from here, Your Majesty, and sadly keep me in Bath, just as they did my father."

The king gave a sniff, glanced at Portia, and sniffed some more. "You need to try harder, Debden."

"I shall endeavor to do that, Your Majesty."

As the king clearly couldn't think of anything else to say, and with Leo making no effort to fill the void and Portia too overwhelmed to speak, they were ushered along by a palace aide.

"Is that it?" she whispered as Leo led their backward shuffle into the opulent reception room that was filled with people who were all, to her relief, as and if not more ridiculously dressed than she was.

"Hopefully." He wrapped her hand around his arm when they could finally turn and maneuvered her deftly through the crowd toward his mother and sisters who had already found the refreshments. "Now we just have to make excruciating small talk until the king decides to leave to gamble and drink with his cronies and we can escape."

"How long does that usually take?"

"You might as well ask how long a piece of string is because it could be one hour and it could very well be six."

"Six hours wearing this tower of feathers doesn't bear thinking about when my scalp is already screaming in protest. I swear your mother has secured it with at least five million pins." All of which were digging into her skin. "Never mind that I look like an idiot."

"You look beautiful, Portia, just as you always do—despite the feathers." And since that lovely compliment wasn't enough, he then slanted her a glance and a sinful secret smile that revealed just the merest hint of his distracting dimples. "You did well just then, by the way. You didn't dodge the question, looked him dead in the eye, and didn't seem the least bit intimidated by his disdain. I was proud of you."

"Thank you." That final compliment somehow meant the world. "But to my utter disgust, I will admit only to you that I was intimidated." She took a moment to properly take in her grand surroundings and all the bejeweled guests. "I've never been in a palace before nor met royalty."

"Now that you have, what do you think?"

"I think the palace is lovely."

He chuckled. "A very diplomatic and reassuringly Portia-like answer."

"Leo . . ." Because her lips still tingled from his kiss, she searched for the right way to casually ask him why he had done it, but the dowager beckoned them over.

"There's the happy couple!" To Portia's complete horror, her mother-in-law was now surrounded by a flock of feathered ladies all sporting superior expressions as they stared at her as if she had two heads. "So many people are dying to meet your lovely new wife, Leo."

"I'll just bet they are," he replied for Portia's ears only. His warm breath causing wholly improper goose bumps to erupt on her skin before he escorted her into the lions' den. "Just remember, as *my* duchess you now outrank almost everyone in this room." His hand slipped softly to the small of her back in a proprietorial gesture he had never used before, and she could not help hoping that it wasn't just part of the show he wanted to put on. "Do not be afraid to use that rank and look down that pretty nose of yours to remind them of it, should the need arise. Which it will, my darling."

My darling.

Two words that somehow held the power to unsettle her as much, if not more, than his out-of-the-blue kiss just had.

Two hours later and the royal reception was still in full swing and showing no signs of winding down. With Leo and his mother watching Emilia like a hawk because she had taken an obvious interest in a handsome officer dressed in his full regimental finery, and Abigail ensconced in a serious conversation with two equally serious-looking young women, Portia decided to seek some respite in the retiring room. She needed a few moments to sit down, regroup, and rest her aching head. It was exhausting being on her best behavior while being judged by all and sundry. And judged she very much had been by almost everyone who pretended to be delighted to make her acquaintance.

She was also exhausted by the weight of her silly court attire, which now seemed to drag her down more with each passing minute, and thoroughly sick to the back teeth of the awful feathers practically riveted to her head. Thanks to them, she had no choice but to keep her chin up and her shoulders back as there was no way of supporting the precarious structure otherwise.

Despite her discomfort, her gaze still drifted to Leo as she escaped. Just as it had repeatedly since they had arrived. And just as it had each time she had looked at him since, her pulse quickened and an odd yearning engulfed her. One that no amount of her practical, logical, and cynical lectures to herself would stop.

She blamed the kiss for her current preoccupation with him. It might not have been as thorough a kiss as their first one, but it was just as potent. That brief peck had certainly affected her enough that her mind couldn't dislodge it. It was genuinely all she could think about.

Maybe that was why he had done it?

Simply to distract her so that she wouldn't feel quite so intimidated by her surroundings and the alien company? In which case, common sense dictated that she shouldn't read too much into it or expect it to happen again. Or worse, weave fanciful, romantic notions about it meaning something that common sense dictated she had no place even contemplating.

The only problem was that her common sense had chosen today of all days to desert her, and something uncharacteristically hopeful had apparently taken its place. Thanks, no doubt, to all the silly romantic notions Kitty had put in her head.

Alongside Leo's kiss.

And that off-the-cuff and likely wholly innocuous "my darling" that her stupid heart wanted to believe was significant.

Urgh! What the hell was the matter with her?

Fortunately, the retiring room was blessedly quiet, even the usually hovering maid was missing, so she found a spare chair, pulled the privacy curtain around her, and gratefully rested the side of her confused and aching head against the paneling.

As the cool wood took some of the unwelcome weight off her shoulders, Portia used her fingers to massage the parts of her throbbing scalp that she could get at in between all the hairpins and wondered why none of the other ladies present were also here doing the same. She had not expected to develop any respect for the king's many female hangers-on, especially the really pompous ones, but it took a special kind of fortitude to sport one of these ridiculous court headdresses for hours on end and still keep the small talk flowing. She even quite admired some of them for being able to converse animatedly about nothing in such a prolonged and seamless manner.

That was not a talent she possessed.

She could lecture, she could educate, she could be pithy, she could be curious, and she could argue, but Portia couldn't be effortlessly charming. She was just, as Leo said, too prickly. Whereas he could, despite his loathing of this sort of gathering. That made her question if the aristocracy were born with such a gift or if they received lessons from the cradle?

Perhaps, if they did end up stuck together for all eternity, he might give her some lessons? She would feel less out of her depth in his world if she could be both pithy and charming like his mother was.

An errant thought that made her smile.

A distant clock struck the hour, reminding her that she really couldn't spend much more time in the retiring room, no matter how tempting a prospect it was. With a sigh, she lifted her heavy head from its wooden pillow and rose, only to discover that one of her dratted feathers was caught on a splinter or a proud nail or something. Instinctively, she tugged her head to release it and managed to dislodge half of her headdress in the process.

Instantly, her artful but hideously stiff coiffure shifted as the cumbersome feathered monstrosity listed ominously to the left, wrenching yet more pins from her scalp as it did so. To stop gravity taking over, she had to grab the dratted thing with both hands as she stumbled to fix the damage in the mirror.

Her refection confirmed what she could already feel and that a landslide had occurred on her head. One doomed to get worse unless she could quickly reverse the subsidence.

While supporting the full weight of the feathers in one hand, she used her other to extract as many pins as she could from her hair before she tried to reuse them to resecure it. A feat that took ten minutes at least and that, when she finally let go to inspect her handiwork, hadn't actually worked at all because the hated feathers refused to stay upright and drooped.

That was when Portia admitted defeat and decided that her giant, dead pet ostrich needed the help of someone else if it stood any chance of coming back to life. However, with still no maid in sight, the only way to summon help without making a public spectacle of herself was to urgently seek a palace servant. Preferably one with experience in collapsed coiffures.

Once again steadying her feathers with both hands, she gingerly poked her head out of the door of the retiring room to locate one and was confronted with a worried-looking Leo instead.

"Hallelujah!" He threw up his palms. "You have been in there forever and I was worried sick that someone had upset you!" Then he must have noticed her expression because he frowned and looked ready to kill someone. "Have they?"

"There has been an incident with my headdress." To prove that, she let go and watched his eyes rapidly follow the feathers on their descent toward her ear. "I need help pinning it back in place." She beckoned him to come into the retiring room and he shook his head.

"I can't enter the ladies' retiring room!"

"Well I certainly cannot go back out there looking like this." She jabbed a finger at the packed royal court. "So you are going to have to. Or you go and find someone more useful who can rescue me in my hour of need!"

He hovered in indecision briefly. "Let's find another room and I'll give it a go."

While she held her headdress, he bundled up her train and spirited them both along the quiet hallway well away from prying eyes, randomly checking doors as they went.

All were locked.

They hurried down a side corridor and after three more attempts, finally found a room that was not only open, but lit. It was filled with green baize tables all with waiting packs of cards and gaming tokens piled neatly on them, but by the pyramid of champagne glasses, the chilling bottles in vast ice buckets and the freshly laid buffet, it would not be vacant for long. Because this was clearly where the king and his cronies would soon come to gamble.

"What do I need to do?" Leo peered at the top of her head warily. "Only while I am happy to be your knight in shining armor in your hour of need, I shall give you fair warning that my only experience with hairpins comes from removing them. I have never ever had any cause to stick one back in."

"How do you know how to remove a hairpin and not insert one?" That question popped out before she thought about it and they both winced at the same time. In her case, because unwelcome images of him passionately undressing another woman immediately made her irrationally jealous. "On second thought, don't answer that." She pushed her hair and feathers back where they were supposed to be with the same force as she tried to banish the flash of jealousy. "There is this pocket contraption beneath the cap that you need to slide in between the hairpins and my hair to anchor it in place. It was too fiddly for me to do on my own." She bent at the knees so he could inspect it. "Do you see?"

"Just about."

Leo set to work, tugging out random pins that were doing nothing now and trying to reinsert them, but he quickly got frustrated. "This is like a Chinese puzzle!" He poked a pin in and stabbed her in the head.

"Ouch!"

"Sorry—but I can't see. The pins are dark, your hair is darker, and I desperately need more light." He scanned the room, then spied two large candelabra on the mantelpiece that flanked an enormous Oriental vase filled with flowers. Behind them was the added bonus of a mirror above it that amplified the candlelight. "Let's move over there."

They shuffled to the mantelpiece, she hunched, and he went to work again.

"Aha!" He grinned after a few more failed attempts. "That's better. I can finally see how this ridiculous contraption works." He stepped closer. Too close because she could feel the heat of his body and smell the subtle but seductively spicy scent of his cologne as he studied the still-pinned side of her headdress and meticulously tried to emulate it on the flapping side. "It seems you have to bend the bottom of the pin over the top." Which was all well and good, but each time he twisted a pin, the roots of her hair screamed in protest.

The front done to his satisfaction, he eventually turned her to face the mirror, then tilted her head forward over the mantelpiece so that he could pin the back. "You were wrong about the five million pins." He sounded frustrated as he repeated the awkward process. "There are at least six million in here."

"Your mother instructed her maid to put double the usual amount in because my hair is so slippery." In the absence of his cologne, something in this room smelled seriously acrid, but not enough to stop her noticing every single time his hips accidentally brushed against her bottom as he struggled with a particularly stubborn pin. It struck her as a good a time as any to ask him about the kiss because she didn't have to look at him while she did it. "Leo . . . before . . . outside . . ." His fingers paused as if he knew what was coming. "Why did you kiss me?"

"It seemed like the right thing to do at the time."

"Oh," she said, still not sure what that meant. "So it was an act of mercy?"

"Not really."

"Then what was it?"

"I don't know." Unhelpful. "But I enjoyed it." So had she, but that wasn't the point. "Done," he suddenly said stepping back. "Or at least I think it is. Test your feathers, wife."

Off-kilter, Portia lifted her head to stare at his handiwork in the mirror and was relieved to see that her dead ostrich once again pointed north. "Thank y—" She screeched as she spotted a worrying plume of gray smoke puffing out of the top of the tallest feather, then automatically tried to wrench the headdress from the six million hairpins that secured it to her scalp again. "I'm on fire!"

Something Leo had apparently already noticed too because with widened eyes and a yelp of his own, he immediately grabbed the vase of flowers, yanked the blooms out, and threw all the water at her.

Chapter

THIRTY

With hindsight, as Portia spluttered in shock, Leo realized he probably could have clapped the paltry flames out rather than douse Portia in a giant vase full of water. But he had panicked and acted on instinct.

Now she was a sodden mess standing in a puddle as she blinked at him open-mouthed. Her sooty eyelashes were spiked with moisture and the ridiculously tall fan of ostrich feathers were now a limp and dripping arc of broken spines.

"Thanks a lot, Leo!" That came out of severely gritted teeth. "As I do not think that there is a bit of me left that isn't now thoroughly drenched!"

Still holding the vase, he scanned the length of her and smiled sheepishly because she was right. The already tight bodice of her gown now molded to her like a second skin and the enormous water stain on the heavy silk brocade of her skirt rendered the fabric several shades darker than the rest of the dress. It had also done something bizarre to the once artful drape that had made it collapse on one side. "But on the bright side, at least your head isn't on fire."

"It wouldn't have been on fire in the first place if you hadn't bent me into the candelabra!"

"Also true." He wanted to laugh because she did look funny, but bit it back because she was clearly distressed about it. "My apologies."

"Now I am going to a be a laughingstock on top of an unwelcome spectacle, aren't I? All the newspapers tomorrow are going to be calling me the Drenched Duchess rather than the Delinquent Duchess. The stupid, clumsy, and common upstart who had no place being in a palace and certainly has no clue how to behave like a real lady while they tolerated her presence."

He wished he could deny that, but knew that was exactly what would happen if anyone here caught a glimpse of her. "Not if we sneak out without anyone seeing us, they won't."

"How do you suppose we manage that with half of Mayfair in attendance, genius?"

"Well . . ." He scratched his head as he surveyed the room. "There is a window over there that we can climb out of, and I am sure we'll find a suitable route to freedom once we're outside."

She grabbed the edge of her sodden train and shook it in her fist. "You want me to climb out of that skinny window in this cumbersome gown?"

"It's either that, or we take our chances back out in that corridor."

"Marvelous." She stomped over to it, her lovely eyes shooting him daggers as he wrestled with the ancient latch and flung it open. "Please tell me there isn't a hideous drop right onto the street."

Leo leaned out to do some reconnaissance. "Thankfully, this leads to an empty courtyard." He held out his hand. "But there is a bit of a drop so I'll have to lower you down."

"This just gets better and better." She took his hand and allowed him to lift her onto the sill, then they both had to fight with her skirts so that she could fling her legs over it. A sight he couldn't help enjoying. Almost as much as he had enjoyed hearing how flummoxed his impromptu kiss of a few hours ago still made her. She stared down at the drop dubiously. "Now what?"

"Twist slightly and hold my hands tight, then gently ease yourself over and I'll hang on for grim death until your feet touch the ground."

"Or you drop me."

"I won't drop you, Portia, I promise. I would allow my arms to dislocate from my shoulders before I let you fall."

"Huh!" was her response to that, but she did as he suggested.

With much grunting and groaning on both of their parts, she successfully made it to the ground without injury and immediately started grumbling about the indignity, as well as her heavy wet dress and stupid, ruined feathers that were all thanks to him. She glared up at him as he flung his first leg over the sill and wagged her finger at him like a stern schoolmistress. "If I catch pneumonia after you soaked me and I die, do not be in doubt that I shall find a way to come back and haunt you, Leopold Sloane!"

That was when he heard approaching voices.

Lots of approaching voices his angry, ranting wife was unaware of.

"First you get me charged for a crime I didn't commit and then you try to drown me!"

"Shhhh." He gave her a warning look as he jerked his head behind to try to convey that they were about to have company, but she took umbrage at his tone.

"Don't you dare shush me, Leo! I am not and never will be a blindly obedient chattel and—"

"Spare me the lecture," he hissed, "because the king's cronies are coming!"

Her eyes and mouth widened to saucers but the doorknob had begun to turn before he could get his second leg over, so Leo had no choice but to take a leap of faith and throw himself out. And for some reason, Portia tried to catch him and got caught in her wet train, so they both ended up on their backsides on the gravel just as all the king's cronies spilled inside the cardroom.

In silent, tacit agreement, they scrambled on their hands and knees out of sight of the window before he helped her up. Then hand in hand, and with a handful of soggy train each, they hugged the wall as they hurried for cover under one of the archways.

It took Leo a minute to get his bearings.

"The main entrance is just behind us, and we want to avoid that, but we might be able to find another exit that isn't quite so public."

"If we are able to break back into the palace from this courtyard, that is." Being an eternal cynic, Portia wasn't convinced. "Then hope to find an unlocked side door despite the king currently being here and his doors being heavily guarded."

"I will get us out, oh ye of little faith." He tested a door and grinned smugly as he swept his arm toward it. "Look—no locks and no guards."

"But we are back in the palace where someone will see me."

Leo ignored that to sniff the air. "I can smell baking, can't you?"

"What has that got to do with the price of fish?" Portia was too busy being annoyed at him to be able to think beyond it. Something that reminded him so much about how his happily married parents had always bickered that it gave him a bit more hope for them.

"It means that there is a kitchen nearby and where there is a kitchen, there is usually a servant who can be bribed." He grabbed the full weight of her ruined train and followed the scent of baking bread, tugging her along behind him with a face like thunder.

It wasn't long before they heard the hustle and bustle of the kitchen, so he left Portia huddled out of sight in a dark corner and strode in. The first person to spy him was a young scullery maid who couldn't have been much more than fourteen.

"Excuse me." He shot her his most charming smile. "I don't suppose you could show me a way out of the palace where nobody will see me leave?" He subtly showed her a shiny silver crown as an incentive, which was probably more than she earned in a week.

"Of course, sir." She bobbed a curtsy, checked that nobody else had spotted the coin, and scurried past him, suddenly eager to help. Once out of earshot of her coworkers, she said, "The servants' entrance will take you straight out on to Stable Yard Road, just off Cleveland Row."

"Excellent—just give me a second to grab my wife, who if anyone asks, you haven't ever seen." Leo placed the crown into the girl's palm and winked. "Try not to notice the state she is in either as it's all my fault and a bit of a sore point."

To give the young maid credit, she did not blink an eye when she spotted Portia and, true to her word, within minutes they were safely on the street outside without another soul seeing them.

"Didn't I tell you that I would get you out?" He hurried her into a deserted side street and tugged her into the first decent sized doorway they passed. "Now take off those ruined feathers before any pedestrians spot you."

"Why don't you take them off seeing as you are apparently such an expert at *removing* hairpins while I try and detach this stupid train?" If he was not mistaken, there was more than a hint of jealousy in her snippy tone. "I'll be swifter on my feet if I am not dragging ten years of sopping wet brocade behind me."

He knew that he shouldn't build his hopes up when all he had was two paragraphs of an unfinished essay to go on, but he could not help being pleased by her reaction. "You say that as if my previous experience with hairpins bothers you."

"I can assure you that I have no interest whatsoever in the many notches on your bedpost, Leo." Except her face said differently, despite how she tried to cover her irritation by yanking at some fastening at her hip. "I'm sure there are plenty of women out there daft enough to positively throw themselves at you, what with your illustrious title and all."

She refused to look at him even when he started removing her hairpins and so he could not resist teasing her a little bit more. "It is hardly my fault that not every woman has your visceral aversion to *being* with a duke. Some even find me charming as well as impressively ducal. In fact, it's just you that finds me abhorrent."

Something ripped as she tugged hard on her train, and she huffed. "I don't find you abhorrent, Leo. I never have. I just have a problem with all this." One of her arms swept back toward the palace as if he suddenly owned it. "The fundamental principles of your world conflict with mine."

"So it is more my title you don't want to be with and not the man?"

She didn't deny it and more hope sprung eternal. "Things would be simpler if you were just Leo."

"I am just Leo—only Leo also happens to be a duke."

"Do we have to talk about this now?"

Yes, they very much did if that was the only thing keeping them apart. "Tell me, now that you have a title too, *your grace*, do you suddenly feel less like Portia?"

"That's different. I came by mine by accident."

"Because I insisted that my father plant me in my mother's womb when he did?"

She huffed again as her train finally detached and she let it fall to the ground while she put her hands on her hips. "I am aware that my arguments do not appear logical to you—"

"That's because they aren't the least bit logical. Which for someone who usually constructs such brilliant arguments, is odd, don't you think?"

"They make perfect sense to me. Just as they would make perfect sense to anyone else like me."

"Hypocrites, you mean?" Before she could rail at him for that, Leo decided to rip her flimsy argument to shreds first, seeing as she enjoyed a well-constructed one. "Because in one breath, despite everything you know about me and everything we've been through together, you still rigidly stick to your mantra of all dukes are bad. Then in the other, you say that this would all be much simpler if I was just Leo. Which I am, but heaven forbid you give me any credit for that. Or do you believe that I am just like everyone in there?" He jerked his thumb back to the palace. "Because if you do, I should like to hear your evidence. And while we are on the subject of *in there*, do you seriously believe that all aristocrats are the same? That none can be decent? None can be nice? All are self-serving, selfish, and utterly irredeemable? Only it strikes me that you are the worst sort of hypocrite if you claim not to want a revolution because you want equality for all *except* the aristocracy, which, frankly, isn't fair." He extracted the last of the hairpins and thrust her the ruined headdress so he could put his hands on his own hips. "And if it's not that, then all your nonsensical objections can only boil down to one thing—that it isn't your rigid principles that bother you, more the way you feel about me that does. *I* bother you. The concept of *us* bothers you."

"That is the most ridiculous thing that I have ever—" He closed the distance between them and swallowed the end of her sentence in a kiss. Another test that she failed with flying colors because she sighed into his mouth and kissed him right back without a moment's hesitation.

As there was no way he was going to stop her, Leo happily lost himself in it the second she wound her arms around his neck, tugging her flush against him so that they could both deepen it. And they did. However, unlike their first kiss in his garden back in Bath that heated quickly and then burned out of control, they both seemed keen to savor this one. Holding just enough back that they could take it all in and enjoy the slow buildup of passion as they explored each other properly with lips and teeth before their tongues tangled. When they finally did, she moaned softly as she arched against him, not the least bit bothered by how obviously aroused his body was.

Her lips stilled but she did not push him away. "Let me guess. . . . You thought that was the right thing to do just then?"

"Unequivocally." He let his lips whisper over hers again and she couldn't resist joining in. "You kissed me back, didn't you?" He kissed her again. "You keep kissing me back. Why is that?"

Rather than answer, she sidestepped. "We probably shouldn't be doing this. It will only complicate things."

"I couldn't care less." Leo nibbled his way along her jaw to her ear. "Especially when this is clearly what we both want."

She didn't deny that either. "And then what?" She tilted her neck to grant him better access. "What if feelings get involved and muddy the—" He pulled away to stare at her.

"You don't already think that the waters between us are well and truly muddied and feelings are involved?" He knew his were. But hers? Something was holding her back and he wanted it gone. "Would you resist this if I were just Leo?" She exhaled in defeat and shook her head, so he pressed his advantage. "Then stop trying to overcomplicate things. I am just Leo and you know it."

She smoothed her palms over his lapels but still did not pull away. "You sound like my best friend Kitty."

The *"Is it possible that Kitty is correct and I have foolishly fallen in love?"* Kitty, and possibly his new best friend too? "Your friend Kitty is clearly a very wise woman."

A comment that made her instantly smile. "If you knew anything about Kitty, you would appreciate that nothing could be further from the truth. Kitty is a dreamer. A hopeless romantic. One of life's eternal optimists."

"Yet you, the eternal cynic, consider her not just a friend but your *best* friend." He now had the overwhelming suspicion that if he kept pushing her into a corner, Portia would fight tooth and nail to get out of it and cease wavering. The last thing he wanted now that some progress had been made was to encourage her to become even more entrenched in whatever misconception she was wedded to. So he stepped back and shrugged out of his coat so he could drape it around her damp shoulders. Then he wrapped her hand around his arm and led her out of the doorway, hoping a slow walk home while the sun romantically set around them might help his cause more. "Why is that, when birds of a feather are supposed to flock together?"

"I know." She scrunched up her face as if she couldn't understand it either. "A cynic shouldn't have anything in common with such a sunny optimist. But it gets worse because I am a realist and she is a dreamer. I am very organized, reasoned, purposeful, and driven."

"You don't say."

Her pretty eyes narrowed again in mock affront. "Whereas Kitty is as disorganized and distracted as it is possible to be. She is the sort who blurts out whatever random thought pops into her head before she considers whether it is appropriate to say aloud. The sort who would forget her head if it wasn't screwed on and very definitely the sort who would be late for her own funeral. Our friendship makes no sense, but I like to think we balance each other out."

"They do also say that opposites attract." Much like dukes and chaperones.

"They do too. But Kitty and I both love to write, so we do have something fundamental in common."

"Does she write pithy seditious essays that put the world to rights too?"

That made Portia laugh. "Not even slightly. Kitty writes fairy tales—but not the sort for children, if you know what I mean." She pulled a scandalized face.

"I am afraid I don't."

"She writes salacious novels." She slanted him an equally salacious glance filled with all sorts of sinful promise. "The sort that involve damsels in distress and knights in shining armor who sweep those damsels off their feet and kiss them until they are breathless." Her eye roll this time was amused. "While simultaneously dealing with all manner of hijinks and peril before they skip off into the sunset together to live happily ever after."

"We both know how much you disapprove of even the concept of a damsel in distress when you are quite capable of saving yourself."

"Or so I thought—until I needed you to save me. More times than I care to count." She offered him a faux irritated smile while her eyes still sparkled with mischief. "Which still galls, by the way, even if most of your attempts have fallen well shy of the mark."

"Well shy?" He clutched at his heart, which was feeling much lighter. "That wounds."

"Do I need to list them?" She began to count them off on her fingers. "You saved me from a falling bookcase and then ended up unable to walk for almost two weeks."

"But you were unharmed so I shall chalk that one up as a success."

"Hmm." For someone who purported to disapprove of the aristocracy, she did imperious so well. "Then you told me to plead guilty to a crime I did not commit and got me a criminal record."

"But I got you safely out of that prison unmolested."

She waggled her ring finger with his slim gold band on it. "Then you turned the constable against me and I ended up arrested the very next day."

"But I still saved you from a convict ship."

"Which I wouldn't have been destined to be on if you hadn't made me plead guilty to the first charge."

"Semantics."

"And today you tried to drown me and destroyed my lovely feathers."

"Better those awful feathers than your lovely hair." Leo snuggled closer as they sauntered onto Piccadilly. "And you missed one because I seem to recall that I also managed to rescue you after you got yourself impaled on my wall."

"Because that ended so well."

"It did right up until you had a conniption about me being a duke and ran away. Before that, we were all over each other. Tearing at each other's clothes and seconds away from—"

"Gracious, haven't we wandered far from our original topic? When I was supposed to be telling you about Kitty."

That missish outburst made him chuckle. "Coward."

Her lips twitched but other than that she was determined to ignore him. "As much as the unromantic cynic in me wants to hate what Kitty writes, I actually really enjoy it. She might be the world's most useless timekeeper and unreliable governess, but Kitty Blackstone certainly knows how to write a ripping yarn. She sends me her chapters to critique and, as her skills as a salacious novelist have improved over time, I find myself critiquing less and waiting impatiently for the next chapter to arrive in the post so that I can find out what happens to her knight and damsel next."

"I would like to meet her. She sounds like fun." More importantly, she sounded like an ally.

"She is and I know she is keen to meet you too."

"You've told her about me?" He didn't expect her to tell him why she had been compelled to start that essay with Kitty's name in the question, but he suspected her friend understood better than anyone why Portia's heart was wary.

"Nothing good of course, seeing as I disapprove of all dukes on principle, but enough that she has annoyingly started to refer to you as my knight in shining armor." She frowned as if thoroughly disgusted. "She is going to adore you."

"What's not to adore?" Leo grinned just so that he could show her his dimples, seeing as he knew she liked them so much. "It's a wonder you can resist me." Then he nudged her playfully with his elbow. "Not that you just did, of course, and not that I am complaining. Feel free to *not* resist me with impunity whenever the urge arises again, because I guarantee that I shall always be game if you are." To prove that, he tugged her closer and quickly kissed her and then, because that was nowhere near enough, indulged in a more lingering one as well while they were still walking.

Her eyes narrowed. "Why are you suddenly flirting with me so outrageously?"

"It seems like the right thing to do at this time." He sighed, ready to be honest, seeing as the stakes were so high and time was running out. "And because I am tired of us arguing and being angry at each other when we have both been in the wrong while trying to do right.

I want things to be like they were when we were friends." He stopped and tugged her to face him. "And because I want to."

"And if I don't want you to?"

He hauled her close and thoroughly plundered her obviously willing mouth. "You are just going to have to suffer it for as long as we last."

Chapter
THIRTY-ONE

They took a convoluted walk back to Berkeley Square through the empty backstreets and quiet parks, chatting amiably about everything and nothing and stopping to kiss more times than was wise. Each time that he tugged her closer, Portia tried to tell herself that she was playing with fire, and each time that sensible voice in her head fell on increasingly deaf ears. Leo seemed determined to seduce her and she seemed just as determined to let him.

By the time they climbed the steps at the front of the house and he kissed her again before a footman opened the door, she was riper for the picking than she had ever been in her life. Kitty's incendiary words about enjoying the benefits of marriage while they lasted were ringing in her ears while something decidedly wanton was happening to all the nerve endings between her legs.

He led her to the foot of the stairs. "Shall I send up a maid to help you out of that wet dress?" They both knew what he was really asking.

"I would rather you did." Portia barely recognized her own voice. It was so needy and willing.

His blue eyes instantly darkened with desire. "So would I."

His hand rested on the small of her back as they climbed the stairs, and he laced his fingers in hers at the top of them. Neither of them spoke as he led her along the landing and then into his room. Words seemed unnecessary. Especially as she didn't want either of them to say anything that might inadvertently shatter the spell they were under. This truce was too new to risk testing it.

He let go of her to turn the key in the lock, then leaned back against the door. "Are you sure about this? Only if you—" It was her turn to close the distance between them.

"Just shut up and kiss me."

And he did, only this time and to her hungry body's complete delight, he held nothing back. It was a deep, decadent, and thoroughly carnal kiss that seemed to involve every bit of him because she experienced it from her lips to her toes. Her breasts were flattened against the solid wall of his chest while his erection pressed insistently into her lower body. So hard and ready that she could feel it through all her layers of petticoats and heavy brocade. He filled his hands with the cheeks of her bottom and dragged her hips still closer.

Needing the heat of his bare skin against hers, Portia pushed his coat from his shoulders and he briefly let go of her backside so he could wrestle his arms from the sleeves while she set about the buttons on his waistcoat. No sooner had that hit the floor than he yanked off his cravat and stripped out of his shirt in one impressively fluid movement.

His chest was a thing of beauty, firm and smooth and dusted with dark golden hair that narrowed and arrowed through his navel on its seductive route below the waistband of his trousers. Portia traced it all with flattened hands while he watched her progress with stormy, desire-filled eyes. She trailed one finger down the middle of his abdomen to the bulge that called to her and screamed for her to be brazen.

She pressed her palm against it and he moaned, his eyes scrunching shut as she explored the tantalizing shape of him over his clothes. When that wasn't enough and curiosity got the better of her, she slipped her hand beneath the waistband and reveled in his involuntary shudder when her fingertips found the silken skin stretched so taut over his rigid manhood.

He sucked in an erratic breath and his eyelids fluttered open as she gently caressed the whole length of him. "Do you like that?" She wasn't entirely sure what she was doing but she wanted to do it right. One of the benefits of having Kitty as a friend is that Kitty had always managed to find the sort of books that contained a great many lurid details about what went on between a man and a woman in the bedchamber. All of those books had stated that men enjoyed very much being touched here. It surprised her how much she enjoyed it too. His shape, his hardness, the heat that his aroused body created.

The way she undid him.

"What do you think?" A nerve in his tight jaw ticked as he choked out every word. One of his hands covered hers over the fabric as the other fumbled with the buttons of his falls. "Hold me."

"Like this?" Her hand slipped lower to cup his testicles and he groaned. "Or like this?" She wrapped her fingers around his shaft and adored watching his eyes slam closed again as his erection jerked within the confines of her closed hand and she tentatively stroked it.

"Either or." He kissed her hard until he could endure it no longer and wrenched his mouth away. "I need you out of that dress now." Leo had never looked quite so ferocious or so desperate and that thrilled her.

"Then relieve me of it."

She turned, presenting him with the laces that held her gown together, expecting him to go straight to them as they both wanted, but instead his fingers went to her hair and he tormented them both by gently removing every hairpin. When her still-damp hair hung heavily down her back, he brushed it all to one side, then with her back to him, he slipped his arms around her waist and kissed her neck and shoulders. "Do you like this, Portia?"

"Yes."

"And what about this?" One of his big hands cupped her womanhood over her skirts.

A stupid question when she instantly arched her hips against it. "Yes."

"Would you like me to touch you like you just touched me?"

Suddenly, it felt as though she might explode if he didn't. "Yes please."

While his teeth teased her earlobe, he took his time hoisting her heavy skirt up as if he knew that every single second of delay made the wanton nerves between her legs throb more and more with anticipation.

The cool night air whispered over her bare skin, torturing her still more, but Leo refused to touch her until she was completely exposed below the waist. His hand cupped her again possessively. "You have no idea how many times I have yearned to do this." He sounded as undone as she felt as he dipped his finger between her shamelessly slick folds and immediately found a spot that made her knees weak as he caressed it. "You're so wet."

"Is that a bad thing?"

He choked out a sound, part chuckle, part groan. "It is the best thing." And to prove that, he used just the pad of his talented, wicked index finger and her moisture to create unspeakable amounts of pleasure. Then, each time that she thought that it could not possibly feel any more wonderful, he gently increased the pressure and the tempo until she was writhing and bucking against his hand.

A curious soul could not read one of Kitty's scandalous books and not touch herself, so Portia knew where this was going, but it had never felt this intense or so utterly sublime before. Whatever peak Leo was taking her to was one that she knew she hadn't yet visited, and all at once she was in a hurry to get there. As if he sensed that, he twisted them both so that she faced the long mirror in the corner where he watched her intently as she began to come apart. Oddly, even though she had never bared herself like this in front of a man and would usually balk at the idea of being so vulnerable before one, she wanted his eyes on her. Wanted him to witness what he did to her. What he was doing to her.

Why was that?

"Oh my god, Leo . . ." She was so close. So dangerously close.

And then it hit her.

Wave after wave of sensations that pulsed from her core and radiated ruthlessly down every single nerve ending. A cascade of ecstasy that left her tumbling back against him, witless, as she cried his name like a benediction.

When she finally floated back to earth, his reflection in the mirror was awed but smug. And so hungry for her that it took her breath away all over again. "I am going to explode unless you are naked and on your back right this minute." Oddly after what had just happened to her, so was Portia.

"Then get me out of this stupid dress."

He set to work on her laces with gloriously clumsy fingers that made Portia feel powerful. As his frustration built, so did hers, and she tried to help him but the fastenings appeared to have fused themselves closed thanks to all the water he had doused them in.

"They're stuck bloody fast!" She adored that he sounded so desperate. "I hate this damned dress." He stepped back, his breathing erratic, and raked an agitated hand through his already mussed hair. "I fear desperate times call for desperate measures." He stalked toward his nightstand where the bellpull was.

"Please tell me that you are not going to call for help?" Because that would be mortifying.

"Don't be daft, woman." He snatched something up and stalked back to her, then right in front of her wary eyes, he flicked open his razor. "I'm going to cut you out of the damned thing." Then, before she could argue, he spun her around and did just that. The blade was so sharp that it sliced through her sodden laces like butter, and before she knew it, her cumbersome court gown was a puddle at her feet.

He didn't bother even attempting to untie the ribbons at the front of her tight stays, and simply sliced through them too. Closely followed by the shoulder seams of both that and her thin chemise. With a wolfish grin, he snapped the razor closed and tossed it, then ripped every stitch of her undergarments away.

Instinctively, Portia almost covered herself with her hands, but the way Leo's gaze appreciatively raked her body made her just stand there while he took it all in.

"Bloody hell but you're beautiful." The reverence in his voice made her believe him. "Come here." She wasn't usually one who responded well to an order but she liked that one. Liked more how utterly divine it felt to finally feel his skin against hers.

When he kissed her, it was with a hunger that she had never experienced before and he thoroughly plundered her mouth as they staggered to the bed. He pushed her backward onto the mattress, his hungry eyes still raking her up and down as he dispensed with his breeches. His uncaged erection drew her eyes like a moth to a flame and held her gaze for the longest time before she dragged it up to his face, wondering why he still hadn't joined her on the bed so he could put it to excellent use. "What's the matter?"

"I'm just giving you time to change your mind. . . . Are you sure you want to do this?"

His thoughtfulness both humbled her and melted her heart. "I am going to explode if we don't." She reached out her hand and he smiled as he took it, then laughed as she yanked him onto the bed on top of her. "But you should probably know that you are my first. Just in case you were wondering."

He stared deep into her eyes and swallowed as if that humbled him, before his dimples slowly emerged on either side of the most sinful smile she had ever seen. "And you should probably know that I fully intend to be your last too. Just in case you were wondering."

His kiss felt both decadent and poignant and Portia happily lost herself in it as fresh desire kindled anew. He tore his lips from hers to worship every inch of her with them instead. He started with her breasts, which died and went to heaven as he suckled her nipples to sharp points. Then he kissed his way down her abdomen, the inside of her thigh and her calf on one side, before he went back up the other way on her other leg. His tongue found that wanton, greedy nubbin of nerves at the precise moment it screamed for more attention, and in no time she was writhing against his mouth with one of her hands tangled in his hair while the other fisted the sheets. Unbelievably ready to climax again despite just experiencing the most monumental one of her life.

She was right on the cusp when he shifted position and completely covered her with his body and his breathing was just as labored. But because the wretch was noble to his core, he once again hesitated. "You need to invite me in, Portia. I need to know that you are sure."

"Take me," was all she said and he did. Sliding into her with one smooth but gentle thrust.

Bizarrely, despite expecting it to, the intrusion didn't hurt at all. She was too wet and too ready for her body to more than register a moment's shock that he was buried all the way inside her. That evaporated the second he began to move inside her and all she could think was how perfect it felt. How perfectly they fitted together. Moved together. Melded together. Almost as if she had been made for him and him for her because even their hearts seemed to beat in complete synchronicity.

Then all at once, any thoughts at all became impossible because nothing else mattered beyond where their bodies joined and how that joining made her body rejoice. Only this time, when she tumbled into exquisite oblivion, he was right there with her. Staring all the way into her soul and calling her his darling as they touched heaven together.

Chapter THIRTY-TWO

Breakfast was in full swing when she strode into the room a strategic ten minutes before Leo, hoping that she didn't look like a woman as thoroughly and gloriously ravished as she was. Repeatedly. "Good morning." They hadn't talked about what last night meant, or even if it meant anything, but Portia and Leo had both agreed that it probably wasn't wise to get his mother's hopes up.

Letitia's teacup paused midway to her lips while both Abigail and Emilia stared at Portia with interest. "Good afternoon." It was obvious that they all already had suspicions. "Am I allowed to ask what happened to you and Leo last night after you abandoned us so scandalously at the palace in the middle of His Majesty's reception?"

"There was an incident." While she intended to keep a great deal of what had happened last night a secret, she had to give her prying mother-in-law something. "A catastrophic incident with my feathers." Portia might not have Kitty's talent for telling a ripping yarn, but all three ladies were in fits of giggles by the time Leo arrived in the breakfast room with the morning post a good ten minutes later.

Letitia abruptly stopped laughing to glare at him. "Did you really set your poor wife's head alight and then try to drown her in several gallons of water?"

"Sadly, I am guilty as charged. But in my defense, they were extenuating circumstances and not all of them were of my making." He flicked through the letters and began distributing them. Most went first to his mother. "Word of your triumphant return to town has clearly got out as they all feel like invitations." He tossed two down on the table in front of his chair. "Only bills for me."

Then he handed the final one to his sister, who, to Portia's mind, did a very poor job of hiding that it had come from her beloved Percy because she cracked it open straightaway and struggled not to sigh aloud.

"Who is that from?" Leo was already suspicious.

"Nobody."

"That's a big soppy grin for a nobody." To all intents and purposes, he wandered to the covered tureens on the sideboard to help himself to some food, but Portia just knew the lovely morning was about to take a very bad turn when Leo snatched the missive from his sister's hand.

Abigail tried to grab it but he had already read all that he needed to. "This is from Percival Bloody Digby!" His rage was as instant as it was predictable.

"Give that back!" Abigail shot up from her seat, ready for a fight. "It is private and none of your business!"

"This is absolutely my business!" He scrunched the letter in his fist and jabbed the air between them. "How many times do I have to forbid you from having anything to do with that dangerous scoundrel before you deign to listen?" Then, because the red mist had descended, and he had quite forgotten how to be reasonable, he decided that laying the law down was his only option. "Well no more, Abigail! While you live under my roof, you will abide by my rules and it will be a cold day in hell before I ever allow you anywhere near that ne'er-do-well ever again!"

And off he went in typical overbearing Leo fashion, slamming the door behind him, leaving Abigail on the brink of tears and everyone else stunned by the ferociousness of his outburst.

"I'll go talk to him." Portia stayed Letitia who was about to do just that, and scurried after him down the hall.

The walls shook as he slammed his study door but for once Portia did not knock on it.

"Did you honestly think that that was the best response to the situation?"

"I do not need a lecture from you to tell me how to deal with *my* family."

"Too bad because they are currently *my* family too so you are going to get one."

"Do not—"

"Oh stick a sock in it, Leo! You are wasting your breath if you think all your overbearing bluster will intimidate me. The day that I do not speak up for an injustice will be the day that pigs fly!"

"Injustice?" He had the temerity to look outraged as he waved his arms in the air. "What the hell is unjust about trying to keep my baby sister safe from the clutches of a dangerous revolutionary?"

"Well, as I am not sure where to start with that ludicrous set of accusations, I shall begin with your misunderstanding of basic words." She stalked to the bookshelf and grabbed a dictionary that she quickly thumbed through. "'Revolutionary—a person who *advocates* or *takes part in* a revolution.'" She slapped the book down on his desk so he could read what she just had. "If we ignore, for one moment, that the last revolution to take place in this country was the English Civil War which ended almost two hundred years ago, Percy has never advocated for revolution in his life! He is a reformer." In case Leo struggled to understand the difference, she rifled for that entry in the dictionary too. "'Reformer—a person dedicated to the improvement or amendment of things that are wrong, corrupt, or unsatisfactory.'"

He opened his mouth to speak but she cut him off. "As for needing to keep Abigail safe from his dangerous clutches, have you quite forgotten that twice in quick succession your sister has put herself in danger? The first expressly against Percy's wishes and the second entirely without his knowledge!" She wagged her finger like the governess she used to be when one of her charges had disappointed her. "And finally, what sort of a narrow-minded, arrogant, and insufferable fool thinks that the most sensible way to break up two people who are hopelessly in love is to forbid them from ever seeing each other again? Because that worked so well on your parents when your grandfather forbade them from a liaison, didn't it? Or am I mistaken and they did not make a baby out of wedlock and then run away to Gretna Green at the first opportunity when they were both just a few months older than Abigail is now?"

She shook her head and sighed. "I know that you feel responsible for her safety and I suspect you have done ever since she fell out of that tree, but all you are succeeding in doing is pushing Abigail and Percy together. All the while pushing more of a wedge between you and your sister than there needs to be. Don't make her hate you, Leo. Especially when you are too good a man to be hated."

He raised his finger to wag it and then dropped it to his side. "Then how am I supposed to keep her out of harm's way when she seems hell-bent to keep running toward it since she met him?"

"Is there a chance that Abigail's involvement in the reform movement and her love for Percy are two entirely separate things?"

"Oh let me see . . ." In the absence of a real argument, he resorted to sarcasm. "He's a reformer and she's a reformer so . . ." He tapped his chin as if it were a great conundrum.

"He's a liberal-minded person with a strong social conscience and so is she. And so, unless it has escaped your notice, are you."

"And your point is?"

"That you and your sister are both your father's children. That you cannot, no matter how much you rant and rave and lay down the law, possibly win this, so you must compromise. Learn to meet people halfway. I appreciate the concept is anathema to you because you are obsessed with being in control, but there aren't many people in this world who are as stubborn as you are and one of them is your sister."

"It is a man's job to protect those under his care."

"Just as it is apparently a wife's job to make her husband a better man, so please try to listen to me in your usual rational and reasoned way because this deaf, irrational, and irate version of you isn't the slightest bit helpful." His brows furrowed but he seemed to be calming down. "I know you carry this huge burden of guilt for what happened to Abigail on your watch all those years ago, Leo, but you are not that careless sixteen-year-old boy any longer." The irony wasn't lost on Portia that they had both set themselves on a rigid path of righteousness at the same age that likely wasn't the right path for them to still be on.

"And your sister isn't a silly little girl with fluff for brains anymore either. Time marches forward. Things change. People mature. But we all, one way or another, have to become who we are meant to become alongside those we are meant to become them with. Your headstrong sister will likely still marry Percy whether you approve or not, so what you need to decide before it is too late is if you want to be a part of her future or not. Because you are currently losing her and you know it."

He sunk into his chair as if all the fight had gone out of him, so she kissed the top of his head. "Perhaps it is time for you to release Abigail from *your* clutches, Leo, and trust that she might know what is best for her far better than you do? I guarantee if you let her go, she won't go far. She loves you too much to ever truly leave you."

As that seemed as good a moment as any to leave him to pickle in his own juices for a while, she headed back to the breakfast room where Abigail's heartbreak had, unsurprisingly, turned to anger. "I take it that as he is not with you, my overbearing brother has refused to see any sense?" Then, exactly like him, she stood up ready to knock some into him herself.

"Give him some time and I am sure that . . ." Portia's words trailed off as Leo reappeared.

As Abigail prepared to pounce, he held out Percy's letter like an olive branch. "I apologize for taking this. You are right. Your private correspondence isn't any of my business." Then, as his sister's jaw dropped to the floor, he made a concession that even Portia could not have possibly expected so soon on the back of his temper tantrum. "If you are serious about your Mr. Digby and he is serious about courting you, you should invite him to dine with us one evening when we get back to Bath. I should like to get to know my beloved sister's fiancé before he joins our family."

Then, as everyone blinked at him in shock, he took his own seat at the table. Only Portia was aware that he reached for her hand beneath the tablecloth and held it as if his life depended on it while his mother tactfully changed the subject.

Chapter
THIRTY-THREE

"Remind me again why we are here?" Leo caressed her fingers where they rested in the crook of his arm as they walked through Hyde Park, no doubt fully aware of the effect it was having on Portia's increasingly wayward body. "Because if you had pleaded a headache like I suggested half an hour ago, we could have spent the entire afternoon making love in a blissfully empty house instead. We travel back to Bath tomorrow, so it will be at least a week before I can have my wicked way with you in the afternoon again."

"Because it is apparently a family tradition that you and your sisters take a boat out on the Serpentine whenever you are all in London. And, more importantly, your mother also decreed that the entire Sloane family should promenade this afternoon to prove to the rest of the ton that we do not give a jot what any of them think of us."

A decree that had come about because yet another gossip column had spread some unfounded speculation about the Delinquent Duchess of Debden. This one suggesting that she and Leo hadn't caused the king grave offense by absconding early from his court reception five days ago, like all the other scandal rags had intimated. But had instead been forcibly removed by the palace guards because Portia had insulted the king when she had been presented to him by stating that she could not wait until he was deposed in a revolution. "And we cannot waste every afternoon in bed just because you have suddenly become insatiable." Although she did rather enjoy that he couldn't seem to get enough of her—almost as much as she enjoyed what they did in bed at all hours of the day.

"I seem to recall that yesterday afternoon, it was you who insisted that I have my wicked way with you, so I am not the only insatiable one." He pretended to be put out by that. "Technically your wifely duty is to honor me with your body. You are my chattel, after all, and took a vow to obey me, so you will only have yourself to blame if I lapse into extramarital original sin because you have denied me my conjugal rights in a timely enough manner."

Portia rolled her eyes at his teasing tone because one thing that she had learned about her duke this week was that he loved to flirt, and he especially loved to flirt in an outrageously naughty and provocative manner designed to get a rise out of her. "You exercised your conjugal rights with me not half an hour ago, so that will just have to tide you over until I deign to suffer your touch again." They both knew that no sufferance was involved. All he had had to do was kiss her neck while she attempted to don the hat that went with her new duchess-ified walking dress, and the next moment she had been riding him like a stallion, as the telltale creases in her skirts were testament. "Or go find another woman who will service you in my stead. That shouldn't be too much trouble for a man who is as well schooled in hairpin removal as you are. What sort of an idle duke doesn't have a mistress or three on the side?"

"I fear you've ruined me for all other women, wife, so only you will do."

That was another thing that he had taken to doing. Constantly reminding her that they were wed. It was most disconcerting when there was still every chance that they might not be soon. Neither of them had mentioned the annulment on this unexpected honeymoon they were enjoying away from their stark reality. Nor had they mentioned feelings or anything to do with the future. Preferring instead to languish in the gloriously carnal limbo that this week in Mayfair had afforded them. Leo had, however, made sure every single time that their bodies joined to ensure that there was minimal chance of him making her pregnant, so she supposed that spoke volumes. They were basically having a transient, passionate affair rather than a marriage, and she told herself that was ultimately for the best. She would enjoy it while it lasted and refuse to allow any of her growing regret or indecision about their current situation spoil what time they had left.

"Debden!" An older man waved Leo down. "I thought you were supposed to be on your way back to Bath?" He looked familiar and Portia struggled to place him. "Or have your plans changed since we spoke at the palace?"

That was where she had seen him! He was one of the many brocaded and pomaded peers who had waylaid Leo at the king's reception.

"We leave first thing tomorrow."

"You cannot postpone it until the day after? Only we need your support."

"We both know that there is more chance of hell freezing over than that bill you want to propose even being considered in the current climate, whether I speak up for it or not." Leo smiled politely. "But it was good to see you, Gray." With that, they continued walking.

"Gray, as in Earl Gray?"

"The very one."

"The Earl Gray who is a vocal supporter of all manner of parliamentary reforms."

Leo sighed. "Yes."

"What bill is he proposing?"

"One that is so large, unwieldy, and unfocused that I am not altogether sure what its purpose is beyond putting the cat among the pigeons."

"It's a reform bill, isn't it?"

"Right now, it is more a ragtag collection of grievances covering everything from rotten boroughs to workers' rights, a change in the poor law to an extension of the franchise with some repeals to the Bloody Code thrown in. In other words, it's a typical, disorganized, and poorly thought-out Whig muddle, and it just doesn't have the support within the party, let alone Parliament, beyond Lord Gray's closest circle to be any more than that."

"It sounds to me like it could be something one day."

"And when it is, I will throw my support and my valuable time right behind it. Until then, these speculative debates are as useful as shouting into the wind."

"So what you are really saying is that you cannot be bothered to waste your breath on what is morally right unless you are in a majority?" And suddenly Portia was incensed at his attitude. "When surely, it would be more useful to add your voice to the cause and convince more parliamentarians of the right of what Lord Gray is proposing, so that eventually there are so many voices shouting into the wind that not even Parliament can drown them out?" She resisted the overwhelming urge to shake him by his distracting shoulders. "You are a powerful and privileged peer after all and one of the rare three percent who have any say when the rest of us in the voiceless ninety-seven percent have no say whatsoever. Shame on you, Leo!"

He was silent for the longest time. "Is this another example of my wife trying to make me a better man?"

"I know that you are a good man, Leo. The foundations are all there. All I am doing is giving you a gentle nudge to remind you of it."

"There was nothing gentle about that lecture, madam." Then he huffed in resignation. "But I shall concede that you made a valid point."

"And?"

"And if it makes you happy, I will attend the damned debate."

"It does make me happy." She snuggled his arm to prove it. "What difference does another night in Mayfair make in the grand scheme of things?"

"Easy for you to say when you do not have to suffer the chaotic, idiotic, patience-testing circus that is the House of Lords tomorrow afternoon."

"If I could be there to lend my voice to the wind alongside you I would. But I shall be there in spirit, husband. Cheering you and this noble lost cause on from the comfort of my pointless embroidery chair like a dutiful but oppressed and voiceless chattel should."

He chuckled as they followed the path. "I'm really not sure that a duchess can complain about being a chattel, Portia. Especially when you now sit at the very top of that voiceless ninety-seven percent. A duchess can have great influence if she wields her power well enough, and not only by nagging her poor husband."

"Doing what? Knitting socks, making up baskets for the poor?" Portia scoffed, unsure where this was going but happy to play along. "Looking pretty while I hang on my superior husband's arm while never opening my big mouth?"

"Sarah Churchill, the Duchess of Marlborough, campaigned tirelessly for Whig causes and was Queen Anne's main counsel. Georgiana, the scandalous Duchess of Devonshire, was also a political activist and philosophical influencer who lived and breathed the reforming ideals of John Locke and Rousseau. To such an extent that the public loved her so the government had to listen to her on occasion. So many duchesses and marchionesses and countesses are patrons of all manner of laudable things from hospitals to schools, and I guarantee that there will be an aristocratic woman spearheading the current fight against child labor, improving factory and mining conditions, and all manner of sweeping reforms that are urgently needed. Women who use their privilege as a platform and the finances at their disposal as a weapon and, while I agree that it might be slow, as change so often is, in the end they really make a difference."

All valid arguments—but why was he suddenly making them? "And your labored point is?"

"That you can do more good for the causes you hold dear as the

Duchess of Debden than you ever could as Portia Kendall, so maybe you should consider staying a duchess? Till death do us part?"

Of all the things she had expected Leo to say today, "till death do us part" wasn't one of them. "What?" *Was he seriously suggesting what she thought he was suggesting?* "How is me using and abusing your title the least bit fair on you?"

"Leo!" A giggling Emilia had already reached the pontoon several yards ahead to secure them a boat. "Stop dawdling! It's your turn to row!"

"Isn't it always?" he yelled back as he extricated himself from Portia's arm. Then, without another word, he left her to jog toward the girls.

"Leo!" Portia dashed after him, still reeling. "Leopold Sloane!" He turned, still moving—albeit backward—and smiled. Making no effort whatsoever to stop like she wanted. "Are you honestly suggesting that we stay married?"

His dimples flashed. "Of course I am, my darling."

"But Leo—" She would not be bamboozled by mischievous dimples and seductive *my darling*s. "Be serious."

"I have never been more serious." And all of a sudden, his smile conveyed that. "If it helps, for context, you should probably also know that I am head over heels in love with you and have been since the beginning. Probably, truth be told, since you first took my breath away at your interview." Then, despite having just knocked her sideways, he turned back to the boats again and quickened his pace.

As if rowing aimlessly across the Serpentine was somehow more pressing than them having any further conversation about the staggering and monumental confession he had just made.

Portia stopped dead, her sensible head reeling and her stupid heart singing.

He loved her.

Leo loved her!

What the hell was she supposed to do about that?

Chapter THIRTY-FOUR

Leo decided to leave Portia to mull for the rest of the afternoon and made sure they didn't have a single moment alone until the five of them arrived back home after the park. She was oddly silent and he had no idea if that was a good or a bad sign, but he was glad that he had told her. He had wanted to for days and had almost bared his heart during numerous passionate encounters, but held back. Reasoning that any declaration made in the heat of the moment would give his clever wife a reason to doubt the earnestness of the words.

Now, like the accused in the dock awaiting the deliberating jury's return, he was nervous as to what her verdict would be.

"Who fancies some tea?" asked his mother as she climbed the front steps.

"Me," answered Portia without a second's hesitation and with a furtive glance his way, which all rather suggested she was either putting off telling him the bad news or the jury was still out.

"Your grace?" A man suddenly wandered toward them on the pavement, his hat respectfully in his hands. "I presume you are the Duke of Debden?"

"I am." But Leo was certain he had never seen this fellow in his life. "Can I help you?"

"I am Mr. Walker. Mr. Robert Walker of Soho. You recently purchased one of my machines and I wanted to check that it met with your satisfaction?"

"Oh." What bloody awful timing. "Yes. Of course." Leo placed a hand on the small of his wife's back to usher her up the steps and out of earshot, but she was having none of it and planted her feet. Her eyes were also suspiciously narrowed. "It arrived in perfect order, sir."

"That is good to know." Like Portia, Mr. Walker showed no signs of moving. "One worries when such an expensive piece of equipment travels so many miles on the water. Bath is such a long way from London."

"Indeed, it is but it came at record speed with no hiccups at all. Thank you so much for taking the trouble to check." Leo inclined his head to signal that this impromptu meeting was done while racking his brains for a suitable lie to tell Portia to explain the strange conversation as he practically pushed her up the steps. Would she believe he had ordered a new plow from London? Or a threshing machine perhaps? Or a—

She stopped dead on the top step and spun around. "Robert Walker of Soho? You make printing presses, don't you, Mr. Walker?"

"I do indeed," said their unwelcome visitor, his chest puffing with pride. "I like to think that we make the best printing presses in the entire country."

Her gaze flicked to Leo and he could see the cogs of her clever mind working overtime. "You are licensed to make Stanhope presses, I believe, Mr. Walker?" Except the dark brow that quirked in question quirked at Leo instead of their guest.

"We do others, of course, but the Stanhope is in a league of its own." Oblivious that one of Leo's secrets was now unraveling in front of his wife like knitting, Mr. Walker was only too happy to expand. "Especially when it comes to printing things in large quantities—like newspapers. Can I inquire as to what provincial newspaper you needed the press for, your grace?" He turned to Leo and for effect, Portia did too.

"Er . . ."

Portia gave him a hard nudge before she answered in Leo's stead. "*Equitas*, I'll wager. Although he is prone to be annoyingly coy about his apparent philanthropy to that publication."

"Ah," said Mr. Walker. "Your secret is safe with me, your grace." The man tapped the side of his nose. "But in my humble opinion, it is a worthy publication, to be sure, and one I am glad my printing presses are now associated with. Although it does explain why you needed a new one so fast. Raided again, was it?"

"Of course." There was a clipped edge to Portia's voice. "And everything in it smashed to smithereens because some in the government prefer the public not to be informed of important issues that concern them, while the rest cannot be bothered to find the time to fight for them."

"Indeed. Our government needs more good men like you to stand up for what is right, your grace."

"You are so right, Mr. Walker." She skewered Leo with her glare. "The more good men who shout into the wind, the more chance we all have of things being changed." That unsubtle dig delivered, Portia beamed at Mr. Walker. "Thank you for taking the trouble of stopping by, sir."

When the unwelcome visitor finally bid them both good day, Portia stomped inside and spoke to his mother rather than Leo. "As it appears that your confounding son and I need to have an urgent conversation, we won't now be joining you for tea, Letitia." Then she glared at him again before she marched up the stairs, expecting him to follow.

Her hands were on her hips by the time he reached her bedchamber and she used her foot to kick the door closed behind him. "Well . . . aren't you just full of surprises today?" He could not tell if she was angry or not and that was disconcerting. "Were you ever going to tell me that it was you who replaced *Equitas*'s broken printing press?"

"Probably not."

That answer made her glare intensify. "And you replaced it at doubtless eye-watering expense because?"

"I can afford to and it seemed like the right thing to do when I felt somewhat responsible for Nolley's venom toward the newspaper. And because . . ." He huffed, realizing that she wouldn't accept anything but the whole truth. "It broke my heart to witness how upset all his wanton destruction made you."

"I thought we had agreed to keep no more secrets from one another?" She was clearly peeved that he had, despite his recently revealed largesse to her beloved newspaper. "Or was that a one-sided edict that only I was supposed to abide by?"

"Of course it wasn't one-sided." Her foot began to tap. "But in my defense . . ." He had already bared his heart so it was pointless pretending otherwise. Especially when she had him over a barrel. "For pity's sake, I am in love with you, Portia! I didn't want you feeling any more beholden to me than you already do."

She said nothing. Folded her arms. Walked to the window.

Sighed.

"Why do you have to be such a gallingly wonderful human being?" When she turned, her eyes were stormy as she walked toward him. "Why couldn't you have been a typical, entitled, pompous, and wholly dislikeable duke like I wanted you to be?"

He shrugged, not sure where this was going. "Sorry."

Her finger prodded his chest. "You've been nothing but an enormous and unwelcome complication to me, Leopold Sloane. How dare you upend my life and force me to reevaluate staunch beliefs that I have held for all my adult life?"

"Should I apologize again?"

"No." Her hands flattened against his chest a moment before she pressed her mouth against his, then as she kissed him, she set to work on the buttons of his waistcoat. "If you don't mind, I am going to have to have my wicked way with you now."

"Of course I don't mind." He happily kissed her back until he realized that he was still none the wiser as to the way she felt about him. Still in wretched, hopeful limbo. "But—" He tore his lips from hers and held her at arm's length. "I need to know what that means."

She looked down, unable to meet his eye, and that made him brace himself for bad news. "I've been laboring over you—us—for a week, Leo. To the point where I've picked up my pen more times than I can count so that I could organize all my conflicting feelings in an essay and nothing would come."

It seemed prudent not to mention that he knew that. Especially as he was desperate to hear her say the words to him rather than read them clandestinely. And because she was obviously still angry at him for the printing press secret he had stupidly kept. If that had made her rant, then the knowledge that he had repeatedly invaded her privacy would likely make her explode with rage. So he stayed quiet and hoped beyond hope that this moment would signal the turning point he craved with all his besotted heart.

"I've no logical arguments against you, beyond you being a duke, and no arguments for why I cannot continue to resist you, Leo, despite all my rigid political principles. That has never happened to me before." She stepped forward, laying her head against his chest and wrapping her arms around his waist, seeking comfort. Something this bold and independent woman had never done before. "Until I realized the reason I had nothing was the only objection that I had was your title, and the only reason that I had no supporting arguments to talk me out of my love for you was because . . ." She squeezed him tighter. "I've been stubbornly suppressing them all. You are an overbearing, heavy-handed, insufferable, aristocratic man—and against all my better judgment, and against all my steadfast objections to being someone's wife, I have fallen head over heels in love with you too."

Leo took a moment to let that sink in. To revel in it. Thank the heavens for it. Then he lifted her chin so that he could see her lovely face. "Does that mean you'll stay my duchess?"

"It means that I am prepared to give us a go."

"I'll take that." Their next kiss was the most poignant and utterly perfect of his life, because both their hearts were involved.

Once it was done, he lifted her up and carried her to the bed, then reverently undressed her on the mattress. As their passion built, even that was different.

Every touch felt significant.

Every word was treasured.

For the first time in their married life, he finally understood what the vow meant to honor someone with your body, because they told each other that irrefutable truth over and over again with every single kiss. Every single caress. Every relieved and grateful sigh.

Before he pushed his body inside hers, however, he wanted to be sure before he gave all of himself to her and potentially closed off her last escape route. "Can I come inside you, Portia?"

"Yes." She sighed that as she smiled against his lips. "As much as it surprises me to say it, or how much the consequences of it were never something I ever considered before you swooped in and flummoxed me, I would like that very much."

Chapter
THIRTY-FIVE

Leo had quite the spring in his step when they ventured downstairs several hours later. The world brighter and his heart so full it was fit to burst. Better still, his head finally seemed like his own once more. Thanks to the marvelous distraction of Portia, he hadn't worried about a damn thing all week and, now that he had conquered those intrusive demons that had plagued him for weeks, he felt lighter too. In fact, with all his worries gone, everything in his garden was rosy and he couldn't have been happier about it.

He escorted his wife—the love of his life—to the drawing room where the rest of his womenfolk were sequestered and then went to leave. An intention that incurred the wrath of his mother.

"Where do you think you are going when dinner is in less than ten minutes?"

"I just have a few accounts to sign off."

"Can't they wait until tomorrow seeing as you have postponed our leaving."

"Not really. Portia is insistent that I shout into the wind tomorrow afternoon and that futile chore is bound to overrun."

"By that," said his lovely, passionate wife with a roll of her eyes, "He means that he is attending an important debate in the House of Lords tomorrow to support Earl Gray's latest reform bill, and he doesn't know when it will end."

The mere mention of the reforming Gray started Abigail off, so he left her and Portia discussing the many injustices that the government needed to fix and headed to his study.

Thanks to his ardent quest to woo his wife, he had barely visited his study all week, so he wasn't surprised to see the neat pile of post waiting for him on his desk. He did a quick flick through, separating out all the bills so that he could arrange to have them paid, and tossing all the Mayfair invitations on the fire seeing as they were imminently headed home to Bath ready to start their new life together proper as man and wife. He almost put his regular weekly copy of *Equitas* to one side so that he could read it on the long journey home, but paused. Wondering why the hell he had still neglected to yet mention to Portia that he had subscribed to her beloved seditious rag for years, as had his father before him? It was hardly a state secret after all, and now that they were being completely honest with each other and no longer kept secrets, holding something so unimportant back seemed daft.

He snatched it up, curious to see if the new printing press he had bought them had improved the look of it, and cracked the seal to unfold it. Then grinned because Mr. Walker's superior machine had indeed made it look crisper and cleaner and somehow more professional, and he knew that would delight his lovely wife.

The headlines especially, really stood out. His gaze automatically went to the opinion piece first.

Does the government's suppression of dissent really work? The headline asked in true Portia fashion and he experienced a sense of pride that *Equitas* had decided to continue writing that bold first column like an essay the way his clever wife used to.

But then he started to read it, and his blood ran cold as there was only one pen that wrote with such aplomb.

Two years ago, when a peaceful but large protest gathered in St. Peter's Field in Lancashire asking for

parliamentary reforms, the embarrassed government sent the army in to break it up. It turned into a senseless bloodbath that has haunted all of us since. Instead of learning from that tragic mistake and making some concessions, the government instead set about tightening all the laws suppressing anything that it sees as a threat to its power and imposed harsh penalties on anyone who dared challenge the status quo. I am sure that they believed that was the best way forward at the time; however, as time marches on, instead of preventing another bloodbath, I would argue that all that they have succeeded in doing is making another Peterloo Massacre inevitable.

As his hair follicles twitched in preparation of standing on end at the mention of the Peterloo Massacre, Leo felt himself spiral into the all-consuming anger, fear, and blind panic that he had hoped and prayed he was done with.

He sucked in a calming breath and tried to be rational.

They were just words.

Truthful words.

Compelling words because she had such a way with them.

This was who she was. What she did.

Her essence. As much a part of her as her beautiful smile and bold personality. Her heart and soul. Everything he loved so much about his wonderful, unconventional duchess.

This behavior wasn't rational. And it wasn't him, dammit! At least not the usual him. Just because she had written another article did not mean that she had snuck out of the house and crossed the city alone in the small hours, for goodness' sake. She hadn't been attacked by a villain in the shadows any more than she had been at that tragic Peterloo protest, so he shouldn't allow his imagination to run riot like this.

For a moment, the tight bands of fear around his chest eased at that logic. Then all at once they constricted tighter as a vivid image appeared in his mind that was so real it merged into his reality. Of Portia's limp body being carried home. Covered in blood caused by an overzealous soldier's sharp sword.

Breathless.

Lifeless.

Her passionate heart stopped and his shattered into a million pieces.

One that instantly sucked him into a vortex of panic that was so strong it squeezed all the air from his lungs.

He didn't remember going back to the drawing room and barely registered the stunned faces of his family inside when he pushed the door open with such force the walls shook.

"How dare you!" He thrust the newspaper at his wife. "I didn't save you from a convict ship bound for Botany Bay so that you could continue to endanger your life writing bloody sedition!"

She swallowed as she glanced down at the offending article but didn't deny being its author. "Sir William was shorthanded and asked me to do it."

"And I expressly asked you if you were writing it again when I spotted those ink stains and you denied it! You lied to my face yet again. After all we've been through. After all I have done for you. And you have the nerve to pull me up for keeping a secret—but at least I didn't lie as well!" That betrayal hurt almost as much as the prospect of her violent death did. "You claimed you were only writing letters to your friends."

"I'm sorry." She did a reasonable job of looking sorry too, but he didn't believe it. "I shouldn't have lied to you about it."

"You shouldn't have bloody done it!" He began to pace, aware that he had been sucked down too deep in the spiral to see reason, but too far gone to stop spewing venom. "You should have just stuck to writing essays about my blasted dimples or whether or not bloody Kitty was right and you'd foolishly fallen in love with me!"

"Leo . . ." She caught his hand. "I . . ." Then she dropped it like a hot coal. "How did you know that I wrote those exact words? Unless . . ." Her eyes widened. "You read my private papers, didn't you?" She began to back away from him as horror replaced contrition. "You spied on my most personal and private thoughts and barefacedly lied to me about it?"

"So I lied!" He hated the petulant and overbearing way that he sounded but couldn't seem to stop himself. The panic was too overwhelming. The fear it had created was too strong. "You do it enough!"

"How could you?" She was gazing at him with such wounded horror that he couldn't stand it. "When you knew—you knew—that I would rather die than allow anyone to read them?" Then a wounded cry escaped and she covered it with her hand. "And then you used them to control me? How *dare* you?

He should have fallen to his knees then and begged for forgiveness. Explained to her that he wasn't being rational. That he had lost himself, somehow, and loathed it. Confessed that he had only read the first paragraph of both of those essays and would never, ever, betray her in the way that she now seemed to think that he had.

Instead, it was the irrational monster who answered. "You are my wife, Portia, so of course I dared." He walked toward her with his arms waving and hating himself every step of the way. "And I reserve the right, as your husband, to insist that you start behaving like one!"

"By doing what you say and not writing sedition?" Horror turned to outrage as she held up her ring finger. "Do you honestly think that this will stop me?" She ripped his ring off and jabbed it in the air between them. "I wave placards and write sedition, Leo!" Defiant, she met him head on. "That is what I do. That is who I am. If I cannot then—" She tossed the ring at him. "I refuse to remain your wife for another second! Whether we get an annulment or not!" If he was panicked before, those words sucked him into a new and wildly spiraling cyclone of hell.

"Over my dead body!"

"Don't tempt me, Leo!" Before he could speak, before he could apologize, she hammered in the death knell. "Good luck controlling a wife who has already left you!"

And with that, she stormed out. Leaving him fighting to breathe as the panic actually threatened to suffocate him this time.

Leo had to bend double just to be able to suck in some air.

"Well," said Abigail, "You made a monumental hash of that, big brother, didn't you?"

The worst thing was that he knew he had.

"And he accuses me of having no common sense when my head is turned." That came from Emilia who had bent to his level and was studying him as if he were something peculiar under a microscope. "When I have never, even in my silliest moments, done anything as monumentally stupid as that." She stroked his hair. "Do you need me to fetch the smelling salts, Leo? Only you look as though you are having a touch of the vapors."

He supposed he did, braced as he was with his hands against his knees, sucking in huge gulps of air while the room was spinning around him and his life spun out of control.

"Oh god. What have I done?" *He had to fix this!* He hoisted himself upright and lunged to follow Portia but his mother blocked the door. "Sit down and calm down, Leo, or I swear to god I'll murder you myself!" She pointed at a chair. "Before I let you go anywhere and cause even more damage, you need to first work out what the hell is currently going on in that thick head of yours, because whatever it is"—she gestured to the state of him—"this isn't right!"

As much as he hated to admit it, he knew his mother was correct.

Chapter
THIRTY-SIX

"And here we are yet again." Miss Prentice poured Portia a fortifying cup of tea as the dawn filtered through the window. She had been back at the school all night after her awful fight with Leo and, to her utter disgust, spent most of it in tears. "Trying to pick up the pieces after another one of my protégées has had their heart broken by a stupid man."

"It has been a bit of a year for it." Kitty, who had had her arm around Portia for most of the night, sighed. "First Georgie came back in tears, then Lottie, and now you. But as things turned out all right for our friends, I am hopeful your duke will come up trumps too. You'll see. He'll come hammering on the door soon begging your forgiveness and you'll both live happily ever after."

"It's over, Kitty." How on earth could it not be after last night? "Leo isn't the man I thought he was, and I certainly cannot be the woman he wants me to be. Our marriage was a huge mistake." She had a feeling he realized that too because he hadn't attempted to follow her upstairs last night to apologize after she had stormed off and he hadn't come looking for her after she had fled Berkeley Square a scant half an hour after. It didn't matter that she had sneaked out the back gate without anybody knowing, at some point, somebody must have noticed that she was missing and still he hadn't come.

To begin with, foolishly, she had so hoped that he would too. But then, she'd had hours to think and to ruminate before she had come to the sad but inevitable conclusion that this was for the best. Expecting her never to write again was like expecting her not to breathe and so she was glad that he had shown his true colors to her before it was too late.

"I am going to catch the morning post back to Bath and get on with my life."

"He might not allow you to do that," said Miss Prentice. "You need to be prepared for that too. Whether you want to be or not, you are his wife still and the law is on his side."

"If I have to change my name and go into hiding to escape him, I will. The only way I will ever abide by his dictatorial rules is if he imprisons me and chains me to the bedpost, and even if he does, I shan't stop plotting a way out." She was speaking about Leo now as if he were a monster, which he wasn't—usually—and that broke her heart some more. Because either she had been a complete, irrational, lovesick fool or he hadn't been at all what she had believed him to be from the outset, and neither option was palatable.

"He's going to fix this, Portia, I promise." The hopelessly romantic Kitty seemed determined to cling to that, irrespective of the evidence. "So try not to harden your heart against him too much now to give him a chance."

"I disagree." Always the pragmatic voice of reason, Miss P sighed. "The sooner Portia hardens her heart, the sooner it will mend." Cynical advice that Portia would have normally welcomed, except today it just felt like another blow. "And it will mend, dear, I promise. Especially if you bury yourself in work."

There was a light tap on the parlor door before one of the current students of Miss Prentice's School for Young Ladies entered. "This just arrived, Miss P." She held out a letter. "It is for the duchess."

The duchess! What a laughable title to still possess when she had already lost her duke.

Portia took it and then just stared at it because she recognized Leo's handwriting.

"It is from him, isn't it?" Typically, Kitty was beside herself with joy. "Read it."

Portia shook her head and slipped the missive under her legs where she didn't have to see it. "Whatever it says, it changes nothing, so I shall read it on the post later."

"Oh for goodness' sake!" Before Portia could brace herself, Kitty pushed her sideways and grabbed it, then dashed to the other side of the room so that she could rip it open.

"Give that back!" Portia went to snatch it and her friend lunged for the fire poker and wielded it between them like a weapon.

"He saved you from a prison hulk bound for Botany Bay, so the least you can do is hear what he has to say."

"She's right, dear," said Miss P. "Whatever it says, you have to hear it, even if it does change nothing."

"Fine." Portia folded her arms and hardened her heart. "But I can assure you that my mind is made up."

Still wielding the poker, Kitty cracked the seal one-handed and shook the letter open. "*My darling Portia* . . . Well, that's a promising and romantic start."

"Just get it over with, Kitty—without any additional commentary."

"My darling Portia." Kitty could not resist sighing at that. "I think we can both agree that what happened last night was an epic disaster and I know that saying sorry again—whether in person or via letter—doesn't even come close to fixing the damage that I have foolishly done. Therefore, as I know how much stock you put in them especially when it involves a conundrum, I thought it best to write you an essay instead. Please read it. Leo."

"That's it?" It was hardly the groveling, on-bended-knee apology that Portia had secretly hoped for.

Kitty frowned as she turned the page. "No. It appears that he has indeed written an essay." She held the page up for Portia to see.

Should the Duchess of Debden give the idiotic Duke of Debden a second chance?

Portia snatched it from Kitty's hand and began to read.

I think that there can be no doubt that I behaved like the worst sort of idiot last night, and while there is no excuse for my dreadful behavior, I have done a great deal of soul-searching since my extraordinary wife left me. And, perhaps foolishly, I still hope that she can find it in her heart to come back to me. Sadly, I do not have her wonderful way with words, but here are my reasons why I think that she should.

It goes without saying that I love her but I will say it again anyway. From the first moment I met Portia, and despite all her glowering disapproval that day, she called to my soul. She felt like the missing piece of a puzzle. My other half. The thing that I hadn't realized I needed but had to have once I did. That is why I kept her by my side when she first wanted to leave me and why I insisted that she marry me when it looked like the law was going to take her away. I could pretend to both of us that it was the only way to keep her safe, and perhaps it was at the time, or that I felt beholden to her for pushing her into accepting that first conviction, but neither of those things were my true motivation for making Portia Kendall my wife. Nor, in case anyone was wondering, did I marry her before I knew what she had done.

I knew she wrote sedition when we took those vows and I didn't care.

In truth, I don't care now.

I love the way my clever wife writes. I love the way her brilliant mind works. I love the questions that she poses. I love the way she constructs an argument, backs it with irrefutable evidence, and comes to a reasoned conclusion. I especially love her pithy turn of phrase, which I like to think I am a bit of an expert on now that I have read every single published essay that she has ever written. My wife is a woman of strong convictions who never shies away from them. I have no right to ask her to compromise them in any way like I did last night.

Which I suppose brings me to last night and why I so spectacularly overreacted. Something my pride would rather not do as I want the woman I love to think that I am her strong and steadfast knight in shining armor, not a hero with feet of clay. But as dignity is overrated, especially where love is concerned, I need to confess how I instead became more of a duke in distress than the man she deserves.

But to do that, I need to first go back a month or so to a time before we'd met. To the day when my sister's fiancé carried her bleeding body back into my house after she had been injured at a protest. A day that turned out to be profound for all the wrong reasons because it affected me in a way that has plagued me ever since.

I do not know why, but for some reason my mind decided to combine what happened to Abigail that day with what had happened to her when she fell out of that tree and nearly died all those years ago—not a giant leap to make, I suppose, as there were some similarities. However, on top of that, my mind decided to throw in a million possible catastrophes too. What-ifs that literally made my hair stand on end because every single one of them seemed to end with my sister dead, and I do not think my luscious locks have fully stood down since. It's difficult to describe the blind and irrational panic that one random incident caused or how real those imagined scenarios felt to me and, because I had no other clue how to banish it, I dragged my entire family to Bath against their will to keep them safe.

My clever wife witnessed me do that again last week after Percy's letter arrived, when thankfully she was able to yank me out of the spiral of panic that had sucked me in, and used her irrefutable logic to put me back on an even keel.

But the irrational panic returned again last night when I read her latest column in Equitas. *I saw the word Peterloo and the whirlpool sucked me straight back down again. Only this time, instead of Abigail's limp and lifeless body, all I could picture was my wife's. Slain by an overzealous soldier because she dared to stand up for what was right. Or murdered by some monster as she walked alone across the city to get to her beloved newspaper. Then, even though I knew I was handling it wrong, all I could think of was keeping her safe and the only way, in my blind panic, that I thought I could do that was to rant and rave and lay down the law.*

Was that irrational?

Yes.

Was it fair?

Absolutely not.

As to me spying on you, my dearest, darling Portia, by reading your most personal thoughts . . .

While I am ashamed to admit that I am guilty as charged, you should also know that all I have read are the opening paragraphs of two of those private essays. One when I peeked inside your trunk to check that your papers were still inside it. The other because it was out in the open on your nightstand and I am only human and was a man hopelessly in love with a woman who I was convinced would never love me back. So when I saw that question which you had posed yourself, in desperation I had to know if you had decided if your friend Kitty was correct and you did feel more for me than an overwhelming attraction to my distracting dimples.

Did I use what little I read to control you? Of course I didn't. But in the spirit of there being no more secrets between us ever again, I will admit to perhaps flashing my dimples at you a bit more.

Portia—love of my life—I know how much your writing means to you, and I have no right to attempt to make you stop. In truth, I'd much rather you didn't because your words are brilliant and so pertinent and gloriously pithy in their accuracy that the world needs to hear them. Hell, you can even wave a placard covered in them on the floor of the House of Lords if you want to, so long as you are not in any danger.

So how about I meet you halfway? You carry on waving your placards and writing sedition with my full support and in return, you agree to the following non-negotiable caveats for the sake of my oversensitive hair follicles:

1. You never keep what you are doing from me again. I might not like it, I might rant and rave, and I might also have an irrational conniption like I did last night, but I will calm down. I always do. Especially when I have you to lecture me back to reason.

2. You never walk all the way home unaccompanied after dark again. We have a carriage, and I have legs, and both are always at your disposal.

3. And finally, you put your name loud and proud at the top of every seditious article that you write. In case you need reminding of it, my love, it is Portia Sloane. Aside from that fact that I am infinitely proud of my clever wife and want her to have the recognition that she deserves, the authorities can arrest Portia Kendall—but they wouldn't dare lay a finger on the Duchess of Debden.

In conclusion, if any of the above goes some way to convincing you that I am not an utter dead loss that you are best shot of, I would be delighted to make a groveling apology to you in person after I have finished shouting into the wind this afternoon, where I will beg on bended knee that you consider taking me back. Obviously, if you remain unconvinced, I will get you that annulment because I selfishly want all of you, Portia, and do not want to settle for anything less than your heart, body, and soul. I will also, irrespective of your ultimate decision, continue on my quest to get your first conviction quashed. Not only because it is the right thing to do, and because I want Nolley to pay dearly for what he did to you, but because

I promised you that I would do so and I have taken every single vow I have ever said to you seriously. And did I already mention that I love you?

Leo xx

Portia slumped back onto the sofa as Kitty and Miss P read the essay, so off-kilter she didn't know what to think or which way was up.

Being an eternal optimist, Kitty of course took all of Leo's words at face value. "That is the most heart-wrenching and beautiful essay ever written, so obviously, you have to go back to him!"

"But what if they are just words, Kitty? Words mean nothing without deeds to back them up and Leo is clever enough to know precisely what to say to get under my skin." And to mine straight through to her silly heart that willed her to be more like Kitty and just accept his pretty words at face value. "He also often says one thing and then entirely behaves to the contrary like he did last night. I need to be sure that he means them—really means them—before I even consider going back."

"Then put your knight in shining armor to the test like the damsels did of old. Give him a challenge to test his mettle. A proper trial by ordeal."

"And how exactly do I do that?" Portia stared down at the letter again, at all of Leo's pretty words for any clue what to do, and suddenly had an epiphany. "There is one thing we could try . . . but I'd need your help with it."

"Whatever it is, let's do it now!" The hopelessly romantic Kitty was, of course, up like a shot.

"You might regret agreeing when you find out what I have in mind." Portia smiled sheepishly as her friend began to frown. "Because I'll give you fair warning that it is very definitely illegal."

Chapter THIRTY-SEVEN

If there was one positive of being in the chaotic circus that was called the House of Lords, it was that it gave Leo something to do other than anxiously wearing a groove in his study floor from his constant pacing. He had paced miles since last night, probably at least a hundred of them, and no amount of pacing had calmed his anxiety any while he waited for the hands on the clock to move.

"Thank you for coming." Lord Gray shook his hand before they took their seats. "We need all the voices of support we can get if we are ever going to get any sort of reforms through this lot."

As the din was currently so loud in the House, Leo decided it would be a bloody miracle if any voice was heard today, but smiled politely. "I am always happy to support a worthy cause." And seeing as this one was Portia's, it really didn't get more worthy. He glanced around all the braying lords and wondered what she would make of it. Because if this disorganized cacophony represented the most powerful few of the pitiful three percent of the entire population considered worthy enough to have a vote, it was a wonder they still had a country left, let alone a government. It had to change. Of that he was in no doubt.

As the Lord Chancellor entered in the traditional formal procession, the other lords finally quieted while he positioned himself on the speaker's woolsack. Then, as was also tradition, all hell broke loose as everyone fought for air. It took over an hour for Lord Gray to find a gap in the noise long enough to propose his bill. "My lords temperate, I come to you today to seek urgent reform for . . ." He had to really shout to list those reforms because most of the house had erupted into jeers of disapproval. To his credit, he refused to allow them to detract him from his message and managed to get most of the salient points out in the next interminable hour before the proposal was opened up for general debate.

Just as Leo had anticipated, there was little support for the bill in the house, but he had made a promise to his wife to shout into the wind, so shout into it he would. He enthusiastically stood each time the floor was yielded, but it took another half an hour before he could be heard.

As he knew he only had a few minutes to make his point, he started with something attention-grabbing. "The longer this house puts off reforming, the more chance there is of our country being swept by revolution. The voiceless masses are sick and tired of being ignored and, worse, bullied into submission by Draconian laws made by the privileged elite whose only purpose is to ensure that they do not have to concede even a crumb of that privilege." That garnered a few boos, but Leo was a man on a mission and raised a righteous finger in the air, which he jabbed at the worst offenders. "Mark my words, gentlemen, unless we extend the franchise beyond those few men lucky enough to own more than forty shillings' worth of land—which equates to a paltry three percent of the adult population—then this house will be lucky to survive the end of the century." While the Whigs, who were severely outnumbered, cheered their agreement, the rest of the lords jeered.

However, as a Tory attempted to rip apart what Leo had just said, there was a commotion on the other side of the floor that seemed to draw more attention. Everyone stood to get a better view, so it took Leo a little while to catch a glimpse of it himself.

Until he saw a bedsheet sheet daubed in giant red letters that was being held in the air.

LORDS!

USE YOUR IMMENSE AND UNFAIR PRIVILEGE TO DO SOME GOOD FOR A CHANGE AND VOTE FOR

REFORM

As there was some sort of fracas going on behind that sheet, it appeared that they had a protestor on the floor. One who clearly had no right to be in the room.

Two guards had hold of the brave fool, who appeared to be putting up quite the fight. One of the guards suddenly bent as if winded and the protestor broke free. The surprisingly slight fellow then dashed toward the terrified Lord Chancellor trailing their makeshift banner behind them.

Both guards lunged, but the plucky protestor sidestepped them before either could grab him, and, in doing, lost his hat. Then the whole house erupted in outrage as a long mane of near jet-black hair tumbled to the protestor's waist.

Hair that Leo was only too familiar with.

"It's only a bloody woman!" exclaimed Lord Gray beside him.

"I'm afraid it's worse than that," said Leo as he tried to clamber over the row of seats and lords in front of him to get to her. "It's my bloody wife!" And bugger him but he was oddly proud of her. Only Portia was fearless enough to pull off a stunt this outrageous.

He had no idea how the clever minx had managed to get in, but by the men's attire that she was currently sporting and the ridiculous black mustache that she had glued on her lovely face, she had somehow managed it. Although how anyone could ever confuse her for a man was laughable as aside from her hair, she filled her waistcoat and breeches far too well for there to be any doubt about her sex.

The guards had restrained her by the time he got anywhere close and were trying their best to drag her out—not that Portia was complying. She hung like a deadweight from her captured elbows and dug her trailing heels into the floor, repeatedly shouting "Vote for reform!" as if her life depended on it right up until he skidded to a stop in front of her.

"Hello, wife."

"Hello, husband."

They both enjoyed the way the guards' eyes widened at that unexpected bombshell as a million stunned whispers ricocheted around the chamber. As her captors let her go, an unusual hush settled in this space that was rarely ever quiet as all the lords craned their ears to hear. "What the blazes do you think you are doing?"

She stuck out her chin, defiant. "You did say that you didn't care if I waved a placard on the floor of the House of Lords."

"I did." He nodded, impressed at her sheer bloody nerve, but also humbled and relieved that she was here because he recognized a challenge—and a second chance—when he saw one. This was a test and one he could not afford to fail, no matter how much his protective instincts urged him to drag her to safety. How he handled this situation would determine their future. "But I feel duty bound to point out that is a sheet and not a placard." He flicked his finger toward it, matter-of-fact.

"Semantics." She wanted to smile. It hovered at the corners of her lips, but she suppressed it. "I had too much to say to fit on a placard, never mind that I never would have been able to smuggle one of those in under my coat. And . . ." Suddenly she didn't look so cocksure. "I wanted categoric proof that you meant what you said." There was hope in her lovely eyes. Hope for him, hope for them, and that meant the world.

"Debden!" The Lord Chancellor's voice bellowed from the woolsack. "Control your wife!"

"You control her." Leo tossed that over his shoulder, then grinned at Portia. "I've given up trying."

Her smile broke free then and he basked in it. "I very much

enjoyed your essay. It wasn't as good as one of mine, of course, but it wasn't bad for a duke."

He accepted that compliment with an amused nod. "I am very much enjoying your mustache but I am not sure it suits a duchess."

"I am not a typical duchess."

"Thank the Lord for it." He leaned forward and placed a soft kiss on her ridiculously hairy top lip. Then for her ears only, he whispered, "Am I forgiven?"

"I suppose so." She brushed a loving hand down his lapel. "Are you going to escort me to safety now?"

"Do you want me to?"

"I'd prefer the irony, and the publicity, of being dragged out of the building."

"And so you should be. Heaven forbid they ever allow a woman here in Parliament. Even a duchess. Society might crumble." Leo took a deep breath and did one of the hardest things he had ever done in his life. He stepped back. "I'll leave you to it then."

She beamed as she unfurled her banner again while the guards shuffled from foot to foot unsure what the hell to do next. "I was proud of you today, Leo. Even if you were shouting into the wind."

"I am proud of you every day, my darling." He took another step back so that she and the cause she held so dear could have their moment to shout into the wind too, but could not help being a little bit overprotective and overbearing as he passed one of the guards. "When you drag her out, which you *will* very much have to because she will not leave otherwise, know that if I find one single bruise on her body, you will have me to personally answer to."

She raised her rebellious fist to the heavens as he turned and sauntered back to his seat. "Vote for reform!" Portia's voice echoed through the rafters. "Votes for all!"

"Will somebody get that damned woman out of here!" yelled the Lord Chancellor.

Leo heard the scuffle, but he ignored it.

She was making a stand, and it was his place as her dutiful husband to allow her to make it without interference. Especially as she seemed to be much more adept at shouting into the wind than he was.

"Leo!" He turned only because she called.

Portia was sitting on the floor, her heels squeaking loudly against the floorboards as they slid her on her bottom backward toward the door. But she was laughing, her dark eyes dancing with affection, determination, and mirth. Her hair was a riotous mane, and her ridiculous mustache was now skewed and making its way across her cheek. He was going to enjoy peeling that thing off later with the rest of her clothes. "You were right about one thing in that substandard essay that you wrote."

"Just the one?"

She tumbled backward but still held her banner aloft as they attempted to drag her out of the chamber. "Where love is concerned, and much to my complete disgust, it turns out that dignity really is overrated!"

Acknowledgments

There are certain books, and especially certain characters, that when you try to write them, refuse to be written until everything is on the exact right path. This book began like that because I had one clear idea for the way it was supposed to go from the outset, but Portia, this story's tenacious leading lady, was determined to go another. Being equally as stubborn, that meant that she and I entered into quite a battle until we both realized that we each had to compromise a little to make this story work.

During that turbulent time, while I was banging my head against my desk and Portia flatly refused to comply, I commiserated with the usual suspects. My go-to people who always have my back when this writing malarky gets tough.

First and foremost is the long-suffering Mr. H. He understands nothing about writing a book, tends to measure success in the number of words written rather than the quality of those words, and has, annoyingly, broken down my writing process into five distinct phases. But he does understand, after thirty-plus (glorious) years together and thirty-plus books, that PHASE 3 is where I am at my most distraught. Therefore, despite his infuriating habit of reassuring me that this is "classic Phase 3" (which I am sure one day will actually lead to divorce), he also reliably tells me that I've got this. That he believes in me and that this too shall pass—and it pains me to admit that he is always right.

Secondly, and I've also dedicated this book to her, my very good friend Jean Fullerton, who was also writing a particularly non-compliant book at the same time as I was at war with Portia, so we helped each other through it. Obviously, the other three reprobates who make up my writing support group, Lucy, Alison, and Liam, get their obligatory thank-yous too. Our regular pub dinners and raucous writing retreats are always a balm to my soul. Huge thanks obviously go to my wonderful agent, Kevan Lyon, and my fabulous editor, Sallie Lotz.

But finally, because this book is all about the people who relentlessly stand up for what is right—even if that means that they are the lonely voice shouting into the wind—I want to thank everyone who has fought so hard for the freedoms that I get to enjoy today.

About the Author

Kat Moran Photography

When **Virginia Heath** was a little girl, it took her ages to fall asleep, so she made up stories in her head to help pass the time while she was staring at the ceiling. As she got older, the stories became more complicated, sometimes taking weeks to get to the happy ending. Then one day, she decided to embrace the insomnia and start writing them down. Now her Regency rom-coms (including the Wild Warriners and Merriwell Sisters series) are published in many languages across the globe. Thirty-two books and four Romantic Novel of the Year Award nominations later, it still takes her forever to fall asleep.